The Slayer had

With the flagon in one hand and the baby in the other, she stared helplessly up at him.

"Will you be all right?" he asked.

She swallowed hard. Nay, she would not be all right. She would be flayed for a fraud and a liar. He would see through her flimsy disguise to the ugly truth that brought her here.

He stood so close that the candle's flame was doubly reflected in his eyes. His gaze devoured her. Clarise's blood ran cold as she waited for judgment to come crashing down.

"He seems content," he said, focusing again on the locket.

The words flowed over her, diluting her terror. God have mercy, had she actually deceived him?

Danger's Promise

Marliss Moon

JOVE BOOKS, NEW YORK

DANGER'S PROMISE

A Jove Book / published by arrangement with
the author

PRINTING HISTORY
Jove edition / March 2002

All rights reserved.
Copyright © 2002 by Marliss Arruda.
Cover art by Donald Case.
This book, or parts thereof, may not be reproduced
in any form without permission.
For information address: The Berkley Publishing Group,
a division of Penguin Putnam Inc.,
375 Hudson Street, New York, New York 10014.

Visit our website at
www.penguinputnam.com

ISBN: 0-515-13275-6

A JOVE BOOK®
Jove Books are published by The Berkley Publishing Group,
a division of Penguin Putnam Inc.,
375 Hudson Street, New York, New York 10014.
JOVE and the "J" design
are trademarks belonging to Penguin Putnam Inc.

PRINTED IN THE UNITED STATES OF AMERICA

10 9 8 7 6 5 4 3 2 1

With special thanks to my best friend and proofreader, Sydney Baily-Gould. You stood by me through many long years and many poor manuscripts. You deserve all the credit for this one!

For Alan, my soul mate. Thank you for believing.

For all my children and stepchildren: Conrad and Chauncey; Corey, Bryan and Tricia. May your lives be filled with magic and grace.

Chapter One

In battle, he fought like a man possessed. To the enemy, he gave no quarter. His *nom de guerre* sent shivers of horror down the spines of common folk. Yet, reflected in the gray depths of his newborn's eyes, the Slayer looked like an ordinary man. A profoundly humbled man.

His baby had inherited his swarthy coloring and his stubborn nature, given that he was still alive. He was little more than a bundle of slippery limbs, but his chest swelled on a healthy breath, and his fists resembled iron mallets. With a wail that bounded off the ceiling and magnified, Simon heralded his own birth. Beyond the shutters, thunder boomed and lightning crackled.

The Slayer nearly smiled. Simon de la Croix would be the next Baron of Helmesly, not a bastard warrior like his father. Not a man forced to fight for all he had.

The portal burst open, startling the baby into silence. A draft beat up the torchlight and illumined the flapping sleeves of the midwife as she rushed into the chamber.

"Give me the babe!" screeched the wizened woman. She reached for him with her shriveled hands. "I must baptize it at once!"

Christian lifted his son above the woman's reach. A pox on the midwife! Did she think Simon marked for the devil? "I told you to leave," he said in his quietest voice.

The old woman stilled, her eyes moving beyond him to the lifeless form of the Slayer's wife. "Mother of God, what have ye done?" she whispered.

Christian felt his horror bubble up, and he quickly squashed it down. "What have I done?" he snarled. "I've done naught but save my son from perishing with his mother. 'Twas you who let her die. Get you out before I think to imprison you for murder!"

The midwife blanched and scurried backward. Hastily she gathered her belongings: bottles of draughts and tisanes, knives and needles. They clanged together in the earthenware bowl as she scuttled from the room. With a furtive look, she darted away.

The door closed behind her. In the silence that followed, Christian heard the thudding of his own heart. His disbelieving gaze drifted about the room, touching on the mutilated body of his wife, the rosary beads lying useless in her palm, the half-embroidered altar cloth upon the chair. At last he looked down at the baby in his arms. Simon returned his gaze intently.

"Your mother is dead," Christian whispered. *And I feel 'tis my fault.*

Until the midwife came, her labor had been unremarkable. Genrose had suffered the pangs of childbirth with the same saintly silence that she'd suffered her husband. Then, oh, so subtly, she had faded with the dying light of day.

There is naught more I can do, the midwife had declared. *These things are in God's hands.*

The words perturbed him even now. Christian had cast the woman from the room and dared to alter fate's design. He had cut Simon free of his fleshy prison, and even cut the cord that tied the baby to his ill-fated mother. And the baby had lived!

Lowering his son into the box of waiting linens, he

wrapped him carefully against the cold. Simon held still, uncritical of his father's ministrations. His somber gaze demanded something of him—a mother most likely.

With a deep breath Christian called upon the ruthlessness that had given him his *nom de guerre,* the Slayer of Helmesly. Then he turned to the task of rolling his lady's corpse in cloth. It took all the sheets on the bed, plus those folded on the chest, to staunch the blood still spilling from her body. His movements were deft with practice. Yet in all his experience of war, he had never felt so sickened by his actions, so keenly plagued by guilt.

Had he loved the lady who had died to give him a son?

In the act of covering Genrose's face, he hesitated. Her quiet features were hardly even known to him. She had been as pure as a novice when he'd wed her a year ago. Then, as now, he'd been unworthy of her sacrifice. His only comfort was the certainty that she was happier with God than she had been with him.

The baby gave a whimper in his cradle. Christian hurried to the box, worried that his son might yet be snatched away from him.

Who would nurture Simon? Who would feed him? The questions hit him like the broadside of a sword. Wiping the blood from his hands, he scooped the baby up and paced the length of the chamber.

Simon ceased to fret, his bright eyes watchful. The rain began to pelt the shutters. A knock sounded at the door.

"Enter."

Sir Roger edged into the torchlight. The droplets on his cloak gleamed like diamonds as he ran an eye over the nightmarish scene. "My lord, you are covered in blood!" the middle-aged knight exclaimed, shutting the portal behind him.

Sir Roger's tilted smile was not in evidence tonight. The scars that forked like veins upon his face paled as he approached. He stopped before his lord, and his gaze fell to the swaddled infant. "A boy, my lord?" he queried gently.

"His name is Simon. He will inherit his grandfather's title," Christian answered, though Roger already knew his motives for marrying the baron's daughter.

Gray eyes flicked once to the bed, then back to the baby. "I know not what to say," confessed the knight.

"Say nothing." Christian felt as if he wore a mask upon his face. Spots burst and swam before his eyes. "Tell me how the defense goes at Glenmyre."

"The news isn't good, my lord," Sir Roger warned.

"Say it." The struggle over Glenmyre was escalating into war. Between domestic matters and military preoccupations, Christian had little time for rest. "What has Ferguson done now?"

"He rode upon Glenmyre at dusk, when the peasants were returning from the fields. He slew them all."

Christian swore viciously at the Scot's perfidy. "How many dead?" he demanded.

"Nineteen men."

A familiar queasiness turned Christian's stomach. The Scotsman's atrocities reminded him of his own past. Feeling his knees go weak, he thrust the baby at his vassal. "Find a nurse for my son," he commanded. "I will ride to Glenmyre to bolster our defense."

He took several steps toward the door, then turned to regard the dismal chamber. "See that my lady is buried alongside her parents," he instructed.

Sir Roger looked older with an infant clutched to his hauberk. "As you will, sire," he assured his lord.

Christian grasped the latch. "Ethelred must bury her. Do not let news of her death reach Abbot Gilbert."

Again, Sir Roger nodded, and the Slayer took his leave. The lord's chamber opened to a gallery, which overlooked the hall. Below, the servants gathered, awaiting news of the birth. As Christian clutched the balustrade for balance, the light of the fire pit deepened the bloodstains on his tunic.

The servants looked up at him in one accord. Shock flared in their eyes. At their collective gasp, he fell back into the shadows. Too late, he realized they were thinking of the abbot's prophesy, cried out within the chapel just nine months ago.

Mark me well, people of Helmesly. This virgin bride will be slain by her husband!

Nay, not he! Christian longed to defend his innocence, but his protests would fall on deaf ears. The servants wouldn't take his word over that of a cleric. He would never win their loyalty now.

He turned to the courtyard, seeking rain to wash the blood from his clothes. But before he reached the solitude of the tower stairs, a servant's whisper rose with the smoke from the fire pit.

"Mother of God, he has killed Her Ladyship! Did ye see the blood?"

With blisters burning her feet, Clarise DuBoise tackled the hill to the Abbey of Rievaulx. The abbey commanded a view at the height of a crag, rising from the stalks of purple heather to lord over the valley below. Its walls seemed to waver in the hot July haze. She would not admit it was her vision blurring.

For two long days the sun had sat upon her shoulders and sucked the moisture from her moth. Beneath the cloth hiding her hair, Clarise's scalp was drenched with sweat. The gown that disguised her as a peasant chafed her limbs where her shift failed to cover her. Her slippers were worn to tatters. She was lucky to be alive.

Ferguson, her stepfather, hadn't cared about the dangers of the road when he'd cast her out upon her mission. He knew the threat to kill her mother and sisters was enough to ensure that she would fight to survive any hardship.

Ferguson had instructed her to go straight to the Slayer's castle. *Ye mon gain admission to Helmesly as a freed serf in need o' work,* he'd commanded. *Drop the powder into his drink at the first chance ye get. If the Slayer isn't dead in two months' time, I'll hang yer mother an' sisters in the court-yard.*

There were others he could have sent in her stead, men and women more adept at subterfuge. But Ferguson had a reason for sending Clarise to do his dirty work. She had attempted to avenge her father's murder numerous times. Her sharp, strategic mind made her an ever-present danger to Ferguson. He could not control her except from afar.

The toxic powder was concealed in a pendant that hung on a chain about her neck. Clarise felt the weight of the pendant swing between her breasts as she pushed her way up the abbey's hill. Ferguson's plan was sneaky and cold-blooded. It was riddled with flaws. The likelihood that she would be exposed and hanged for spying was high, but that did not cause Ferguson any great concern. Clarise was as dispensable as her mother and sisters.

Only one alternative existed to the plan: that Alec could help her. Six months ago Alec had been Clarise's betrothed; now he was a monk. The wedding would have taken place last Christmas, had the Slayer of Helmsly not attacked without warning on the eve of the nuptials. In a bloody assault he had killed Alec's father, prompting Alec to flee to Rievaulx Abbey in fear of his life. Clarise's dream of escaping her stepfather's clutches through marriage had been crushed.

She told herself Alec would stay at Rievaulx only a short while. He was a knight, after all, not a man of the cloth. But the days turned to weeks and then to months. In letters too many to count, she pleaded for Alec to take up his sword and rescue her family from the Scot's abuses. Until now, her efforts had been in vain.

Today she would petition him in person. How could Alec refuse to help when she told him of Ferguson's threat to kill her family? Honor dictated that he summon an army and challenge her stepfather once and for all.

The scent of cooked meat wafted from a nearby village, distracting Clarise from her introspection. Her stomach gave an empty growl, but she ignored it. The monks would feed her at Rievaulx.

Her footsteps faltered as she approached the abbey's only gate. The wall that rose toward the cloudless sky reminded her of her father's tomb. It was hewn from the same gray stone.

Alec is here, she reminded herself, shaking off her sudden foreboding. When he saw her in person, he would remember his love for her. He would be her hero once again.

The only way to signal her presence was to tug on a bell rope. At the bell's high jingle, the peephole snapped open. "Aye?" came a voice from the folds of a cowl.

Clarise greeted the faceless monk in Latin. "I must share a word with Alec Monteign."

The monk showed no reaction to her words. "We have an illness here. The abbey is quarantined," he said stoically.

Alarm rippled over her. "What manner of illness is it?" she demanded. Without Alec's help, she would have no choice but to execute her mission.

"Fever," said the monk shortly. "Boils and lesions."

Clarise repressed the urge to cover her mouth with one corner of her headdress. "Nonetheless, I must speak with Alec." Desperation made her dizzy. She blinked her eyes to clear her vision, and when she opened them, the monk was gone.

Where did he go? Clarise stood tiptoe and peered into the abbey's courtyard. The cobbled square looked strangely abandoned. An inscription over a pair of double doors drew her gaze. *Hic laborant fratres crucis,* said the message. *Here labor brothers of the cross.*

No one labored now. Neither did they tend the vineyards outside the abbey's walls. The rows of trellises stood bereft of vine or grape. She was left with the dampening suspicion that she'd come to the wrong place for help.

The sound of footsteps echoed off the courtyard. Another man approached the gate. He did not wear a cowl over his dark, tonsured hair but a stole that designated him an abbot.

Clarise's hopes took wing, then plummeted as his black gaze skewered her through the little opening.

"You should not be here," he informed her cryptically. "There is a great scourge within these walls."

"I wish only to speak with Alec Monteign," she said deferentially.

"Brother Alec tends the sick. He cannot be interrupted."

"He isn't ill, then?" she asked, hopeful once again.

"Not yet." The abbot spoke with no inflection in his voice. She couldn't tell if he was angry or dispassionate.

"I was once his betrothed, Your Grace," Clarise rushed to explain. "If he knew I had come so far, I am certain he would want to—"

His gaze had sharpened with her words. "Remove the cloth, so that I might see you," he interrupted.

Clarise eased the kerchief from her flame-colored hair. The abbot put jeweled fingers to his mouth and gasped with recognition. "I know you," he said in a voice so intimate her innards seemed to curdle. "You are the one who has written Alec words of defilement and temptation."

"But, Your Grace," she protested, realizing he made reference to her many letters. "I merely reasoned with his choice—"

"Silence!" he hissed. He stepped back suddenly, his face lost to shadow. "You are a woman, an ancestor of Eve. You would lure Alec from his holy vows," he insisted.

"Not true!" she cried. "I have come for . . . for . . ." She stuttered, for in truth, she *had* come to lead Alec from the Church. "I have come for sanctuary," she amended. It was a means to gain entrance; she had nowhere else to turn.

The abbot pressed himself to the gate. In a wolfish smile he bared his teeth. "Sanctuary?" he repeated. Then his head fell back as laughter, harsh and mirthless, rose from his throat. "Is that what you call it?" Suddenly he was deathly serious. "Horatio!" he snarled over his shoulder.

The man who'd answered the gate loomed behind him. "Show this woman your face," the abbot commanded.

The monk pulled the hood from his head.

Clarise sucked in a breath of horror. The man's face was speckled with lesions. Puss oozed from every pore. The wounds seemed to weep, lining his cheeks in flaky traces. She changed her mind at once about wanting to enter.

"Does this look like refuge to you?" the abbot inquired. There was a mad gleam in his onyx eyes.

Clarise drew her kerchief closer to her nose. She swallowed hard as the vision of illness threatened to upend her empty stomach. "Let Alec go," she begged. "He is the only one who can help me, Your Grace. I have great need of him."

"I am sure you do," said the abbot with oily implication. "Nonetheless, he cannot leave. Until the illness runs its course, no one leaves. You run the risk of infection yourself."

She stepped back instinctively. "I am going now," she said.

"Just a moment," the abbot ordered. "It comes to mind that Horatio might have infected you already. We cannot contribute to the spread of disease. Can we, Horatio?"

"Nay, Your Grace." The monk seemed to smirk.

Clarise looked from one man to the other. She weighed the benefit of seeing Alec against the risk of being stricken. "I must go," she repeated, staggering backward several paces as she pulled her head covering into place. "I will call again when the illness is gone." She could not afford to be locked in the abbey's walls indefinitely. Ferguson had given her two months' time to accomplish her assignment. After that, her mother and sisters' lives were forfeit.

With a nameless fear she turned and hurried down the grassy slope. As the earth dropped sharply beneath her feet, she began to run, desperate to put distance between herself and the sickness that polluted the abbey. She pinched her slippers with her toes, skirting hollows and leaping over rocks as she raced toward the river and the trading town at its shore.

Clarise dived into the midst of traffic. A trail of carts and traders swept her along. The cheerful throng was headed toward the market at the river's edge. To her relief, there was no sign of illness in the sweating faces of those who milled around her.

The busy air of the market town contrasted sharply with the deathlike stillness of the abbey. Stalls and tents crowded the grassy riverbank. Tables overflowed with goods brought from other places—leather, samite, mink, trinkets, and jewels. Clarise stumbled through the throng, dismayed by the turn of events.

The scent of meat pies lured her toward the food stands. Ducklings sizzled over spits. Barrels swelled with luscious fruit. Over the shouts of the hawkers she heard her stomach rumble.

"Have a gooseberry?" a kind old lady offered, extending her the prickly ball of fruit.

"Thank you!" Clarise ripped off the skin with her teeth and stuffed the juicy globe in her mouth.

Now what? she wondered. It had never occurred to her that the Abbey of Rievaulx would be anything but a haven of refuge. Alec had flown there to keep from being murdered by the Slayer. Yet illness now despoiled the place, and the abbot's strange behavior made it all the more frightening.

She thought of Alex, trapped behind the walls. He must be desperate to leave! But until the illness ran its course, he could not. Perhaps he'd never even received her letters. The abbot could have kept them to himself, fearing Alec would rescind his vows if he knew of Clarise's desperate situation.

She seized the explanation with relief. While it meant that Alec knew little of her plight, it also meant that he might still help her. *If* she found a way to reach him.

How long until the quarantine was lifted? Could she afford to bide her time in this trading town while every day brought her mother and sisters closer to death?

The sound of one woman scolding another roused her

from her thoughts. "Megan, are ye mad?" hissed the woman, tugging at the other's elbow. "Do ye want to live at Helmesly and be nursemaid to the Slayer's son?"

At the Slayer's name, Clarise gave a guilty start. She followed the direction of the women's stares and spied a man sitting astride a horse. The man wore no armor in the afternoon heat. By the hopeless look on his battle-scarred face, he hadn't met with any luck in his search for a nurse.

That can't be the Slayer, Clarise thought, swallowing hard. A gooseberry seed moved painfully down her throat. As the women moved hurriedly away, whispering to themselves, Clarise eyed the Slayer's representative.

The Slayer had spawned a son on the baron's daughter. Ferguson wouldn't like that at all, she thought with a faint smile. Yet it made her mission that much easier. For the sake of her mother and sisters, she needed to approach the knight and offer her services as a nurse.

I am not equipped to feed a baby, she silently resisted. Yet that was not exactly true. She'd fed her youngest sister goat's milk when their mother suffered the birth fever. It wasn't an impossible task. Besides, she couldn't stay in this trading town indefinitely, waiting for the quarantine to lift.

With leaden feet, Clarise crossed the grassy expanse that separated her from the horseman.

The man caught sight of her and stared with interest. To her relief, he did not appear to be a vicious warrior. Below a full head of graying hair, his eyes were light and keen. Though his face was crosshatched by scars, one end of his mouth was caught up in a perpetual smile, giving him a congenial look. He dismounted as she approached him.

"Are you in search of a nurse?" she asked in the Saxon tongue. As Ferguson had suggested, she would play the part of a freed serf.

He took hold of his animal's bridle. "I am," he said, giving her a quick but thorough inspection.

"I can care for the baby," she offered, sounding more certain than she felt.

He gave her a skeptical look. "Where is your child?"

My child? Mary's blood, she was supposed to have birthed a child! "It . . . it died of fever just a day ago."

The knight's expression turned sympathetic. "And you would care for another," he finished gently. "What does your husband think?"

Husband? She balked at the unexpected question. Having not intended to go through with Ferguson's plan, she'd given little thought to what she would say under the circumstances. "I have no husband," she answered automatically. At the knight's odd look she added, "He died in a skirmish."

The knight frowned and paused. "You have suffered much for one so young," he said.

His sympathy gave her courage. It would be easier than she thought to find her way into the Slayer's home. "I have no money," she added pathetically. "No way of feeding myself. Please, take me to Helmesly Castle. Let me care for the baby."

The man looked dazed by her enthusiasm. "Very well," he said. "You wish to go now?"

"Aye, right now." Her hopes rose anew. The hoary knight had fallen for her tale.

"Have you nothing to bring with you?"

"My goods were sold to cover my husband's debts," she said, thinking quickly.

"What is your name?"

"Clare," she improvised. "Clare Crucis." The last word from the inscription at the abbey sprang to her lips. She congratulated herself for being so clever.

"I am Sir Roger de Saintonge," said the knight. He inclined a slight bow. "Shall we go?"

She approached the white destrier with mixed eagerness and dread. Sir Roger spanned her waist, tossing her pillion into the saddle. "You are not afraid of horses," he remarked.

She shook her head and realized belatedly that most peasants *were* afraid of the giant warhorses. She would have to remember to think like a commoner.

The knight led his mount by the bridle through the thinning crowds. Clarise kept her gaze fixed on the road they were taking. It was a well-trodden path leading away from the town and abbey.

As they wound around a series of low hills, the Abbey of Rievaulx dropped from view. The hope that Alec would save her from her dreaded task died a painful death. Either she advanced Ferguson's evil plot, or her mother and sisters would be put to death.

Oblivious to her desperate thoughts, the knight strode alongside the horse, keeping hold of the reins. The sun sank lower into the troughs of the hills, bringing Clarise the worry that she might be alone with him come nightfall.

"How far is it to Helmesly?" she inquired.

He slanted her a startled look. She realized with dismay that she'd spoken in the language of the upper class.

"You speak French!" he commented. His eyes gleamed with interest. "And you're not from Abbingdon, are you?"

Her spirits sank to new depths. She was not as adept at subterfuge as she'd imagined. "I served in a Norman household," she muttered, as that was the only logical answer. Few peasants, free or bound, knew how to speak Norman French.

"Which household?"

Ferguson had instructed her not to mention Heathersgill. "Glenmyre," she said, naming Alec's estate. It was best to keep close to the truth, she told herself.

"Ah," said the knight, looking suddenly grave. Crickets added a melody to the tempo of the horse's iron shoes. "Was your husband one of the peasants recently killed?" he inquired gently.

As he persisted in speaking French, she answered in the same, being more at ease with her first tongue. "Nay," she said slowly, though she knew the peasants to which he referred. Just before she left, Ferguson had boasted that he'd cut the peasant population at Glenmyre in half. She had no wish to be associated with that slaughter. "As I said, my husband was killed in a skirmish."

They continued the journey in silence. Clarise used the time to sketch a rough history for herself. She imagined what it would be like to care for a warlord's baby. *Rather like playing nursemaid to the devil's spawn,* she thought, recalling what she knew of the Slayer.

The mercenary had once been the master-at-arms for the Baron of Helmesly. The baron had wed him to his only daughter and then departed Helmesly on pilgrimage to Canterbury, leaving the Slayer behind as his seneschal. Rumor had it that the Slayer had plotted to kill the baron and his lady wife, for they did not return alive from their pilgrimage but in coffins. The Slayer was left ruling Helmesly, not as rightful lord but as a usurper.

Much the way Ferguson had acquired Heathersgill, Clarise thought with a sneer.

She cautioned herself to disguise her disdain. In masquerading as a freed serf, she would need to be humble and respectful. "What is the Slayer's proper name?" she asked, realizing she didn't even know it.

The knight looked up at her sharply. "Have a care that he doesn't hear you call him that," he warned. "He doesn't like the name Slayer."

Clarise paled at the warning.

"His name is Christian de la Croix," answered the knight, "and despite what people say of him, he is a devout man."

Christian of the Cross? She nearly hooted aloud at the devout name. With difficulty she swallowed the lunatic laughter in her throat. Still, she couldn't resist questioning the knight. "How comes it, then, that they call him the Slayer? Did he not kill every living soul at Wendesby, or is that a lie?"

The knight's crooked smile flattened to a seam. "If you value your post as the baby's nurse, you had best keep silent on the subject."

She bit her tongue at the reprimand and looked away. The knight was clearly loyal to his liege lord. She would do well to be cautious in his company.

Gazing toward the horizon, she sought sign of a fortress standing over the next hill. For just a second she imagined what it would be like if Sir Roger spoke true. What if the Slayer weren't the monster rumor painted him to be? What if he hadn't killed anyone at Wendesby, or the Baron of Helmesly, or even Alec's father?

She shook her head at her wishful thinking. There were far more villains in this world than good men. She'd be doing everyone a favor to rid the borderlands of the notorious Slayer. If she wished to see her mother and sisters alive, she had best accomplish her task and do it quickly.

Chapter Two

"'Tis beautiful," Clarise admitted with surprise.

"Aye, it is," Sir Roger concurred.

The object of their admiration stood in a field of wild-flowers, just behind a swift-running moat. In the coppery hues of evening, the moat was a golden disk from which the outer wall rose clifflike. It stood at least twenty hands high and twelve feet thick. The entire castle had been built on ancient earthworks, making the second wall visible as well.

The inner wall was flanked by towers. *Four of them!* Clarise marveled. Her own family's home of Heathersgill touted just one tall building. The closer Sir Roger urged them, the more overawed she became. With the sun plunging down behind the castle, shadows engulfed the draw-bridge. She felt as if she were being swallowed into the maw of a great beast.

They clattered over the moat. "Diverted from the River Rye Derwent!" Sir Roger shouted over the burbling water.

Clarise recalled that Helmesly had been built after the Norman acquisition to protect England from Scottish incursions. The ruling barons had been powerful men, fervently loyal to successive kings. Yet the man who ruled it now was nothing but a bastard seneschal.

They stopped before the gatehouse. Clarise shrank into

the saddle, eyeing the window slits with the fear of being recognized. Feeling sharp, suspicious gazes on her person, she tied her kerchief more securely beneath her chin. Yet Sir Roger's hail was answered at once. The portcullis rumbled upward, and their passing went unchallenged.

In the outer ward she cast eyes to the outer bailey. Bobbing helms betrayed the Slayer's vigilance. In the grassy enclosure stood a practice yard and archery run, attended by a handful of knights who continued to drill, though bats wheeled overhead. She knew already that a number of his fighting men remained at Glenmyre, yet he did not look ill prepared to defend this stronghold.

There was no bustling trade at Helmesly as there had been in Abbingdon. No venders, no craftsmen, no laughing children. It was a warrior's paradise.

Passing through a second gate, they came to the inner ward. The keep stood squarely before them, rising nearly to the height of the towers at either corner. It loomed into the evening sky, abutted by supporting arches. Smaller buildings huddled at its base in no apparent order, yet each was immaculately kept. No filth grimed the cobbles; no stench fouled the air.

Neither was there sign of human life. A red fire glowed in the smithy's hovel. From the mews came the screech of a hunting bird. The scent of hops wafted from the brewery house. Yet not a soul traversed the courtyard.

"Where is everyone?" Clarise wondered aloud.

"Within," Sir Roger said, helping her from the saddle.

He left her for a moment to duck into the stables. His answer told her nothing. She took note of where to find his horse should it suddenly become necessary to leave. Then she hunted for signs of a nanny goat.

She told herself she wouldn't linger long. But until she slipped the powder in the Slayer's drink, she would need to be convincing. If she were caught feeding the baby goat's milk, her identity would be called into question. She didn't doubt the Slayer had ways to make a prisoner talk.

In a distant pen a mud-caked sow nursed her offspring. Chickens pecked in another enclosure. There wasn't a nanny goat in sight.

Sir Roger emerged from the stables. "Lord Christian is back from Glenmyre," he announced with cheer. "His horse is here. He will be pleased that I have found a nurse at last."

How nice, thought Clarise, her stomach cramping. "Do you house goats here?" she rushed to inquire. Sir Roger was leading the way to the forebuilding of the main keep. "I have a fondness for goat's milk," she said, running to keep up with him.

He slanted her a tolerant look. "I find it sour."

"'Tis good for one's health," she argued, mounting the stairs by his side. "You *do* have goats, here, do you not?" she asked again. What would she do if the man said no?

"Several," came the heartening reply. "You shall have milk to quench your thirst," he promised. A moment later he swung wide the doors to the great hall and motioned for her to enter.

The grandeur of the hall chased all thoughts of goat's milk from her head. Clarise stepped into an enormous chamber. Its high arched ceiling soared above the first and second levels. A gallery coursed the length of the inner wall. The last hint of daylight glowed in the four tall windows opposite.

Clarise drew up short. Not a single tapestry, urn, or silver tray relieved the starkness. The hall was clean beyond compare but lacked the personal touches that made it welcoming.

A murmuring of voices drew her gaze to a clutch of servants lining the benches. A minstrel, sitting with his back to the door, plucked dejectedly upon his lute, while his audience looked on. At Clarise's entrance they turned their heads to regard her, their faces reflecting only vague curiosity.

"Did someone die?" she whispered, working at the knot beneath her chin.

Sir Roger spared her a distracted glance. "Did I not tell

you? My lady died in childbirth. 'Tis the reason I was sent for a nurse."

Clarise's stomach tightened. The baby's mother was dead? And she was supposed to kill its father as well? "I'm sorry to hear that," she said automatically. "They must have loved her greatly to cease their labors."

"Aye, they did," Sir Roger said with a sigh. "But this particular gathering is an indication of my lord's temperament. They herd together like sheep to avoid an encounter with him."

She nearly rent the cloth in her hands. "What . . . what does that mean, exactly?" But he was already mounting the stairs to the second level. With leaden feet she chased after him.

The tales of horror inspired by the Slayer bubbled in the cauldron of her mind. In laying waste to Wendesby six years past, he'd burned the village to ash and killed the innocents that ran before the flames. His own people huddled in the hall in fear of him, and she had just joined their oppressed ranks. Was she mad?

With every step Clarise's feet grew heavier. What if he recognized her from some previous visit to Heathersgill? She quickly redonned the kerchief to conceal her hair. Gazing at the second level, she faltered to a halt. She couldn't do it. She feared she would be caught and executed in a matter of hours.

"I have a terrible thirst," she called, stopping Sir Roger midway up the stairs. "Might I have the milk you promised me?"

Roger leaned over the balustrade and called to the servants. "Dame Maeve!" An elderly woman withdrew from the gathering, her harsh face softened by the mellow light. "Have a servant bring up a mug of goat's milk for our nurse, Dame Crucis."

"Aye, sir."

"Boil it first, if you please," Clarise added, knowing that part to be crucial.

Dame Maeve thinned her lips, but taking up her keys, she turned to fulfill the request.

"You give orders with accustomed ease," Sir Roger remarked. He indicated that they should follow the length of the gallery where a servant worked to light a torch. Shadows had already leaked into the upper levels. Clarise felt like a lamb being drawn to slaughter.

"My husband was a lenient man," she said, offering him a breathless explanation. She followed him along the gallery and down a long and narrow hall. They came to the twisting stairs of one of the four towers. Here the shadows thickened into blackness.

"Lord Christian must be in a rage if his servants won't approach him," she gasped, dreading the encounter to come.

"My lord is a reasonable man," Sir Roger threw out to comfort her.

But the sounds coming from the level above belied his tale. The cacophony of a wailing infant and a bellowing man blended in an awful duet. The Slayer's angry roar shot through Clarise like a poisoned arrow. She felt as though he were railing at her and not some hapless servant. Curiosity alone carried her up the remaining steps.

"Blood of the Saints, wench!" he shouted. "Cease this infernal sniveling and think of something else. My son is starving. Will you listen to his cries!"

"M'lord, I've done naught else for the last ten hours," whimpered the servant in Anglicized Norman. "He ne wille take the milk. I've tried it for days, now. Please ask nay more of me."

"You will scrub the garderobes for the rest of your life if you fail to make him drink!"

Clarise pitied the poor woman, but at the same time the distress in the Slayer's tone was palpable. No father, good or evil, would want his son to die.

Sir Roger chose that moment to propel her through the open door. "Lord Christian," he called over the din. "Your troubles are over, sire. This is the nurse you bade me find. Clare Crucis."

Clarise skidded to a halt before the most enormous creature she had ever seen. Her first instinct was to draw back, and she trod Sir Roger's toe as he barred the exit. The nursery seemed exceedingly small, or maybe its proportions had shrunk in the presence of the giant.

So this was the man she was to kill!

The Slayer stood before the open window. Half his body was illumined by the lingering glow of sunlight; the other half concealed in shadow. He was long of limb, broad in the shoulders, packed with muscle. His hair defined the color black as it hung in waves to his shoulders. Midnight eyebrows scowled over a long, straight nose.

He was younger than she'd imagined. The clean lines of his face—the half she could see—were shockingly handsome. The soft light revealed unblemished skin, tanned to the color of a nutmeg. The lines of his cheek and jaw were forceful. His eyelashes were absurdly long.

On the other side of his face, a glittering eye pierced the gloom. *Green.* His eyes were a light gray-green. They seemed to burn the air from her lungs as he stared at her. She read intelligence in their depths, followed by a sensual consideration that made her skin grow tight.

She would have known this man had they met as strangers on the open road. What man but the Slayer could be so utterly *dark?* His alert stance betrayed a lifetime of training. His body was honed and powerful. He was still wearing his chain mail, as though loath to shed the mantle of war. She hoped the powder in her pendant was enough to kill him.

"Of the cross?" he drawled, his voice blessedly quieter than it had been seconds before. His tone was touched with humor, an attractive sound coming from a man who would order her execution if he learned who she was.

After a moment's incomprehension, she realized he made

reference to the surname she'd invented, Crucis, yet she
failed to see the humor in it.

The warlord flashed his vassal a smile. With teeth gleaming white, his smile was like a jag of lightning in a sullen
sky. It took Clarise's breath away.

Unaware of her amazement, he added, "You have done
well in your search, Sir Roger. This damsel even bears my
name." His cool gaze ran over her, and she felt a tingling of
awareness.

"Christian de la Croix, madam," he introduced himself.
He sketched a bow—more for mockery than courtesy. But
it gave her the time she needed to understand his amusement. The name she'd given herself was the same as his, but
in Latin. She couldn't believe she'd overlooked that detail.

A fluke, she told herself, sinking to a curtsy. She knew an
overriding need to remove herself from his scrutiny, to run
as far and as fast as possible. Surely he could see the guilt
on her face! The pendant burned like the flames of hell
against her chest.

The baby's cries told her what to do next. His wails were
raw and desperate. She turned to comfort him and encountered the weeping maidservant.

"You may go," Clarise murmured. The girl snatched up
her skirts and ran, nearly toppling Sir Roger as she launched
herself through the door.

With a trembling in the pit of her belly, Clarise reached
into the cradle and lifted the baby. She settled him in her
arms and thrust her awareness of the Slayer aside. This child
was her alibi, her reason for being. If she convinced the men
she was caring for the baby, she would avert suspicion long
enough to do what was necessary.

The shrieking subsided. Clarise found herself the focus
of a bottomless, gray gaze. A tiny, heart-shaped face was
framed in a cowl of thick blankets. *He doesn't look like the
spawn of the devil* was her first thought.

She noticed suddenly that he was bundled so tightly perspiration drenched his swaddling. Oh, poor mite, she

thought, clicking her tongue at the incompetence of others. She eased the material from around his limbs and freed his hot head. With that, the infant grew peaceful. A tender wind blew across Clarise's heart. The babe felt natural in her arms, a precious burden. She turned toward the window, needing to see the baby better.

Though barely days old, from what she understood, he was cast in the image of his father. She could now see that he boasted a head of black hair. His little mouth trembled with the memory of distress, but he made no sound.

Tenderness gave way to uncertainty. Thus far, she had only thought of herself and her own safety. This child's very life rested in her hands! What if she failed in her attempts to feed him? What if she left him orphaned with no one to ensure his survival?

Hiding her concerns, Clarise ducked her head and kissed the baby's cheek. She felt the wetness of his tears on her mouth. Unthinking, she pulled the kerchief from her own head and dabbed at the silken cheek. From behind, she heard a sharp intake of breath, and she turned.

Christian couldn't help but stare. Clare Crucis had wrought the miracle of Simon's silence. She had burst into the room like a sunbeam, dispelling his fear that his son might die. As she moved toward the window, she'd removed her head covering, and he could see that her hair was the color of a flame, her eyes like honey. He could not prevent himself from hissing in a breath of appreciation. She glanced at him warily, then lowered her eyes again to study his infant son.

Christian feasted his gaze on her lovely profile—sculpted cheekbones, a delicate nose, lips so soft as to make a man weep. Yet her expression of tenderness was the quality that arrested him most.

"What is his name?" she asked, her accent nearly continental. He could only assume she had served a Norman family since birth.

"Simon." He had to clear his throat. "Go on, feed him,"

he urged. "He is half starved." The baby gave a start at the sound of his voice. To Christian's amazement, the nurse took note of this and frowned.

"The child must nurse in private, my lord. Kindly leave us and be assured that he will hunger no more."

Christian felt his jaw slacken. He glanced at Sir Roger to see if he had heard the woman right. His vassal merely grinned.

By God's right eye, the woman had just dismissed him from the room! He could think of no one—man or woman—who had dared such a thing before.

The novelty of it aroused him instantly.

Clarise was forced to mask her desperation. Hadn't the warriors heard her? They behaved as if they were pegged to the stone floor, doomed to grow shadows on the wall. She stepped closer to reason with the pair.

The Slayer stood a full head higher than his vassal. His scowl alone would frighten the fleas off a hound, but she could not afford to be intimidated. If the men did not leave, her masquerade would end ere it began.

"Am I not to be given privacy?" she asked, her tone implying she would leave her post, if such were true.

Sir Roger shook his curly head. "My lord, we must talk," he announced, backing out the door.

This announcement dragged the Slayer's gaze from Clarise to the empty portal. But Saintonge was gone. The Slayer held his ground.

Clarise regarded him with acute awareness. The sky outside the window had deepened to azure. She could see nothing of his features now. As the baby threatened to sob again, she clutched him more tightly and prayed the Slayer would leave.

"Feed my son," he said peremptorily.

Panic bloomed in her breast. "I . . . I require privacy," she stammered. What purpose could the warlord have other than to watch her bare her breasts? She gave a thought to Ferguson's treatment of female servants, and her blood abruptly thinned.

The floor was turning liquid under her feet. She cast about for a place to sit. But it was too late. She felt herself falling.

She never saw the Slayer move. But in the next second he was holding her upright. Strong arms banded around her, pinning both her and the baby to his chest. She struggled instinctively, panicked by the thought of being at his mercy. He dragged her toward an alcove and deposited her on a stool, where she shrank away, clutching Simon for protection.

"You are ill," the warrior announced. He loomed over her, an unformed shadow.

"Nay!" Clarise protested strongly. A vision of Horatio's festered face sprang to mind. "'Tis merely that I haven't eaten in a while."

Silence followed her answer. "I will see that you get some food at once," he offered unexpectedly.

She opened her mouth to thank him, but he was already striding away, his boots ringing on the stone floor. Clarise waited until he was gone, and then she dashed to the cradle to seek the nursing skin that the servant must have used. She would need it as much as that woman had in order to feed little Simon.

She could see nothing in the blackened chamber. Cursing at the lack of tapers, she felt inside the cradle and along the floor. At last she found what she was looking for, but the bladder was full of milk, and the milk smelled rancid.

By the time the Slayer returned, Simon was livid with rage. Nothing short of a full stomach would satisfy him. Clarise sat on the stool, her back against the wall, her heart hammering her throat. She was certain her hours were numbered. The Slayer would kill her for failing to comfort his son.

A candle illumined the Slayer's face as he crouched to place the tray upon the floor. He had brought her a crust of bread, a wedge of cheese, and the goat's milk. Saliva rushed into Clarise's mouth, despite her anxiety. She prayed Dame Maeve had let the milk boil long enough.

Glancing at the Slayer, she found him staring at her. The shock of seeing both sides of his face left her speechless. A scar creased his left cheek, running from eye to jaw. The seam was smooth, telling her the wound was an old one and well tended. Yet it marred the perfect symmetry of his face. Some might say it made him ugly.

As though privy to her thoughts, a scowl pressed down on his forehead, carving menace into his features. Clarise looked away and murmured her thanks. Simon wailed.

"Supper is being prepared," growled the mercenary. He straightened and stepped away to where the ring of light reached only to his shoulders. "You will eat again straightways. Please do hurry," he urged. "My son is crazed with hunger."

Clarise grabbed a chunk of bread and stuffed it in her mouth. The lord's courtesy abated her terror just enough that she could feel how hungry she was. He stepped away from the alcove, leaving her in semiseclusion, but he didn't leave the nursery. She heard him pause before the window, dominated by the dark of night.

She was truly in a quandary, now. She had managed to dump the sour milk outside the window, but she could scarcely refill the nursing skin with the Slayer in the same room. How, she wondered, would she get the fresh milk down the baby's throat?

The seconds stretched by. The warlord remained by the window, presumably to give her privacy.

Simon sobbed until his tears dampened her bodice. With a feeling that none of this could be real, Clarise dipped a finger in the milk and offered it to the baby. He nuzzled the offering, then screamed when little came of his exertions.

"How goes it?" the Slayer demanded over Simon's piercing note.

She heard him take a step toward the alcove, and she

tensed with alarm. With no alternative, she tugged at the laces on her bodice. "All will be fine," she assured him. For authenticity's sake, she pushed the material apart and offered a breast to the inconsolable baby.

Simon fastened on so fiercely that she had to swallow a cry of pain. By some miracle, his enthusiasm silenced him. It felt strange indeed to have a baby tugging at her breast. He didn't seem to mind that he was getting nothing from his efforts. To be held, to be pacified was enough for now.

Grateful for the momentary respite, Clarise let out a pent-up breath. Exhaustion swamped her. She sat more heavily on the three-legged stool and lifted the mug to taste the formula herself. She was pleased to note that it had been boiled for some time.

The crush of rushes under the sole of a boot had her pricking her ears. Clarise dragged her eyelids upward. The warlord stood an arm's span away, his gray-green gaze on the pendant that lay between her naked breasts.

Chapter Three

The Slayer had joined her in the little alcove. Clarise gasped with surprise and promptly sucked milk down her lungs. She succumbed to a fit of coughing. With the flagon in one hand and the baby in the other, she stared helplessly up at the warlord, her eyes stinging.

"Will you be all right?" he asked as she wheezed for breath.

She swallowed hard. Nay, she would not be all right. She would be flayed for a fraud and a liar. He would see straight through her flimsy disguise to the ugly truth that brought her here.

He stood so close that the candle's flame was doubly reflected in his eyes. His eyes saw *everything*. Clarise's blood ran cold as she waited for judgment to come crashing down.

"He seems content," he said, focusing again on the locket.

The words flowed over her, diluting her terror. God have mercy, had she actually deceived him? One knot at a time, her muscles relaxed.

Was he looking at the pendant to avoid looking at her breasts? She glanced down to see how suspect the hollow ball appeared.

"'Tis unusual for a servant to wear jewelry," he said, causing her heart to pound. "Is it gold?"

"Oh, nay," she replied, hastily covering the locket with the fabric of her gown. "My mother gave it to me. 'Tis naught but bronze."

"Your mother?" he repeated. "And who was she?"

Did his narrowed gaze betray suspicion? "Jeannie Crucis," Clarise supplied. "She was a peasant."

"Why is it you speak like a noblewoman?" he demanded.

She struggled to subdue her galloping heart. "My ancestors were Saxon nobles," she told him, grasping at straws. "When the Normans seized our home, our family served them, learning their language."

"You practiced speaking like a lady?"

There was genuine skepticism in his voice this time. "I'm a freed serf," she insisted. But she knew that he did not believe her tale. She would stick to it as long as she had to, and then she would be gone. If she lived that long, the man before her would be dead.

"Whence do you hail?" he asked, giving her no time to think.

"From Glenmyre," she answered, wishing he would cease his interrogation.

Glenmyre. The name rolling off the woman's tongue sent Christian's spirits plummeting. He turned away as shards of darkness wormed their way beneath his skin.

He resumed his place by the window, letting the night air take the edge off his self-incrimination. Genrose, his saintly wife, had died for his ambitions. Nineteen peasant women wept for the loss of their husbands. Glenmyre's fields would go to seed without hands to farm it. He was a plague to them all. *A Slayer who butchered the lambs.*

Behind him, Clare Crucis shifted. Simon emitted a wail, one that was immediately muffled. The baby's grunt of pleasure was followed by little sucking noises, sounds that tempted Christian to thank God out loud. Here, at last, was something good. He had been certain God would take his son from him. He'd expected it.

But an angel interceded on Simon's behalf. Hope pulsed anew in his breast—not for himself, but for Simon's future, Simon's soul. Unless there was more to this angel than met the eye.

"Did your husband die defending Glenmyre from my attack?" he inquired. Silence exploded in the tiny chamber, and he feared he had his answer. The woman had a motive for vengeance.

"He . . . he died in a skirmish," she finally answered.

Christian searched his mind. There had been several skirmishes at Glenmyre, but no loss of life until just recently. "He must have been in Ferguson's slaughter, then," he surmised, realizing the full extent of Clare's suffering. Here was a widow of one of the slain peasants. "I am sorry I wasn't there to prevent it," he added awkwardly. "I was called away for the birth of my son."

Clarise gnawed the inside of her lip. She'd told Sir Roger that her husband was not one of those unfortunate peasants. Should she correct the warlord's assumption? Now that she considered it, it made sense to say her husband had been killed in Ferguson's attack, for then it followed to reason that she would turn to the Slayer—her overlord—for protection and sustenance.

Christian waited for the woman to answer him. Perhaps she was too bereaved to speak. He pictured her bowed over his baby, overwhelmed by her recent loss. Guilt cut deeply into him. "The Scot has no respect for human life," he growled. The words offered only hollow comfort. It was *his* fault the peasants were slain, but there was nothing he could do to bring her husband back.

The silence in the chamber grew oppressive. He longed to hear her honeyed voice again. Seldom did he come across a soul willing to converse with him. "Why did you journey south?" he prompted. "Why did you come to Helmesly?" It was a two-day walk from Glenmyre, perhaps farther. The road offered untold perils.

"I could stay no longer." He was relieved to hear resignation in her tone and not weeping. "'Twas logical that I come to Helmesly, as you are now the ruler of Glenmyre. I came to . . . to serve you as I can."

Her observation caused him to remember the fateful day he rode upon Glenmyre. Monteign's forces had spilled over a hill without warning. There was no time for words, no time for explaining. Monteign thought he was defending himself from attack. He fought like a lion, ignoring the banner of peace that Christian's flagman had frantically waved. Despite effort to subdue Monteign without undue bloodshed, the lord of Glenmyre had died and his soldiers had laid down their arms in surrender.

Ignorant of the warlord's weighty thoughts, Clarise struggled to keep her eyes open. She sensed that the Slayer had finished questioning her. Miraculously she'd survived the initial round. With wildflowers sweetening the evening air and the rhythmic tugging at her breast, she was lulled into a false sense of security. Any moment now she might fall asleep.

Through the bloom of light at her feet, the warlord's rasping voice reached her again. "I am sorry for the death of your lord, Monteign."

She could not credit the quiet apology. She must have misheard him.

"I'd heard rumors of an alliance between Monteign and Ferguson. I only meant to question him about the matter."

"An alliance?" Reality jarred Clarise to wakefulness. Her heart lurched against her breastbone.

"'Twas a marriage, between Monteign's only son and Ferguson's stepdaughter."

Her stomach slowly twisted. Her scalp tingled. *He couldn't have guessed who she was already!*

"I was told to confront Monteign and put an offer to him that was better than Ferguson's. The sight of our soldiers must have confused him. He ambushed us as we came over the hill. We had no choice but to fight. He ignored our signal for a truce."

Stunned, Clarise digested this new information. She'd always assumed that the Slayer had seized Glenmyre by force. This was the first she'd heard of an attempt at negotiations, but perhaps he was lying to her. Men's recollections of battle were inevitably skewed.

"Tell me," he added, sounding reflective. "What was Monteign like? What kind of lord was he?"

The question left her reeling. *Did the Slayer feel remorse for his sins?*

She summoned a picture of Alec's father. "He was a father to his people," she replied. "He was fair, yet stern with them. He was stubborn, too, and loyal to his friends."

"And was he friends with Ferguson?"

She swallowed against the dryness in her throat. "I . . . I don't know. I was only a servant. However, I . . ." Did she dare say more, to admit to any kind of knowledge? "I rather think he feared Ferguson more than anything."

All at once it was quiet on the other side of the partition, and the quiet was profound.

"Dame Crucis, would you like fresh clothing?"

The question was the last thing Clarise expected. She was certain he had guessed who she was and was preparing to kill her.

Clothing? She looked down at her worn smock. "Please," she replied, dazed that he would even concern himself.

She heard him move to the door. Straining to see beyond the alcove, she perceived the outline of his powerful frame.

"I expect you to sup with me once you've refreshed yourself. Bring my son with you."

With that peremptory order, the shadow melted into the darkness, and Clarise was left alone with the baby. She pondered the words she'd shared with his father. No matter how she turned them over in her mind, she was left with one burning impression: The Slayer wasn't the barbaric warrior she'd believed. His intelligence made him a double-edged sword. And something else . . . he seemed to actually have compassion and remorse—rare qualities indeed for a man of such fearsome repute.

How was she to poison such a man without losing her own life, or worse yet, her soul to eternal hellfire?

Christian shifted his legs under the table and encountered the wolfhound bellycrawling beneath it. The dog did not belong on the dais, but the presence at his feet was comforting. Since no one but the dog dared get so close, he let the interloper stay.

The discordant twangs bouncing off the ceiling drew his disbelieving gaze. Christian stared at the multicolored tunic of the minstrel and admitted he had erred. Three days ago he'd believed the presence of a minstrel would lighten the spirits of the servants. But the notes tumbling from the boy's instrument were more of an irritant than entertainment. Christian tried to shut his ears to the noise. Now he knew why the hound hid beneath the table.

Shifting his attention to Peter, he wondered perversely what the page would drop tonight. Peter lived in terror of the seneschal's temper, and his fear put him in peril of dropping the water bowl. Even now candlelight shivered on the water's surface. If he dropped the bowl, the Slayer would yell. 'Twas a self-fulfilling prophecy.

Christian growled and glanced toward the gallery. No sign of the new nurse yet. Perhaps the servants had whispered his sins in her ears, and she cowered in her chamber, loathing the prospect of his company. What of it? Everyone feared him. It was inevitable that she would come to fear him, also.

Still, he thought, peering into the ale that was the color of her eyes, he hoped she wouldn't. Her unflinching attitude was a novelty to him. It had been so long since anyone besides Sir Roger had told him what to do. *Kindly leave us.*

Could the woman really be a freed serf? She sounded like a bloody queen.

Now she was late for supper, exacerbating his desire to look at her again. He entertained himself by wondering which of her many attributes appealed most to him. Was it her eyes or her mouth? Her habit of chewing on her bottom lip had caused immediate stirrings in his loins. And those breasts! Ah, how he marveled at those full pale globes. He found himself irrationally jealous of his son, who got to suck on them.

Where was the wench? For that matter, where was his master-at-arms? Christian sat alone, insulated from his serfs by the rift that widened to unbreachable proportions after his lady's passing. Genrose had visited the peasants' cottages and tended to their needs. He could not compete with the devotion they were used to. He could not begin to emulate it.

He swirled his drink, feeling guilty for something that had been beyond his powers, irritable for the caterwauling coming from the minstrel's lute. Several soldiers at the boards grumbled over supper's delay.

At last Sir Roger sidled along the dais to take his seat beside the empty lady's chair. He greeted Christian with his usual aplomb and held out his goblet to be filled.

Christian waited for what he thought was a reasonable span of time. "You wished to tell me something of the nurse, Saintonge?" he inquired casually.

Sir Roger sent a meaningful glance toward the musician. "How long are we going to put up with this?" he asked, ignoring his liege's opening.

Christian didn't want to discuss the minstrel. "Dismiss him tomorrow," he said curtly. "What was it you were going to say about the nurse?" he asked, betraying his impatience.

"A veritable pearl in an oyster, eh, my lord?" Sir Roger stalled.

Christian checked his reply. With his wife not in the ground a week, it didn't seem appropriate to comment one way or the other. But if Clare were a pearl, then Genrose might have been a slab of marble. He squashed the unkind thought.

"Did she tell where she is from?" Sir Roger added, his eyebrows nudging upward.

"Glenmyre," Christian assented with a grunt.

"Yet you trust her with your son." The knight watched his lord's expression. "Her husband was killed in a skirmish, you know."

Christian nodded his head. "He was one of the peasants Ferguson killed."

Sir Roger gave him a funny look. "Nay, I asked her if that were so, and she denied it," he retorted unexpectedly.

The noise from the lute faded into the background. Christian frowned and searched his memory. "She led me to believe such *was* just the case. That is why she came here, because she couldn't bear to remain at Glenmyre any longer."

Sir Roger's gray eyes narrowed. "I'd say we have a slight discrepancy," he said lightly. "What more did she tell you?"

"In her own words, she said she came to serve me, as I am now the ruler of Glenmyre."

"Serve you?" the knight repeated, a hint of ribaldry in his eyes.

Christian ignored it, though in his mind's eye he imagined her serving him in exactly the same way. "Is she suspect?" he asked his vassal. Sir Roger had a gift for sensing danger. If the woman were a spy, his man would soon know it.

"I'm not sure," Saintonge surprised him by replying. He scraped the bristles of his new beard. "I know she is not what she professes to be. Her speech betrays her. She is no more a freed serf than you or I are high-born princes. The woman is a Norman, if not a lady outright."

It was nice to have his suspicions corroborated. Yet if the woman lied to them, then chances were she intended some mischief. "I'd better check on Simon." He rose quickly from his chair.

Sir Roger clapped a hand to his wrist. "Peace, my liege. A man stands guard over the baby. Sit you down and eat for a change."

Christian eased back into his oak chair. "You left a guard alone with her?" The notion unsettled him. He knew firsthand the willpower it took not to stare at the nurse's breasts.

"'Tis only Sir Gregory," Sir Roger said, naming the oldest knight in their service.

Christian was mollified, but only slightly. He signaled to Peter to bring the water bowl. "He had best keep his eyes to himself," he muttered, dipping his hands. "Marked you how the woman spoke to me?" he couldn't help but add. It had been years since he'd shared a casual conversation with any woman, the most recent being with his mother nigh ten years ago.

"Mayhap she has yet to hear the rumors of your bloody past," drawled the knight.

"She knows them," he insisted. "I saw the fear on her face when she beheld my scar."

"Then she is either brave or foolish."

Trenchers of starling and pork pie made their way to the high table. "Where is the wench?" Christian wondered aloud. "I bade her sup with us."

"Likely sleeping," said Saintonge. "She was dead on her feet when I found her."

Ah, yes, she'd fainted in his arms. Christian savored the memory of her softness against his armor. He ought to have thought of her welfare, but he was not as astute as Saintonge where women were concerned. Catching the eye of Dame Maeve, he waved her forward. "See you what the nurse is doing," he commanded.

The woman pinched her lips. She gave the air a sniff as she turned to do his bidding.

What? Christian wondered, staring after her. He decided he should have asked a lowlier servant. The steward's wife had better things to do than charge up and down the stairs.

It was no secret that she was the true source of efficiency behind the simple-minded steward.

Harold, panicked by his wife's desertion, began to pace
before the dais. His white hair bobbed like a rooster's comb
as he oversaw the food's distribution. The minstrel fell
wisely silent as the men dug into their trenchers.

The meal progressed slowly. Christian looked up, happy
to see the steward's wife approaching the table at last.

"My lord, the woman is sleeping, and I was unable to
awaken her," she said with more deference.

"Well, what about my son? Who watches him?"

"The babe sleeps, also, and a knight stands guard outside
his door."

"All is well with the world," Sir Roger added with distinct cynicism.

"Kindly prepare a tray for her," Christian requested of the
woman, "as I would not have her starve. I will carry it up
myself," he added, eager to share words with the woman.

"She is fond of boiled goat's milk," said Saintonge from
the side of his mouth.

Christian indicated that the milk be added to the fare.
Dame Maeve affirmed the order and moved away, calling
instructions to the pages as she hastened to the kitchen.

"So," Sir Roger said, reaching for his goblet. "You will
deliver the tray yourself."

"I mean to question her, 'tis all," Christian groused. "We
know that she has lied to us. I mean to discover why."

"The answer depends on what she truly is," his vassal
reasoned. "If one goes by her speech alone, she could be a
damned Parisian." He deftly fingered his knife.

"Then she's a lady," Christian reasoned. "But what would
a lady be doing traipsing through the countryside in search
of work? 'Tis impossible."

"'Tis possible if she bore her baby out of wedlock," Sir
Roger countered.

Her baby. Christian had forgotten that the woman had to
have given birth first in order to have milk. God's blood. Not

only had she lost a husband recently but also a child. Having experienced that kind of loss himself, he felt a ribbon of pity wind through his heart. At least he was capable of such a basic emotion, poor woman. Had he been crass to her? He could have been more thoughtful.

He put the pieces together slowly. "So, if she bore a babe out of wedlock, then mayhap she lies about the husband."

"'Twould explain the inconsistencies," Sir Roger countered. He tapped the side of his goblet with his knife and narrowed his eyes. "Which brings up an entirely new possibility," he murmured, after a moment of intense reflection.

"And that is?" Christian prompted.

"Perhaps she was a courtesan, a leman—"

"A mistress!" said Christian. Now, this explanation he preferred, for he could feel less guilty about the woman's loss. "Aye, that would explain her candor with me, the jewelry that she wore about her neck," he added with enthusiasm. "She said it was bronze, but I know the difference." He remembered staring at the pendant to keep from ogling the woman's wares.

"It also explains why she bore a child out of wedlock, why she has come to *serve* you as overlord of Glenmyre." Sir Roger imbued the word with all its baser connotations.

Christian felt his ardor rise. The woman had come to serve him in the absence of her former lord. All at once, his excitement dimmed. "That means . . ." He reached for his wine, needing to chase a bitter taste from his tongue.

"That she might have been Monteign's leman," Saintonge supplied.

Christian thrust the unpleasant image from his mind. Monteign had been a big and burly man, more than twice Clare Crucis's age.

They sat for a moment in private contemplation.

"Do you think she seeks a new protector?" Christian dared to ask.

Sir Roger wiped the sheen of grease from his chin. "We have taken our guesses to extremes," he replied, crushing his lord's burgeoning hopes. "She might also be a spy, sent to take stock of our defenses. Or to avenge a husband's death."

Those same fears had coursed Christian's mind like muddy rivers, sullying the relief that Simon had been saved. "I will get the truth from her yet," he vowed, hurrying to finish.

With eagerness whittling away his appetite, he abandoned his trencher and stood. The knight's parting caution echoed in his head as he took the tray from Maeve and carried it up the stairs.

Try subtlety, my lord. It works better than threat.

The room that Clare had been allotted stood adjacent to the nursery. Christian approached the knight who was supposed to be standing guard. Sir Gregory sat on the floor with his back to the wall and his head between his knees. He snored loud enough to herald an army.

"God's toes!" Christian muttered, battling the urge to jerk the old man to his feet. He stepped over him instead and snatched the torch from the holder. Angling himself into the nurse's room, he held the torch aloft and looked around.

Dame Crucis lay on the high mattress, fast asleep. By all appearances, she'd intended to join him. She wore the gown he'd found in his late mother-in-law's discarded wardrobe. A brush lay loosely in her palm. It appeared that she had simply wilted onto the bedcovers, lulled by the warmth of the brazier.

In the innocent posture of sleep, she didn't look capable of spawning any mischief. She did, however, fit the description of a female valued for her womanly charms. Brushed to smoothness, her hair poured fire over the bleached pillowcase. She had bathed the dust from her body, revealing pale, soft flesh beneath. The room smelled of lavender and woman.

Even in a dress more suited to a matron, she possessed a sensual allure. The turquoise bodice strained across her breasts, its laces scarcely meeting. Christian's gaze moved from her tiny waist to the flare of her hips. Her skirts molded the shapely length of her splayed thighs, invited his gaze to fall into the indent between them. How simple it was to imagine himself moving over her, pressing himself into her vulnerable core.

Christian gave himself a mental shake. He could not afford to blind himself with lust until he knew the woman's purpose.

The cry of his infant penetrated the wall of the nursery. Clare Crucis stirred but failed to waken. Witnessing the extent of her exhaustion, Christian placed the tray beside the bed and carried the torch to the nursery, stepping over the knight, who blocked the corridor.

The vision that awaited him brought choked denial to his throat. Simon lay naked in his box, his skin nearly blue with cold. The swaddling had been taken off him and tossed over the end of the cradle. He wore no soiling cloth, and the crib was wet with urine.

Christian threw the swaddling over his screaming son and caught him up. "Hush," he soothed, rubbing the baby's limbs to speed the return of warmth. The infant's distress filled him with helpless rage.

How long had Simon lain there shivering? Had Clare Crucis done this to him? By God, he would tear her limb from limb if he saw guilt upon the nurse's face! But first he would teach that doddering, old knight not to sleep on the job.

With his temples throbbing, he girded his baby's loins in a fresh soiling cloth and swaddled him as best he could. His ministrations only enraged the infant more. Simon's fists broke free of the inept swaddling, and he bellowed loud enough to make the chamber echo.

Sir Gregory muttered in protest as Christian stalked into the hall. "Get up!" the warlord snapped, prodding the man with his toe.

The knight threw his head up suddenly, smacking it

against the wall. With a cry of pain, he scrambled to his feet, muttering unintelligibly.

"Someone took the swaddling off my son," Christian told him in a voice that made his own blood run cold.

Sir Gregory's mouth fell open. "Oh!" he cried. "I . . . I . . . I didn't see anything."

"Of course not, you sluggard," Christian snarled. "You were sleeping! Go and tell Sir Roger what just happened, and stay well away from me!"

"Aye, m'lord," quaked Sir Gregory. He hobbled away with a hand pressed to the growing lump on his head.

Christian glared after him. With some portion of his wrath thus exorcised, he turned to the nurse's chamber. 'Twould have been a simple thing for her to perpetrate this mischief. His blood boiled at the thought. Recalling Sir Roger's advice, however, he tempered his rage and pledged himself to subtlety.

The baby still wailed, but the woman slept on as Christian entered the chamber. He stared at her in angry disbelief, then deposited Simon by her hip. The baby grasped her gown and turned his cheek in a desperate search for milk. Christian watched his futile efforts for a moment. Then he put his hand on the woman's shoulder and shook her hard.

Chapter Four

*C*larise pushed herself to run faster, but her legs kept tangling in her skirts. The hallways of Heathersgill seemed endless as she raced for the courtyard. At last she burst through the oak door. It was nearly too late. Her mother and sisters were lined up on the gallows with kerchiefs covering their eyes. They would die because she failed to do what Ferguson had commanded.

"Stop!" she screamed, racing across the cobbled area. The Scot was standing on the platform behind them. At her cry of protest her stepfather grinned through his flaming beard and shoved the stool out from her mother's feet. Jeanette dropped abruptly, then dangled like a doll on the end of a rope.

"Nay!" Clarise screamed through a tight throat. "You bloody bastard! Murderer!"

The sound of her own voice snatched her from her dream. Her eyes flew wide in time to see a shadow looming over her, but it wasn't Ferguson. She gasped and scrambled backward. The man was immense. Something small jerked against her hip. Its wail of distress oriented her at once.

She realized with horror that she had just called the Slayer a murderer. In the wavering orange light, she could barely make out his features.

"'Tis I," he rasped, ignoring the epithet, at least for the time being. "Simon is hungry. You were sleeping and failed to wake to his cries."

The accusation in his voice made her scalp tingle. He'd come *alone* to her chambers? Couldn't a servant be sent to awaken her?

"Your pardon." She tried to decipher the mercenary's mood. Anger seemed to emanate from his tense form, and she tried to guess the reason for it. "I was combing my hair." She lifted the brush she still clutched in her hand. "I must have fallen asleep." Perhaps he was upset that she hadn't joined him at supper.

It was no excuse, but after her bath, the warmth of the brazier had left her so drowsy, she sank onto the feather mattress, grateful that she hadn't been given a straw one, and that had been her last thought.

You were sleeping and failed to hear his cries. "Oh, the saints, I beg your pardon!" It was her sloth that angered him, of course! She reached for the baby at once, pressing him to her breast. Would the Slayer dismiss her? Would all hope of saving her family be dashed because she'd succumbed to exhaustion?

The moment she lifted him, Simon quieted. Clarise kissed his petal-soft cheek, grateful for the baby's cooperation. Her gaze slid warily to his watchful father. To her dismay, the Slayer seated himself on the corner of the bed. The mattress dipped and the bed ropes creaked.

"You have a way with him," he growled. The words would have eased her fears if not accompanied by that same threatening undertone.

"Th-thank you," she stammered. "He is easy to love, as most babies are."

Silence stretched over the next minute, interrupted only by a soft crackle from the brazier.

"Did you take the blankets off my son?" he asked.

The question came unexpectedly, like a cut from a razor. "I'm sorry?" She didn't understand.

"I found my son, just now, with no swaddling to warm him and no soiling cloth, either. He was naked and shivering."

She stared dumbfounded at the warlord. With his face in shadow, she could make out only two features: his rock-hard chin and glowing eyes. He had spoken through his teeth.

The breath in Clarise's lungs evaporated. "I swear to you, I left him swaddled in clean linens. He was sleeping contentedly." Her thighs tensed with the urge to flee. "Lord de la Croix," she gasped, picking up speed as she begged for mercy, "I swear it on my soul I would never hurt this babe. You must believe me! Someone else must have slipped into the nursery intending to harm him."

A breeze blew softly through the window, and the torchlight brightened, revealing his face—one side like an angel's, the other slashed from eye to jaw. He searched her face to see if she lied. Then he gave a little nod, as though accepting her word. "I will have your oath, Dame Crucis, that no harm will befall my son when he is with you," he said, with far less violence. "I am surrounded by those who wish him ill. He is heir to the land that others covet."

His words made her think of Ferguson. She considered, not for the first time, that the Scot would also want the baby dead, for Simon was the rightful heir to the seat of Helmesly. She looked down at the innocent infant, stricken by the thought of him murdered. Had Ferguson also sent someone to kill the baby?

She rebelled at the thought. "I will protect him with my life," she heard herself say, and she found that she meant it.

Clarise grew suddenly aware that the Slayer's thigh was touching her knee. She could feel the heat of him through the linen fabric of her skirts. This was far too intimate. She was boxed in a little room with a warrior who watched her every move. There was every chance that he would realize her deceit if she didn't guard her words and actions carefully.

"Thank you for bringing Simon to my chamber," she

said, encouraging him to leave. "He will sleep in this room with me if you prefer."

"I prefer it so," said the warlord, giving her permission to move the cradle to her chambers.

She adjusted the baby, as though preparing to nurse, but the Slayer didn't budge. "Since my son is content to be held, you should eat. You must have nourishment to feed him." He stood up and retrieved a tray from the nearby chest.

Clarise noticed for the first time the aroma of pastry. Her gaze fell greedily to the meat pie in a crusty shell. To the side was a cup of Frumenty pudding. Her stomach gave a hollow rumble.

Hearing it, the Slayer flashed her the same brief smile she'd seen before and placed the tray by her bent legs. "Eat," he invited, sitting more comfortably at the end of the mattress.

With the smile encouraging her, she attacked the food with gusto. Even while leaning over the now quiet baby, she managed to consume as much as her stomach could contain. She scraped the last bit of pudding from the cup and licked her spoon clean.

The warlord watched her every move with his gray-green eyes. Simon's little fists clutched the fabric of her bodice, but for his part, the baby seemed content. Clarise eyed the goat's milk—the only drink upon the tray. She was relieved not to have to ask for it again. But given the warlord's vigilance, she feared she would have to drink it herself.

"My vassal swears that you are fond of goat's milk," he remarked.

"Very fond." She smothered a burp. "However, I shall have to save it for later. I'm exceedingly full."

"Wine, then," he suggested, coming to his feet. "You must have something to drink."

"I am fine, truly." She wished he would simply leave the room. The man made her nervous.

"There is wine in the conservatory," he insisted. " 'Tis no trouble at all to fetch it."

She watched with dismay as he left the chamber. Why was the Slayer so solicitous, she wondered, when he'd just questioned her about the care she'd given his son? A rash of goose bumps prickled her skin. Perhaps he meant to drug her with wine, first, and then he would question her.

She seized advantage of his absence to pull the nursing skin from beneath the pillow. She filled the vessel for a second time, having had success with it earlier. Then she put it back beneath the pillow and waited for the Slayer's return. Her pulse tapped against her eardrums. She could hear no evidence of a guard standing outside the nursery door. *What has become of Sir Gregory?* she wondered.

At last she heard the unmistakable tread of the warlord. He stepped through the doorway, bearing an earthenware bottle and a silver goblet.

"Forgive me, lord," she hastened to say, "but I was so thirsty I drank the milk after all. I've no need of wine, now."

He halted in his tracks, his black brows sinking slowly over the ridge of his nose. Clarise cringed at her unfortunate timing. With torchlight licking over him, the man looked huge, dangerous, and angry. She was insane to think she could manipulate him.

"You will share it with me," he insisted on a growl.

Simon responded to his father's threat with a shriek. Clarise nearly smiled at the baby. "I have to feed your son," she informed him, seizing the excuse.

He stalked to the high bed. "Then we will speak whilst you nurse him," he insisted.

Her full stomach began to churn. Her deception would be put to the test again.

She laid the baby deliberately in the shadows and turned her back on the seneschal to loosen her bodice as before. Reclining by Simon, she pretended to latch him to a breast. Instead, she pulled the nursing skin from its hiding place and stuck the tip into Simon's mouth, counting on the shadows to hide it. The baby latched on as eagerly as before.

Scarcely breathing, Clarise eyed the Slayer's shadow,

cast by torchlight onto the bed curtain before her. She saw him raise an arm, saw the wine's reflection sparkle as he filled his goblet. Stoneware clinked against the floor. Then he propped a shoulder on the bedpost.

"Tell me something, Dame Crucis," he murmured in a voice buttressed by determination. "Was your husband recently killed by Ferguson, as you led me to believe, or was he slain in a different skirmish? Or could it be you lied on both accounts?"

The cool inquiry turned her cold, then hot. *Mercy, but it hadn't taken them long to notice the discrepancy.* She cursed herself for not sticking to her original story. Now he would question her until she broke down and told the truth. Her disguise was a flimsy one indeed.

"I never had a husband," she admitted, seeing that option as the best solution to her needs.

"Ah." He sounded happy to hear it. "Then what brings you here?" he finally asked.

Panic fluttered up and down her spine. "I told you, I could stay at Glenmyre no longer."

"Why?" he asked predictably.

"I was ashamed," she said, making up her answers as she went along. Luckily, this little bit seemed to fit.

"Ashamed to bear a child out of wedlock?" he asked mildly.

"Aye."

"What line of work did you do before?" This was asked in almost pleasant tones.

Clarise relaxed a bit. The warlord was certainly more sociable than she'd imagined him to be. "Well, I was, er, a reading tutor," she replied. She winced the moment the words were out, for she'd never heard of a woman performing such work.

"Is that why you speak French so well?"

"I studied French at a convent." 'Twas logical, she told herself.

"Which one?"

"St. Giles," she said firmly. She'd made the name up.

"I've never heard of St. Giles, though my mother is the Abbess of St. Cecily."

Her tongue stuck to the roof of her mouth, refusing to mire her any deeper. His mother was a *nun*? Nay, she must have misheard him.

"Tell me the truth now, Clare," he cajoled. His voice grew compelling and seductive. "Why did you come here?"

The blood rushed frantically through her. She was tempted to tell him everything—he hadn't believed her lies anyway. Yet her dream seemed to warn her that defying Ferguson would result in the death of her mother and sisters. If she apprised the Slayer of the truth, their lives would be forfeit. She could say nothing of her purpose.

"I needed work and wages, 'tis all," she helplessly insisted.

"Are you here to avenge me on someone's behalf?" he pressed, the seductive tenor of his voice cooling abruptly.

"*What!*" she cried, wondering if he knew the truth all along. Had he simply ben toying with her?"

"Are you a spy, sent to take account of my men and weapons?"

Worse and worse. "Of course not!" she cried. She twisted her head around in order to persuade him of her innocence. The nursing skin slipped from Simon's mouth, and the baby let loose a high-pitched cry.

The Slayer frowned with concern, then began to unfold. *He's going to stand!* Clarise realized with paralyzing fear. *He'll see what I'm doing!* She shoved the nursing skin beneath the pillow, and Simon raged at the sudden deprivation.

"What goes wrong?" the lord demanded. "Why is he not sucking?" In addition to towering over the bed, he felt inclined to raise his voice. Simon responded in kind, his cries growing louder.

Under the threat of doom, Clarise raised her own voice. "He must have quiet, my lord!" she informed him firmly.

"Please, sit down and I will calm him!" Her imperious suggestion brought an incredulous look to the Slayer's face.

Very slowly he put the goblet on the floor. Simon roared in Clarise's right ear. The Slayer's shadow fell across the bed. She realized he was crawling onto the mattress, over her. His long fingers sank into the pillow on either side of her head. She had visions of the bladder spewing milk onto the sheets.

Ignoring Simon's cries, the Slayer lowered his face until his eyes were level with her own. *This is it,* Clarise considered. Shock slipped over her with the feel of hot oil. *He will force me now, and I will be helpless to stop him.*

She willed her eyes to shut, but the scar that raked the length of his cheek held her spellbound. His body was so close that she could smell a hint of juniper mixed with the fruity scent of wine.

"Let us settle one thing now," he told her in a voice as hard as the links of armor he'd thankfully shed. "Simon is heir to the Baronetcy of Helmesly, and that is more than I will ever be. To be baron, he must first survive his infancy. He must have the best care, the best food, the *best* this world can offer. Do I make myself very clear, Dame Crucis?"

"Yes!" she gasped, struck by his honesty.

"You of all people should understand how I would feel if something were to happen to him." A flicker of sympathy showed in his face as he said those words.

I, of all people? She tried to grasp what he was saying. He could only be referring to the babe she was supposedly grieving.

With a start of surprise, she realized he felt pity for her loss. Not only was he sympathetic, but instead of threatening her with physical violence, he'd listed his hopes and fears regarding Simon. With his words the lens of fright dropped briefly away, and Clarise found herself looking at a real human being, a vulnerable man.

A very big and powerful warrior-man. She grew suddenly aware of his hard, honed body hovering over her.

"Very clear, my lord," she whispered, her voice deserting her.

"In exchange for your service to my son, you will enjoy my protection," he added. "You will sleep on this feathered bed, eat in my hall, and wear the gowns that I give you. Do you question this arrangement?"

"Nay." She could hardly see past him for the breadth of his shoulders. His arms bulged on either side of her. His neck was thick and corded with muscle. *Ferguson wouldn't stand a chance against him,* came the errant thought.

He flashed her his unexpected smile. "Good," he said, looking suddenly more intent. His gaze shifted to her mouth.

It was then Clarise remembered that her bodice was unlaced. So did he. His gaze traveled lower, where the tight material thrust her full breasts upward. The breath wedged deep in her throat. He did not bother this time to keep his gaze on the pendant. In reaction to his hot stare, her nipples crowned. She couldn't help it.

"By God, you would tempt a man to madness," he muttered.

The words sobered her instantly. Did he think she was *tempting* him? She lifted hands to his shoulder and pushed with agitation, but he didn't budge.

"Is something wrong?" he asked, taking note of her reaction. The baby curled his fists in her hair and screamed. "Ah, Simon wants you to himself," he concluded, seeing her wince.

To her melting relief, he lifted himself a fraction higher. Then, just as she expected him to step off the bed, he dipped his head. Clarise's eyes flew wide. In a gesture as shocking as it was unexpected, he rasped his tongue over her nipple.

Once.

Lightning shot up her spine. She gasped, drawing back into the mattress. The Slayer straightened from the bed. He looked as dazed by his temerity as she was. Dull red color crept toward his cheekbones. "We will speak again," he warned, falling back on bluster. "And I will have honest answers from you next time."

With a scowl gathering on his forehead, he retrieved the goblet and pitcher and exited the chamber.

Clarise watched the open doorway in the event that the Slayer returned. To pacify the unhappy baby, she retrieved the nursing skin, which was thankfully unharmed, and stuck it in his mouth. The pendant swayed momentarily against her arm, reminding her again of the nightmare she'd awakened from. She realized with astonishment that she could never bring herself to poison the Slayer.

The man was too decent, too clever, too *virile* to be dispatched at an early age. He'd had the opportunity to take her by force, and he'd restrained himself. Ferguson would never have let such an opportunity pass. She could not kill the Slayer—not even to save the lives of those she loved.

Dazed by the revelation, Clarise watched little Simon suckling happily, unknowing of all the evil in the world. She'd gotten herself deep into a cover that served no purpose at all but to give her shelter and food. Yet she couldn't leave now, not when the baby needed her. There had to be another way!

She would try to contact Alec one more time. Alec owed her a boon for abandoning her at the altar. As soon as she got word to him, Alec would raise an army on her behalf and challenge Ferguson's right to Heathersgill. Alec would be her champion yet. She had not given up on him.

It was well past dawn when Clarise awoke. She had missed the morning meal. She had slept until the sun rose high enough to leap the outer wall and pierce the crack between the bed drapes. She opened one eye and groaned. *Alas, it was not a dream.*

She was dwelling in the castle of the Slayer. The welfare of the future baron rested on her narrow shoulders. She had her work cut out for her, given the number of times Simon had awakened for a feeding.

And if that were not enough, her virtue was also at stake. The memory of the Slayer's caress made her groan again. He'd made it shockingly clear that he desired her. And though she knew in her heart that she could never poison him, she had no intention of becoming the Slayer's lover. The mere thought made her break out in a sudden sweat. She kicked off the covers to relieve the heat.

There was no denying reality. She had wedged herself into a situation from which there was little chance of escaping unscathed, unless she dared admit who she was. To do that was sheer foolery. Given the antipathy between the Slayer and the Scot, she would quickly become the Slayer's hostage. He would think he had the upper hand until he learned that Ferguson wouldn't pay a shilling for her return. Ferguson would then do what he'd threatened in the first place—hang her mother and sisters in the courtyard.

Since forcing her mother into marriage a year ago, the Scot had taken all that he wanted from Jeanette, and then cast her aside. The marriage had given him the legitimacy he needed to rule Heathersgill without the peasants' revolting. Now that he'd established his foothold, Jeanette and her daughters were dispensable.

With her eyes still closed, Clarise drew her strength from the knowledge of their desperate plight. Jeanette was likely in her rose garden this morning, where she drifted like a wraith among the bloodred blooms. Since her beloved Edward's death, she'd been mad with grief, scarcely sparing a thought for her three daughters.

Merry, of course, would be hiding in the woods outside the castle walls, where she would not fall prey to Ferguson's men-at-arms. In the forest she sought poisonous herbs for her herbal. Clarise was not the only one who plotted Ferguson's demise, but the wily Scot had all his food tasted before a morsel ever passed his lips. Merry had only succeeded in poisoning a number of men-at-arms.

Kyndra, who was six, was the only daughter who seemed oblivious to the changes in their lives since Ferguson first killed their father. Covered in filth and grime, Kyndra would be playing in the buttery with the servants' children.

Clarise drew a deep breath and let it out again. Somehow, some way, she would find a means to save them all. But she would not sell her soul to the devil to do it. She would not poison the Slayer of Helmesly.

Nor could she tell him who she was. As long as the warrior believed she nursed his son, she was safe. She would stick to her flimsy disguise and pray that he would question her no further. Simon seemed content to drink the goat's milk, and all she had to do was ensure a steady supply for him while endeavoring to reach Alec.

Clarise whipped back the bed curtain and put her feet to the floor. The sight of a tray inside her door gave her pause. It was laden with cheese and bread and—God be praised— milk for Simon. She rubbed a grain of sleep from one eye. The necessity of finding the source of the goat's milk could be put off for a little while. First she would tend to the matter of reaching Alec.

The baby awoke at the sounds of her stirring. She fed him the milk until he burped with repletion. Then she changed his soiling cloth, adjusted his swaddling, and viewed her own reflection in a square of hammered steel.

Dark circles rimmed her eyes. Her hair was a tangled mess and her gown wrinkled from wearing it to bed. While her vanity protested, she knew she would be safer this way. She looked the part of a harried nurse, not a tempting female. The Slayer would look elsewhere to assuage his amorous needs.

Thrusting aside the memory of his tongue at her breast, she left the room with his baby in her arms and hailed the first person to cross her path. "Good morrow," she called to a girl staggering under a load of clean linens.

Rays of sunlight poured through the crossloops, splashing warmth onto the folded sheets. Blue eyes set in a pretty face peered around the pile. "Ye art the new nurse!" the girl exclaimed in the English tongue.

"Dame Crucis," Clarise supplied. "You may call me Clare." Instantly she saw the resemblance between this girl and the one who'd tended Simon earlier.

"I am Nell," the girl said eagerly. "Me sister Sarah gives thanks that ye haffe come." Her gaze fell to Simon. "Sarah raised all eight of us when oure mum and da died. But not e'en Sarah knew how to comfort the wee master. 'Tis a miracle ye haffe wrought. Ye saved me sister from a fate most dire."

The word *dire* hung in the air between them. Clarise glanced down the deserted hallway and stepped closer to the girl. "What happens when the Slayer is angry?" she whispered, recalling the sharpness in the warlord's eyes. "Does he . . . maim his servants?"

The color drained from Nell's round cheeks. "Sarah tol' me ne'er to speak on it!" she whispered back. "Pardon, madam. Dame Maeve wille be sore vexed with me, do I tarry longer." She slipped past Clarise with her teetering load.

Struck by the girl's palpable fear, Clarise nearly forgot her purpose in questioning her. "Just a moment," she called out, halting the maid at the stairs. "Can you tell me the way to the chapel? I missed matins this morning."

Nell cast her gaze to the floor. "The chapel is in the forebuilding, but it hast ne been used since Our Ladyship wed the lord," she admitted, clearly crushed by that circumstance.

Clarise kept her disappointment guarded. "You mean, there's no priest here?" She required a priest to convey her message to Alec. Merry's blood! Her spirits took an abrupt downward turn.

The girl sadly shook her head.

"Well, how do you confess?"

Nell brightened. "The Abbot of Revesby visits Rievaulx once a week. We confess to him."

"The Abbot of Revesby comes to Rievaulx? But there's already an abbot at Rievaulx."

"Aye, but he ne speaketh English like the Abbot of Revesby doth."

Clarise had doubts about enlisting an abbot's help. "Is this Abbot of Revesby a kindly man?" she asked, recalling the malignant glimmer in the Abbot of Rievaulx's black eyes.

"A truly holy man, he be. He hath many differences with the Abbot of Rievaulx," Nell added, seeing her wary expression. "Would ye like to come with us on Friday? Most folk walken to Abbingdon to hear his words."

So there was a way to contact Alec, but it would take some time. "I would like to come with you," Clarise replied, though she had doubts that the Slayer would let her go. Hadn't she sworn to keep vigilant watch over Simon?

Thanking the laundry maid, Clarise bid her good day and followed a wing of the castle toward the east tower. With no luck in enlisting the aid of a priest, she tackled the next most pressing need: finding the source of the milk Simon drank. She couldn't ask for a mug every time the baby hungered.

The more Clarise wandered, the more the size of Helmesly impressed itself on her mind. It had been built to house the king and all his men, should the baron be blessed by King Stephen's presence. Yet as she peered into the guest chambers, she found them all wanting. The beds had been stripped of their drapes. The embroidered cushions had been plucked from the chairs. The chests were gutted. The torch holders were devoid of torches. *Had the goods been sold to pay for weapons?* she wondered.

She found herself comparing Helmesly with her own ravaged home. Ferguson had set fire to the hall one day while brawling with his second-in-command. The roof now had holes that the rain poured through, a circumstance that pained her heart whenever she thought of it.

In her father's day Heathersgill had been a lovely stronghold, built at the highest point of the Cleveland Hills, making sieges almost impossible. The only way to take the

keep was by trickery. And that was how Ferguson had come
to claim it for himself.

If her father could see what had become of their home,
she thought, her heart compressed with grief. If he saw his
lovely wife, wasted to a skeleton, her hair cut to jagged
lengths, his ghost would haunt the wall walks.

If something should ever happen to me, he'd often told
Clarise, *protect your mother and sisters as best you can.*
He'd raised her much like a son, which explained why he
had laid such a burden at her feet. And he could never have
predicted that his death would come so soon, while Clarise
was yet a maid with no husband to call upon for military
might. Nonetheless, she felt that she had failed him. Oh,
she'd failed him.

If there had been any way to stop Ferguson from over-
taking the keep, she would have done it. But with a false
smile and a humble request for shelter, the Scot had wormed
his way into the gates. No one had suspected his intent to
poison the lord, then sever Edward's head from his body.
Ferguson had raped Clarise's mother, then laid claim to the
castle himself. No one could have stopped him. Still, Clarise
blamed herself for the ruination of her family and her home.

Simon mewled in her arms, rousing her from such
painful reflections. She hurried toward the eastern tower,
hoping it would speed her to the kitchens. There, she would
feign an interest in livestock and discover where the nanny
goat was housed.

Clarise had almost reached the ground level when the jin-
gling of keys alerted her to Dame Maeve's approach. The
grim-faced servant drew up short at the sight of the nurse in
the dim stairwell.

"What are you doing here?" she demanded, clutching her
chatelaine as a sign of her power.

Clarise quelled the impulse to check the woman's tone.
The steward's wife was a superior servant. She would be
wise to establish a friendship with the woman.

"Does this tower lead to the kitchens?" she meekly inquired.

"Nay," said Dame Maeve flatly. "Why? Have ye need of aught?"

"Actually, I missed the morning meal," Clarise lied. She would determine if Dame Maeve were responsible for the tray in her room or someone else.

"Then you should get up earlier," the woman snapped.

"The lord has instructed me to eat well—"

"He is seneschal, not the lord," Dame Maeve corrected her.

Clarise wondered if the woman's gray hair dared escape the knot on her head. "I see," she said. "*The Slayer* has instructed me to eat well." She used the taboo sobriquet to fluster the old woman. "I was hoping for a bit of bread and some milk to stave off my hunger."

The woman turned as still as stone. Her eyes hardened to match her frame. "You are a fool to use that name lightly," she muttered. "Do you know how this babe came into the world?" With a long bony finger she made to prod Simon in the belly, but Clarise turned her body to protect him. "He was cut from his mother's belly while my lady yet lived."

A chill swept through Clarise. She'd been told that Simon's mother died in childbirth. No one had mentioned such butchery.

"I don't believe you," she said, rubbing the baby's back to comfort herself as much as Simon.

"Ask anyone," insisted the steward's wife. "We all saw the blood on his tunic. Her body was still warm when I went to clean the chamber."

"None of this is my concern," Clarise insisted, thrusting aside the horrific image. "But the baby is. I must have nourishment to feed him. And I must have it now."

Dame Maeve drew herself up. "Your request will be relayed," she said, glaring at her.

"And bread and milk brought to my chamber?" She was pressing her luck now.

The steward's wife pushed past her, muttering commentary on the sin of sloth as she stormed up the stairs. Clarise listened to the click of her efficient footsteps. She had meant to make a friend of the steward's wife. Instead, she'd likely made a foe. With no hope of reaching the kitchens by this avenue, she turned back the way she had come, seeking her chamber, for Simon showed signs of getting hungry.

The light repast was brought to her door with impressive speed. The page who'd brought it also conveyed a message from the master-at-arms, enjoining her to share the midday meal with him.

Clarise declined Sir Roger's offer. *We will speak again,* the Slayer had warned her. *And I will have honest answers from you next time.* Not if she succeeded in avoiding him, he wouldn't. She refused to be caught between the two of them at the noon repast. Instead, she fed Simon with the milk and nibbled at the loaf, hoping to make it last.

The sound of a horseman leaving the stables spurred her to the window. Looking down, she caught a glimpse of the warlord's black hair as he guided his mount through the gate. The sight of the Slayer in full armor made her stand at attention. She held her breath, waiting for him to reappear on the road outside the castle walls.

As he thundered into view, she watched with silent awe. He was armed to the teeth and striking out with purpose.

Where was he going at midday? And why did she feel disappointment to see him leaving? The more distance between them, the safer she was. And yet she wished, perversely, that he would stay where she could keep an eye on him.

Dressed in armor, he looked every inch the warlord. The chain mail that girded his broad chest was hewn from dark iron links that nullified the sun's rays. The leather scabbard across his back was black, as was the hilt of his sword and the knee-high boots. Even the shield that she couldn't see was black—or so she'd heard—with a small white cross on the upper left corner.

She'd always thought his device a sacrilege. Now that she knew his name, she understood the cross, in part. Yet the man had no priest in his castle. He was anything but devout—though Sir Roger had insisted to the contrary.

Still, she knew in her heart that she couldn't poison him. Warlord or not, he was still Simon's father. Helmesly would be lost without his iron rule, just as Ferguson desired. And she would not be party to such violent destruction.

She caught up the pendant that hung from her neck and studied it. The gold globe seemed to symbolize Ferguson's power over the lives of the DeBoise women. Clarise curled her lip in scorn. She would not be subject to Ferguson's whim any longer.

Very deliberately she pulled the chain off over her head. With a flick of her thumb, she unhooked the clasp that kept it closed and swung the chamber open. Lethal powder sat in the silk-lined interior, looking as harmless as a pinch of salt. Clarise extended her arm and held it out the window. With a twist of her wrist, the powder slipped free and sailed lightly into the wind.

Clarise felt a great weight ease from her shoulders. She snapped the locket shut and looped the chain over her head once more. Then she turned to inspect her lonely chamber. It solved nothing to sequester herself with Simon. She would eat with the master-at-arms, after all. Perhaps Sir Roger knew a priest who could bear a message to Alec.

Chapter Five

After hurriedly feeding the baby, Clarise placed Simon in his cradle and hefted them both. Though the burden was heavy, she struggled to carry both the baby and the box down the tower stairs. After all, she had promised the Slayer her vigilance.

Sir Roger hastened to her rescue the moment he saw her on the gallery. "Dame Crucis, you should summon a servant," he scolded as he took the cradle from her hands.

They descended the broad stairs together, drawing the gazes of servants who scurried under Maeve's stern eye.

"Where would you have me put this?" the knight inquired.

"As close to the dais as possible. Let us pray that Simon remains asleep."

"I trust you are rested," he huffed as they neared the high table.

Clarise murmured something to the affirmative. She took approving note of the ready table, the neat appearance of the pages, the freshness of the rushes under her feet. Maeve performed her husband's duties with daunting skill.

"Lord Christian looked for you again this morning," the knight confided, putting down the box. "But I advised him to let you sleep." He straightened and looked directly at her face. "You still look tired."

Clarise turned away from his probing gaze. "The little baron woke me more than once," she told him. For all his chivalry, she sensed a search for answers in the knight's silvery orbs. She hoped she could put his suspicions to rest.

"Come and sit by me," he invited, gesturing toward the high table. "My lord is gone from the castle for the day, and there is no one but the minstrel to entertain me."

As if by cue, the discordant twang of a lute rose toward the rafters. Clarise glanced toward the source of the discord and saw the minstrel she had seen once before seated at a bench on the far end of the hall. He burst suddenly into song, plucking an accompaniment that might have belonged to a different tune altogether.

Apprehension stirred the hairs on her forearms. There was something familiar about the man, she thought, staring at him harder.

"Fear you not," Sir Roger said, mistaking her expression for disdain. "These are his last hours at Helmesly," he divulged. "I will send him on his way after supper, with coin enough to speed him to his next destination." He tipped her a smile and helped her up the dais steps.

She was glad to hear it. The last thing she needed right now was to run into someone who knew her. She turned her attention to the two men already seated at the table. Sir Roger introduced them as Hagar, guardian of the dungeons, and Harold the steward, husband to Dame Maeve.

When neither man acknowledged her polite greeting, she looked to Sir Roger for an explanation. "Hagar is deaf," he informed belatedly, "and Harold lives in his own world. Your gracefulness denotes breeding, however," he added lightly.

She gave him a thin smile. The knight was mocking her disguise as a freed serf. She hoped she could keep the truth from him, as she had kept it from the Slayer.

Sir Roger helped her into a chair, then occupied the seat

beside her, leaving the lord's and lady's places empty. He nodded to the water bearer, and the meal began. The scent of trout broiled in almond sauce preceded the pages as they bore the main course to the high table.

Men-at-arms still trudged to the trestles from the practice yards. Sweaty and exhausted, they straggled in, groaning audibly at the sight of the minstrel and casting curious glances toward the high table. Clarise kept her eyes downcast as they whispered among themselves to discover who she was.

"Did you live in Glenmyre all your life?" Sir Roger asked. At the same time he divided their trencher in half, giving her the choicest portion of the fish.

She braced herself for another round of questions. "Aye, all my life, except for the years I spent studying at St. Judes."

"You mean St. Giles," he offered helpfully.

Clarise colored furiously. He'd caught her right away in the web of her own words. "Aye, St. Giles," she muttered, stabbing at her fish with her two-tined fork.

Sir Roger dabbed his mouth with the edge of the table linen. "Dame Crucis," he said softly, "you have heard, no doubt, that my lord will kill anyone who crosses him."

She forced herself to chew, though the trout began to taste like dirt in her mouth. The knight was clearly warning her to be forthright. To save herself, she retreated behind a wall of silence.

Saintonge drove his point home. "He respects honesty in any man," he added, "or woman."

She resisted the urge to shake her head. She could never tell the Slayer who she was, for in jeopardizing her own life, she jeopardized the lives of those she loved. "Where has the seneschal gone?" she asked, changing the topic abruptly.

The gleam in Sir Roger's eyes warned her that he saw straight through the ploy. "To Rievaulx," he said shortly.

The unexpected answer brought her senses to alert. "But

the abbey is quarantined. I went there for shelter and was turned away."

Sir Roger ripped off a portion of his trencher and dipped it in sauce. "I know," he said, with anger coloring his tone. "'Tis supposedly riddled by a great scourge."

"Oh, it is," she assured him. "I saw the effects of it myself." Her stomach turned at the recollection of Horatio's ravaged face.

The knight leaned back until his chair creaked. "My lord means to call at the gate, not to enter. He is looking for a monk there." His silvery gaze swiveled toward her face. "Alec Monteign. You must know him, coming from Glenmyre," he added casually.

Clarise glanced to the cradle to disguise her sudden panic. Simon was dozing, giving her no excuse to flee. "Aye, of course. He heeded a call to the brotherhood after the . . . the seneschal took possession of Glenmyre." She had nearly said *the Slayer.*

"Just so. What do you know of the man?"

She tore off a bit of her own bread. "He's a good man," she said evasively. "Why do you ask?"

The knight looked at her directly. "'Tis a matter of great importance, affecting the lives of many," he replied. "One day you may be able to return to Glenmyre"—he paused and sipped his wine—"to do whatever it is that you did before."

She ignored his deliberate sarcasm. "What do you mean?" she demanded. "Are you suggesting that Alec might rightly rule in his father's stead?" Hope fluttered anew.

The knight smiled enigmatically. "Mayhap," he said, raising her hopes, "but then, mayhap not. Who can explain the devotion of an eremite?"

To Clarise, it sounded like a leading question. Sir Roger was eager to explore her allegiance to Alec. Likely, everything he had to say was designed to trap her into revealing her loyalties.

She clicked her mouth shut and silently counseled herself

not to speak of the past again. The conversation moved to safer topics: the lax attitude of King Stephen and the recent antics of his dubious heir.

As the sweetmeats approached the table, Clarise summoned the courage to ask, "Sir Roger, why is there no priest here?" Seeing his questioning look, she added, "'Tis my custom to confess once a week."

Something suggestive flickered in his eyes. "Are you such a sinner, then?"

The strange question gave her pause. "Let us just say that I have a conscience," she finally answered. "Why is there no priest?"

His perpetual smile became a grimace. "An interdict was imposed on Helmesly not too long ago. The only sacraments that may be administered here are baptism and extreme unction. 'Twould serve no purpose to have a priest."

"I see," she said, reeling with surprise. "And who imposed the interdict? The Abbot of Rievaulx?"

"An accurate guess."

"But why?" she persisted.

He popped a sweetmeat in his mouth. "Who knows?" he muttered. "It gives him pleasure to spread discontent."

Hearing the irritation in his voice, Clarise glanced toward Simon's cradle and saw that the baby was fussing. "Sir Knight, I thank you for your gracious company. The baby wakes, and I have sworn to give him my undivided attention." She was anxious to retire to her room and ponder her next move.

"Join me," he said, trapping her hand momentarily under his, "at the evening meal. The minstrel will be gone, and our ears will be left at peace."

She gave a noncommittal reply. The knight was too astute by far. If she spoke at any length with him, she knew her story would buckle and the truth would be revealed.

He pulled back her chair, then called a youth to assist her with the cradle. As Clarise trailed Peter toward the stairs, they passed the minstrel who plucked at his strings in a futile attempt to make harmony. The young man's gaze rose to capture hers, and shock slammed through her, bringing her to a sudden halt. By God, she knew him after all!

His name was Rowan. He was the son of Kendal, Ferguson's second-in-command. No doubt he'd been sent to Helmesly to ensure that Clarise fulfilled her sinister purpose.

Mischief sparkled in Rowan's eyes. Without warning, he launched into a ballad extolling the beauty of "The Fiery-Haired Lady."

Clarise's heart began to pound in earnest. She glanced about the hall and realized she was now the center of attention. Knowing she would draw more speculation by ignoring the boy, she listened to his song with outward courtesy.

Inwardly she felt herself quaking. Rowan's ballad was laden with hidden meanings. It was the story of a king's mistress, hung for betraying him and revealing secrets to his enemy. This was Ferguson's way of warning her, she thought, feeling her anger burn. He was likening himself to the king and her to the fiery-haired mistress.

Clarise's throat felt suddenly parched. She swallowed hard against the dryness. The nightmare she'd dreamed last night replayed itself in her mind.

Mercifully, the song came to an end. Rowan offered her a mocking smile, one that held an unmistakable warning. Pretending to be flattered, Clarise clapped for him. A smattering of applause punctuated the hall. She turned stiffly away, encouraging Peter under her breath to move out smartly.

Halfway up the broad staircase, Clarise dared a glance over her shoulder. Two pairs of eyes in particular watched her retreat. One was dark and mocking, the other light and speculative.

Frustration pricked the backs of her eyeballs. Everywhere she turned, men sought to control her destiny. All she wanted was to give her family back their freedom. And there wasn't even a priest at Helmesly to help her!

•   •   •

Clarise sheltered Simon's eyes from the sunlight drenching the inner bailey. The afternoon was uncomfortably hot, and she missed the breeze wafting from the meadow to cool her third-story chamber. But she would not reenter the keep until she'd accomplished her tasks. She had two birds to kill and only one stone to see it done.

Under the guise of introducing the baby to the castle folk, she managed to locate the livestock shelters near the kitchen. Two nanny goats bleated in alarm as she peered through the shelter door. The nearest entrance to the castle was a short dash away. Getting milk straight from the source would not present a problem, she determined, so long as she could do it without attracting notice.

Her spirits sank briefly at the need for so much secrecy. Still, she thought, rallying, her masquerade would be over the moment Alec learned of her plight. Perhaps with the Abbot of Revesby visiting on Friday, she would have more luck in getting word to him.

With one bird slain, she resumed her walk around the castle courtyard, keeping a vigilant eye on the only gate. Rowan would be leaving this very afternoon, dismissed for his poor playing. She could not resist the urge to gloat over his failure to infiltrate the castle as she had. She would need to convince him that she would soon be poisoning the Slayer. That way Rowan would have nothing but good news to deliver to Ferguson.

She crossed sedately to the stables where a rough-hewn laborer pounded shoes on a plow horse. "Have you met the little baron yet?" she inquired, guessing the man to be the stable master.

The laborer straightened and wiped his brow. Frowning suspiciously, he stepped from the horse to peer at the bundle in Clarise's arms. Simon resembled a sleeping cherub with lashes feathering his rounded cheeks. The stable master's visage softened. "He has the look of his mother," he growled, turning away.

Clarise hid a satisfied smile. Though the people of Helmsley found it easy to resent their seneschal, they couldn't bring themselves to hate a baby. Simon might be still an infant, but it was good to foster the loyalty of the people he would one day rule.

Enjoying a moment of misplaced pride, she almost overlooked the minstrel's surreptitious departure. Rowan hastened toward the gate, clutching his lute to his chest. As he cast a wary glance over one shoulder, he caught sight of Clarise heading him off. He drew up short, his lips drawn back in a crafty smile.

"Lady Clarise," he said, ignoring her hissed warning not to speak her name.

"You make a sorry minstrel, Rowan," she informed him, casting a scathing look at his festive attire.

"You wound me, lady," he said, clearly not meaning it. "Did you have something of any import to tell me?"

Clarise was conscious of several curious gazes being cast their way. She would need to keep their meeting brief to avert suspicion. "I want you to take a message to Ferguson for me," she told him in a hushed voice. "Tell him all is going according to plan. At the earliest convenience the deed will be done."

Rowan narrowed his eyes. "What took you so long in getting here?" he demanded. "I was at Helmsley two full days before you showed up."

"I got lost," she lied. "Then a farmer gave me a ride in his cart, and he took me in the wrong direction."

"Humph," grunted Rowan. "Ye had best not try something foolish."

"Like what?" she wanted to know. "You know that I have no choice in this matter."

He gave her a careless shrug, making it clear that the lives of her family meant nothing to him.

She knew a vicious urge to wound him. "You should have practiced on that lute of yours before you came here," she needled. "Ferguson won't be pleased to see you back so soon."

Rowan smirked with self-confidence. "I got what I needed to make my stay worthwhile," he confided.

His words pricked her curiosity. "What do you mean?"

The minstrel leaned closer to share a confidence. "There are others here who would gladly see the Slayer replaced." He patted his covered lute the way she patted Simon. "Now," he said straightening, "see to it that you follow Ferguson's orders soon. Don't make a liar of me," he cautioned, turning away.

Clarise watched with relief as he walked through the shadow of the barbican. Rowan would tell Ferguson what he wanted to hear. He would not be tempted to cut short the deadline that he'd given her.

As casually as possible, she turned and strolled toward the keep.

The sound of a furious gallop roused Clarise from the bed where she lay humming to Simon. Leaving him, she ran to the window and peered through the purple twilight to locate the horseman thundering over the meadow. Even in the semidarkness the silhouette of the Slayer could not be mistaken for any other. He guided his mount toward the open draw, where she briefly lost sight of him.

He appeared again in the outer ward and veered toward the lists. At the edge of the field, he halted his horse in a patch of dusky shadow.

What was he doing? Clarise's knees trembled to know that he was back. She recalled, without wanting to, the feel of his tongue gliding over her breast. She wondered at his purpose in visiting the abbey. Was it possible he would actually return Glenmyre to Alec? What sort of warlord made such generous concessions?

She leaned out of the window in order to see the Slayer better. The sky, like the mercenary, was of mixed character tonight. The horizon, where the sun had set, was pink, then violet merging into indigo. Black night threatened to swallow the whole of it. *Was he good or evil, or some volatile blend of both?*

The warlord urged his horse toward the lances hung on rungs at one end of the list. In a graceful movement he caught up a spear and tested the weight of its tip. Then he turned his horse toward the entrance of the run.

This was a *fête des armes,* Clarise guessed, against an unseen enemy. There were no gay banners snapping in the breeze. The air was still. The shadow of the Slayer and his steed lay across the grass, like the fantastical centaur in the books her father used to read. She imagined the clarion of a trumpet as he closed the visor on his helm. An unseen handkerchief fluttered in the air and fell. The Slayer was off.

So thickly were the shadows settling on the ground that his horse simply disappeared. The warlord galloped as though flying through air. He focused fully on the stuffed target at the end of the run. In the tattoo of the horse's hooves she could hear his force and speed. In the set of his broad shoulders, she could see determination, power in the arm now raising the tip of the lance.

The Slayer targeted his weapon on the dummy's nonexistent heart and, in the next instant, ran it through.

The straw figure was ripped from its place atop a pole. It dangled limply on his lance until the warlord shook it off. Clarise's knees knocked together. There had been fury and frustration in the Slayer's attack. She imagined those two emotions turned upon herself, and her mouth went dry.

Are you a spy, sent to take account of my men and weapons? She let the windowsill take her weight. If only she could earn his trust.

With fluid motions the warlord replaced the lance, patted the neck of his stallion, and headed toward the inner gate. Clarise's vantage was such that she could also see into the courtyard, to the very spot where she had spoken to Rowan earlier. Several torches had been left blazing in expectation of the seneschal's late arrival.

She glanced back at the bed. Simon was staring at the patterns of light flickering on the bed canopy. For the moment he could be left unattended.

She turned to the window again to mark the Slayer's approach. A youth, probably a squire, ran forward to catch his master's reins. The Slayer freed the latches of his helmet and tossed it at the boy. But the squire fumbled the catch, and the helm went clanging to the cobbles.

The boy froze in terror. Three stories in the air Clarise bit off a fingernail down to the quick.

"What ho, my lord?" Sir Roger's cheerful hail shattered the tense moment. The master-at-arms popped through an archway of the garrison and into view. He drew up short at the sight of the Slayer's scowl. "No success in getting past the abbot, then," he said, sizing up the situation.

Clarise strained her ears for the seneschal's reply. The still silence of the early evening and the empty yard caused the men's voices to carry clearly to her window. She gleaned that the abbot was ill and refusing visitors. The warlord swung down from the back of his giant horse.

"'Twas nothing less than you expected," Sir Roger cajoled. He hesitated a moment. "Or did aught else go awry?"

The Slayer's chain mail gleamed with the oil with which it had been scrubbed. "I take it you sent the minstrel away," he growled, in a voice thick with disgust.

"He left this afternoon," affirmed the knight.

"Did he inform you of his destination?"

Sir Roger hesitated. "No, my liege."

"Did anyone think to search his possessions before he left?"

Silence answered for the knight.

The Slayer turned toward his horse and pulled a length of parchment from beneath his saddle. "He was carrying this inside his lute," he added, unrolling it for his vassal's inspection. Clarise caught a glimpse of a drawing in the flickering light. She pressed a hand to her thudding heart. Rowan had said he'd made his stay worthwhile. Clearly he thought he'd gotten away with stealing sketchings of Helmesly's interior defenses.

The Slayer rolled up the parchment with furious but fluid motions. "He was heading straight for Heathersgill," he added through his teeth.

Clarise strained her ears as the warlord's volume dimmed to scarcely more than a murmur. "Henceforth no one enters or leaves this stronghold without being thoroughly searched. I want to know how the minstrel got his hands on these designs!" He shoved them out for his vassal to take.

"We will soon find out, my lord," Sir Roger promised him. "What did you do with the boy? We will question him."

The seneschal tugged off a gauntlet, one finger at a time. "I killed him," he said at last, in a voice as emotionless as death. "'Twas an accident."

Clarise's vision blurred as the words seeped into her brain. The Slayer muttered something in defense of his butchery. She shook her head in denial as she struggled to assess the impact of this news. Rowan was dead, cut down by the Slayer for being a spy. It was true that Kendal's son was sly and utterly without honor, but he'd gone without armor and could not even defend himself! To kill him was a cold-blooded act indeed.

She thought of something still more horrible. What if Rowan blurted the truth of her identity before he died? She might be hanged for a spy within the hour.

Paralyzed by the window, Clarise watched the warlord stalk toward the keep and disappear. *Was he coming after her?*

As if sensing her alarm, Sir Roger looked up and caught her gaze. She steeled herself to keep from ducking out of sight. Forcing a smile, she raised a hand in casual salute.

The knight did not wave back. Nor did he return her smile, but stared at her solemnly and with suspicion.

Clarise turned and stumbled toward the bed. Crawling onto the mattress, she hugged Simon to her breast and sought comfort in the warmth of his tiny body. The image of the straw dummy flashed through her mind. The Slayer had killed Rowan without a trial. What made her think he would hear her tale with any compassion whatsoever?

Moonlight shimmered through the cracks of the shutters, exacerbating Clarise's inability to sleep. Simon, who had squirmed fitfully for hours, was peaceful at last. Scarcely a drop of milk remained in the earthenware mug beside the bed.

Clarise stared at the shadows forming on her bed curtain and listened for the fall of approaching footsteps. She was certain the Slayer would visit her tonight.

Minutes stretched into hours, and still no midnight visitation. Just when she succumbed to the weight of her eyelids, the groaning of the hinges brought her senses back to wakefulness.

She snapped her eyes shut again and forced herself to breathe evenly. The sound of her pounding heart blended with the stirring of rushes. The air in the boxed bed moved as the curtain was pulled aside. She saw the faint illumination of moonlight through her eyelids. Someone was looking down at her. And she knew who it was.

The blood in her veins crystallized. She waited for him to waken her, her lungs starved for oxygen. Would he give her a chance to pour out her tale, or would he simply strike her down as he had Rowan?

Simon was in the bed beside her, she reminded herself. Surely he wouldn't want to spatter blood all over his baby.

"Clare Crucis," he called her in a voice that sounded faintly slurred from drink.

She didn't answer him. She was scared if she spoke that she'd admit who she was and beg for mercy. And worse, the truth would spread like a quick blazing fire and it would only be a matter of days before Ferguson caught wind of her betrayal. She just needed time enough to reach Alec.

To her relief, the mercenary didn't call her again. He

stood silently beside her bed. She could scarcely hear him breathing. Fear of the unknown kept her motionless.

Christian blinked to clear his vision. He wished he hadn't drunk a full bottle of wine to drown the memory of this day's work. He wanted to see the nurse more clearly.

Besides, it would take more than a bottle of wine to forget that he'd snuffed out yet another life. Doing so unintentionally made it no less difficult to bear. He should have realized that the boy wore no armor, no helmet to protect his head. One slap with the broadside of his sword had sent him sprawling to the earth. It was simple misfortune that his head had hit a rock and cracked his skull wide open.

Christian sucked in a breath at the memory and let it out again. He couldn't help but consider that he had been a young man once, and in the name of service to his father, he had done things more awful than steal the sketches of a castle.

"I didn't mean for it to happen," he muttered hoarsely. The sound of his voice in the quiet chamber startled him. He'd had more to drink than was wise.

This was not the time to question the woman, though that had been his intent when he entered the room. Several witnesses had seen her speaking with the minstrel at the gate. Others claimed he'd sung her a ballad filled with hidden meaning. He had more than enough reason to doubt that Clare Crucis had come to Helmesly just to serve him. More likely, her purpose was a sinister one.

His gaze fell to the chain about her neck. The ball-shaped pendant lay against one breast. Since first laying eyes on it, its odd shape and the clasp had made him wonder what use it served. Perhaps she carried in it the ashes of a saint, or a sweet-smelling spice . . . or a deadly poison.

With fingers that trembled slightly, Christian extended his hand and captured the golden ball. He worked the clasp with his thumbnail, determined now to see what lay inside. The two halves of the pendant swung apart, revealing a hollow. He tipped it to one side, then rubbed his index finger in the silk-lined interior. The locket was empty.

Warm relief pooled in his gut as he closed the pendant shut. This did not mean the woman was innocent, he reminded himself. And yet, gazing at her peaceful profile, at the curve of her jaw in the moonlight, he couldn't bring himself to believe that she meant him any harm. He preferred to believe—as he had from the first—that she was sent by design, to save Simon's life. And possibly to save the Slayer's soul.

The hope still throbbed in him. Bathed in moonlight, she looked capable of casting out a hoard of demons. Her legs were drawn up trustingly, like a child's. One arm curled protectively around the sleeping form of his son. They lay together as if they belonged.

She was beautiful to behold, a goddess with long, fiery tresses. He didn't want to believe that she had anything to do with Ferguson or the struggle over Glenmyre. It chafed him to think it.

Sir Roger would question the girl tomorrow. The master-at-arms was more adept with words, more skilled at eliciting a slip of the tongue. But for his part, Christian would sleep one more night with the illusion that there was hope for him and the new life he dreamed of. The baby prospered in his nurse's care. With that sole assurance, he exited the chamber.

Clarise listened to the sound of his retreating footsteps. As soon as she thought it safe, she gasped air into her lungs and let it out in a sob of relief. A layer of sweat coated her skin. She threw back the sheet to cool herself.

He hadn't killed her.

He'd opened the pendant that she'd emptied yesterday and found nothing, thank God. Other than that, he'd done nothing but stare at her in her sleep and utter those wrenching words, *I didn't mean for it to happen.* Had he been referring to Rowan's death? Or was it something else—the death of Simon's mother, perhaps? With so many matters on his conscience, it could have been anything.

All she knew for certain was that he'd let her live a few more hours.

It must have been because his son was in the bed. She nuzzled the baby, grateful for the lifeline that existed between them. Perhaps the Slayer would spare her because he knew that Simon needed her.

With thanks for small mercies, Clarise closed her eyes and sighed. Once she was certain the Slayer had sought his own bed, she would rise and execute her plan. Tonight she would find more milk for the baby. Whatever happened, she could not let Simon starve.

Chapter Six

Clarise awoke with a start. She could not remember falling asleep, but she realized nearly at once that the opportunity to fulfill her plans had nearly escaped her.

It was no longer dark. The sky through the open window was imbued with silvery light. If she didn't hurry, the castle folk would soon be up and stirring. The baby would awaken, too, expecting milk to fill his small, but ever-ravenous stomach.

Scolding herself for sleeping so late, Clarise slipped from the sheets and sought her slippers. She had left her gown on in anticipation of her mission. All that was left was to determine what to do with Simon.

She couldn't bring him with her, for if he woke, his cries would rouse the servants. But if the warlord learned that his son was left alone, even for a moment, his faith in her would be destroyed. If she were caught skulking through the castle in the dark, his suspicions would multiply like the plague.

She decided to leave Simon behind. An empty corridor beckoned her from the bedchamber. The tower was lost to darkness but for the barest glow in the window slits. She sped unnoticed past the Slayer's solar, down the steps of the main stairs and through the great hall: Only Alfred the wolfhound remarked her passing from his place beside the fire pit. He raised his head, studying her through yellow eyes.

Clarise exited the keep through the door that was closest to the livestock pens. In the breezeway separating the castle from the kitchens, she hesitated, looking for signs of life. A crow regarded her from the peat roof of the latter. No one else appeared to be awake.

The scent of yeast and drying herbs made her stomach growl as she hurried past the kitchens. She turned toward the animal enclosure and the less appealing stench of manure. Straw snapped crisply beneath her slippers as she pushed open the door of the goat shed. She could just make out two pairs of eyes reflecting the light she let into the pen.

Clarise reached for one of the pails hanging overhead. She dragged a stool close with her foot and backed a spotted goat into the corner.

The nanny goat tensed, mistrustful of a stranger. Clarise wasted precious minutes soothing the animal whose milk would not flow freely unless it accepted her touch.

By the time Clarise began to get results, a rooster was crowing in the yard. Knowing that servants would soon be heading to their chores, she quickened her pace.

She had filled the pail halfway when the sound of women's voices arrested her. Two of them were talking near the entrance to the kitchens.

"He killed the minstrel? Just because he couldn't play?"

"'Tis what Maeve told me. Struck him down where he stood."

Clarise frowned at the inaccurate gossip. Rowan had been caught carrying important papers in his lute. Espionage was a crime punishable by death, though murder was a bit excessive given the boy's lack of defense.

Reminded that she might well become the next victim, Clarise rose to her feet and hefted the pail. Peering out of the enclosure, she determined it was safe to leave the pen, so long as she kept to the shadows of the garden wall.

The milk sloshed loudly in her bucket as she scurried for

cover. All the while she strained to hear the conversation
coming from the kitchen door. She could just make out a
young girl and a plump cook conversing by the hearth they
worked to light. To her amazement, she realized *she* was
now the topic of their conversation.

"Well, who is she?" the girl wanted to know.

The cook shrugged her massive shoulders. "She were
seen sharin' words with the minstrel yesterday. They say
she's a spy as well, which means the seneschal will kill her,
too. That's what Maeve thinks."

Clarise's eyes widened. She nearly tripped over her own
two feet.

"Well, I don't think her a spy. I think she's beautiful,"
said the girl. "Me sister Nell says she's a gentlewoman."

The girl was clearly kin to Nell and Sarah. Clarise was
grateful for the vote of confidence, even if it came from an
insignificant source.

"She might be a noblewoman for the airs she gives herself," the cook replied, "but Maeve says she's a leman. She
overheard Sir Roger say it."

Clarise stopped in her tracks. She, a leman? A nobleman's mistress?

Surprise rooted her beside the bed of ivy. She considered
the rumor, disdaining it at first for its inaccuracy. Yet she
understood why the knight had come to his conclusion.
She'd supposedly given birth to a child out of wedlock. And
she'd claimed no family, no allegiance to anyone.

Just as suddenly she realized the idea had merit. Indeed,
it gave her the perfect excuse for coming to Helmesly.
Moreover, it explained Rowan's song about the king's mistress, for she could say that he had recognized her as . . . as
Monteign's mistress. She could barely swallow the thought
of carnal relations with Alec's father. Yet it was the best solution all around.

Still, if she didn't get back inside the keep, it wouldn't
matter what story she gave. She glanced toward the rising
sun, dismayed to find it peeking over the garden wall.

In the kitchen the servants moved away from the hearth to tend other tasks. Clarise dashed to the entrance and yanked open the door.

Thankfully, no one stood in the corridor that sped her to the great hall. There, she found Harold setting up the trestle tables one by one. *He lives in his own world,* Sir Roger had said. Clarise put that assessment squarely to the test and walked briskly toward the stairs. The steward never once looked up from his work.

She adjusted her grip on the pail and picked up speed. Her heart threatened to explode from her chest as she passed the Slayer's solar and ran up the twisting tower stairs. Once within her chamber, she leaned weakly against the door and gasped for breath. She'd done it, thank the saints! And she would never, ever fetch milk at such a risky time again.

The baby, bless his heart, was still asleep. Clarise dropped a kiss on his cheek and went to light the brazier. She would steam the milk in the pail until it boiled. When Simon awoke, the formula would be ready for him.

Thoughts ricocheted within her mind as she went about her business. She would construct an identity based on the gossip she'd just heard. Her plan to cultivate the Slayer's trust had been shaken but not destroyed. She would rise above suspicion yet.

There was still time left in Ferguson's ultimatum . . . if she could only get word to Alec!

Clarise pressed the pillow over her ear. A pig squealed as though running from the cleaver. Hens clucked. The smithy's hammer clanged, and the room was hot. She kicked off the blanket and admitted defeat. It was useless to try to sleep any longer.

The few hours' rest she had gotten since dawn would have to sustain her in the hours to come.

With a lingering stretch, she braced herself for what was certain to be a trying day. Fresh air wafted from the window, cooling her bare calves. She wondered where the air was coming from when she had closed the shutters intentionally.

Someone must have opened them.

She lifted her head off the pillow and found her fears confirmed. The Slayer stood beside her bed with one hand upon the bedpost. His gray-green gaze pinned her to the mattress.

"Do you always enter women's chambers without knocking?" she snapped, forgetting for the moment who he was.

"Do you always sleep so late?" he countered, with an even stare.

She noticed the stillness in him right away, and she sat up with a start. "Is it Simon?" she asked, directing her attention to the baby, now asleep in his cradle. She saw at once that he was snuggled in his swaddling and sleeping soundly.

"Nay," said the Slayer. "He is peaceful. The midday meal is being served, and I would have you join us."

The inevitability of the confrontation made her stomach clench. The warlord was impatient for answers, yet she doubted her ability to eat well and spin lies at the same time. "As you wish," she said, resigned to getting it over with.

She tended first to Simon. By luck alone she'd pulled the nursing skin from his mouth and tucked it out of sight. Evidence of the early-morning feeding would have ruined her disguise.

As she put her legs over the end of the bed, she noticed the wrinkled state of her gown. She didn't look the part of a leman.

As if thinking the same thing, the warlord asked, "Why do you sleep in your clothes?"

"My chemise is being laundered, and I have nothing else to wear."

"Sleep naked," he suggested.

She glanced at him sharply and was not surprised to see the watchfulness in his light green eyes. Now that she'd heard the rumors, she understood his reason for such suggestive words. This was as good a time as any to corroborate his suspicions. "To what purpose should I sleep naked," she asked, meeting his gaze boldly, "when I sleep alone?" She raised her eyebrows at him.

Her pitch clearly worked, for a glimmer of interest entered the warrior's eyes. He raked the length of her rumpled gown. "That's an easy problem to remedy," he drawled.

Alarm bells tolled in her head. "Oh, I forgot. I don't sleep alone, do I? I sleep with Simon now." She mustn't let the Slayer think her favors were available for the asking. The mere notion sent panic swirling through her. The man was too large, too powerful, and by far too male. Today he wore a charcoal tunic that strained over the breadth of his chest. The sleeves were rolled back to reveal a dusting of hair on his powerful forearms. Black leggings hugged his long, muscular thighs.

She tore her gaze away. "Well, I'm up," she said, coming to her feet. "Give me a moment to refresh myself and I will join you in the hall anon."

"I wish to escort you," he replied implacably. "You have tarried long enough."

She weighed the wisdom of resisting him with the necessity of earning his charity. "As you will." Shaking out a protective sheet, she lifted the sleeping baby and laid him on the bed. "Kindly wet this for me," she instructed the Slayer, handing him a cloth, "and squeeze out the excess water."

To her relief, he complied without protest. While his back was turned, she shoved the nursing skin farther under the bedcovers. She was glad she'd had the foresight to leave the pail inside the chest.

The warlord handed her the moistened cloth. The baby lurched into wakefulness as she placed it against his bottom. "He has a rash," she commented, not knowing what else to say. "Perhaps Sarah knows of an ointment that will soothe him. Did you know she raised all eight of her siblings?" She realized she was rambling, and she clamped her mouth shut.

"My servants don't share confidences with me," admitted the mercenary shortly.

Clarise tossed the soiled linens into the basket Nell had set aside for her. She couldn't resist giving him the tiniest bit of advice. "Perhaps you should speak with them first. Good servants don't initiate conversations."

He accepted her words without comment, though his eyebrows rose from their scowling line.

Clarise diapered the baby in fresh cloth, then dressed him in a gown of finest lawn. At last she spared a thought for her own pressing needs. "Here," she said, thrusting Simon at his father. "Hold him for a moment, please."

Their skin brushed as he put out his hands to accept the baby. Clarise hurried for the door, disturbed by the warm, smooth texture of the Slayer's skin.

"Where are you going?" he called as she stepped into the corridor. There was a hint of panic in his tone.

She neither slowed her step nor answered him. There were some matters that were best kept private.

Abandoned, Christian gazed with consternation at his gowned son, who stared back at him with equal trepidation. It took a full minute to realize that the baby wouldn't cry. Confidence reemerged, and Christian began to enjoy the close encounter.

He noticed right away that his baby's cheeks were fuller. A link of fear fell away, making him breathe a sigh of gratitude. The nurse had saved his son from sure starvation. Even if Roger found she were a spy, he knew he couldn't punish her. He owed Clare Crucis for saving Simon's life.

He studied his son's features, his tiny nose and watchful eyes. He could hardly believe that something so perfect had sprung from his loins. The awakening he'd felt at Simon's birth was not fleeting revelation. The desire to be a good father burned in him like a steady flame.

He pressed a finger to Simon's palm and received a hearty squeeze. Amazement coursed through his veins. The urge to laugh made his throat tickle.

He glanced toward the empty doorway, relieved that no one had overheard his rusty chuckle. The nurse was dawdling, he thought, with exasperation. She'd had time enough to recover from her travels. Now was the time for honesty. If she were linked to the minstrel's subterfuge in any way, they would know it today.

Still, he had his doubts. Perhaps it was wishful thinking, but the thoughts flickering in the nurse's eyes were not shifty thoughts. There were times when she was truly afraid of him, but they were few and far between. Rather, she watched him as if assessing him. He hoped it meant she was toying with the notion of coming to his bed. His blood quickened at the thought.

He growled in irritation at her delay. The sooner the truth of the matter was unburied, the sooner he would know if his burgeoning desire would find release. It had been so long, so long since a woman had held him tenderly.

Ignoring the heaviness in his groin, he turned his attention back to Simon. The future Baron of Helmesly, he thought with bone-deep satisfaction. No one would call his son a bastard. He would be loved by all and, in turn, rule his vast demesne with justice and might.

Clarise lingered in the garderobe for as long as she dared. With the water that trickled through a pipe from a cistern on the roof, she wet a sponge and rubbed it on the harsh lye soap. The tales that she would tell today left her feeling less than wholesome. She gave herself a cat bath, then scrubbed her teeth and plaited her hair.

In vain she tried to smooth the rumpled dress, yet it didn't really matter what she looked like, she decided, ceasing to groom herself. She might confess to having been a man's mistress, but that didn't mean she had to look the part.

Helping herself to a few stolen moments, she gathered her thoughts before returning to her chamber. She didn't like to have to lie, and she prayed that Monteign's soul would forgive her. She had always thought of him as her future father-in-law, and she was certain he had viewed her as a daughter. Nonetheless, this was the surest way to avert suspicion. The Slayer had come too close, too many times, to guessing who she really was.

Returning slowly to her chamber, she drew up short at the scene that awaited her. The Slayer had seated himself on the chest in which the pail of milk was stowed. With the baby in his arms, he looked halfway tamed, but for the locks of dark hair falling to his shoulders as he gazed intently down at his son.

She approached them cautiously and took in Simon's rapt expression. "He wants to be like you," she said, intending her words to be a compliment.

The warlord's head came up swiftly. "Why the devil would he want that?" He gave her his fiercest scowl.

She would have thought the answer was obvious. "You're a mighty warrior, the best there is."

His eyes narrowed as he fixed them fully on her.

She realized she'd revealed too much of her own fascination for the man. "All boys want to be like their father," she added belatedly.

He gave a smile that was more a baring of his teeth. "Not all," he refuted.

She remembered suddenly that the warlord was a bastard. She wondered if he'd even known his father.

He must have read the question in her eyes. "My father was the Wolf of Wendesby," he said in a voice as harsh as the lye soap she'd just used.

Clarise's brain stuttered at the news. "The Wolf? But . . . that means you—"

"Killed him," he finished for her. He rose swiftly, causing the baby to fling out his little arms.

Not just the Wolf, but every other living soul at Wendesby.

Clarise watched him stalk to the door. My God, she thought. Wasn't it enough that he'd killed the Lady Genrose and the minstrel, too? Every time she thought the warlord worth redemption, she discovered another flaw in him.

She remembered suddenly that they would need the cradle. She called him back.

He rounded on her with amazement. "Aren't you afraid to talk to me now?" he snarled.

In the light of what she had just learned, she ought to be. Her ears still rang with the knowledge of who his father was: a Danish warlord who'd ravaged the countryside during her father's era. "Should I be?" she dared to ask, holding her breath as she awaited his answer.

His gray-green eyes burned with an emotion she couldn't understand. "You and Saintonge are the only people who ever speak to me."

The admission was as unexpected as it was pitiful. It came to her in a flash that this man was lonely. "Why did you kill your father?" she pressed, wanting desperately to hear a reasonable reply.

The muscles of his chest flexed beneath the linen tunic. "'Tisn't a matter I discuss with strangers."

She felt a peculiar twinge in her chest. "I just want to . . . to . . ." She shrugged, unable to voice the warring emotions inside of her, both disdain for his actions and sympathy for his plight. Added to those was the alarming knowledge that she didn't want him to consider her *a stranger*. "I am trying to understand you, Christian de la Croix," she admitted, her voice quavering.

The mask of anger slipped briefly from his face, usurped by surprise. Just as quickly he veiled his gaze, bending to place Simon in his cradle. "I am what you see," he said quietly. With that, he lifted the cradle effortlessly and turned away to carry it to the hall.

Clarise trailed close behind. Her gaze strayed to the wild locks of his hair. The black strands looked soft to the touch. The scent of juniper trailed after him, betraying that he had bathed recently. The breadth of his shoulders blocked her view of the stairwell entirely. *I am what you see,* he'd said.

What she saw was an awesome warrior, a man possessed by demons, a lonely man. She needed his strength and experience. But asking for his help was like bargaining with the very devil. If anyone could free her family from Ferguson, it was this man. But she would have to sell her soul to him to gain their liberation. And she wasn't quite brave enough to do it.

What would the Slayer do if he learned she was Clarise DuBoise, the stepdaughter of his archrival? What made her think that she might even have the chance to bargain with him at all? Perhaps he would strike her dead the moment he discovered the truth.

If only Alec could receive the Slayer's offer! Then she would be spared the necessity of playing a fallen woman. Then she would have a champion worthy of her admiration. She struggled a moment to construct a vision of Alec's boy-like face. She found she could not; the memory of him seemed to have faded. The only face that came to mind was slashed by a scar and framed by hair the color of night.

Chapter Seven

Clarise's gaze was drawn to the high table where Sir Roger stood with a gyrfalcon on his gloved hand. He was dressed for hunting in a pea green tunic and soft hide boots. He met her gaze and smiled, placing the falcon on the back of his chair. Its silver jesses jangled as it scooted free, scenting the air with an open beak. Clarise felt suddenly like its prey.

She lifted her chin and walked straight to the high table. The story she would offer was a credible one. She had nothing to fear from the master-at-arms. As the Slayer lowered the cradle beside the dais, Clarise reached in and plucked the baby free.

"What are you doing?" he asked.

"Your son is wide-awake," she said. "If you want to hear him screaming, then I will leave him in his bed. Elsewise, I must hold him."

She had another reason for wanting to hold the baby. The more accustomed the Slayer was to seeing Simon in her arms, the more secure her future.

The warrior gave a shrug and put a hand beneath her elbow to help her up the dais steps. She could feel the latent power in his fingertips. An unexpected thrill chased up her spine.

"Good day, Sir Roger," she greeted the knight with outward confidence. "It appears you are going hunting," she added.

The knight's eyes gleamed like silver platters. "I am, damsel," he replied. "Do you like to hunt?"

"I enjoy the challenge as much as any man," came her retort.

"Would you care to come with me today?"

She knew the offer was simply a gesture. "I'm afraid I have a baron to watch," she replied. "I have vowed to take good care of him."

The knight acknowledged her answer with a crooked smile. "Please sit," he said, holding out a chair. Both men helped to push the heavy chair into place. The Slayer seated himself on her left side, boxing her into the space between them. She realized with a start that she was sitting in the lady's chair.

What game were they up to? she wondered. Her heart beat erratically as she assessed the reaction of the pages carrying out the meal. The servants appeared outraged.

"Gentlemen," she said, addressing her companions firmly. "You do the servants an injustice by seating me in the lady's chair. Kindly seat me elsewhere."

"We have questions to put to you," the knight replied in the same steely tone. "And we would both do so at once."

She hesitated a split second. "Suit yourselves," she said, setting Simon in her lap. "If your servants are displeased, I warrant you they will find a way to let you know." She turned her attention to the baby, who seemed content to gaze at the azure tablecloth.

Sir Roger and his lord shared looks.

"Let us eat," the Slayer growled. He nodded at the waterbearer, and the boy approached them with the bowl to dip their fingers. Clarise noted that the basin trembled in Peter's freckled hands. Here was another servant afraid of his master.

Pages swarmed into the hall, carrying with them an

aroma of cooked meat and thyme. Thanks to Maeve's efficiency, the food was still steaming. But Clarise's appetite had dwindled. She regarded the trencher of venison, boiled in milk and whole wheat, and wondered how she would eat it.

As he had done yesterday, Sir Roger cut their trencher in half, giving her the choicest portion of the fare. The Slayer got a whole trencher to himself. She had scarcely taken a bite when he nudged her with his shoulder and said, "I visited the abbey yesterday."

Knowing that already, she nodded and kept chewing. The warmth of his shoulder burned through the sleeve of her gown.

"There is an inscription over one of the doors," he added casually. "It bears your name—Crucis."

Her heart forgot to beat. Could a simple word give her away? "In truth?" she murmured, trying to sound bored.

On her right side Sir Roger called her name. "Dame Crucis, what was that song the minstrel sang to you yesterday?"

The men weren't wasting any time. "'Twas 'The Fiery-Haired Lady,'" she replied. "Have you never heard it?"

"Perhaps I have. The words sounded different this time."

She had nothing to say to that observation.

"Did you know the minstrel?" he persisted.

"I cannot say that I did."

"You cannot say? Or you did not know him? Please be clearer in your answer, madam."

She was already weary of this questioning and it had scarcely begun. She laid down her spoon abruptly. "Yes, let us be perfectly frank with one another. The minstrel knew me, it seems, but I never knew the minstrel before my arrival at Helmesly, and I will never see him again, thanks to your lord's enthusiasm with a blade." She sensed, rather than saw, the Slayer stiffen beside her. "My encounter with the man was merely circumstantial. The mockery that he made of me with his song deserved a good tongue-lashing, and that is what I gave him."

Her forthright answer left both men temporarily mute. Sir Roger was the first to recover. "What was it about his song, Dame Crucis, that so displeased you?"

Clarise gathered herself to speak the necessary lies. "'Twas a reference to my past, Sir Knight. The minstrel knew me as Clare de Bouvais. I was Richard Monteign's mistress."

The silence that followed her pronouncement brought color streaking to her cheeks. She was certain every ear in the great hall had overheard her. Pages froze with interest. The men-at-arms quit guzzling their beer to peer over the tops of their mugs. She could only imagine the expressions on her companions' faces, as she couldn't bring herself to look at them.

Sir Roger cleared his throat. "Lady Clare de Bouvais?" he asked, clearly recognizing the prestigious surname.

Clarise was pleased to hear his chagrin. "Aye, Sir Knight. I am Alec's second cousin—the daughter of a third son who was cousin to Lord Monteign."

"But how did you . . . ?"

"Become his mistress?" she finished when he floundered for the words. She wondered how many paternosters she would have to say to be forgiven her lies. "I came to my uncle's keep when I was only eight. After my aunt died, I was the only female remaining the household. I regret to say that Monteign turned his sights on me."

Following these daring words, Clarise held her breath. She hoped her story would be believed, for much of it was based on fact. The cousin of Alec's who had lived with the family for years had left in disgrace and with child, only it was the stable master who had compromised her, not Monteign.

To her left, the Slayer hissed a stream of deprecations under his breath. She had clearly provoked an emotion in him so strong as to be nearly palpable.

Sir Roger persisted with his questions. "Why didn't you tell us this earlier?" he demanded. "Why accept the lot of a commoner when your blood entitles you to more?" He sounded offended on her behalf.

Clarise was prepared for that query. "When I told you that I hailed from Glenmyre, Sir Roger, I saw suspicion in your eyes. You thought I'd come to avenge Monteign's death. I assure you that my uncle meant very little to me."

The Slayer spoke forcefully on her left. "You spoke highly of him the other night," he accused. The thunder in his tone gave Simon a start. The baby's face crumpled, and he began to wail.

"Kindly lower your voice, my lord," Clarise scolded. She placed the baby against her shoulder and patted his back. "Monteign was good to his people—in that I did not lie. But I hold no allegiance to a man who compromised my virtue."

Her words reduced the men to silence. The noises in the hall seemed unnaturally loud as she waited for their reaction. The Slayer took a swig of his wine. Sir Roger toyed with his knife. "Why did you call yourself Clare Crucis?" the knight finally asked.

"'Tis obvious. Six months ago I went to the abbey for protection, along with my cousin Alec. I stayed until the illness . . ." she stuttered over the next few words, finding them the hardest to say, "until my infant took ill and died. I took my name from the inscription at the abbey, rather than use my given name."

"Yet why make up a name?" the knight demanded. "Why not return to your family to help you?"

"My family has cast me out," she said shortly. "I am no longer marriageable. They have no use for me."

"Because you bore a child," he persisted.

"Exactly." She did not wish to linger on that part of her tale.

"Are you certain it died of the scourge?"

"Leave her be!" the Slayer suddenly interrupted.

Clarise started at the fury in his voice. She swiveled her head to study his thunderous profile. The spoon in his hand looked in danger of being bent upon itself.

"Leave her be," he repeated, more quietly.

Sir Roger ducked his head and dug into his trencher.

The meal progressed with scarcely a word more spoken. At the end of the table Hagar belched and patted his belly. Harold slurped the broth off his spoon. Both the seneschal and his master-at-arms were thoughtfully silent.

Clarise was relieved to see the ewer of spiced wine making its way to the table, signaling the meal's end. The tension swirling about her made eating impossible. She planned to enjoy a sip of wine, then excuse herself with the need to nurse Simon. The men would want some privacy in which to discuss her news.

Peter edged along the back of the dais to fill their goblets one by one. From the corner of her eye Clarise watched him reach for the cup she shared with Roger. A stream of garnet liquid rushed into the vessel. She could not have predicted any more than Peter that the gyrfalcon would suddenly flare his wings, knocking his arm aside.

The newly filled goblet sprang from Peter's grasp. Wine shot through the air, spattering Clarise's chest and Simon's backside. The goblet bounced musically from the dais to the floor.

Clarise gasped in surprise. The baby screamed in alarm. The gyrfalcon, panicked by the uproar, beat his powerful wings to escape the chaos, but his jesses held him fast.

"Clumsy youth!" Sir Roger scolded, attempting to calm the raptor.

The Slayer rose like a thundercloud, saying nothing. Clarise took one look at the ashen page and shot to her feet to protect him. "'Twas not his fault," she declared.

The warrior ran an astonished look over her ruined gown. The men-at-arms ogled the scene from the benches below. Servants froze in expectation of violence.

The Slayer's gaze cut to Peter. "Clean up this mess," he snapped. He jerked his head, and the youth reached for the linens Dame Maeve held out to him, nearly spilling the rest of the wine in the process.

"'Twas not his fault," Clarise repeated as the boy stuttered his apologies.

The Slayer glared at her, and she realized it was neither
the spilled wine nor the ruined gown that irked him. No, it
had more to do with accepting her new identity. She saw
anger, even loathing in his eyes, but as best she could tell it
was not directed at her.

"You will need a new gown," he commented, his gaze
falling to her sodden chest. A similarly savage but unrelated
emotion flashed in his eyes.

It was then that she realized her breasts were clearly vis-
ible beneath the wet fabric. The warlord had noticed it, too.
Needing to sever the intensity of his gaze, Clarise used
Simon as a shield.

"Come," he added, signaling that they would leave the
table.

Sir Roger stood as they skirted his ruffled falcon. "I am
sorry, lady, for the inquisition," he said. The words were
awkward and tentative. He was still uncertain of her tale.

Clarise threw him an understanding smile. "Your job is to
defend your lord," she assured him, "and in so doing, you
must be suspicious of everyone. Rest assured that I came
here for protection, nothing more." At least that was the case
now that she would not do Ferguson's bidding.

The tension in the knight's face eased, making him look
younger. "You are safe here," he said sincerely.

Clarise dared a peek at the Slayer's face as he drew her
toward the stairs. It seemed all at once that he was cloaked
in predatory silence. She felt threatened by the simple touch
of his fingertips as he escorted her to the stairs.

"Change him," the warlord instructed, letting her go. "I
will send more gowns to your chamber. You may choose
those that please you."

His narrowed gaze dared her to decline his generous
offer. She passed an uncertain moment, wondering if the
Slayer assumed, because of her story, that she was now *his*
mistress by default.

Peter rushed toward them with the cradle, and the question went unspoken. With eyes wide and mouth dry, Clarise turned and followed Peter up the stairs.

She hated the niggling suspicion that she'd just dug herself a deeper hole.

Clarise studied the gowns that Nell had draped over the chest, the bed, and the new dressing partition. There were ten in all, in every shade and color of nature: blue, orange, saffron, purple, and green. They were fashioned out of wool and linen, precious cotton and silk. Some were shot with silver thread; others embroidered with ribbons, tassels, and lace. They came with matching slippers, all a bit too big. She had never seen such luxurious clothing in her life.

"Did they belong to Lady Genrose?" she asked with sudden reluctance.

"Oh, nay, milady," Nell assured her. "These were Lady Eppingham's, the baron's wife. She loved to look the part, if ye know what I mean."

Clarise recalled the rumor that the Slayer had killed the baron and his wife on their pilgrimage to Canterbury. "What happened to her?" she asked, wanting to hear Nell's version of the story. She ran a hand over a length of lustrous silk.

"She died with her husband on pilgrimage," the girl predictably answered. "They got nay farther than Tewksbury when they fell fiercely ill. 'Twas the food they ate in an inn, someone said. An awful way to die, do ye not agree?"

Clarise gave a delicate shiver. "Wholeheartedly," she said.

"Which will ye wear first, milady?" Nell prompted, eager to test her wings as a lady's maid.

Clarise deliberated a moment. In accepting these gowns from Christian de la Croix, she was in effect accepting her new role in the castle. Was it the role of a guest and a lady, or did he expect her to be his mistress? Either way, she had no choice. The turquoise gown could not be salvaged.

"The saffron one," she decided at last. She liked the way

the sleeves fell away from the arm and draped toward the floor.

"Perfect!" Nell exclaimed.

Clarise withdrew behind the dressing partition that had been dragged into her chamber by two young boys. After peeling off the wine-stained gown, she submitted to Nell's pampering as the maid wiped her down with lavender water. Before Nell could catch a glimpse of the pale stripes across her back, Clarise tugged on a clean shift. The marks that Ferguson had placed there would be hard to explain in light of her story.

Moments later Clarise examined her reflection in the looking glass. The mirror was too small to tell her much about the gown's fit, but the saffron color turned her eyes to liquid gold. *I look more like a leman than a nurse now,* came the troubling thought.

"Ye look lovely, lady," the maid enthused. "I knew ye was gentry the second I laid eyes on ye. Wille ye still be wantin' to come with the servants to Abbingdon on Friday?" she asked.

Clarise was counting on it. Everything she had done and said depended on her ability to reach Alec. "I would like to, very much," she answered. Whether the Slayer would let her go was another question altogether.

Nell chattered enthusiastically as she combed her lady's hair. Clarise, who had begun to fear that she would never be left alone, was relieved to hear a knock at the door.

Her maid went to answer it. "My lord," she squeaked, stepping to one side.

The Slayer ducked beneath the lintel and drew up short. Clarise experienced his stare as a bolt of lightning striking her from the sky.

"I wish to speak with you," he said in a voice that was oddly reserved.

"That will be all, Nell."

The girl dragged herself from the chamber. Wisely she left the door ajar. Clarise stood up from her seat on the chest.

She felt her newly brushed hair swing softly at her hips. She was relieved to see the predatory glint gone from the seneschal's eyes. In its place was a brooding thoughtfulness.

He looked away to locate Simon. Approaching the cradle, he studied the rise and fall of his baby's back. Clarise had found just enough time to feed him before Nell's arrival with the gowns.

"So peaceful," he remarked in an envious tone. He lifted his gaze and caught her curious regard. "I came to apologize," he admitted unexpectedly.

She cut him short. "Lord Christian, you have been most generous with me. Please, don't . . ." *apologize!* She felt her neck grow warm with shame. All she had done was further deceive him.

He stepped to the window where a family of pigeons roosted on a jutting ledge. A green-necked pigeon hobbled along the corbel. "You must think me little better than Monteign," he added, frowning at the bird.

It took her a moment to realize he was talking about the caress he'd placed on her breast. It was hardly the same as forcing a woman against her will. In stammering words she told him so.

He glanced at her and looked away again. "I see no difference," he said, unforgiving of his own actions. She wondered briefly if that was the cause of his previous anger. "There is something else I want you to know."

Her eyes were drawn briefly to his scar as he clenched his jaw. "What is it?" she asked, watching him closely.

"I didn't kill my wife."

The statement was so stark that she froze in the face of it.

"I know what my servants have told you," he continued, breaking away to pace the length of the chamber. Darkness seemed to settle over him, though perhaps it was just a cloud blotting the sunlight. "They told you that I cut her open while she still breathed. Is that not so?" He paused and looked at her. The crease between his eyebrows had taken up permanent residence.

Clarise said the only words that came to mind. "Why are you telling me this?" She was baffled by the man's intentions.

"You said you were trying to understand me."

So she had. And she was beginning to do just that. He was a lonely man, indeed, if her opinion meant that much. The hunger that had been in his eyes before returned as he approached her, stopping just an arm's reach away.

"I didn't kill her," he repeated, his searching gaze begging her to believe him. "She stoped breathing, and then I cut Simon free."

Clarise swallowed heavily at the vision his words created. "I believe you," she said, quite sure he wasn't lying. After all, why would he kill the woman who gave him and his son legitimacy?

"Nor did I mean to kill Monteign," he added, almost as if he were seeking absolution for all his sins. "I told you that he ambushed us as we came to Glenmyre to strike a peaceable agreement."

She looked at his face, at the hope shining in his eyes. "And the minstrel?" she prompted. "Was that also an accident?"

"Yes!" he said, with controlled intensity.

She shook her head and looked away. "You ask much of me, lord, if you wish me to believe you blameless in all this." Especially considering he'd admitted to killing his own father, she added silently.

"I never said that I was blameless," he added, more subdued.

Clarise glanced back at him. There was something about the Slayer that she couldn't put her finger on. Something eluded her still.

"Why did you come here for protection?" he asked her suddenly. "Why not Monteign's ally, Ferguson?"

She flinched at the mention of Ferguson's name. "Ferguson was not an ally," she replied as neutrally as possible. "Monteign feared him, just as he feared you."

"But Monteign was willing to ally himself with Ferguson. He would have seen his own son wed to Ferguson's stepdaughter." His gaze narrowed as he added, "You said you knew nothing of it the other night," he accused.

She wondered if he could see the pulse hammering at the base of her neck. "I will tell you what I know," she promised. "The betrothal had been arranged years ago by Monteign and Ferguson's predecessor, Edward DuBoise. Ferguson found it convenient to acknowledge it, as it would gain him an ally and a surer foothold in the region. Thanks to your . . . *intervention,* the wedding never took place."

He frowned at her, perhaps astute enough to hear the bitterness behind her words. His gaze followed the sweeping sleeves of her gown. "You look lovely in that. Like a true lady." His voice took on a regretful timbre. "But such is your birthright. Your nobility cannot be taken away from you no matter what . . ." He trailed off.

No matter what anyone does to me, she finished his sentence silently. For him, a bastard, such issues of birthright and nobility were clearly often on his mind.

He moved awkwardly to the window, giving her the chance to breathe again. She marveled at his change in attitude toward her. Whereas before he was watchful and wary, he was now incredibly forthcoming, even friendly with her. Any moment now she expected him to offer her a place as his mistress. She hoped he would not be furious when she refused him.

"My wife wore naught but gray."

Clarise searched her mind for an appropriate response to the unexpected admission. "The servants speak highly of her," she replied, clasping her hands before her.

The mercenary gazed out at the flower-dotted meadow. "She was a saint," he quietly divulged. "She wanted to be a nun, but as her father's only child, 'twas up to her to produce an heir."

Clarise heard more in his words than what he was actually saying. "Such is the lot of a noblewoman," she pointed out, implying that nobility didn't come without a price.

She ran a gaze over the warlord's powerful back and long legs. His virility struck her anew as he planted his feet apart and squared his shoulders. Genrose must have been terrified to wed him. Clarise felt suddenly sorry for Simon's mother, as well as the warrior. Their joining must have been painful for them both.

With his next sentence the Slayer confirmed her conclusions. "She was afraid of me," he admitted. He turned around, leaning a shoulder against the shutters. "She allowed me my husbandly right just once. That was the night that Simon was conceived."

Clarise's eyebrows rose toward her hairline. In her mind's eye she pictured the mercenary taking his marital rights with the pristine Genrose. He would have waited patiently for the daughter of a nobleman to be ready and then . . . but instead, she saw herself, lying flat on her back as his dark head came down, his mouth licking fire at her breasts, his thighs spreading hers. Her knees went weak to the point that she feared they would give out completely. "Why you?" she asked, shifting the focus of their conversation slightly. "Her father might have wed her to someone else." As soon as she said it, she realized it was a mistake.

"Someone with better lineage, you mean," he said, his eyes narrowing. "You wonder how a bastard like me came to marry a baron's daughter."

The savagery in his tone did not frighten her as much as it had before. "The thought did cross my mind," she admitted frankly.

He eased his backside onto the window ledge. "The Baron of Helmsly had no sons, as I said. Yet he balked at the idea of leaving his lands to the Church, since he disliked the Abbot of Rievaulx so intensely. I was already safeguarding his lands as his master-at-arms. 'Twas a logical step to consider me for his daughter. He reasoned, should anything happen to him, that it would take a strong arm to protect the baronetcy for his grandson and heir."

Clarise inclined her head. "That is sound reasoning," she agreed. She touched the tip of her tongue to her upper lip. "However, there is a rumor," she dared to add, "that you had the baron killed while he was away on pilgrimage." She watched the Slayer's reaction carefully.

The look in his eyes became downright frosty. "I have no ambition to be Baron of Helmesly," he informed her. "That right belongs to my son."

She had no doubt he spoke honestly. The man seemed truly offended to be accused of killing his in-laws. She wondered why he didn't actively combat such rumors. "The baron was right, then," she decided, "to choose you for a son-in-law. If not for you, Simon would have no chance."

Her vote of confidence brought that same startled look to his eyes that she'd glimpsed before. "I could say the same for you," he retorted gruffly. "You saved Simon's life by coming here. For that I thank you."

She forced a smile, though she really felt like cringing. Blessed Mary, what would happen if he learned she was feeding his son plain goat's milk! Worse yet, if he learned that she had come to Helmesly to poison him! God help her then.

"Tell me about you," he asked, tipping his head slightly to one side. "What makes you so outspoken, so brave?" His eyes now burned with interest.

Flushed by the intensity of his gaze, Clarise averted her face. "Oh, I suppose I was raised much like a boy." She thought of her father and a knot swelled in her throat. "My . . . tutors encouraged me to learn by questioning, as Socrates did. I was taught always to have an opinion and to speak my mind." It was even possible her father asked too much of her. His request that she protect her mother and sisters was proving impossible to fulfill.

"Were you educated with your cousin?"

It took her a second to realize he meant Alec. "Aye," she said. "We did everything together."

"Was he as"—he cast about for a word—"as spirited as you?"

She gave in to the urge to laugh. "Nay, Alec is a lamb. He was always preoccupied with moral issues, yet he would do anything his father requested of him. One time Monteign told him to steal back a sheep that had wandered onto the holding of a villein. Alec went straightways to the villein and paid him five denarii to get the sheep back. He believes that people should have a common share in all things; therefore, the sheep, having strayed onto the freeman's lands, was his. Yet on the other hand, Alec could not defy his father's wishes."

The Slayer seemed to mull over her tale. "He sounds like a goodly man," he decided, frowning.

"Better cannot be found," she agreed. She quirked an eyebrow at him. "But why do you ask?"

Instead of answering, the Slayer put another question to her. "Is he strong enough to defend his lands from Ferguson?"

Clarise reeled at the implications. "Is that what you intend to do?" she asked. "Give him back his lands?" Sir Roger had hinted at the possibility, but she hadn't believed it. The gesture was too magnanimous for a warlord.

"I told you, I had no intention of seizing Glenmyre in the first place. But with Monteign dead and Alec gone, I feared that Ferguson would seize it. Now I'm embroiled in war that drains my weapons and my men. I have a castle of my own to run and no time to indulge Ferguson in his savage games. Yet I am loath to let the Scot take the birthright of young Monteign. I'd gladly give Glenmyre back to Alec, aye."

Clarise drew a breath to steady her soaring optimism. Alec still Lord of Glenmyre! Surely he would seize the opportunity to claim his inheritance. The moment he emerged from the abbey, she could appeal to him to challenge Ferguson and save her family. "Alec earned his spurs when he was just sixteen," she heard herself boast. "He is young and strong. He won a good number of tourneys a year ago."

The Slayer nodded, then looked away. "A year ago," he repeated, looking grim.

"What is it?" she asked, fearful that he would suddenly retract his offer.

"How much training do you think he does at the abbey?" he inquired, looking at her.

Her optimism plummeted like a partridge with an arrow through its heart. "None at all," she guessed.

"Also, there is the illness to think of," he continued. "Should Alec be stricken by the scourge and survive, he will be much the weaker for it."

Clarise felt a flutter of alarm. Without Alec, who would be her champion? She would have to admit to the Slayer who she really was. In her desperation she would have to ask him for his aid and admit to all the lies she'd spun.

"Nonetheless," the warlord added with more force, "Alec should rule Glenmyre. I have tried to get word to him, but the abbot professes to be ill, and the monk at the gate will not convey a message for me."

"Then you should go about it another way," Clarise suggested. She was about to mention the Abbot of Revesby's name when the Slayer stood up, taking a step that brought him suddenly closer. She locked her knees to keep from backing up. Whatever she was going to say died forgotten on her tongue.

The Slayer's shadow folded over her, immense and cool. "I have to go now," he said, cutting their conversation abruptly short. "When Sir Roger hunts, I train the men."

She forced a response through a tight throat. "I imagine you enjoy that," she said breathlessly.

He gave her one of his rare smiles, one that nearly blinded her with its brilliance. "I do," he admitted. His hand came up and captured a length of her hair. He let it slip through his fingers, apparently pleased with its texture.

Clarise swallowed convulsively. She did not understand

the thrill that chased down her neck and shortened her breath.

"I won't hurt you," he promised, seeing her shudder. He caught up one strand of her hair and brought it close to her face. He lightly trailed the curl over her neck and her chin. The cool glide of her hair caressed her lips, sending pleasure rippling across her entire body.

She looked in his eyes for an explanation. What she saw there made her heart miss a beat. Banked behind a wall of wistful longing was a fire of raging desire.

Panicked by the height of the flames, she forced herself to say something, as silence would only encourage him. "I think you should go now," she told him, speaking through stiff lips. "I'm no longer any man's mistress."

He dropped her hair as though scalded. For a stricken moment he stared at her, the tan on his face paling. With a muttered apology, he turned away and fled through the open portal without a word or a backward glance.

Clarise went to the window to cool her heated cheeks. The warlord's visit had left her shaken and disturbed. At least she no longer feared that he would ravish her. Her status as a lady, albeit a sullied one, protected her somehow. That meant he was guided by a code of ethics, making him a better man than Ferguson, which she had guessed already.

Yet at the same time, her response to his touch revealed a frightening truth: she was attracted to him. Not only did his skill with a sword hold fascination for her, but the man himself was luring her along a frightening path that threatened her identity. She reminded herself that she was not a mistress by trade, but a lady, the beloved daughter of Edward DuBoise.

Furthermore, she was Alec Monteign's betrothed. Alec was going to be her champion. And yet she felt the inexorable pull of the Slayer, bringing her closer and closer to admitting the truth, to casting herself on his mercy.

As the Slayer had pointed out, Alec had not trained for war in more than six months. He was exposed to illness on a daily basis. What would she do if Alec were too weak to destroy Ferguson before he carried out his threat?

The sound of someone crossing the courtyard drew her gaze outside. She caught sight of the warlord striding through the first set of gates toward the practice yard. Her sudden shortness of breath was unmistakable.

As he walked, he pulled his tunic off over his head. A light sweat broke out on her skin as he emerged again, looping the strap of his scabbard over his bare chest. Even with the practice yard a good distance away, she could see the well-defined muscles under his sun-bronzed skin. He had traded his chausses for a pair of braies that sat low on his hips. He was a giant of a man, yet perfectly put together, she admitted, feasting her eyes.

The Slayer motioned for the men in the practice yard to form a circle around him. In a smooth motion, he pulled his broadsword from the scabbard. The length of steel flung bursts of sunlight into the air as he hefted it and swung it casually. Clarise guessed that it weighed nearly two stone. The men-at-arms gave him a wide berth.

The warlord waved the weapon in a series of graceful arcs. The blade twisted left, right, down, up, then swooped in a lethal arc that would cleave a man from shoulder to groin.

As he performed the drill a second time, she imagined Ferguson standing helpless before the onslaught. The Scot would struggle to raise his double-edged ax in his defense. As the blade came down, she imagined him crumpling to the grass that would turn red with blood. She spun around and blinked to clear the vivid daydream.

Alec would take care of it for her, she vowed. There wasn't any need to admit to the warlord who she was.

And yet, deep in her heart, Clarise had a feeling it was only a matter of time before she would need to beg the Slayer's mercy and call upon his might.

Chapter Eight

"The saints and the apostles!" Nell exclaimed, helping her mistress into the tub.

Clarise did not have to ask the reason for Nell's sudden outburst. She'd taken great pains to shield her lady's maid from viewing the stripes on her back, but the task was impossible with Nell hovering so close at all hours. Though the wounds were old and near to fading altogether, it was obvious that the marks hadn't fallen there by accident.

"'Tis nothing," Clarise assured her. She would have to rush this bath and send Nell away promptly. Simon was thrashing mightily within his cradle. She had just enough milk for one more feeding. Then it was off to the goat pen to procure more for him.

"But, my lady, ye haffe been beaten!" Nell cried. "Who dared do such a thing to ye?"

Clarise put a toe in the water, testing its heat. "Perhaps I will tell you one day, Nell," she admitted, turning her head to give the servant a stern look. "But for now I cannot. You must tell no one about these marks." She cringed at the necessity of having to tell more lies. "Promise me," she added firmly.

Nell gave a reluctant nod. "I promise, milady," she whispered. "I be right good at keeping secrets," she assured her.

"I ne did tell ye how the seneschal killed our Lady Genrose, did I?"

"No, you kept that well to yourself," Clarise drawled with irony. She stepped into the steaming water, hissing as it burned her thighs.

The girl clasped a hand to her mouth. "Oh!" she cried. "I just told ye."

"That's all right." Clarise assured her. "I have heard the story already." She lowered herself into the fragrant bath.

"'Tis nay a story," the maid insisted, propping her hands on her waist. "He plucked the babe out whilst she still breathed. We heard her screams, we did."

"Nonsense." Clarise wondered why she felt moved to defend the warlord. She had nothing but his word that he hadn't killed his wife. "No one mentioned a scream before now. You made that up." She scooped up a sponge and began to lather it with soap.

Nell seemed to search her memory. "Mayhap I did," she relented.

With her face averted, Clarise rolled her eyes. Nell's imagination didn't bode well for her own secrets. She sensed the culmination of her own deceit coming steadily closer. "I would like to take a bath alone," she informed the maid. "You may come later when I'm done."

"Aye, milady. May I wash yer hair?"

"I'll take care of it."

Nell left the room, reluctant to return to her less glamorous chore of laundering.

Many hours later, smelling of lavender and sleeping in her newly laundered chemise, Clarise's eyes sprang open. A fleck of moonlight had fallen on her face, reminding her to waken. She sat up slowly. Simon was sleeping in his cradle for a change. He had yet to rouse for a midnight feeding. If he did, she would have nothing to feed him. The pail was empty as it usually was by this late hour.

She dragged herself from bed. The servants would have sought their pallets by now. It was time to make her move.

Opening the chest, she retracted the empty pail. She wriggled her feet into her slippers and set out on another perilous quest for goat's milk.

This is truly madness, she thought, not for the first time. Her stomach endured a familiar uneasiness as she slinked through the darkened castle and out the rear door. She edged cautiously around the kitchen and arrived at the animal pen. The ground seemed to glow under the incandescent moon. A fresh layer of straw crunched beneath her feet.

At least the goat was used to producing at this time, she comforted herself. The door to the pen gave an agonizing groan. She pinpointed the two nanny goats by the whites of their eyes. The one with the dark patch on its side was her favorite. As she stalked it, her foot came in contact with a bucket.

The full pail sloshed but didn't tip. She bent down to examine it.

It was a full bucket of goat's milk, fresh from the udder if its warmth was any indication. She dipped her finger and tasted it. Sour, just like Roger said.

Who would be so careless as to forget a pail of milk? She straightened and eyed the bucket thoughtfully. One of the milkmaids must have left it behind.

Why waste the time of milking a goat when she ran the risk that Simon would awaken? What if he were crying even now, drawing the unwanted concern of his father? Mere stone could not disguise the baby's volume.

Making a quick decision, Clarise snatched up the bucket and hastened back into the castle. Remembering the fall of Troy from Homer's famous volume, she hoped she wouldn't regret this gift the way the Trojans regretted the gift horse and the enemies who lay concealed within it.

"Lady Clare!"

Clarise winced openly and ground to a halt. She'd been tiptoeing past the Slayer's solar, hoping not to gain his notice. It was Friday afternoon, and the servants were sched-

uled to leave for Abbingdon at any time. This was her big
chance to enlist the Abbot Revesby's aid in getting word to
Alec.

"My lord?" she inquired, stepping closer to the open
doorway.

The warlord was seated at a writing table, quill in hand.
Sunlight streamed through the window behind him, framing
his torso in a haze of gold. He looked different, she noticed,
and then she realized why. He wore a bleached undershirt
and no tunic. She'd never seen him in white. He looked like
the archangel Gabriel.

Until he looked up. The scar on his face betrayed an inner
tension that was entirely at odds with an angel's serenity.
"Call me Christian," he demanded, stabbing the inkwell
with the tip of his quill. He paused to take in her appearance.

She wore a different gown today, a smock of forest green
with a satin ribbon that laced up the front. His gaze fell to
the sling she carried against her hip. "Where are you
going?" he added sharply.

She rubbed her moist palms against her linen skirt. "I
would like to go to Abbingdon to hear the Abbot of Revesby
preach," she replied, holding her breath.

"With my son in a sling?" His eyebrows predictably lowered.

"He will come to no harm," she assured him. "I go in the
company of many servants, even men-at-arms, to keep us
safe."

"My son does not pass outside these walls," the Slayer
quietly explained. His expression was stern enough to make
her fidget.

"But I wish to confess," she insisted, fighting to keep her
tone mild. "Is there another here who may watch Simon in
my stead?"

The warlord clenched his jaw. The scar on his cheek became more pronounced. "What if he hungers whilst you are
gone?" he queried. "'Tis an hour's walk in either direction,

and I have no horses docile enough that you could ride with a babe."

"Then I will take him with me and nurse him on the road." A full bottle of milk was tucked inside the sling, thanks to the bucket she'd discovered last night.

The Slayer laid down the quill and scrutinized the scratches on the parchment. "Are you so devout, then?" he asked, frowning mightily.

She sensed the struggle within him. He was trying to be fair. "My lord, you have no priest here," she pointed out.

He looked up at her then. "What sins have you committed that you must confess?"

"That is between me and God," she retorted sharply. Frustration welled within her. He had no idea how important this mission was to her. The Abbot of Revesby was not due to visit again for another month. In the meantime, every day brought her mother and sisters closer to death. "Oh, just forbid me to go and have done with it then!" she snapped. She threw him a glare and was halfway down the gallery when he called her back.

"Lady Clare."

She slowed to a halt but refused to turn around.

"Please stay," she heard him beg.

His deep voice pitched on such a humble note was her undoing. Turning slowly, she stalked back to the door with her mouth compressed. "Why?" she demanded.

"I need your help." He gestured to the vellum sitting on his desk. "'Tis a letter to Alec. Since I'm unable to speak to him in person, I will put my offer on parchment and see it delivered."

A letter to Alec? Maybe she need not ask the Abbot of Revesby after all! Adjusting the sling on her hip, Clarise ventured into the Slayer's solar.

The room was a very different place than the rest of the castle. Here, rich blue tapestries padded the walls. The rushes under her feet were woven into a thick mat. At one end of the room stood a massive bed, draped in blue velvet.

At the other end was his writing table and a chest laden with manuscripts.

The sight of so many books distracted her. "Oh!" she exclaimed, stepping over to the chest to admire the jeweled covers. "*Proverbs of Solomon,*" she cooed, picking up a book and reading the titles of its lengthy poems. "*History of the English,*" she added, putting it down. "Where did you get these?" She hoped he wouldn't say he'd acquired them in his sieges.

"They were a gift from the abbot you just mentioned. Ethelred illustrated them when he was master novice at Rievaulx."

"Ethelred," she echoed him. "You know him well enough to use his first name?"

"He wed me to Genrose," said the warlord shortly.

With that simple admission, Clarise's hope for help expired. Was there no way around her troublesome quandary? Perhaps this letter would finally put the matter to rest. "What did you need my help with?" she reminded him.

The Slayer glanced around. "Let me find you a stool."

"Simon will wake if I sit," she declined. It was true. The minute she held still, the baby rose from his slumbers. He seemed especially agitated today. She stood by the table, swaying softly to keep him lulled.

The warlord seemed distracted by her movements. He sat behind his desk and forced his gaze downward. "Let me read what I have already written. 'Amiable and God-fearing knight, Greetings from your humble neighbor and friend, Christian de la Croix, and wishes for good health . . . '" His eyebrows sank so low they formed an unbroken line over his eyes. Half a minute of silence ensued. Clarise gazed in consternation at the rigid warlord. "Is that how you address a man whose father you have murdered?" he finally asked, in a voice gritty with remorse.

Compassion flooded her. While sunlight sat brightly on his shoulders, shame also weighed them down. He looked forlorn, clutching the quill as though his words alone would redeem him. "Give me the words," she heard him mutter.

She knew an insane urge to shelter the beast. "You must apologize," she instructed him. The letter would have to be worded carefully. If Alec accepted the warlord's offer, he would need a wife to help him rule Glenmyre. But was he strong enough to defend her? she wondered disloyally. "Confess your guilt," she instructed, "and accept full blame for killing Monteign. He will respect your honesty."

She noted, absently, that the Slayer's lashes rimmed his eyes the way Simon's did. He took up his quill and began to write.

His handwriting was forceful and sweeping. Black ink bled into the vellum as the Slayer worded his apology. His hand seemed to tremble slightly. She could not read what he wrote, as the script was upside down and some distance from herself. The words were for Alec—and perhaps even God, if he meant them true enough.

When he lifted his gaze to look at her, she was surprised by the honesty in his gray-green eyes. She was suddenly convinced that he hadn't killed his wife. People simply delighted in keeping the rumor alive.

"Shall I mention you?" the Slayer asked.

Alec would need to know where to find her. "Please do," she answered, wondering why she wasn't thrilled at the prospect of Alec's rescue. "Tell him Cousin Clare dwells safely at Helmesly, caring for your son in exchange for your protection."

It would take Alec a moment to puzzle through that statement, but then he would arrive at the conclusion that Clarise had taken up residence at Helmesly, using an alias to hide her identity. Curiosity would then bring him to Helmesly to ask for her. The sooner he came the better, she thought, chewing on her bottom lip.

The quill scratched away at the parchment. It stopped just as suddenly, and the Slayer looked up at her. "I take it he knows what his father did to you," he guessed, the lines of his face hardening with disapproval.

Guilt rose up in her like bile. How she hated to be reminded of her deceit, especially when the warlord seemed so genuinely concerned. "Of course," she said tightly. "We went to Rievaulx together." The moment the words were out, she regretted them. With his letter the Slayer was unburdening his soul. Why not confess her own sins now and tell him who she really was? Her pulse accelerated at the thought. Could she afford to pass up such an opportunity, with the Slayer in such an amenable mood?

"Forgive me," he said, stabbing at the inkhorn, unknowing of her thoughts. "It must be a painful matter to discuss. My own mother was raped, you know, by my father."

She didn't know. But his admission stirred her curiosity.

"She was a nun at the time, a novice gathering herbs outside the convent walls," he added, gazing down at his work. "A lone rider surprised her and took her by force. He boasted that he'd defiled a child of the Christian God, and he told her his name—Dirk of Wendesby." He made another stab at the inkwell.

Clarise remembered clearly the tales her father had told of that heathen warlord. How horrible for an innocent novice to be debauched by a man who held no law to be higher than his own.

"My mother endured the shame of bearing a child when she was supposed to be chaste," he continued, his mouth twisting with bitterness. "Fortunately, her superiors were compassionate and refrained from casting her from their order. She gave birth to me within the convent walls, and I remained there, to the age of twelve."

Amazement and understanding came to Clarise in the same instant. No wonder Sir Roger had called his lord devout. The man had grown up in a convent, of all places!

""When I was twelve," he continued, his voice flattening with tension, "my mother fostered me to a nearby family. I wasn't told that the lord of the house was my father." He broke off, waiting to see her comprehension. "'Twas an act of forgiveness, she told me later." Though his face was now a mask of ruthlessness, she saw the pinch of pain overtake him briefly.

Horror followed in the wake of amazement. Why would the nun want such a man to raise her child? And yet this tale explained why the Slayer was a man of contradictions, a fascinating blend of good and evil. "I don't understand," she said. "Why give you up to him?"

His jaw muscles bulged. "She thought he would change for the better once he knew me." A frosty look entered his eyes, and she knew he was reliving painful memories.

It took little insight to realize the Wolf had mistreated his son. Clarise felt for the boy he was then. Every child deserved a father like her own, a man who had doted on his daughters and adored his wife. "I'm so sorry for you," she told him, feeling the sting of tears in her eyes. She blinked them back, surprised by the depth of her empathy.

The Slayer gave her a searching look. "You need not pity me," he said, straightening his spine. "I had the benefit of a good education, and my father, despite his failings, made me strong. Without his training I would not have become a master-at-arms here." He gave her a grimace that was meant to pass as a smile, then he applied himself to finishing his letter.

With her heart pounding, Clarise realized the time had come to tell the truth. Surely this man was capable of mercy, for that was a virtue his mother would have taught him. She would begin by telling him how her own father had been slain, and then he would know that she had no allegiance to Ferguson. Other than her lies, she had nothing to be ashamed of. She'd refused to poison the Slayer, and she had brought Simon from the brink of starvation. The Slayer's punishment, if any, was bound to be light, she reasoned.

The warrior's tongue appeared at the edge of his lip. Seeing it, Clarise's stomach performed a cartwheel. She remembered the banked desire smoldering in his eyes. *What would it be like to be kissed by him?* she wondered, distracted from her resolution.

He glanced up in time to catch her considering look. It was too late to disguise the direction of her gaze. A smile kicked up the edges of his mouth. "Did I swear you would be safe with me?" he inquired, his eyes sparkling.

Her voice deserted her, and she gave a jerky nod.

"Pity." He looked down again, melting wax to form a seal.

The lightness of his tone was unexpected. Clarise gave a laugh that was half relief, half amusement. Suddenly she was not afraid to tell him anything—even that she'd substituted goat's milk for the precious breast milk she was unable to give.

With a shy smile he looked up at her. "I like you, lady," he admitted, astonishing her with his honesty.

Flustered and beset with guilt, she could say nothing by way of reply. She realized, suddenly, that Simon was stirring. From the bundle at her hip rose a garbled cry. It wasn't like any other cry she'd heard from him before. Clarise plucked the blanket off the baby, giving him air.

Simon did not look happy. With concern knifing through her, she touched her fingers to his cheek.

"What is it?" the Slayer demanded, noting her expression. He rose to his feet and peered down into the sling at his son.

It was worse than she feared. Simon's skin was burning to the touch, his face beet-red with fever. "God's mercy," she whispered. "He has taken ill!"

She looked up in time to see the warlord's Adam's apple rise and fall. He put his hands out. "Let me have him," he demanded.

Keeping the full nursing bladder out of sight, she wedged her hands beneath the baby and passed him carefully to his father. Simon's eyes were opened but glazed. Again, he issued a cry that sent anxiety twisting through Clarise's heart.

"What can we do?" she begged, raising an uneasy gaze to the Slayer's face.

Only once before had she seen such a stricken look on a man. Her father had worn that look the moment he realized he'd been poisoned.

"From the cold," the Slayer rasped, staring down at his son. "The other night, when I found him naked . . . he was so cold."

"Yet he has thrived since then," she pointed out, touching Simon's burning cheek.

"Someone in this castle is responsible," the warlord growled. He sounded capable of killing with his bare hands. He glanced up at her then, his eyes now an icy gray. "*You* have reason to avenge me," he accused.

She threw her arms around her body, feeling suddenly defenseless. How could he think she would harm Simon— or any baby? My God, she had just been on the verge of telling him who she was! If he reacted so rashly to Simon's illness, what would he have done had she confessed her true identity?

"I did not do this," she said succinctly. She looked the Slayer squarely in the eyes. "Now, what can we do for him? Can we send for a physic?"

He dismissed her suggestion with a shake of his head. "I trust no one in these parts," he said shortly.

"Not even a wise woman from the village? A midwife mayhap?"

At the mention of the midwife, his eyes flared with outrage. "The midwife gets her herbs from the abbey. The scourge may spread from there to here. Nay!" he thundered. "I will care for him here. I will bring his cradle to my room and watch over him. You will stay with me until he is well again."

The underlying threat was plain. Until the baby recovered, she would remain suspect in the Slayer's eyes. Inwardly she cringed. This was the side of him that terrified his servants and made him a lonely man.

"Of course I will," she retorted, defying his temper as her own anger flared. "But we must have medicine to save him. The illness has to be purged from his body. We cannot save him *alone*."

"What do you suggest we do?" he snarled.

Beneath the blustering tone, she heard a thread of desperation and she answered more reasonably. "I will ask Nell or Sarah what they know of healing. Those two are loyal to Simon; I know it."

"Go fetch them, then." He skewered her with a warning look. "But you'd best come back," he threatened.

She whirled on him, her entire body trembling with distress. "I happen to love your son," she countered, her voice breaking on the final word. With that, she raced through the door to find help. For love alone she would do all that she could to ensure that the baby lived. Only then might she herself be saved.

Christian was used to sleepless nights. More times than he could count, he'd stood watch beneath the heavens and not succumbed to drowsiness. The Wolf had molded him into a disciplined soldier. Like a smithy, he had hammered his son into an instrument that felt neither pain nor deprivation. The Wolf had taught him that mercy to the enemy could be fatal, that might prevailed, and morality was the great tormenter of souls.

In one hideous night's work Christian had implemented every tool of war that the Wolf had taught him. He had killed his father in his very own bedchamber. He had slaughtered the Wolf's men who came after him. He had set fire to Wendesby, and the smoke had killed both women and children. At the time he'd felt no remorse, only blinding fury. That was the night he had learned the Wolf was his father—a vicious, war-loving Dane.

Remorse had found him before the dawn. Fury faded in a matter of hours. Now the screams of innocents haunted him nightly. His soul bled with remorse for the slaughter committed by his hand. And sleep was no longer a refuge for him, but a place of anguish.

His envious gaze fell to the sleeping nurse. Lady Clare suffered no affliction like his. After hours of silent vigil, she had wilted onto the floor beside the baby's box, her head resting on an out-flung arm. Her body was curved around Simon's cradle as though protecting him, even in her sleep.

Christian gazed at her in the light of the sputtering tallow lamps, and his bitterness softened at the miracle of what he saw. This woman was no enemy. She could not have been the one to steal the covers off his son. In the past twelve hours she, Nell, and Sarah had devoted themselves to Simon's welfare. Fear was not their motivation, but rather love.

Clare had spoken the truth when she said she loved his son. Her appearance at Helmesly had saved Simon from starvation. And after tonight he could only believe that fate had delivered her to his stronghold for a purpose. Could she possibly bring herself to love the Slayer, too?

One of the lamps dimmed, telling him the wick was drowning. It was well past midnight. He rose from his desk and crossed to the open window. A brief spell of rain had passed, leaving thick patches of mist floating above the land. It looked like fleecy sheep were dotting the meadow. He closed the shutters and moved to the baby's cradle.

Simon had suffered pains that could only be communicated through his cries. Nell could not supply fresh cloths at the same rate that Simon soiled them. Together, he and Clare had forced the infusion blended by the servants down the baby's throat. They'd dispelled the evil humors, causing Simon to purge whatever ailed him.

The baby's suffering had left Christian pale with helplessness. He relived the fear that Simon would be snatched away, that his strange and lonely marriage had been for naught.

Clare, with her tender and efficient touch, had brought the baby through the worst of it. Her voice, her consolation, had done as much to comfort Christian as it had his baby. Gratitude swelled in Christian's heart.

Kneeling by the cradle, he turned his attention to his son. Simon's skin was waxen, his eyelids sunken and bruised. Bending his head, Christian found a prayer on his lips.

He had not prayed for more than thirteen years—not since the Wolf discovered the altar he had built in a corner of the stable. Christian had been mocked for his piety and flogged for seeking help from anyone, even God.

Helpless men pray, Dirk of Wendesby had scoffed.

I am helpless. There was nothing within the range of Christian's powers that would save his infant's life. The choice was entirely up to providence.

Hot tears pooled in his eyes as he begged the Almighty to spare Simon. A part of him still felt that he was wasting his time. He didn't deserve a son.

Clarise found the floor unbearably hard. With her shoulder paining her and her arm growing numb, she stirred from slumber. The sound of fervent whispers brought her fully awake. She shifted slightly and cracked an eye. Lord Christian was kneeling over the cradle. In the faint bluish light she saw that his head was bent. His hands gripped the wooden box.

He is praying, she realized with amazement. And his Latin was perfect.

A rush of empathy brought a lump to her throat. She gazed at him for what seemed an eternity. He was an enigma to her! One moment he struck her as merciless and fear-inspiring. The next he demonstrated a deep streak of honor and generosity. He was well read, with nearly as many books in his solar as her father had owned.

Ignoring her discomfort, she decided not to disturb him. He needed peace in his heart more than anyone she'd ever met. Besides, it pleased her to watch him, to know that he was just as human as she was. At last her eyelids grew weighted and drifted shut.

Moments later she felt herself being lifted. The unyielding floor dropped away, and she sank into a feather mattress. It was the Slayer's bed, she realized in her semiconscious state. Yet she felt no fear of ravishment. *I like you,* he had said to her today. The simple proclamation offered reassurance in spite of how quickly he'd accused her of making Simon ill.

Christian gazed at the graceful figure in his bed. Her scent clung to him from the brief moment he'd held her in his arms. She smelled of lavender and woman. Her scent was comforting in the same way that his mother's sweet smell had been when he was small.

She murmured in approval of her newfound comfort and snuggled into the coverlet. Her bosom rose and fell with a sigh. He remembered the lush perfection of her breasts. Poor woman, she had been misused by a man, just as his mother had. He had no right to entertain the thoughts that sizzled through his mind each time he looked at her.

With a self-directed sneer he turned away. All he could think of lately was possessing the woman for himself. That made him no better than Monteign, no nobler than his father.

Making his way to the tallow lamp, he snuffed the flame. Then he moved toward the far side of the bed, where he hoped he wouldn't reach for Lady Clare in his sleep. Something unseen lay in his path. He tripped over the cloth object, then bent down to retrieve it.

In the sooty darkness he identified the sling that Clare had carried Simon in. Something soft and heavy was caught in the material's folds. His hands closed over a pouch of some kind. The slosh of liquid helped him realize what it was.

It was the same nursing skin Sarah had used without success before Clare's intervention. As he clutched the smooth vessel, his mind began to churn. What would a nurse need with such a tool? Had she given Simon milk that was not her own?

The question unearthed new doubts. Had the milk been

rancid? Had it been tampered with somehow? The doubts, like maggots, began to gnaw at his newfound faith.

Could his son have been poisoned?

Nay, he could not believe it! The woman had just demonstrated the depths of her devotion. She would never have poisoned his son.

Resolve hardened the warlord's jaw. Because of her devotion to Simon today, he would let her sleep. But she would have to account for the nursing skin the moment she awakened on the morrow.

Chapter Nine

Soft yellow light penetrated Clarise's eyelids. The gentle cooing of a pigeon came from somewhere close by. In the courtyard a supply wagon rumbled over the cobbles. Reluctantly she opened her eyes. She could not remember for a moment where she was. Then she recognized the Slayer's solar. She was lying in his bed.

Her gaze jumped to the warlord, who was sleeping silently beside her. His jaw was dark with unshaved bristles. A streak of hair had fallen over his forehead, softening the severity of his brow. The scarred half of his face was buried in the pillow. She was struck by how handsome he looked without the flaw, how young.

Her gaze wandered from the powerful curve of his cheekbone to his stubbornly square chin. His mouth fascinated her. She wondered again what it would be like to kiss him.

And then she remembered Simon.

Holding her breath, she turned over and dropped her feet to the floor. She peered wide-eyed into the cradle, terrified that she would find the baby dead.

He looked utterly at peace. At the telltale rise and fall of his chest, the breath rushed out of her lungs. She touched a finger to Simon's cheek. His skin was cool. The fever was gone.

With a cry of joy Clarise spun around on the bed, jarring the warlord into wakefulness. He sprang up, gripped her by the shoulders, and slammed her to the mattress before she uttered a word.

She found herself pinned beneath his rock-hard body, the breath pushed from her lungs. As she struggled to inhale, the scent of juniper and manliness washed over her. The heat of his body seeped through her clothing and warmed her skin. Christian looked just as astonished as she was to find that they were pressed together, chest to thigh.

Putting his hands to the bed, he lifted some of his weight, but not all of it. His alert gaze centered on her lips. "My apologies," he said, not sounding at all contrite. And then he rolled away.

Clarise felt robbed of something. It took her a second to remember the reason for her joy. She sat up and seized the Slayer's white shirt, noting how soft it felt against his muscled arm. "Simon's fever is gone!" she cried. She bounced to her knees and gestured at the cradle. "Look! He sleeps peacefully."

Hope kindled in the warlord's eyes. He scooted across the bed and leaned over the cradle to study his son. She remembered his fervent prayers of last night, and she was certain they'd been answered. Tears of gratitude sprang to her eyes.

"Praise God," said the Slayer hoarsely. He glanced at her then, catching sight of her damp gaze. A long-fingered hand came up and wiped away the tear that had seeped over her lashes. "Is this happiness?" he asked.

His thumb was warm and calloused. As it stroked her cheek, she experienced a melting sensation and leaned unconsciously toward his palm. "I am grateful Simon is restored to good health. I so was afraid," she pushed the confession through her throat, "that you would blame me if . . ." She couldn't finish the thought.

He nodded as if understanding, but he looked away, his

eyes narrowing. "You have practiced some deceit," he accused quietly.

The blood slipped from her face in an instant. What had he discovered? "Deceit?" she repeated. "What do you mean?" She was amazed that her voice remained so steady.

He flung himself off the bed and bent to collect the cloth sling from the floor. "I found this," he said, holding up the nursing skin.

The breath in Clarise's lungs evaporated, but her mind produced another lie quickly. "You will note that it's full," she said. "I carried it thinking Simon might cry on the way to Abbingdon and I could assuage him without . . . without stopping."

"Did he drink any of it?" he demanded harshly.

She found she couldn't deny it. "He had a little. Apparently it didn't agree with him," she added faintly.

The Slayer dropped the bottle as if it were a venomous serpent. He stalked to a basin and splashed water on his face.

Clarise felt like a piece of fraying rope. A moment ago she'd thought that the root of her deceit had been detected, but it had only been a small part of her complex lie. And the Slayer was furious with her for just that small transgression. How would he react to learn that goat's milk was all the baby ever got?

He turned around, then, dragging a towel over his face. His expression was irritated but not murderous. "From now on, Simon will only take nourishment at your breast," he warned. "He is the next Baron of Helmesly, by God. He will not take milk from a goat that eats anything to cross its path!" His volume rose so that by the end of the sentence he was practically yelling.

Clarise lowered her gaze to the baby. She felt she deserved his chastisement. "I am sorry, my lord," she choked out. Guilt cut deeply into her heart as she realized the milk had very likely been the reason for Simon's affliction. Had it just been rancid? Or had someone possibly poisoned it?

Her pallor must have convinced the Slayer of her contrition. He tossed aside the cloth and strode toward the bed to sit beside her.

She glanced at him warily.

"I don't mean to be harsh," he said, propping his elbows on his knees. He frowned down at his feet, his scar distinctly pale upon his cheek.

With surprise, she realized he felt sorry for having just raised his voice at her. She rushed to reassure him. "Nay, you were right to be angry. 'Twas my fault. I must guard him more closely."

He turned his head then, his gaze probing. "Why do you love him?" he inquired with genuine puzzlement.

She pulled back and frowned at him. "Why?" She glanced at the baby. "How could I not? He is innocent, he is beautiful. Look at him!" She gestured to Simon.

The warlord glanced at his son, then back at her. "*You* are beautiful," he corrected her roughly. His eyes warmed to a clear, bottomless green. "And I thank you for loving him." He leaned toward her unexpectedly and pressed his mouth to hers. Clarise gave a start of surprise, her eyes flying wide.

His lips felt just as she'd imagined, warm and firm. He put brief and gentle pressure on her mouth and then withdrew, taking away the promise of more.

She felt as though she'd been doused in a warm, fragrant rain that abruptly stopped. The Slayer had just kissed her! She could only stare at him, amazed that she wanted to be kissed again.

"A kiss of thanks," he explained, waiting.

She *needed* to be kissed again.

Without thinking of the consequences, she slipped her hands into the long strands of his hair and pulled him back for more. She had kissed Alec to convey the depths of her love and willingness to wed him. In this instance, she had nothing in mind but to feel the Slayer's mouth on hers and the thrill of courting danger.

He held perfectly still, his breath quick and shallow, while she placed feathery kisses upon his mouth, along his bottom lip, and at the corners. Flushed and confused that he was not responding, she pulled back, chagrined by her boldness.

He slowly raised a hand and captured her jaw, keeping her motionless. His eyes flashed a warning, and then he lowered his head and the assault became his.

His kiss was surprisingly gentle, given the steely strength of his fingers on her face. He fused his lips softly to hers. The contradiction of gentleness and strength brought heat coursing through her veins. With focused intent he added pressure to his fingers, causing her jaw to fall open. With great tenderness the Slayer slipped his tongue between her parted lips and slowly, thoroughly explored her mouth.

Caught up in a whirlpool of dizzy delight, Clarise gripped his shoulders. Never had she known a kiss could be so sweet, so intoxicating. When the Slayer lifted his head, she made a sound of protest.

With a look of bemusement he studied her flushed face and bright eyes. His fingers moved from her jaw to slide across her slightly parted lips, and his own face darkened with desire. He lowered his head again and kissed her with sudden, unrestrained force.

Shocked by his sudden savagery, Clarise clung to him, her heart pounding with expectation. His erotic plunge and retreat was nearly more than she could stand. It left her breathless and squirming and desperate for some unknown relief.

He pressed her smoothly back against the pillows, and she sank into the softness, disoriented. The room seemed to wheel behind her eyelids as their mouths merged again. She was vaguely gratified to feel the hard length of him against her. She strained upward, needing to feel more, her breasts aching with some vague hunger.

His hand molded her hip and slid along the indentation of her waist. His touch inflamed the strange, new restlessness that was building in her. His hand closed suddenly over the swell of her breast, and she gasped in surprise and pleasure.

The memory of his tongue gliding over her nipple caused it to rise toward his palm as though beckoned. With a groan, the warrior squeezed her tenderly. Then he tore his lips from hers and nipped her shoulder through the material of her gown.

The light sting intensified her sensitivity. His mouth moved lower. Suddenly he was grazing her erect nipple with his teeth. She moaned aloud at the stabbing pleasure. Then he closed his mouth over the linen bodice and sucked, straight through the moistened fabric, his mouth hot and insistent.

Clarise cried out in mixed astonishment and delight. She sank her fingers into his hair, confused by the mixed urge to push him away and pull him closer. "My lord, you must stop," she begged in a voice without substance. She realized now this was moving too far, too fast.

His mouth moved stealthily upward and kissed her into acquiescence. She briefly forgot her concerns; after all, kissing could cause no harm. But then he pressed his hips against her, and the enormous proof of his arousal brought her quickly to her senses.

With sudden alarm she began to struggle. "Let me go," she begged, between his kisses. In retrospect she realized she should never have encouraged his attentions. She should never have fallen asleep in his chamber, should never have let him put her in his bed. "Please, release me at once!"

The Slayer lifted his head. He stared at her stricken face and frowned. And then he thrust himself away. Whatever he might have said, whether in apology or in anger, was forestalled by a pounding at the door. He leaped from the bed and went to answer it.

At least he had the presence of mind to shield her from the caller's view. She could only imagine what she looked like with her hair in disarray and her clothes disheveled!

"My lord," Sir Roger rapped out. "Our spies say Ferguson will strike Glenmyre at dawn tomorrow."

The warlord seemed to grow in size as he gripped the

door latch. "Tell Justin to ready my horse. I will speak with you anon. Let me dress."

He shut the portal quietly. Clarise slipped to the edge of the bed and wrapped her arms over her torso to keep herself from trembling. Without looking at her, the warlord moved toward his boots. He stamped his feet inside them and laced them up without a word. Silence grew to unbearable proportions. When he straightened again, he seemed to have made a decision.

"Watch over Simon carefully," he instructed, scowling so fiercely she was tempted to flinch. "No one may tend him but you," he added.

"How long will you be gone?" The knowledge that he was off to fight Ferguson filled her with excitement and trepidation. Maybe he would kill the Scot without her asking him to do so.

The muscles in his jaw clenched rhythmically. "I know not." He studied her defensive posture, then he sighed almost despairingly. "Will you kiss me when I return?" he asked.

The request was almost boyish in its uncertainty. She was tempted to say yes, if only to reassure him. Part of her longed to resume their passionate kisses! She had never tasted anything like them. But she had no intention of offering her favors in exchange for his sword arm. She was the daughter of a nobleman, not the leman she professed to be.

She looked away, wishing she could blurt the truth. 'Twas safest to say nothing at all, she decided.

"I see," he said, reaching for his belt. In a furious gesture he slung the strip of leather against the bedpost. The resulting crack made her leap with alarm. The baby came awake with a gasp. The warlord snatched up a charcoal-colored tunic and strode to the door.

Simon began to cry. "Lord Christian," Clarise called out as she reached for the baby.

When he looked at her, his anger was subdued. "Aye, what?" he asked, taking in the two of them.

"Be careful. Ferguson uses alchemy as a weapon. But I suppose you know that already."

His gaze narrowed with interest. "What do *you* know of it?" he demanded.

The truth quivered on her tongue, but his volatile temper made her loath to confess it now. "I told you, Monteign feared Ferguson and his trickery. Beware the powders that he uses to spread fire. Beware any ruse for peace, for he will use deceit to gain advantage."

He pondered her words in silence, seeming to take them to heart. Then, with a brusque nod, he left the room.

Her thoughts ran after him. She found herself wishing him the best possible outcome, fearing for his life. If only he could kill Ferguson in the conflict to come! Then her family would be free, and then she would dare to tell him who she was, knowing Ferguson could not learn of her betrayal.

Suddenly she realized she should have told him the truth after all. Wasn't the Slayer going to Glenmyre? The people of Glenmyre would unknowingly expose her, for there had never been a Clare de Bouvais in their midst, only an Isabeux by that name.

She looked at Simon with consternation. Aye, she should have told him who she was. Instead, she'd lied and lied again, simply to avoid the Slayer's wrath. With those lies she'd sealed her own uncertain fate, whatever it might be.

Several mornings later Clarise parted the cupboards of the lord's conservatory and eyed the stale bread with lukewarm enthusiasm. This was what she got for sleeping so late and missing the morning meal. Her late-night exploits to the goat pen had left her exhausted.

On three more instances she had found the same offering of milk awaiting her. With every discovery her skin tightened and a chill washed over her. She was certain someone knew of her masquerade. But who? And how could they know when Nell was the only one to enter her chamber?

Since Simon had fallen ill, Clarise knew better than to

use the milk. She'd dumped the bucket in the corner of the shed and milked the nanny goat herself. She wouldn't take the risk that the offering was poisonous. If a plot was afoot to see Simon murdered, she refused to be party to it.

It was not entirely the baby's fault that she was tired. After stumbling into bed again, she would lie awake, thinking of her family and wondering how they fared in her absence. Often her interference was the only thing that kept Ferguson from cuffing her mother in plain sight of his men. Her vigilance kept Merry from being fondled by the Scottish men-at-arms. The only time that Kyndra bathed was when Clarise toted her, kicking and screaming, to the bathhouse.

She was also preoccupied by thoughts of the Slayer. Word had come from Glenmyre that Ferguson had not attacked on the first day. The warlord remained at Alec's stronghold, ready to defend it if the need arose, free to make inquiries into her background.

The knot in her stomach would not allow for a big breakfast. Clarise poured herself a mug of watered ale and cut a wedge of cheese from a wheel. Carrying her food to the only trestle that hadn't been put away, she adjusted the sling in which she carried Simon and sat down.

The food was tasteless. The reason for her anxiety, she acknowledged, was not whether the Slayer could repel Ferguson's attack. She had confidence in his abilities. It was his reaction to the truth she feared. She ought to have told the warlord who she was before he came to his own conclusions.

Glumly she nibbled on her cheese. A few well-placed questions would expose her. When the peasants were asked if they'd ever heard of a Lady Clare, they would inquire if he didn't mean Clarise, for the names were all too similar. And then they would describe the elaborate betrothal that had taken place there just a month before the Slayer seized Glenmyre.

She'd had ample opportunity to tell Lord Christian the

truth. Because of her reticence, he would likely assume the worst.

What could she do to soften the blow? How could she appease the warlord when he came storming back to Helmesly?

"Oh, oh, oh!"

This cry of lamentation wrenched her gaze to the far end of the hall. Clarise spied Harold pacing before the fire pit, wringing his hands and muttering in distress. She looked around for the source of his worry. Other than the two of them, the hall was deserted. Harold gave another cry of despair, and she abandoned her breakfast to hurry over to him.

"Why, Harold, whatever is the matter?" She put a hand on his shoulder to gain his attention.

The steward looked amazed to see her there. "Oh!" he cried again, halting his frantic pacing. "Lady Clare," he said, staring at her blankly.

"What is it, Harold?" she asked again. "Tell me what is troubling you?" Her first guess was that his overbearing wife had caught him filching pastries from the kitchen, as it was a common occurrence.

"'Tis Doris," he blurted, his color high, his white hair waving as he rocked himself. "She's going to have a baby, a baby."

"Who is Doris?" Clarise asked in bewilderment.

"The cook!" Harold seemed to force the words out.

Immediately Clarise envisioned the heavyset woman who prepared all the meals at Helmesly. Surely she was well beyond her childbearing years. "Are you sure?" she asked.

"The midwife has come. Oh!" he groaned. "She is going to die. Doris is going to die, oh!"

"Calm yourself." She tried to reassure the rattled steward. She brought him a flagon of ale and made him drink it, but still she could make no sense of his prattle. She decided to look into the matter right away. With Simon sleeping in the sling, this was the best time.

Clarise headed straight for the servants' quarters in the

castle's southern wing. A handful of women had gathered outside one of the many tiny chambers. Among their number was Sarah, a brunette version of Nell, looking drawn and pale. "How does she?" Clarise inquired.

Sarah merely shook her head, reluctant to spread poor news. "Dame Maeve haffe summoned the midwife. She be with Doris now," was all she said.

Clarise peeked through the curtain that separated the room from the hall. The sight that greeted her filled her with dismay. Doris lay like a great mountain on her pallet of straw. Her body was covered in sweat, due to the blazing brazier. It was common practice for midwives to heat the chamber to unbearable temperatures. There was no window to open in order to relieve the occupants.

Clarise did not believe that heat encouraged the body to expel a baby any faster. All it caused was premature exhaustion. She stepped into the cell with the intention of extinguishing the brazier's flames. The sight of blood between Doris's legs drew her up short. Her gaze flew with alarm to the midwife's stoic expression.

"Push with the next pain," said the shriveled woman. She had yet to notice Clarise, for her shoulder was positioned toward the door. More than that, a blinding film clouded the woman's right eye.

Doris gave a tortured gasp. The cook's big body tensed with pain. The midwife leaned forward, lifting the blanket. "'Twill soon be over," she predicted, scooting to the edge of her stool.

Clarise could not have moved if the castle fell into ruins around her. The stain on the pallet spread, until it went clear to Doris's ankles. The sight was ghastly, yet the midwife's grip remained steady as she held up the blanket.

Again, Doris was racked with pain.

"Push," urged the midwife. "Push!"

A baby eased out of the passage in a breech position. It had obviously come before its time. Scrawny in size and coated in a cheesy substance, it lay still and silent on the soiled pallet. There was not a sound in the room, other than that of Doris's heavy breathing.

Then the midwife bent low and dragged a metal object from the beaten bowl at her ankles. It was an iron cross.

Clarise took a look at the lifeless baby and the dull cross and fled the room. She succumbed to her sudden need to pull Simon from his sling and hold him close.

An hour later she summoned the courage to visit Doris again. The servants had moved into her cramped chamber, telling Clarise that the cook could stand to have at least one more visitor. The women shuffled aside as she entered, giving her room to kneel at Doris's side. "We suffer with you, Doris," she said, not knowing what else she could possibly say to ease the woman's pain.

Doris closed her eyes. Her doughty face was ashen from the loss of so much blood. "'Tis God's will, my lady," she said bitterly.

Clarise floundered in her helplessness. "What can I do for you?" she dared to ask. She was not the mistress of these people, and yet she felt protective toward them. They had no one to lend an ear to their complaints. No one but the stern Dame Maeve.

A fat tear squeezed between Doris's stubby lashes. Behind Clarise, the servants scuffled near the box that held the dead infant. "Looks just like 'im," someone whispered.

Like who? wondered Clarise. Did they know who the father was?

"If I could have a mass for my babe," the cook finally murmured. "If I could have him buried close, in the castle graveyard, where my mother and brothers lie, 'twould ease my spirit."

It took Clarise a second to understand the significance of Doris's request. Priests would not venture near to Helmesly with the interdict in place. Who would perform the burial?

Her spine stiffened with resolve. The chapel must be restored to use. The servants hungered for Godliness. They seemed to blame their seneschal for their inability to worship. It would be a favor to Lord Christian to open his chapel doors. Finding a priest, however, lay beyond her powers. Perhaps she could convince the Abbot of Revesby to ignore the interdict and perform the necessary sacrament.

"I will do what I can," she heard herself say. And in the same instant, she thought of several improvements she might make at Helmesly before the seneschal returned. Would it help her cause at all to make his castle more welcoming? It might dissuade him from violence, she reasoned, to find his home transformed when he did come back.

She could place a tapestry or two upon the walls, make torches to brighten the great hall, gather flowers to add color. At this juncture she would try anything within her powers to earn his good will.

She felt precisely like a straw dummy hanging in the wind, awaiting the thrust of a lance.

Chapter Ten

With Simon ever present in the sling tied across her shoulders, Clarise carried luncheon for two to the outer ward. The day was growing hotter, much like the situation in which she found herself. She hoped today to make an ally of Sir Roger. If anyone could aid her with her cause, it was he.

She found the knight in the training arena, tightening bowstrings on the arsenal of bows. With no men-at-arms to train, he focused his energies on keeping Helmesly in constant readiness for war. All the fighting men were off with the Slayer at Glenmyre.

Clarise hailed him from a distance and showed him her basket. They found a shady area in the orchard, where Sir Roger spread the blanket under a pear tree. She didn't miss his quizzical look. If his watchfulness were any indication, he knew that she was up to something.

"Have you any news?" she asked to distract him. She pulled Simon from the sling and laid him on his stomach in the center of the blanket.

The knight eased himself down beside her, his joints protesting loudly. "Nay, nothing more than to say that Ferguson has yet to strike. Perhaps he has changed his mind with my lord on site defending Glenmyre." He began to unpack the basket. He lifted out a bit of dry meat and grimaced. "How does the babe today?" he asked.

"Fully recovered," Clarise assured him. She patted Simon on the back. The future baron grunted in an effort to lift his head. There was much to catch the eye. A butterfly settled at the edge of the blanket and fanned its black and yellow wings at him.

Clarise glanced sidelong at the knight to gauge his mood. He appeared more somber than usual. She guessed it must chafe him to linger at Helmesly awaiting summons, but such was his duty as second-in-command.

She began by informing him of Doris's miscarriage. He listened intently, clucking with compassion to hear that the baby was stillborn. Clarise did not miss the pitying glance he sent her way. No doubt he was thinking that she had suffered a similar loss. For the hundredth time she lamented the necessity of that particular lie. "I wonder who the father was," she said out loud. "The servants must know, for one of them whispered that the babe looked just like his father."

"Did you see the babe?"

"Nay," she admitted. She had scarcely been able to glance at the lifeless infant.

"Hmmm," said the knight. "Doris is a spinster."

Which meant that she could be with whomever she pleased, provided she was discreet. "As you can tell, the event will have an impact on the food we eat," she remarked, indicating the meat at which he had already pulled a face. "Doris was the best cook in the castle."

They settled on splitting a capon wing and sharing the wine. "'Twill take her a week or so to recover," she said, accepting the wineskin he handed her. "I could speak to the others about the quality of the fare."

"You had best leave that to Dame Maeve," he warned. "She is jealous of her duties, that one."

Clarise agreed with him and steered the conversation back to the day's events. "Is there only one midwife in these parts?" she asked.

"Aye," he said. "Why?"

"Then the woman I saw this morning must have been the one who oversaw Simon's birth?" She knew she was prying, but she could not imagine the Slayer putting up with the shriveled woman's malpractice.

Saintonge cast her a glowering, sidelong look. "Aye, she was the same," he answered bitterly. "Lady Genrose was fine until that shrew took over," he added.

Clarise took note of his disapproval. "I do not agree with her methods," she felt safe in adding. "Heating the chamber is a heathenish practice. She was insensitive to Doris's pain and seemed not at all dismayed to deliver a stillborn."

"As I said, there are no other midwives." Taking a bite of the bread, he added that the men would grow discontent if they were made to eat such fare.

The time had come to lay her proposition before him. Clarise reached into the basket. "Would you like a sugared almond?" she offered. "'Tis the last one in the kitchens." She held out the confection she had squirreled away for bribery.

His gray eyes narrowed, and his familiar smile took hold of one edge of his mouth. "What do you want?" he asked. "I know you ventured into this heat for something. Out with it."

"'Tis a simple request, really," she assured him.

"Speak it then," he said kindly.

She experienced an inward twinge. Would the knight be so congenial when he learned how very much she had kept from him? "First I need the key to the chapel."

"What!"

"Doris asked that her babe be given a mass," she quickly explained. "She wants him buried in the castle graveyard with the rest of her family. The servants hunger for a spiritual life, Sir Roger. I know that the interdict prohibits services of any kind," she added, cutting off the protest that was certain to come, "but they will be happier with a chapel where they may venture in and pray."

Sir Roger itched a spot inside his collar.

Clarise saw that Simon's eyes had begun to cross as he examined the pattern on the blanket. She put him in a new location.

"Who would bury the babe and say the proper words over his grave?" Saintonge finally asked. His question betrayed at least some consideration.

"Perhaps the Abbot of Revesby would come? The servants think highly of him." She also had personal reasons for wanting to meet the good abbot. If she didn't soon get a hold of Alec, she was doomed to confessing her guilt to Lord Christian.

The knight shook his head. "I doubt he will defy his colleague again."

"Defy? What do you mean?"

He looked displeased with himself for having said so much, then grimaced with resolve to share what he knew. "It was Ethelred who wed Lord Christian and his lady in the very chapel you speak of," he grimly explained. "The Abbot of Rievaulx had refused to marry them, offering no other reason than his differences with the baron. Ethelred petitioned the archbishop and received permission to perform the sacrament in Gilbert's stead."

"Gilbert is the Abbot of Rievaulx?" she asked.

"Aye." He gave her an odd look. "You must not have lingered long at the abbey to have escaped that knowledge."

"I was housed separately from the men," she answered, wincing. *Coward! You should have seized the opportunity to confess to him.*

"Ah. Well, on the day of the wedding, Gilbert discovered Ethelred's betrayal. He tried to stop the ceremony but arrived too late. In a choleric fit, he cried out a warning that has caused a rift between the serfs and their seneschal ever since, just as he meant it to."

"What was it?" Clarise asked, feeling a chill on the top of her head. At last she would know why the folk at Helmesly persisted in fearing their master.

The knight began dumping leftovers in the basket.

"Please tell me," she softly begged him.

He stilled, struggling with himself. "My lord is an honorable man," he told her. The scars stood out starkly on his face.

Clarise felt her eyes sting in response to such loyalty. "I have seen the better side of him," she admitted. And she would doubtless see the worst unless she could soften the blow when it came. "What did Gilbert say?"

Sir Roger looked down at his own callused hand. "He said Lady Genrose would be slain by her husband."

Clarise barely smothered her gasp. A vision of a body desecrated rose up in her mind's eye, and she shook it free.

Sir Roger's eyes flashed with unaccustomed fierceness. "The lady labored long and died in childbirth. Lord Christian saved Simon from dying, also. He never wanted such a fate for his wife!"

She put her own hand over his roughened one. "I believe you," she said convincingly. "I do. And God will reward such loyalty as yours." As she squeezed his fingers, she mourned that their bond of friendship would soon be put to the test. "Gilbert is mad," she added, saying out loud what she had thought the moment she saw the unreal glitter in the abbot's eyes. "When I spoke with him, he left me feeling quite uneasy."

"You may be right," Saintonge agreed. "They say he works night and day pouring over his herbs. Likely he has tried one too many of his concoctions, and it has turned his brain to mush."

Clarise smiled at the knight's imagination. "I don't know why the servants put any credence in the things he has to say," she commented lightly.

His eyes began to crinkle at the corners. His smile took up its post once more. "Helmesly is a happier place for your presence, lady," he told her with feeling. "You have cast your light into my lord's dark heart, and I thank you for it."

So that he wouldn't see the guilt in her face, she lifted her gaze toward the main keep where it stood between its graceful buttresses. To her amazement, contentment flooded her heart when she looked upon its clean lines. How could she feel so connected to a place when the foundation of her existence here was built on sand?

Heathersgill had ceased to be a home after Ferguson usurped her father. For months she'd felt abandoned by Alec, overwhelmed by her family's plight. Now all those feelings were removed from her, by time and distance. It was wrong of her to forget her family.

"Do you know if Alec has made reply to Lord Christian's offer?" she dared to ask. If there were any way to escape her final judgment, she would take it. Alec's chances of defeating Ferguson were not as high as Christian's. But at least she knew him for an honorable man, a kind man.

The knight studied her from beneath his lashes. "There's been no word," he said neutrally.

Sir Roger had praised her for bringing happiness to Helmesly, but he didn't yet trust her with issues of power and politics. She could not forget that underneath his friendly veneer there remained a bond of loyalty, firm and enduring. "Tell me how you came to serve Lord Christian," she heard herself inquire.

Saintonge leaned in with an air of confidence. "I served the Wolf before him."

"His father?" she asked in amazement.

"I didn't know he was his father. Nor did Lord Christian, until later. He came to Wendesby to train as a squire. He was but twelve years old—a slim lad with a vocabulary that had me scratching my head to remember my grammar. He spoke eloquently of angels and apostles and a vision of the future."

Clarise went curiously light-headed. "He was that innocent, then?" she breathed, all ears as she waited for more. "Go on," she said when the knight paused thoughtfully.

"The Wolf refused to recognize him publicly. He kept their kinship a secret, I think because he didn't understand him. He looked at the boy and saw his weakness rather than

his strength. He felt the need to turn the whelp into a warrior."

Oh, nay. She felt a sudden pang for Christian's lost sim-
plicity. "Did Lord Christian take offense to that? Is that
why . . . why he razed his father's demesne six years ago?
Did he hate him so much?"

Sir Roger picked up the baby, whose head had dropped
wearily to the blanket. He held Simon against the hard surface of his iron-linked chest. "My lord was ill treated by his
sire. He was made to sweat and to toil. To train long hours
and then grow hungry. He did not discover that the Wolf was
his father until his half brother taunted him on the lists, calling him a bastard."

Clarise stifled a gasp of sympathy.

"By then I had grown fond of him," the knight continued.
"He was a quick study in the art of warfare. In just a few
years, he had grown as tall and strong as the father who denied him. His sword arm became the stuff of legends. Yet
what I most admired in him was that he never lost his sense
of right and wrong. He had a determined spirit and a streak
of chivalry that the Wolf could not snuff out."

He patted the baby, transferring his loyalty to the Slayer's
child. "That is how he got the scar on his cheek," he recalled. "His father found an altar he had built in one corner
of the stables. He was a Dane, himself, and a godless man.
He ordered Christian chained to a post and whipped. My
lord refused to cry out. He even turned his head to send the
Wolf a defiant look, and the tip of the whip cracked his face.
He was only fifteen."

Clarise touched a finger to her cheek. She could almost
feel the sting of the whip herself. Why, he'd been only a
boy! How could a father treat his flesh and blood so cruelly?
She stared at the knight, aghast.

"Five years later my lord left Wendesby with blood on his
hands. I cannot say that I blame him. All those years he'd
trained under a man he hated. It was too much to learn that
the man was his father.

"When he left, I was afraid he would lose the honor that I cherished in him. So I mounted my horse and followed him. There have been times," the knight said with a sigh, "when I believed the Wolf succeeded in claiming his soul for evil. But lately, I remark more of the Christian I once knew. He is coming back into himself," he decided with a contented nod.

Clarise was enraptured by the tale. She found herself rallying fiercely behind the Slayer of Helmesly. So, she was right in guessing that he was not as ruthless as rumor depicted. Ah, the Saints, she should have trusted her instincts and told him what had brought her to Helmesly. Perhaps if she had, she would now have a champion at her side. As it was, she would have to earn his trust all over again.

"We traveled east," the knight added, recapturing her attention, "and pledged our swords to various lords. The Baron of Helmesly saw Christian fight in a tourney and hired him at once to train his men. A few years later, desiring to go to the Holy Lands and needing to leave his estate in capable hands, the baron betrothed my lord to his only daughter."

Simon, who was finding the unyielding surface of Sir Roger's armor too hard, let out a plaintiff cry. The knight quickly passed him to Clarise. As always, when she took him in her arms, she felt a rush of tenderness for the helpless babe. The fear that her days at Helmesly might be numbered tinged the tenderness with grief. "Sir Roger," she began in a strangled voice, "I . . ."

Someone across the field called out his name at the same time and waved him over.

The knight struggled to his feet, unaware of the confession that hovered on her tongue. "Thank you for the meal," he said. "I pray that Doris soon recovers."

"As do we all," Clarise replied. Perhaps this evening she would get around to admitting to what had brought her to Helmesly. "Er, there's just one more thing, Sir Knight," she added, coming to her own feet. "Could you ask Dame

Maeve to give me the key to the chapel? She won't heed my request." She'd asked the steward's wife herself, but the woman had refused her.

He nodded his head distractedly. "Very well."

"Oh and, er, may I have your permission to make some changes in the castle?"

Now she had his full attention. "Like what?" he asked, scowling suspiciously.

"Well, I think the hall would benefit from the addition of flowers, don't you? And there is an urgent need for more torches to be made, or perhaps you haven't noticed that everyone scuttles about in the darkness? Also, it would not be amiss to hang a tapestry or two."

Sir Roger wiped away the sweat that was dripping from his forehead. He looked quite overwhelmed by her quick suggestions. "Fine, fine," he said, clearly eager to return to such simple things as weapons and their use.

"Thank you," Clarise replied. "Do you know what happened to the tapestries that were there before? Nell says the baron had a number of them hanging in the hall."

The knight's brow wrinkled and then smoothed again. "The Lady Genrose gave them to the poor in honor of her parents' memories, I believe."

"And the silver, too?"

He shrugged. "I suppose."

Clarise could not contain her remark, "Then she managed to live in a convent after all!"

"Indeed," the knight agreed, not missing a beat. Thanking her for lunch again, he strode across the field, returning to his labors. Clarise worked to return Simon to his sling. Then she bent to shake the crumbs from the blanket. If she thought that replacing a few tapestries would ensure the Slayer's forgiveness, she was literally hanging by a thread, she reflected ironically.

Christian couldn't sleep. That circumstance in itself was not a novel one, but this was the third night in a row that he'd awakened in the middle of the night, unable to return to sleep. The tedium of waiting for the darkness to lift taxed his patience.

He lay on a feathered bed in the chamber that once belonged to Alec Monteign, staring at the whitewashed ceiling. The bed curtains had been stripped by the peasants and used for clothing. The shutters had been broken off the window and used for firewood. Nothing prevented the moon from shining through the open window to mock him.

Perhaps he should have slept in the lord's chamber, where the bed was tucked out of the way of the moon's illumination. Yet he'd made it a point never to sit in Monteign's chair nor sleep in his bed. Not only did he worry that the ghost of Alec's father would torment him, he had no wish to exacerbate his relations with the people of Glenmyre. They disliked him well enough as it was.

He sent a hopeful look toward the open window. No hint of dawn yet. Stars paid court to the half-moon's brilliance. Insects chirped in the overgrown yard below. The room was hot and humid. His eyeballs burned, but whenever he lowered his lids, unanswered questions beat against the door of his brain, finding no outlet.

Who was the woman in his castle?

No one at Glenmyre had heard of Clare de Bouvais, only Isabeux de Bouvais, Alec's cousin who had departed years ago after being compromised by the stable master. Monteign had no mistress by the name of Clare. There was nothing that tied Simon's wet nurse to Glenmyre, save the quick looks exchanged by peasants when he questioned them.

They knew something, Christian was certain of it. He was also certain he would be the last to discover what it was. He flung an arm over his eyes and groaned. Was she a spy for the people of Glenmyre, an advocate, or someone else entirely?

A vision of her beauty swam behind his eyelids. As in the flesh, she glowed with purpose and strength. He'd assumed her purpose was to rise above her past. *I am no longer any man's mistress,* she'd told him with haughty disdain. She'd kissed him with passion, then sent him away.

Could it be she was somebody's *wife?* He cursed long and fluently at the mystery. Then he turned and buried his face in the pillow.

Her lips were like rose petals, enticing him with their silken texture. Her passion was a hot spring bubbling just beneath the surface. *He would go mad if he couldn't have her.* But what chance did he stand, scarred as he was—a man guilty of murder?

For the Slayer of Helmesly, passion took place under the cover of darkness. It was done quickly, spuriously, and always with feelings of guilt.

He'd never kissed a woman with the slow, searching sweetness that he'd kissed Lady Clare. Moreover, touching her hadn't left him feeling guilty at all. How could he when she'd pressed herself so eagerly against him?

Why had she ultimately denied him then? *Will you kiss me when I return?* he'd asked. What did her silence mean?

Without his awareness, Christian drifted back to sleep. When he next cracked his eyes, the chamber was saturated with harsh, yellow light. He sat up quickly. Someone was shouting. Leaping from the bed, he rushed to the window. The shouts became clearer.

"Fire! Fire!"

Thrusting his head through the second-story window, he realized that the roofs of the huts below him were smoldering. Chased from their houses, Glenmyre's peasants coughed against the smoke and huddled together. A few brave men struggled to put the fires out. But the water seemed to have no effect on the conflagration. It died with deceptive ease, then sprang up in a great roar. It made no sense, for the roofs had been newly thatched. The only explanation was that they'd been doused with a flammable substance and then set on fire with flaming arrows, volleyed over the wall.

Beware the powders that he uses to spread fire. Clare's

warning echoed in Christian's mind. "*Ferguson*," he ground out, realizing the Scot's long-awaited attack had come at last.

He raked his gaze along the tree line, seeking sight of his enemy in the thickly shadowed pines. One man alone could have thrown packets of flammable powder over the wooden wall, for it was not particularly high. Fortunately the wall itself had been stained with a substance that was resistant to fire. The buildings inside, however, were not protected. Whatever Ferguson had used, it was highly combustible.

"Ferguson!" he roared. His shout was louder than the crackling fire below, so loud that it echoed back at him in mockery. But he was certain the Scots remained nearby, hiding in the distant trees perhaps, hoping that the wall would catch flame.

Suddenly he spied movement in the trees. His soldiers, posted on the wall walks, saw it also and whipped the bolts from their quivers. A solitary figure hurtled toward them. It tumbled into a low-lying area, then rose up again, racing over the earthworks toward Glenmyre's closed gate.

Second by second, the figure took shape. It was not a lone Scot, as he'd first guessed, but a woman, dressed in nothing more than a white shift that molded her slender body as she ran. The sound of her cries rose over the snapping of flames. She was screaming for the gates to be opened.

"Hold your arrows!" Christian called. The men at the battlements heard him. Tension eased on the bowstrings.

Christian snatched up his boots and raced outside to join the soldiers on the wall. "Is she from Glenmyre?" he asked, breathing harshly from his race to the battlements. Smoke billowed thickly from the fire, obscuring his view of the field. For the moment he'd lost sight of the woman, but he could hear her. She was crying out, hysterically.

"I know not," answered one soldier. The other one shrugged.

They were no more familiar with the people of Glenmyre
than he was. Christian shimmied down a ladder and grabbed
a peasant man by the scruff. "Come to the top with us. Tell
me if you know the woman out there."

The man scrambled obediently up the ladder. Meanwhile,
the woman had arrived at the gate. She was pounding at the
oaken barrier with great distress. "Do you know her?" he
shouted, dangling the poor peasant over the edge of the wall.

"I . . . ne do not know," the man wavered. "My vision be
poor. But I . . . I think I do."

"You think so!" Christian raged. This was not the time
for uncertainty. He released the peasant and thrust his fingers through his hair. He did not have time to drag another
peasant up the ladder. He longed to yell out for the gates to
be opened, but wary of a ruse, he decided to be cautious. The
woman could well be a decoy sent by Ferguson to get the
gates open.

He searched the field for any sign that the Scots were
hidden in the grass, rather than the trees, preparing to swarm
forward and take them by surprise. He could see no one.
Still, with Clare's warning ringing in his ears, he was reluctant to open the gate right away.

He leaned over the parapet and peered through the haze
at the woman below him. For a heart-stopping moment he
thought it was Clare herself who bloodied her fists as she
sobbed for entrance. But then he could see that this
woman was older. Her slender bone structure was the
same, as was her hair, only darker. As she threw her body
against the oaken gate, she screamed until her voice was
hoarse. All his instincts to shelter the weak demanded that
he let her in.

"My lord?" queried the soldier he had posted at the gatehouse. Clearly the man suffered the same impulse.

"Wait a moment," Christian answered grimly. He could
not get over his impression that the woman was somehow
related to Clare. A sliver of suspicion began to work its way

beneath his skin. "Crack the gate," he decided. "Let her in and shut it quickly behind her."

"Aye, sir." The soldier bounded into the gatehouse and jogged down the narrow stairs.

Christian heard the shouts below him. It took several men to lift the heavy crossbar from its slot. He hoped they could slam it into place again at once. He heard the crossbar roll to one side. *Not too far,* he cautioned silently.

There came an unmistakable roar of voices. Before his eyes, the very ground seemed to rise as men, disguised by mats of straw across their backs, leaped up and raced to the gate with their swords raised. At the same time the sound of thunder ripped Christian's gaze to the tree line where shadows took the form of distinct silhouettes. Men on horseback exploded across the field in a second wave.

"Close the gate!" he roared down to his men.

They struggled now to shut the gate against the foot soldiers who threw themselves against it to push their way in. Though the woman had been a ruse to get the gates open, she now howled like a cat gone mad, seeming truly distraught that she'd been denied entrance. The crossbar rumbled back into its slot, effectively locking her and the army out. The force of it reverberated under Christian's feet.

He turned his attention to the second wave. The Scots' horses devoured the remaining distance to the wall. Ferguson was easiest to find, betrayed by the burnished beard that jutted from beneath his helm. He wielded his trademark battle-ax in lieu of a sword.

Out of the Scot's leering mouth came the command to halt. His men pulled hard at the reins, out of range of Christian's arrows. Horses reared up in whinnying protest. With a furious gesture, Ferguson roared for his men to retreat and the woman in the shift to return to him.

Christian cursed at his cowardice. "Weapons down!" he called to his men, who had readied their crossbows again.

He did not want the woman accidentally struck while his men sought to pick off the Scots.

The woman refused to come. In reply to Ferguson's orders, several of his soldiers grabbed her and began to drag her away. All the while, they looked over their shoulders, fearful of being struck by the Slayer's arrows.

"Weapons down," Christian repeated.

He watched as Ferguson reached out and yanked the woman up onto the saddle in front of him. Her stricken face was the mold from which Clare's own features had been cast.

With a flash of insight Christian guessed the truth. He recalled the rumors of how Ferguson had seized Heathersgill, killing Edward the Learned and then marrying his widow. Was that she, then? If so, then Clare the wet nurse was Ferguson's stepdaughter. The thought spattered his brains like a blow from a mace. He hadn't realized how much he had wanted to believe in her innocence.

But at the present moment he could not afford to dwell on his discovery. The savage troops withdrew just far enough to where they could gloat as the fires they'd spawned undid all the work that Christian had expended in rebuilding.

Christian bellowed orders to the serfs to herd their livestock into the main keep. The stone wall of the keep would protect them as long as the fire didn't sink its teeth into the timber floor joists. Their primary job was to ensure that the outer wall, which was made of timber, continued to resist the flames.

Rallying the heartier people of Glenmyre, he called them to fight the fire. While it had taken only a handful of men to spawn such mischief, it would take many more to keep the fire from spreading. The Scot was planning to burn them out, then slaughter them all.

Eight hours later they stared in weary stupefaction at what remained of the lesser buildings. Charred timbers rose from postholes like ragged pikes. The walls, the roofs, the contents of the buildings lay in steaming piles of cinder just an arm's length from the main keep. But the outer wall held, keeping the Scots at bay. They'd survived Ferguson's attack with no loss of life, and at last the Scots melted away, sullen with their defeat.

Christian wiped a hand over his blackened face. His limbs ached. He longed to collapse where he stood, but that was an indulgence he would not allow himself. Despite the knowledge that his reparations at Glenmyre had been undone, he felt a sense of accomplishment at having saved the wall and the keep.

The livestock were led from their sanctuary, snorting, stamping, bleating in confusion. He smiled wearily. It was a small victory, but a victory nonetheless.

He had worked side by side with the people of Glenmyre to save their home. The grain had been kept from harm. The water was still clean. In the act of fighting for Glenmyre's future, they had forged a bond of mutual respect. He could see it in their blackened faces, in the steady gazes that turned his way.

"Let us celebrate the saving of the Glenmyre!" he shouted, startling more than a few of his own men.

A rousing cheer rose over the hiss of steaming wood.

"And for every man that joins with me to defeat the Scot, I will build you a wall of stone, so that Ferguson can never burn you out again."

This announcement was followed by another cheer. Three barrels were rolled from the keep's cellar and set upon trestles for the people to help themselves. Ale flowed freely, drowning despair and replacing it with a vision for the future.

Christian waited for the right people to become sotted with drink before he cornered them. What was the name of the woman Alec was going to wed? he asked. What did she look like?

In short time his suspicions had been confirmed. He'd been taken for a fool.

As the sun set that evening, he rooted out a solitary spot on the wallwalk. The sun glowed an angry orange, lighting the tips of the pines like so many tapers. A flock of geese honked noisily overhead as they flapped their way toward Spain and thence to the land of the infidels.

Christian eased his aching back onto a ledge, thankful for the balm of cooler air streaming from the mountains, and raked his fingers through his hair. Some of the longer strands were singed. He would have to cut them.

Oh, but it felt good to take his ease! He dropped his head into his palms. The sound of a woman screaming echoed in his ears. He was able to name her now: Jeanette DuBoise, the mother of the woman in his castle. To see such a fair woman wearing only a shift and crying with such desperation had been shock enough. But the fact that she looked so much like her daughter, Clarise, made it all the more disturbing.

He wished very much that they had managed to let the woman in. What was clearly a ruse to open the gates might also have been her only hope. Ferguson had put her directly in the path of danger, as though he cared not a whit if she were killed.

The thought sickened him.

He dragged his fingers over his face. What was he going to do now? The only thing left to him was war. Ferguson had asked for it by willfully attacking Glenmyre. And yet everything inside him rebelled at the spilling of more blood. He did not care to fight anymore, to add yet more hellish visions to those that paraded through his dreams.

And what of Clare? *Clarise,* he corrected himself. Seeing her mother's situation firsthand, he was certain she could not be loyal to the Scot.

Why had she come to Helmesly, then? Why?

The sun sank lower, and the crickets began to chirp in the high grass between the wall and the tree line. Christian lay down on the wallwalk and closed his eyes.

All he knew for certain was that she hadn't come to

Helmesly to save his son. The hope that God had sent an angel to redeem him was nothing more than fantasy. Clarise had another purpose at his castle altogether. And it wasn't likely a purpose that would benefit his soul.

Chapter Eleven

A thin mist hung in the castle graveyard. The sound of wet earth falling on a wooden casket rose over the sniffles of the heavyset cook as she watched her baby being buried. Clarise huddled with the few servants who dared to test Maeve's patience this morning by shirking their duties. There were no holy words to soothe the spirit of the grieving mother, only the mournful call of a dove as it settled on the wall to observe them.

As the grave was steadily filled, Simon grew impatient for his breakfast. Clarise shifted him to her left shoulder and thought about the meager milk supply in her bedchamber. A bucket of goat's milk was no longer enough to get the baby through a day. How on earth, she wondered, would she manage to procure two buckets without drawing notice?

Simon broke into angry cries as the gravedigger dropped the last clump of earth on the mound and patted it down. Sniffles rose from the more sympathetic women. One of them helped Doris to her feet. Clarise, who needed to break away for a feeding, hurried over to offer the cook a word of encouragement.

"Might I hold him?" the woman asked, her wet gaze falling to the baby's swaddled form.

Clarise was more than happy to let Simon shriek in someone else's ear, at least for the time being. He looked tiny against the woman's robust breasts as she cradled him in her arms. With his mouth wide open, he turned his head, searching hopefully for sustenance.

"He knows that I have milk!" Doris cried with surprise. Her many chins wobbled at the thought of what might have been.

Clarise's eyes widened as a notion hit her. Rather than rush Simon off into the castle, she dawdled in the graveyard while others approached Doris and offered their comfort. "Doris," she called, when the last one moved away. "I have a favor to ask of you."

"Yes, milady?" Doris replied, still holding the squirming Simon.

Clarise hoped it wasn't too much to ask of a grieving woman. "I have so much to do," she began, "making changes in the castle, and I fear that I'm depriving Simon of the proper nourishment. Do you think you might feed him with your own milk on occasion?"

Doris's eyes narrowed with sudden discernment. "Ye have ne milk o' yer own, do ye, milady?" she guessed.

Clarise made a choking sound and looked around, relieved to see that none of the lingering servants were close enough to have overheard. "How do you know that?" she breathed, deciding it was pointless to lie.

Doris rocked the disconsolate Simon. "Nell tolde me that ye hide a pail o' milk in yer chamber."

Of course, thought Clarise, with a grimace. Nell was not the soul of discretion she required in a lady's maid. "Do you know who's been leaving a bucket for me in the goat pen each night?" she asked, still no closer to solving that mystery than she'd been two weeks ago.

"Nay, milady." Doris shook her head. "But I am happy to helpe ye now." She gazed with pleasure at the squalling Simon. "Bring him to me whene'er he hungers, and he will grow plump on my breast, I warrant ye!"

A great weight seemed to rise from Clarise's shoulders.

At the same time a voice of caution whispered in her ear. "I would prefer you to come to my chambers to nurse him. I promised the seneschal my vigilance, and I would stay with you when you do."

"As ye wish, lady."

"Can you come with us now?" Clarise pleaded. It would save her the trouble of feeding Simon herself.

Doris fell into step beside her.

"Will you promise me something?"

The cook looked at her askance.

"Promise you'll not speak of our arrangement to anyone yet," Clarise whispered. "It must appear that I am still Simon's nurse. Very soon, the truth will be known," she added. Her spirits sank as she realized the moment was coming ever closer.

The messenger who'd stamped his way into the hall that morning had announced that the Slayer would be home by nightfall.

Doris paled a bit at the necessity for secrecy, but she nodded nonetheless. "I swear," she said.

Two hours later Clarise surveyed her handiwork from the landing on the stairs. Shortly after her picnic with Sir Roger two weeks ago, she had stumbled on a room full of goods in one of the castle storerooms. Most of the pieces Genrose had supposedly given to the poor still remained, collecting dust. Maeve protested that she'd forgotten about the goods, overwhelmed as she was by the baron and his lady's death. The amazed knight had given Clarise permission to haul it from the cellar for display.

At first the servants had been too paralyzed by the housekeeper's influence to help Clarise bring the goods up. Dame Maeve had secretly threatened them with additional chores, while in the presence of the master-at-arms she was solicitous and helpful. Clarise had found the woman maddening to deal with.

However, when it came to the chapel, servants had come whenever they could sneak away. With additional hands it had taken only a week to coat the ornate woodwork in beeswax. The embroidered kneeling cushions had been washed and replaced under the pews. They had swept up the stale rushes and scrubbed the floor with lye and wood ash. In short time the chapel was fit for worship.

Clarise had then turned her attention to the hall. With an eye toward decorating the walls, she'd enlisted Harold's aid in hanging a tapestry on the gallery wall. She chose the tapestry of a hunt, attended by lords and ladies, complete with comical hounds and red-tailed foxes. Silver trays were hung between the windows where they flung the light of the many torches back into the chamber. Even with the shutters drawn to keep out the gusty rain, the hall appeared as bright as if it were a fair day.

Clarise had placed a pot of flowers on every step of the grand staircase and brightened the high table with a colorful bouquet. She'd plundered the castle gardens and sent servants outside the walls to procure wild roses, savory, and meadow saffron, which now filled the room with their perfume. Oxeye daisies and pink mallow splashed color against the gray stone.

All stood in readiness for the lord's return. The room lacked only the crowning touch—a fire crackling in the fire pit. But with Dame Maeve threatening to complain to Sir Roger, Clarise admitted that a fire might make the room a mite too warm.

Studying the combined effects of her labor, she sought reassurance that the Slayer would be pleased. She had heard that Ferguson had set fire to Glenmyre. While the wall and central keep had held, the rest had been gutted by flame. If Lord Christian had discovered her identity by now, his need to avenge the Scot might well overshadow his reason.

The blare of the gatekeeper's horn shot through her like an arrow. Clarise nearly dropped poor Simon, who was sleeping in her arms. *He's back.* Her first instinct was to flee to her bedchamber and lock the door. But she was not a coward. Aside from a few white lies, she was guilty of no wrongdoing.

Clutching Simon like a shield, Clarise headed to the forebuilding. There, she encountered Harold dawdling at the base of the steps. He seemed reluctant to step through the protective arch and into the pounding rain.

"'Twould put me in a foul mood to travel in this mess," she called out, announcing herself. The thought depressed her further.

"Foul mood," the steward repeated. He glanced at her with something akin to wariness. She could only assume his wife had blistered his ears for doing her bidding this afternoon. She reminded herself that she had promised to read to him in exchange for his help with the tapestry.

Perhaps tomorrow, if the Slayer could forgive her lies.

She found herself wishing she had told Sir Roger who she was. The opportunity had presented itself at nearly every meal. And yet, as she was loath to see the disappointment on his face, she had bitten her tongue. The last time he'd questioned her, weeks ago, he had demonstrated great trust in her. How would he feel to know she'd been misleading him all the while?

In tense silence Clarise waited with the steward at the base of the steps. Sir Roger dashed across the courtyard from the garrison and joined them in a huddle. "Is all in readiness?" he asked, casting her a conspiratorial wink.

She gave him a weak smile. "I pray so," she replied, her voice barely above a whisper. Anxiety was twisting her innards into knots. What if the Slayer didn't like the changes she had made? What if they were viewed as presumptuous?

The clopping of hooves played descant to the spattering rain. They were all astonished to see a lone rider pass through the gate on the top of a donkey. The beast hung its head dolefully against the downpour. The rider was cloaked in a mantle, his hood pulled low over his face.

"'Tis Ethelred!" Sir Roger exclaimed. He ran into the rain to greet the good abbot.

Clarise went weak from a mixture of relief and disappointment. She watched the Abbot of Revesby slide from his mount. She could see that he was quite a little man, coming only to Sir Roger's shoulder. As a stable boy took away his donkey, the two men splashed through the puddles as they raced for shelter.

Clarise had just lit the torch on the stairwell—a true feat with a baby in her arms. She had adopted the habit of carrying a flint with her, as it afforded her pleasure to witness the fruits of her labor.

As she turned around, the abbot shook back the hood of his mantle. He was still a young man, she saw, having pictured him much older. His sandy-colored hair was cropped short. He wore the black garb of an Augustinian monk, yet unlike the Abbot of Rievaulx, he went without a fancy stole. No jewels twinkled on his fingers. Sandals peeked from below the hem of his cloak. She looked into his friendly gaze and found him watching her intently.

"Father, this is Lady Clare, Simon's nurse." Sir Roger made the introductions. "Lady, the esteemed Abbot of Revesby."

"Pleased to meet Your Grace," she murmured, masking the sudden certainty that this man would help her reach Alec if the necessity arose. She hoped it would not.

The abbot's gaze fell upon the bundle in her arms. "This could only be Christian's son!" he exclaimed. "What a mighty one he is already!"

Simon was swaddled in purple silk, a color chosen to complement Clarise's lavender gown. He returned the abbot's praise with a dispassionate stare. Father Ethelred laughed out loud. "A miracle!" he pronounced, chuckling.

Clarise felt her heart swell with love, both for the baby and the cleric who was so clearly pleased to see him. She kissed the curl that grew skyward from the top of Simon's head.

"I have news," announced the abbot happily, "and I would say it without delay. But where is your seneschal?"

"Due to return at any minute," the knight supplied.

"I cannot wait!" Ethelred's blue eyes sparkled. "I have just come from a meeting with the archbishop. The subject of the interdict came up in casual conversation. Archbishop Thurston said that the interdict was never approved by the Holy See. Tomorrow I go to Rievaulx to see the papal seal. If Gilbert fails to produce it, this matter will place him under grave scrutiny."

Ethelred did not seem at all displeased by his colleague's treachery. Clarise recalled that there was rivalry between them.

"Verily?" exclaimed Sir Roger after a moment of astonished silence. "Then it was just an attempt to breed discontent at Helmesly. Gilbert hoped the people here would turn against their seneschal."

"Mayhap so," Ethelred agreed.

"Well, why stand here like knaves when Lady Clare has put the great hall to rights? Our castle is now a welcome place for visitors."

An hour later Clarise had developed a pounding headache. The abbot had been given a room where he would dry out his robes. All she had intended to do was to tell the new head cook that a special meal would have to be drawn up for the cleric, who could not eat meat, except for Sundays. The cook, who'd finally been persuaded to concoct a jellie of fyshe this night, complained to Maeve. The steward's wife intercepted her in the breezeway.

"Lady Clare!" she called in her strident voice.

Rolling her eyes at the woman's tone, Clarise turned, just two steps from an escape into the great hall. "What it is?" she inquired sweetly.

"I see you have taken it upon yourself to perform Harold's duties once again. What the abbot—or for that matter, what anyone—will eat is none of your concern."

"I am certain *Harold* would not mind a little help. You, on the other hand, seem to resent it strongly. I have to wonder why you wield your power like a sword. Even your husband is subject to you."

Maeve drew herself into a rigid line. "Do you wish to play lady, then?" she hissed. "Very well. Let us see if you can take my place. I'm retiring to my chambers," she announced, pivoting sharply. She took her keys with her as she headed toward the servants' hall.

Clarise stared after her with her mouth agape.

This was a setback she hadn't expected. She had hoped to greet the Slayer with poise and elegance from the vantage of the dais, not scurrying around with her hair slipping from the knot on her head, sweating from the heat of the kitchen and the burden of having to tote Simon wherever she went.

Harold, she feared, would be more of a hindrance than a help. He paced before the kitchen exit, wringing his hands and muttering in agitation. Promising once again that she would soon read *Stories of the Saints' Lives* to him, she managed to convince him that they would get along *without* his wife.

In the kitchen the pages and maids milled aimlessly. Hearing them squabble over the order in which they would carry in the food, Clarise pushed into their midst and gave them a lecture worthy of the Empress Matilda. The jostling for position ceased but not the complaints.

She reentered the hall to find the abbot conversing with the reticent steward. He detached himself to approach Clarise.

"Harold tells me that a babe has been buried in the graveyard and awaits the sacrament of burial," said Ethelred.

Clarise was forced to calm a fussing Simon. "Aye, Your Grace. 'Twas the cook Doris's babe, a stillborn. She would be thankful if the proper words could be said over him."

"At dawn tomorrow, then. It should be done at once, now that the interdict has been lifted, so to speak."

"Has Simon been baptized?" Clarise asked, realizing that she didn't even know. He fretted loudly against her shoulder.

"I baptized him the day that I buried his mother," said

Ethelred solemnly, "as Christian had refused the right of the midwife to do so. True," he added under his breath, "the interdict forbade both sacraments at the time, but I never did see the point of it." His hand came up and stroked the soft spot on Simon's head. Immediately the baby quit his hungry mewls. "At the time," Ethelred continued, "I was quite concerned that this babe would not live. You have been a blessing to him," he added, glancing at her sharply. "Where are you from?"

She looked into the abbot's inquisitive gaze and found she couldn't lie. "From Heathersgill," she admitted quietly. "My father was Edward the Learned."

"Keeper of the Books," he elaborated with a smile. "I met him once."

"In truth?" She was astonished to hear it.

"He tutored King David's children in the Scottish court."

"Aye, that he did!"

"I was educated there myself. How does he now?"

Clarise's throat closed with grief; still, she managed to repeat the awful story of Edward's death. It came as a relief to speak of it after guarding her identity so long. "Now Ferguson rules my father's keep as if he were the rightful lord," she added, pained by the knowledge that she had done nothing yet to ensure her mother's and sisters' survival.

Ethelred's face reflected shock. "I am saddened to hear it," he said. "Your mother? Is she well?"

Clarise shook her head. "The selfsame Scot forced my mother to wed him. He abuses my mother at will; my sisters, also."

Ethelred put a hand on either one of her shoulders. "What can I do to help you?" he asked sincerely.

Her hopes took wing. "Is there something that the Church can do? Annul the marriage, perhaps?"

"I will look into it," he promised.

"Your Grace," she added, resisting the urge to cling to his sleeve. "I have yet to tell Christian who I am. You see," she added, lowering her voice, "Ferguson sent me here to poison his enemy. Only I couldn't do it. But if Ferguson learns that I've betrayed him, he will kill my mother and sisters as he has sworn to do."

The abbot looked astounded by such subterfuge. "You haven't told Christian the truth?"

"Not yet," she admitted miserably. "I was afraid that Ferguson would catch wind of it, and the ones I love would be swiftly put to death. Now I have spun so many lies, Lord Christian has every right to be angry, perhaps to throw me out with nowhere else to go, or worse." She tried not to think of what worse might entail.

"You must tell him at once," said Ethelred firmly. "Truth is a better fortress than deceit."

She nodded in agreement of his admonition. The time had come to cast herself on the Slayer's mercy.

Further discussion was curtailed by Sir Roger's presence as he trotted down the steps behind them. No sooner had the knight joined them than the horn trumpeted loudly, announcing the Slayer's return.

"He's here," Sir Roger stated cheerfully.

Oh, God. Clarise gripped the baby so hard he let out a shriek. She had just enough time to cast a final look over the hall, wishing again that she had struck a fire in the hearth, in spite of Maeve's disapproval. But now it was too late. Both the doors to the main entrance crashed open. Into the glare of fifty candles and ten torches stepped the Slayer.

Clarise's eyes flew wide. He looked every inch a warrior tonight—immense, powerful, swathed in black. The links of his armor, dulled with soot, swallowed the light of the torches. His sword hung out of sight beneath a swirling, black cloak. As he threw back the hood, she could see that his hair was cut shorter and plastered wetly to his skull. It looked as if he hadn't shaved in days. His eyes gleamed above the scruffy darkness of his beard.

Christian drew up short and blinked at the unexpected glare. The great hall was ablaze with torches and blinding reflections. Despite the gathering that drew him toward the stairs, he paused a moment to marvel at the changes that had taken place since his departure.

The scent of flowers masked the odor of so much burning tallow. The most immediate difference was the enormous tapestry that hung from the gallery to cover an entire wall. A row of blazing torches drew his gaze toward the high table, covered in snowy linens and bouquets of colorful flowers. On the eastern wall, silver platters, with their polished luster, reflected the gay scene.

The great hall bore little resemblance to the echoing chamber that his wife had made of it. A rush of contentment filled him as he beheld his home transformed. There was no doubt as to who was responsible for the changes. Just as suddenly, bitterness tinged his pleasure. How dare she taunt him with what he longed for most? She hadn't come to shed her light into his morbid world. She'd come for a different reason—to spy or to hide. And yet she teased him with the illusion of what he craved.

He ripped his gaze from the wall hangings and shot her an accusing look. Clarise's eyes reflected hope and fear in equal parts. Her pale face was framed by copper tendrils that had slipped from the knot on her head. Her mouth was slightly parted as if she struggled to inhale. Good, he thought, as betrayal stung him anew. She would do anything to procure his mercy.

A movement next to Clarise dragged his gaze to the cleric standing beside her. "Ethelred!" he exclaimed, surprised to see the abbot in his castle. He hurried forward and extended a wet hand. Water streamed off his cloak onto the fresh rushes. "'Tis a pleasure as always."

"The good abbot has brought us excellent news," Sir Roger interrupted, his smile at the height of crookedness. "You tell him, Father."

Ethelred offered his boyish smile. "The interdict has been lifted from Helmesly," he announced, pumping Christian's hand as if he didn't mean to let it go. "In fact, it never truly existed in the eyes of the mother church, for it lacks the approval of the Holy See. I am going tomorrow to question Gilbert about the matter."

It seemed to Christian as if the hall were suddenly brighter, though that was impossible given its present brilliance. He looked from Ethelred's blue eyes to Sir Roger's happy smile and felt his vocal chords vibrate. The laugh that rasped free was almost an embarrassment. He darted a look at Clarise and found her gazing at him with wonder in her eyes.

He withdrew at once behind a façade of solemnity. "I owe it to you," he said to the abbot, whose hand he still squeezed.

Ethelred let go with a muffled yelp. "Not at all, not at all," he assured him affably. "The matter came up in casual conversation."

Christian nodded. His thoughts had already turned to Lady Clarise, who stared at him like a paralyzed hare. Anger boiled in him anew. She had lied to him so many times that he found himself looking at a stranger. She wasn't from Glenmyre. She was never Monteign's mistress. He didn't know whose child she had born out of wedlock, or had she lied about that, too?

He took a step that brought him close enough to hear her sharp intake of air. Her head tilted back, offering him a clear view of the hollow fluttering at the base of her throat. The fact that she was frightened of him meant that her purpose at Helmesly was a sinister one. She hadn't come for protection or simply to hide.

He leaned over her, allowing his knowledge of the truth to blaze in his eyes. "You and I have much to discuss," he warned her. He was perversely satisfied to see all color slip from her cheeks.

It was the glare of his infant son that distracted him from toying with her further. The baby, swaddled in royal raiment, glowered at him from the throne of Clarise's arms. The little baron looked displeased with his father's behavior.

Christian straightened guiltily. He thrust a finger out for

Simon to squeeze, but the baby ignored him. The frown on his downy brow bespoke of grave disapproval. "He doesn't remember me," he said by way of explanation. Addressing the onlookers, he added, "Give me a moment to wash up, and I'll join you for supper."

Ignoring his vassal's questioning look, he tackled the stairs two at a time. He couldn't help but notice the effort that had been put into ensuring his mercy. On every step there stood a pot of wildflowers, artfully arranged.

Nevertheless, he thought, squaring his shoulders, she would have to pay a price for her deceit. She was guilty of putting a hunger in his heart, and he would not be satisfied until he forged his spirit in her fire.

Chapter Twelve

A murmuring of masculine voices was audible through the closed solar door. Clarise hovered on the gallery, uncertain whether to wait for their conversation to end or to knock. Though she trusted Doris to care for Simon in her stead, she could not leave the baby alone with the cook all evening.

She was eager to put this reckoning with the Slayer behind her. Throughout the meal, she had caught him sending her narrow-eyed looks, and she'd held her breath, awaiting a public denunciation, only it hadn't come. At the same time she'd had to keep an eye on the food's distribution as Harold struggled to perform his duties without his wife.

Following supper, the abbot had excused himself to visit the chapel. The Slayer had scraped back his chair and announced to his second-in-command that they should retire to the solar. Clarise was left to deal with a fussing baby. She withdrew to her own chamber, chafed by the delay in the inevitable confrontation.

Never before was she so hopeful of the Slayer's help. He'd made it clear by his looks that he knew who she was. And yet he hadn't mocked or publicly exposed her. Perhaps all her worries had been for naught.

The door of the solar opened suddenly, and Sir Roger

stepped through it, stopping just short of plowing her down. "Ah!" he exclaimed. "I was just coming to get you ... Clarise DuBoise." At the purposeful mention of her name, she drew a quick breath and searched his face for condemnation. His expression was taut. The smile that hovered perpetually at one corner of his mouth had fled.

"Please," she begged, grabbing his sleeve as he held the door for her, "I never wanted to lie to you. Please understand that I had a very good reason."

"Go in," he said, ignoring her plea, but his tone had mellowed. He gave her what she took to be a pitying look.

Her heart beating with dread, Clarise inched through the portal, expecting the worst. Her gaze flew to the Slayer, who was seated behind his writing table. With the candle behind him, shadows pooled in the hollows of his face, concealing his expression.

She looked back at the knight in a silent plea for his support. But then he shut the door between them, and she was left alone with her nemesis.

Two tallow lamps cast feeble light onto the tapestries. Rain beat loudly on the closed shutters. The room seemed full of menacing shadows, not the least of which was the Slayer himself, dressed in the black tunic he had worn to dinner.

"Where is Simon?" he asked, breaking the stillness.

The hard edge of his tone made her stomach cramp. "With Doris in my chambers," she replied. "I will fetch him right away—"

"Stay," he commanded before she could flee. He propped his elbows on the writing desk and leaned forward. Light rose up his cheekbones, illuminating the scar on his cheek. "You owe me an explanation first," he told her very softly.

To give herself courage, she thought of how he'd come by that scar. "My lord, I will tell you the truth," she promised him, "and you must ask yourself what you would have done in my stead."

"Fair enough." He watched her with a steady gaze.

Clarise clasped her hands together and squeezed them. "A year and three months past Ferguson appeared at our gates, a traveler with just a band of men," she began, saying the words she had rehearsed in expectation of this hour. "They begged my father's hospitality and we gave it, never suspecting how we would be repaid." She took a breath to steady the tremor in her voice.

"That night Ferguson sprinkled poison in my father's drink. He hides his powders in his brooch rings." The memory replayed itself, and the words came more easily. "My father fell from the dais, stricken with pains. The Scots jumped up, catching our knights unawares. They pulled daggers from their boots and killed every man that dwelled in Heathersgill. Then Ferguson took his sword and severed my father's head from his body."

A thundercloud had gathered on the Slayer's forehead. Encouraged by his look of outrage, she sought to convey the depth of her horror. "Ferguson dragged my mother to the upper chambers. She had just seen her husband beheaded and now she was being forced . . ." She put her hands to her ears, hearing the awful screams again. *"Oh, God, I could not stop him from raping her!"* she cried.

The warlord came abruptly to his feet and rounded the table. She was startled to feel his arms band around her. He pulled her gently against him, and the last thread of her self-composure snapped. She tried to master herself, but her grief consumed her. A ragged sob tore free from a place in her that she had kept firmly under wraps. "I am sorry," she wailed, shamed by her loss of control.

"Hush." With no warning, she felt the floor fall away. He lifted her into his arms and carried her to the high bed.

Clarise was vaguely conscious that the warlord had seated himself at the edge of his bed. He scooped her in his lap, cradling her as if she were a babe.

She was helpless to fight her grief. It rolled over her in waves, drowning her in despair. Memories of her gentle father besieged her—how she missed him! The plight of her poor mother and sisters crushed her spirit. She had done all she could to help them, but ultimately she was helpless without a champion.

At last her tears had run their course. Clarise stirred. Her nose was buried in the crook of Christian's neck, where every breath was filled with juniper and musky maleness. Just knowing how near his mouth was to hers left her weak with private yearnings. Yet she realized she could not stay where she was. She had yet to confess her reason for coming to Helmesly.

Lifting her tear-stained face, she looked at him uncertainly. His thoughts seemed far away as he brushed aside the tendrils that had straggled into her eyes. "Why didn't you tell me this before?" he asked, his voice rumbling deep in his chest. "Why did you say you hailed from Glenmyre? You pretended to be a freed serf and then Monteign's leman." The lines of his face grew harsher as he shook his head. "Why so many lies?" he demanded.

Sensitive to his rising ire, she tried to get out of his lap, but the warlord held her fast. His grip became bruising.

"Very well, I'll tell you!" she submitted. "I lied because Ferguson sent me here. Aye!" she cried, seeing the flash of surprise in his eyes. "He sent me to poison you, just as he had poisoned my father."

The Slayer let go of her wrist, only to seize the locket that still dangled from her neck. "Poison me?" he growled. "With this? Did you carry the poison in here?"

"I did once," she admitted, meeting his blazing eyes with the appearance of courage. "He said if you weren't dead in two months' time, then he would hang my mother and sisters."

The horror of that ultimatum left him temporarily speechless. "Where is the poison now?" he asked more gently.

"I poured it out."

"Out? Where?"

"Into the air," she said, gesturing. "'Tis gone. I couldn't do it."

He let the locket fall from his grasp. "Why not?" he asked, tilting his head back to look at her.

Why not? She focused her gaze on the scar he'd received because he was once so devout. "Because you are not evil," she told him simply. "I realized that almost at once," she added.

For a startled moment, he stared at her. Thoughts ebbed and flowed behind his gray-green eyes. Then he released her, all but thrusting her off his lap.

She staggered on her feet, while he himself prowled to the far side of the room. Clarise backed away from him, uncertain of his actions. Should she flee to her room and let him decide her fate? Nay, 'twas better to remain and answer his questions. She could see that he was battling with the knowledge that the woman who had seemed to be Simon's best hope was also the one who'd been sent to kill him.

Locking her trembling knees, she awaited the Slayer's judgment. Her heart beat so heavily that it rocked her lightly on her feet. She watched him as he paced back and forth, casting her disbelieving glances, as though trying to reconcile the woman before him with the one he'd known before.

Clarise's gaze fell to his hands, clenching and unclenching as he stalked in and out of the candlelight. She became aware of a rising sense of sympathy for him. He had just come from salvaging Glenmyre. How must he feel to discover that she too had been sent to undermine him?

"'Twill be all right, my lord," she heard herself soothe. "No harm will come to Simon or to you, I swear it."

He swiveled suddenly and glared at her. "Were you in league with the minstrel?" he demanded in a chilling voice.

She shook her head. "He'd been sent by Ferguson to assure that I arrived at Helmsly and that I fulfilled my evil task, but I had nothing to do with his pilfering. He said there were others who would gladly see you ousted. They were the ones who helped him steal."

The warlord made a sound of disgust and stalked to the window to lean out of it. He gulped down air as though needing its purity. The rain outside spattered the windowsill. Droplets bounced off the stone to wet the warlord's tunic, but he didn't seem to care.

"My lord, there is something more I need to tell you," Clarise admitted. Now that she was baring the truth to him, she wanted no more secrets between them. They would start anew and be guided by honesty as Ethelred had suggested.

He turned around warily. "How could there possibly be more?" he growled.

"'Twill anger you," she acknowledged miserably. "'Tis about Simon. I want you to know that I take full blame for the harm it nearly caused him."

Darkness settled over him. "Go on."

"I never gave him milk of my own," she rushed to confess. "I couldn't, for I have never been with child."

The Slayer's face was expressionless, telling her nothing. "You mean that you always fed him with that nursing skin?" he asked evenly.

"Aye," she confessed, casting herself utterly at his mercy.

His gaze fell to the outline of her bosom, defined by the narrow bodice of her purple gown. "But I saw you nurse him."

"I did that to convince you," she admitted, her breasts tingling beneath his regard. "I needed an excuse to find my way inside of Helmesly. I believed I could care for the babe, because I'd done the same for my youngest sister when our mother suffered the birth fever."

His eyes had narrowed to slits. "Simon deserves better," he stated, through his teeth.

"Which is precisely why Doris feeds him now," she cut him off.

"Doris?" His tone was now incredulous.

"I asked her just this morning, after we buried her baby, if she would nurse Simon in my stead. I believe her to be

most loyal to you," she added. "And I have supervised every
feeding but the one that is taking place right now."

An insurmountable silence settled between them. The
warlord ran his gaze over her lithe form, lingering in a manner that left her feeling exposed. "I suppose you expect me
to help you now," he said, his tone emotionless.

She shifted nervously, wishing the lighting were better.
She knew he must be furious with her, yet his voice now betrayed no emotion whatsoever. "What do you mean?" she
asked.

He couldn't mean he was volunteering to be her champion. Surely she hadn't wasted all this time hiding the truth
from him when she only needed to ask for his help!

He took three quiet steps in her direction, bringing him
within an arm's reach. "I suppose you want me to take up
arms for you," he paraphrased, his eyes like a hawk's as he
scrutinized her face.

Clarise sensed a trap. Perhaps it was the predatory gleam
in his eyes. "You would do that?" she asked, her heart beating unevenly. "Challenge Ferguson for me?" Hope rose like
a bubble before the realist in her squashed it down. "In exchange for what?" she wanted to know.

He hesitated, his gaze dropping to her breasts. "In exchange for a kiss."

His answer brought her to prickling, physical awareness.
He stepped closer still, his shoulders blocking the light of
the tallow lamps completely. His evergreen scent filled her
head, making her suddenly dizzy.

"A . . . a kiss?" she stammered, thinking vaguely that
such an exchange was more than fair. In truth, if he didn't
kiss her now, she would be sorely disappointed. "Very well,
if . . . if you so desire."

He slipped a hand around the back of her neck and pulled
her mouth to his. The taste and texture of him filled her hungry senses. Ever since their first kiss, she'd secretly longed
to be kissed again, in that same plundering way that weak-

ened her knees and brought a moan rising from the depths of her feminine soul.

With his kiss came the glorious realization that she had found a champion at last! The enormous burden she had carried alone was no longer hers to bear. In gratitude, she parted her lips to him, offering him the deepest recesses of her mouth, not protesting when he pulled her deeper into his embrace, his arms like giant manacles, keeping her captive.

Without warning, he lifted her completely off her feet. She realized he was taking her to his bed. Alarm bells tolled in her head, but he stifled her protest with his lips.

Without severing their mouths, he lowered her onto the bed and pressed her slowly back, coming down on top of her. His body, heavy and hard against her, caused excitement to shimmer through her. If any place were dangerous for a maiden to lie, it was beneath this man of brawn, steel, and determination.

With his knee he nudged her legs apart. His thigh settled between hers, causing her to gasp at the intimate intrusion. She tried to speak, but once again he headed off her protest with a deep, disturbing kiss.

He tasted of wine and darkness, and soon she was lost to the dizzying pleasure of his kiss. He'd begun to move against her, his thigh rubbing so subtly against her womanhood that she didn't notice it at first. It was the prodding length of his manhood that roused her to reality.

It dawned on Clarise that Christian de la Croix would not be content with a single kiss, as he'd led her to believe. He intended for her to give him *everything,* her body in exchange for his sword arm!

The realization sent panic streaking through her. She pushed at his shoulders and found him impossible to budge. "Stop!" she cried. "This isn't what you said at all!"

"Shhh," he soothed, "I won't force you, you have my word of honor on it." He lowered his mouth and kissed her again, this time more gently, persuasively.

She believed him to be an honorable man. If he swore not

to force her, then her virtue was safe, wasn't it? She had difficulty answering the question, for she could scarcely think with the dark, insidious pleasure of his kisses stealing over her again.

His thigh, riding against her crotch, further diffused her thoughts.

When she felt the heat of his hand on her ribs, she did not protest, for he had touched her there before. His hand inched higher, and soon he was cupping a plump breast and squeezing gently. Her nipples ached with exquisite sensitivity, so that when he soothed a thumb over the rigid peak, a jolt of pleasure stabbed straight to her womb. Her insides turned liquid. She wondered, ashamedly, if he could feel her moisture between her legs through the fabric of her gown.

She would have a champion! she marveled.anew. Ferguson could never defeat the Slayer. Her hands strayed up his arms to feel the rock-hard muscles bulging there. What a beautiful warrior's body he had, she thought, clinging now to his immense shoulders. The tension in her tightened another notch. She felt utterly restless and needy. She could not pull him close enough to satisfy her. Her skin grew flushed and heated, so that it came as a relief to feel the stays of her dress slip apart. Cool air wafted over her breasts.

"Let me suckle you," the Slayer begged, sliding his mouth downward.

His words left her quivering with longing. She lacked the will to resist him; indeed, she tangled her fingers in his hair and guided his lips to one breast. He took her nipple deep in his mouth, stroking it between the ridge of his tongue and the roof of his mouth.

Clarise gasped for breath. The tension in her was becoming unbearable. She needed relief, a place to focus the overwhelming sensations. By the time she realized he had worked a hand beneath her skirts, his palm was resting on her thigh, squeezing and molding her sleek muscle.

She knew she should protest the violation. He'd said he would not force her, but at this rate, there would be little

force involved. She craved something, craved it so badly
that her heart felt it would jump from her chest. His hand
slid abruptly higher, so that the heel of his palm was touching her woman's hair. She struggled to her elbows, dislodg-
ing her breast from his mouth. "Don't!" she cried, trying to
clamp her legs together.

"I told you already, I won't force you." His voice was as
hypnotizing as the hand, moving now in slow, thorough circles, pressing where she was most sensitive.

The pleasure was so exquisite, so overwhelming, that
further protests died in her throat. She sought the Slayer's
gaze in the shadows of the boxed bed. His eyes glittered
with a sensual intent that snatched her breath away. She realized with deep awareness that he was *touching* her. This
dangerous man whom everyone feared, whose savage
scowls made peasants run for cover, was touching her most
private places and wreaking havoc on her senses.

She gasped at the wanton realization, and her breasts rose
and fell, her nipples so hard that they stabbed the air. The
moisture between her legs was spreading. The Slayer shifted
so that he lay half beside her, half on top. His hand shifted
also, so that it was not his palm that caressed her but his
long, strong fingers. He lowered his head again and kissed
her, stifling the whimper of uncertainty that vibrated her
vocal chords. His fingers traced the delicate petals of her
womanhood.

Lubricated with her moisture, his finger eased neatly into
her passage. At the same time, his thumb pressed against the
nub that pulsed above it.

Clarise ripped her lips from his. "Stop," she begged, dis-
concerted by the unfamiliar tightness. "You mustn't do
that." She was concerned for her maidenhead, a precious
commodity for a maid who wished to be a virgin bride.

"I won't take your maidenhead," he assured her, as if
reading her mind. "'Tis firmly lodged. 'Twould take more
than my finger to break through it."

"Why are you doing this?" she demanded, with belated panic. "You said you only wanted to kiss me."

"I do." He recaptured her mouth. The hot insistence of his tongue was more than she could resist. His finger moved in and out of her, and his tongue mimicked the plunge and retreat, driving her to an instant frenzy. Tension coiled in Clarise's belly. His thumb began to play with the nubbin of flesh that was quivering with excruciating sensitivity.

Clarise forgot to breathe. Something powerful, inexorable, and sweet beyond her imagining threatened to roll over her and wrap around her. Again and again, the Slayer's finger plumbed her softness. Again and again his tongue thrust into her mouth. His thumb slicked mercilessly over her pouting flesh, and then it happened.

She spasmed, rocked by her first climax. It flung her to a place she'd never been before. Stars seemed to flicker behind her eyelids. Her muscles clamped down hard, squeezing, pulling, milking the pleasure that went on, and on, and on.

Then with a ragged sigh, she released the breath she was holding. Her muscles went limp with exhaustion. She spasmed once again as the Slayer's finger slipped out of her. He pulled slowly away, smoothing her skirts down as he did so. Her breasts were still naked, glowing like pale orbs in the semidarkness.

The Slayer slid back so that he was no longer touching her. He lay on his side, waiting, watchful. His eyes glittered with an intensity that could not be disguised by the darkness. The lines of his reclining body looked rigid.

In the painful silence that followed, Clarise scurried to regather her wits. She sat up swiftly, fumbling with the laces at the front of her gown. Her fingers trembled so badly that she could not tie them. Shame burned up her throat and singed her cheeks. She was painfully aware of the Slayer's silent perusal.

How could she have responded with such abandon? She was a maiden, by heaven, still betrothed to Alec Monteign,

should he decide to leave the priesthood. Yet she'd behaved
like the wanton leman she'd once professed to be!

She wanted to die! She wanted to leave Helmesly Castle
and never set eyes on the Slayer again. And yet he'd
promised to take up arms for her, so that was impossible.
She forced herself to focus on their agreement. After all, the
arrangement had just been sealed, hadn't it?

"Now you'll take up arms for me and free my family?"
She was dismayed to find her voice thin.

His hungry gaze caused an unwanted awareness to ripple
through her. "Not quite," he corrected. "First, you'll agree to
be my mistress."

His answer hit her like the broadside of a sword. Clarise
reared back at the unexpectedness of it. "Nay!" she cried in
protest. "You said I owed you a kiss and that was all!"

"The way I look at it, lady, you owe me a great deal more
than a kiss," he retorted on a growl. "You have taken advantage of me since your arrival at my gates. If you want me
to kill Ferguson, you will have to give me something in exchange. What I want is you. All of you."

Her body quivered with excitement, betraying her. Her
mind exploded with rage. A bright red haze rose up before
her eyes. "You lowlife, sneaking bastard," she hissed,
pulling back an arm to strike him.

Moving swifter than a snake, he caught her descending
arm in a grip that was bruising. Just as suddenly he let her
go. She scooted wisely off the bed, surprised to find her legs
so weak as she came to her feet. "How dare you promise me
one thing and then raise the price," she raged, wishing she
could do him lasting harm.

He said nothing at all, frustrating her desire to do battle.

"Oh!" she raged, stamping a foot on the rush mat.
"You . . . you conniving, scheming blackguard! How dare
you blackmail me in such blatant fashion? Why you're nothing but a—"

"Save your breath, lady," he interrupted. "I've been
called those things before. Go on now," he added, jarring her

with his demand that she leave. "Doris must be wondering where you are."

To be thrust from his room was just as humiliating as his ultimatum. With a cry of outrage, Clarise cast her eyes about and spied an earthenware pitcher. Snatching it up, she hurled it with all her might at the Slayer. To her chagrin, it bounced harmlessly on the mattress and landed by his thigh. She wished, then, that it had been full of water. "Go to the devil!" she raged, marching for the door. Tears of humiliation smarted her eyes as she wrenched it open.

She gained small satisfaction in slamming it as hard as she could behind her.

With a low whistle of amazement, Christian fell back against the bed. Clarise's passionate nature was evident not only in her body's response to him but also in her formidable temper. He hoped he had not ruined everything by giving her such an ultimatum. And yet he'd decided that unless Clarise DuBoise was the prize, there was little allure in engaging in a long siege for the purpose of retaking Heathersgill. He already had his hands full with Glenmyre. Such chivalry was for other men, men who couldn't bear to see a damsel in distress. Not he. He wanted to have a palpable reward for his efforts. He wanted Clarise DuBoise's body for his sole possession. He wanted to be on her, over her, in her, and around her, always.

His body throbbed with a hunger too fierce to be ignored. Rolling down the tops of his chausses, he caught up his swollen shaft and eased it up and down. He had brought Clarise to a shattering orgasm! The truth of it exhilarated him; it excited him beyond bearing. Her body had been so responsive, yet so innocent with its tight sheath. He vowed he would have her soon.

The scent still lingered on his hands. He breathed it in, stroking his flesh as he lost himself to his imaginings.

Would she agree to be his mistress? He knew it was no light decision, giving her soul to the Slayer of Helmesly.

Much depended on how badly she wanted Ferguson elimi-
nated.

But for now, he pretended she would tell him yes. Then
tomorrow at this time he would sink his aching shaft into her
softness and know true fulfillment. The thought hurtled him
to a speedy climax. Scalding hot seed spattered his tunic and
wet his hand. He let out a groan, and realized later that he'd
groaned Clarise's name.

Chapter Thirteen

Clarise read aloud the entire chapter on the life of St. Dunstan without absorbing a word of the text.

If you want me to kill Ferguson, you will have to give me something in exchange. What I want is you. All of you.

The Slayer's words reverberated in her head, making other thoughts impossible. She found herself at the end of the chapter with no memory of what she'd read.

Across the trestle table Harold wore a wistful expression. His white hair was bleached by the sunbeams slanting through one of the windows. The lingering aroma of trout griddled in herbs filled the empty hall. Clarise had left Simon safe in Doris's care in order to fulfill her promise to the steward. Reading, he said, was something his niece had done for him. The girl, apparently, had died quite recently.

"Did you like the story?" she asked, wresting his attention from a corner of his mind known only to him.

Harold smiled at her sheepishly. "Aye." He sighed. "You read as well as my lovely Rose."

"Was that your niece?" Clarise asked, closing the book. "Rose, that's a pretty name."

"Our pretty Rose has wilted," he intoned in a singsong voice. His vague blue eyes darkened with loss.

Clarise felt a pang of sympathy for the old man. She

reached across the plank table and touched his hand. "She is with the saints now," she comforted, knowing Harold's fascination for saints and martyrs.

Harold's gaze drifted until it landed on her face. "My Rose had a baby," he told her mournfully. He frowned as though struggling to remember something.

"Did she die in childbirth? 'Tis such a sad thing. Simon's mother also died," she reminded him.

"Not Doris," he said, sounding relieved.

"Nay, Doris is well, thank God. 'Twas her babe that died," she clarified, thinking him confused.

He scratched the bristles on his jaw. "So sad," he echoed her earlier statement. "She was a baby once, my Rose. I rocked her on my knee. Here's your horsey." He clicked his tongue to imitate the clip-clopping of hooves.

"You must have been a wonderful uncle."

"Harold, brother of John," he said, as though introducing himself.

Awareness stirred at the edges of Clarise's mind, but with her thoughts elsewhere, she failed to grasp what it was. Instead, she found herself recalling the conversation she'd shared with the Slayer over breakfast.

She'd had no intention of speaking to him at all, for she had no answer to his ultimatum. But hearing him recount for his men-at-arms Ferguson's attack on Glenmyre, she'd realized he had seen her mother with his own eyes, and she longed for reassuring word of her. "How did my mother look?" she asked, buttering her bread to avoid eye contact. Nonetheless, her face flushed crimson, and she was certain that anyone who looked at her would guess her indignity of the night before.

He had turned his attention from his men to her. "Not well," he'd said with a frown. "She seemed desperate to enter the gates."

Desperate. The word sliced deep into her heart. "Could you not have tried to let her in?" It was useless to hide her dismay.

"I did try, lady." He'd captured her hand, then, the strength of his grip reassuring. "The foot soldiers were too close, and a second wave of men hid in the trees. The most I could do was ensure she didn't get hit by our arrows when Ferguson called her back."

She had almost told the Slayer, then and there, she would accept to be his mistress. Ferguson had put her mother in the direct path of the enemy's arrows! How could she risk the lives of her family by waiting another day?

But pride kept her in check. There was yet another option, one that did not involve the threat to her senses, the indignity of trading her body for the Slayer's aid. With the Abbot of Revesby's help, there was still a chance that she could contact Alec.

The scuffle of sandals roused her to the present. Just then, the good abbot stepped through the rear entrance of the hall. This morning's service, followed by the sacrament of burial for Doris's babe, had afforded no opportunity to catch him alone. Perhaps now, she thought, seizing what might be her only chance.

"Excuse me, Harold." She abandoned the Slayer's book on the table and hastened toward Ethelred. He had spotted her as well, and his face lit up. His short stride was charged with purpose. They met by the empty fire pit.

"Lady Clarise," he greeted her. "I was told to seek your assistance in showing me the herb garden."

"By all means. But I've only stepped foot in it once," she admitted. "I believe Dame Maeve knows more about herbs than I."

"It was she who bid me seek you out," he said, looking puzzled.

"Ah, well, the housekeeper is feeling ill." *Suffering from a case of wounded pride,* she nearly added. "Shall we find the garden now? I would speak with you about a certain matter." She glanced surreptitiously over her shoulder. The hall was deserted at midmorning. The Slayer had left with his master-at-arms to run through drills in the outer ward.

"Lead the way." The good abbot gestured.

"What exactly are you looking for, Your Grace?" she called a moment later. He paced the walkway of crushed seashells, looking hot in his black robe. Sweat dripped from his temples as he peered at the rows of aster, tansy, and feverfew. He stroked his beardless chin in contemplation.

"I wish I knew, lady," he cryptically confessed. His gaze hovered over a bright patch of horehound, then inspected the heavy stalks of foxglove. At last he glanced at Clarise. "Do you know much about healing?" he inquired.

She shook her head regretfully. "Not I, Father. My sister Merry is skilled in the herbal arts. What little I know I learned from her. Why do you ask?" she inquired, feeling a chill despite the heat.

He clasped his hands together and looked away. "'Tis a matter the archbishop has asked me to look into," he answered vaguely. He turned away and paced down another shell-strewn aisle.

Clarise followed his gaze and managed to summon the names of just a few of the plants crowding the narrow beds. Pink lady's mantle, pale Saint-John's-Wort, and purple pennyroyal. There were others, but she could neither name them nor list their qualities.

For the moment Ethelred seemed content with his inspection. He approached her, smiling a bit grimly. "What is it you wished to speak to me about?" he asked.

Clarise's heart began to pound. She had waited so long for a priest to assist her. At the same time she felt as though she were bent on a secret mission, one that the Slayer would disapprove of should he catch wind of it. "Your Grace," she hedged, plucking the folds of her salmon-pink gown. "There is a novice monk at Rievaulx, an old friend of mine. I've been unsuccessful at reaching him, either by letter or in person. I fear," she added, feeling the heat of embarrassment on her cheeks, "that he may be stricken by illness there."

"What is this brother's name?" the abbot asked. His probing blue gaze was not without sympathy, and Clarise took heart.

"Alec Monteign. He was once my betrothed," she admitted, baring all. "He went to Reivaulx six months ago." She was startled to find that the pain of his desertion had miraculously eased.

"I believe I met him once," Ethelred mused. "Is he a man of average stature, with golden hair, light eyes?"

"He is!" she cried. "When did you see him?"

"This winter past. He was newly come to Rievaulx, quite zealous to live the life of an eremite. I remember he approached me and asked me questions about my book."

Alec hadn't shared his religious zeal with her. It came as a surprise to hear of it. Clarise had to wonder if he hadn't agreed to wed her for his father's sake.

"Is it at all possible to get word to him?" she asked, wishing she had more confidence in his skills.

Ethelred thought for a moment. He gave the garden a quick but thorough inspection. Walls surrounded them on every side. The air was saturated with birdsong and the distant gurgling of the moat. "I think I can," he told her quite decisively. "As you know, I will go to Rievaulx to investigate the matter of the interdict. I will look for Alec while I'm there."

"But what if Gilbert denies you entrance? After all, Rievaulx is quarantined. He can say that in your best interest you must keep away."

Ethelred's eyes sparkled with adventure. "I was master novice at Rievaulx for two years. While I was there, I discovered something Gilbert doesn't know."

"And what is that?" she asked.

"A second entrance into the abbey."

"Verily?" She found herself smiling in wonder.

"Aye, in a cave on the side of the abbey hill, there is a hole, big enough for a wild animal or a small man like me. The cave leads to an underground passage and thence to the chamber where I used to gloss Psalters. Now, should Gilbert deny me entrance, I will still find my way inside."

"But what of the illness? You must be careful. They say if you breathe through a satchel of herbs, you won't catch the plague." She looked helplessly at the garden around them.

He patted her hand. "The illness is the least of my concerns," he assured her.

She thought him exceedingly brave. "There is one more thing, Your Grace. Lord Christian wrote Alec a letter in which he offered to return Alec's inheritance to him. Would you ask him if he received the letter and whether he has considered the offer?"

The good abbot's eyes narrowed with sudden comprehension. "Do you hope that he will take up arms on your behalf?"

"I have nowhere else to turn," she admitted, feeling suddenly forlorn, though her chances of getting word to Alec had never been higher.

The abbot frowned in confusion. "I thought perhaps Christian would help you now that you've told him the truth of your plight. Perhaps since you care for his son, he would be willing to reclaim your father's home for you. Have you asked him?"

She looked down at her knotted hands. "I've already asked," she replied, willing herself not to blush. "He refuses to help."

A thoughtful silence followed her words. She glanced up to find his keen gaze on her face. "Would you like me to speak to him?" he offered kindly. "Perhaps I can convince him—"

A hot wave of mortification crested in her cheeks. "Nay, thank you," she refused, not wanting the abbot to know of her humiliating choice. "If you can get word to Alec, you'll have done more than enough."

The abbot nodded gravely. "Then, I'll do my best," he promised.

"When will you go?" Desperation made her bold. She feared the Slayer would try again to persuade her. The thought made her heart race and her mouth go dry.

"Shortly after none's prayers today."

Good. If there was any recourse to the Slayer's proposition, she would know it soon. "Thank you," she told him. "How can I repay you?"

He winked at her as he tightened the sash around his waist. "I was headed to the abbey anyway," he said.

Clarise's spirits rose a notch. "I must go now. Simon is mine for the afternoon."

"A blessed burden," said Ethelred.

He is indeed, thought Clarise. Because of Simon, she was actually thinking of accepting the Slayer's proposition. She had loved the infant from the first. She could not bear the thought of leaving him when the time came to leave Helmesly.

If she left. She refused to accept that the Slayer's touch might influence her. Yet whenever the memory of her ecstasy replayed itself, her bones seemed to melt like butter, and a delicious shudder overtook her. Humiliation could not defeat desire. There was a part of her that would secretly revel in becoming his mistress. A part of her that found the Slayer exciting and fascinating. Only she refused to acknowledge it.

Clarise DuBoise had been born a lady, and a lady she wished to remain. She owed it to her bloodlines to discover if Alec would trade his cleric's robes for a sword. Alec, she thought, would never demand such a price as the Slayer had demanded. He was far too honorable for that.

Abbot Gilbert crushed the purple berries in the large marble mortar, heedless of the juice that spurted stains onto his vestments. The beauty of being an abbot was that no one could take him to task for soiling his clerical garb.

At Rievaulx no monk dared question the things that he did or said. Anyone foolish enough to try was shut away in

a dark cell, with Horatio visiting in short but painful inter-
ludes. These unfortunates rarely survived to speak of the
horrors they'd endured.

Gilbert chuckled and reached for one of the glass vials on
a shelf above him. Of all the chambers in the abbey, this cellar chamber was the most cluttered and unkempt. He preferred it that way. The lack of order encouraged him to think
creatively. As he ground the seeds of the fruit into the pulp,
he looked about his cellar herbal with satisfaction.

In addition to the shelves of corked vials, all of them un-
marked and known only to him by their smell, the room contained a long table where he performed his masterpieces. On
the table were various instruments for heating, mixing, and
separating his creations. Squares of parchment were scattered across his work area. Now and then he jotted down the
ingredients and quantities of his experiments.

Behind him, crates were stacked as high as the wall.
These contained various beasts that snuffled and stirred in
continual despair. Their animal odor blended with the herbs'
perfumes. A pair of foxes lived in one box, a pig in another—the gluttonous creature. It had knocked its slop out
of the bowl, so that it dribbled through the slats of the crate
onto the stone floor.

The smaller boxes held animals ranging from a mouse to
a poisonous lizard. These were the recipients of his experiments. Some of them were wounded or ill when they came
to him. He had healed a few with his herbal remedies—pure
happenstance, he admitted. He had killed the majority.

I will let them go, Gilbert decided with uncharacteristic
magnanimity. In truth, their noise intruded on his thoughts
so often that he would be better off without them. He un-
corked a vial and added a careful drop of anise infusion to
his mixture.

He had no use for beasts anymore. He was skilled enough
to work with humans. As soon as word of the scourge
reached Clairvaux in France, he would dazzle the world by
healing his monks. He savored the vision of his acclaim. No

longer would he be considered a rustic priest, doomed to obscurity in the fells of Yorkshire. Nay, he would have as much fame or more as his colleague Ethelred. And that little man would finally show him some respect!

The familiar beating of a bird's wings caused him to drop his pestle and pivot toward the single window. It was just a narrow vent that filtered the sunlight and kept the room in gloomy illumination. In the aperture at level with the ceiling paced a pigeon, bobbing its iridescent head.

"My clever one!" Gilbert exclaimed, stepping on a stool to reach the sill. "What have you brought me today?" he asked. He reached with stained fingers to free the cord looped over the bird's neck. From the reed that was strung along the cord, he pulled out a tiny piece of parchment.

Archbishop Thurstan denies interdict at Helmesly, he read. *Ethelred comes today to make inquiry.*

Gilbert balled the minuscule letter in his fist and hurled it with fury across the cellar room. "Cursed, meddling man!" he railed, bounding off the stool.

Ethelred had once been a brilliant monk at Rievaulx. Several times during his years as a master novice, Gilbert had been tempted to cast him into the Cell of Castigation. But Ethelred was looked upon favorably by Bernard of Clairvaux. The Augustinian leader had encouraged the master novice's writing to such an extent that Ethelred was released from his rigorous schedule and left alone for hours. Now that he was the Abbot of Revesby, he was Gilbert's social equal. Was there no such thing as justice in the world?

Gilbert trembled with irrational fear. If the interdict were found to be a fake, then his integrity would be called into question.

Wouldn't the illness keep Ethelred away? He paced the length of the cramped chamber, then back again. A thought occurred to him that soothed his anxiety.

He could get rid of the meddling Ethelred once and for all! He would explain to Archbishop Thurstan that Ethelred had fallen ill and died of the scourge. He envisioned the little priest chained to the cellar wall. Horatio would force a liquid laced with malignant herbs down his throat, and that would be the end of him.

The abbot smiled outright and rubbed his hands with anticipation. Aye, Ethelred would get what was coming to him. But that did not prevent the matter of the interdict from coming up again.

Ah, what did it matter? He would think of something to excuse himself. The interdict had failed, in any event. The people at Helmesly should have closed the gates against their evil seneschal, but they were too afraid to defy him. Shunned by the church or not, the Slayer ruled the fortress with an iron hand. And now he had a whelp, a boy with a rightful claim to the lands.

Gilbert sighed in disgust. He had done everything he could to expel the Slayer from Helmesly. It was up to the sender of the messages to do the rest.

Nell gasped in fear and slapped a hand to her heart. "Oh, m'lord, ye gave me such a start!" she exclaimed, flattening herself to the corridor wall. One of the torches lining the passage found a reflection in her golden curls as she gawked at the warlord.

Christian regarded the girl's panic with mild amazement. Would the servants never cease to shrink from him? "Nell, is it?" he asked, summoning an expression that he hoped looked harmless.

She nodded mutely and at the same time forced herself to step away from the wall.

"I hear that you have many siblings and that Sarah raised all of you," he said, utilizing the information Clarise had once fed him.

She nodded her head, looking dazed.

"Were you orphaned?" he prompted.

Again she nodded.

"Have you a plot to call your own?" He realized he should know the answer to his own questions. But between

Ferguson's mischief and domestic demands, he'd put off perusing the castle's ledgers. Harold took care of the bookkeeping—or was it Maeve?

"Nay, sir," the girl finally spoke, gazing at him earnestly. "The baron reclaimed our lands under the Right of Escheat when my da passed away. But he gave us work in the castle and a roof over our heads."

"Then you had no brothers to inherit the land?"

"There be Callum and Aiden, but they were only wee ones at the time."

Christian crossed his arms over his chest. As seneschal, he could distribute the peasants' holdings however he saw fit. "How old are your brothers now?"

"Fifteen an' twelve," she told him, apparently forgetting to fear him.

"Tell Callum and Aiden they will each have a plot to call their own. And if they have an interest, they may take up swords and be trained to fight."

Nell's mouth rounded into a perfect circle. "M'lord, 'twould please them immensely!"

"I'll send for them soon," he promised.

"Thank ye, m'lord!" She bobbed him a curtsy and nearly kissed his hands.

Christian stepped back, unused to such affection. "Is your lady within?" he asked.

Nell hesitated. "I left her with a full tub o' hot water."

"So she's bathing."

"Aye," she said, drawing out the word.

"How long did you know she was feeding Simon goat's milk and not her own?" He threw the question out suddenly, taking her by surprise.

Nell grew pale. "Not long, m'lord. Mayhap a week."

"Then you should have told me a week ago," he chastised. "I'm the seneschal of Helmesly," he added, pointing to his chest. "Lady Clarise could have been a spy."

Nell cast a helpless gaze down the hallway, but no one was coming.

"Who else knew the truth?" he demanded. He felt a little mean, torturing the girl, especially as they'd just had a pleasant exchange.

"Me sister," she admitted mournfully. "An' Doris."

He frowned down at her sternly, letting her stew in her distress a moment longer. "From now on you will come to me with news that bears on Simon's safety."

Nell's eyes flashed with sudden fire. "The Lady Clare— *Clarise* would ne'er think to hurt the babe!" she cried.

Clarise had been at Helmesly, what, about a month? And yet the servants defended her over a man they'd known for years. "Fortunately for you, she has cared well for him," he relented.

Nell swallowed hard, not knowing what to say.

"If I had known her circumstances sooner," he heard himself explain, "I'd have killed Ferguson already." It wasn't exactly a lie. He'd have maneuvered Clarise more swiftly to his bed, and perhaps gone after Ferguson in their latest conflict.

Regret darkened Nell's blue eyes. "I'm sorry," she said, empathizing with her mistress's plight.

Christian jerked his head. "Go about your duties," he said, dismissing her.

She edged thoughtfully past him. Before she'd taken three steps, she stopped and turned around. "There be somethin' ye should know, m'lord," she blurted.

"What's that?" Curiosity rose along with caution.

"The lady hath marks on her back where she haffe been beaten. An' she cries out often when she sleeps." Nell looked miserable for having revealed just that much.

Christian hissed a breath through his teeth. *Ferguson had beaten Clarise?* Anger came to a flash boil. He pictured the burly Scot leaving marks on Clarise's flawless skin, and he couldn't wait to kill the fiend!

But then he reined himself in. Nay, he wouldn't kill the Scot for free. He'd placed a price on his willingness to help. The price was Clarise's body—his for the taking.

He offered the maid a reassuring nod. "You were right to tell me, Nell. She is safe now."

Safe, hah. He was a hypocrite to say so, casting himself in a chivalrous light, as though he meant to defend the lady without recompense. Mercenaries were not chivalrous. They killed for pay. And the price he'd demanded was Clarise's sweet and willing body.

As the maidservant retreated, Christian approached the lady's door. Uneasiness roiled in his stomach. What if she declined his offer? What if she turned him down flat? After all, it must be distasteful for a lady of her breeding to yield to a monster like himself. Perhaps if he sweetened his offer with the promise to restore her home. According to his spies, Ferguson had all but destroyed it.

The sound of splashing water distracted him from his thoughts. He put an ear to the wood and was astonished when its hinges gave way and the door eased slightly open. The view that greeted him through the resulting crack made him freeze like a thief.

Clarise sat in a wooden tub, the water to her shoulders. Her hair was a damp, russet rope mooring her to the floor. The scent of lavender hung sweetly in the air. The brazier snapped with mellow light. She had not seen him, for her back was to the door.

Just as it occurred to him that he should turn away, she perched a long, slim leg on the edge of the tub and reached for the soap.

Like a hungry hound he salivated. He told himself to leave, but for the moment he was spellbound. With lazy movements she began to lather herself, starting with the leg she'd lifted and then switching to the other one. Limb by limb, she rubbed the scented bar into her skin. His fingers itched to follow the same path.

Go now, he told himself. *'Tis bad enough that you take advantage of her circumstances. Must you sink to new depths by spying on her?*

Her head fell back, and she rubbed her neck, sighing

softly as she eased the soap between her breasts. Christian swallowed a groan. Desire pulsed through his body with double vigor. Uncertainty followed close behind. What would he do if she refused him? His need for her could not be slaked by any other woman!

Something pounded on the door of his conscience, demanding to be heard. *This is honor!* shouted the entity. *I demand that you free her family without reward.*

But he ignored it. He was a bastard warlord, not an honorable knight. He needed Clarise DuBoise, and there was no way to get her other than by blackmail. Ladies of her ilk didn't give themselves to baseborn mercenaries.

Unless they proved themselves worthy, replied the voice inside.

She caught up her hair and squeezed it, coiling it on top of her head. Then, without warning, she put her hands on either side of the tub and stood straight up. Christian's gaze fell at once to the pink streaks lining her back. Nell had not been lying. *"Jesu,"* he cursed, unable to keep silent.

She turned with a gasp. "Who's there?" she called, trying to see through the cracked door.

He swiveled guiltily and beat a hasty retreat.

Cur, he called himself, stalking furiously toward his solar. He wanted so badly for her to want him that he had stooped even beneath himself. There was more of his father in him than he cared to admit, he lamented, grinding his teeth.

Yet he *had* to capture her incandescence or else lose himself to the despair that threatened before she came.

In the sanctuary of his solar, Christian dropped his head into his hands, his temples throbbing. A promise to rebuild her home was not enough. Short of offering for her hand, nothing he did could cast his offer into a nobler light.

He straightened abruptly, startled by the workings of his mind. *Offer for her hand?* Nay, the thought was ludicrous! Absurd! The lady would take her own life ere she agreed to wed him. Wouldn't she?

He forced himself to rationalize. There were factors in his favor, not the least of which was Simon, whom she adored. Then, too, he was not without the ability to give her a decent home, to feed and clothe her as befitting her station. Most important, he could give her what she truly desired of him: his sword arm to defend and protect those she loved.

It might just work.

His gaze fell upon a book that lay open on his table. It was Ethelred's *Mirror of Charity,* the latest text brought for Christian's erudition. He and the abbot made a practice of discussing the readings the abbot supplied. They'd had no time on this particular visit. But Ethelred had marked one of the pages with a ribbon in order to draw it to Christian's notice.

Christian dragged the manuscript closer and read the indicated page. His attention was drawn in particular to the closing remarks. *Put off the mantle of self-absorption and embrace the world unselfishly. For God, who sees all things, rewards the righteous heart.*

Christian read the lines three more times. With fingers that had butchered and maimed, he smoothed down a wrinkle in the parchment. It was time for the Slayer of Helmesly to forget his bitter roots. For his son's sake, he could not continue to be a fearsome warlord. Why not do as Ethelred suggested and shuck the mantle of self-absorption? What would it cost him? A mistress, probably.

What would he gain? Perhaps a wife.

God rewards the righteous heart, wrote the abbot. Christian hoped the abbot was right. He didn't want to go through the trouble of redemption and not get what he'd set his sights on: Clarise DuBoise.

Chapter Fourteen

"When did they leave?" Clarise asked Malcolm, who kept the mews.

The aged falconer regarded her through eyes as bright and watchful as the birds he tended. "They left but a second 'fore ye came," he answered in a creaky voice.

She shot him a word of thanks and raced across the treacherous cobbles of the inner ward toward the first gate. Already, she was breathless from this morning's activities. It had all begun at morning prayers when the good abbot failed to show himself.

Clarise had raced to Ethelred's chambers, hoping that she would find him sleeping in exhaustion from his visit to Rievaulx the day before. His chamber was empty. His bed had not been touched.

Agitation fizzed in Clarise's empty belly. Ethelred wasn't safe at Rievaulx. She remembered the mad gleam in Abbot Gilbert's eyes, the festering sores on Horatio's face. If anything had happened to Ethelred, she would blame herself for encouraging him to visit the scourge-ridden abbey.

Clarise had looked for Christian, wanting to apprise him of the circumstances. He had already eaten, she discovered, not finding him in the great hall. She would not break her own fast until she delivered her news to him. If anyone could help the good abbot, it was the Slayer.

"He's gone ahunting," the stable boy had said, yawning with maddening apathy. At last the falconer had more definitive news. If she hurried through the shadowed barbican, she might catch the seneschal and his vassal before they left.

The sun was still creeping skyward at this early hour, promising a warm day as it tinted the air a peachy pink. Swallows dipped and whirled for their breakfast of bugs. A rooster crowed from the henhouse. Clarise caught sight of the Slayer and his master-at-arms disappearing on horseback through the second gate. Sir Roger's gyrfalcon rode on its perch. Its jeweled hood gave a final wink as they passed under the barbican.

"My lord, Sir Knight, wait!" she cried, dampening her slippers on the grass as she raced toward them. They failed to hear her, for the rushing of the moat.

The vigilant gatekeeper gave a blast on his horn, alerting them for her. Lord and vassal turned together at the end of the drawbridge. Their faces reflected alarm to see Clarise chasing after them, her hair flying like a banner.

She slowed to a brisk walk, wary of the Slayer's enormous black mount, snorting impatiently to be on its way. The men were dressed in minimal armor. They bore all the accoutrements needed for a successful hunt, including bow and quiver slung over their shoulders.

"What's amiss?" the warlord asked, his scowl taking up its usual post. "Is it Simon?" He looked ready to return at the least word.

"Not Simon," she assured them, catching her breath. "The Abbot of Revesby. He went to Rievaulx yesterday, and he hasn't returned. Something foul has happened to him, I can feel it."

The Slayer's alarm subsided into something more like consternation. He looked to his vassal for an opinion.

Sir Roger's smile wavered and dipped. "He and Gilbert have never seen eye to eye," commented the knight. "If

Ethelred accused his colleague of dissembling, Gilbert may well have reacted without thinking."

Clarise rubbed away the chill on her arms. She swallowed down the admission that she'd made her own request of the good abbot.

"But Ethelred has the backing of the archbishop," Christian countered. "Gilbert can do nothing to deter him."

Sir Roger gazed off in the direction of Rievaulx. "Still, if Ethelred doesn't return by sunset, we should act."

"I have a bad feeling about this," Clarise repeated, admitting nothing for the time being.

The warlord returned his focus to her. His gaze was still as intense as it had been in the last two days. But a secret light now sparkled in his eyes, making them more green than gray. He seemed happier, almost gay—if such a word could be applied to a man who never laughed. As he stared down at her, his mouth curved in a hint of a smile.

Could he have been the one spying on her bath the other night? she wondered. The thought put butterflies in her stomach. She told herself that she'd imagined the whispered curse and that Nell had left the door cracked.

"Did you not lock the door?" she'd asked the girl, who'd appeared a moment later.

"Nay, milady."

"Did you see anyone in the corridor?"

"Only Lord Christian. He means to make me brothers squires, milady. An' he means to give them both a plot o' land!"

That had been excellent news for Nell. But it also meant the warlord had been skulking in the corridor. Pacing like a fox for a rabbit to come out of its hole.

"We have to hunt," he said now. He still looked secretly pleased. "There will be a feast if we are lucky."

"A feast," she repeated. The lightness of his spirits was contagious, if curious. "And what is the occasion?"

"You will know it soon enough," he said. He turned faintly red beneath his tan.

"Can you not send others to do the hunting?" she asked, thinking of Ethelred. "There must be men-at-arms who would undertake the task."

"Sir Roger's falcon answers only to his call. My men remain at Glenmyre. That leaves only us." He shrugged, looking like a handsome woodsman with a bow on his shoulder.

"Well, go then, but hurry back," she relented. She made to turn away, but then remembered that she wanted to thank him for a recent kindness. "My lord, I thank you for moving Doris to the nursery. I am well rested for the first time in a month." The cook had taken over Simon's midnight feedings, giving Clarise the leisure to sleep.

The warlord's half-smile faded. His expression became quizzical. "I would like to take credit for such thoughtfulness, but it wasn't I."

Not he? Then it could only have been Sir Roger. They both looked to the knight, who shook his head.

Possibly Harold, then, or Dame Maeve. Had the steward's wife tired of their rivalry? Was she ready to make amends? "Do you object, my lord? I will, of course, watch him at all other times."

His gaze caressed her upturned face. "You look better for your rest," he decided kindly. "Doris may stay."

"Thank you."

"I wish to speak with you this afternoon, about my offer," he announced. With those alarming words, he yanked his mount around. The destrier gave his tail a haughty swoosh, and they were away.

From the edge of the drawbridge, Clarise watched the two men cut a fresh path through the knee-high flowers. Daisies and loosestrife swayed beneath an easterly breeze. She only had eyes for the dark-haired warrior who rode so confidently in his seat, his sharp gaze focused on the tree line. She felt a clutching pang in her chest that she attributed to missing breakfast.

What was he going to talk to her about? Likely he wanted an answer right away.

She didn't have an answer yet, though she'd imagined in vivid detail what it would be like to be his mistress. Despite his bloody reputation, she was certain he would treat her well, perhaps even come to feel affection for her. Breed children on her if he so desired.

Or marry again and leave her with her shame.

She recalled the things she had wanted for herself since childhood—the things she'd thought Alec could offer her: a marriage blessed by God, a husband who cherished her, children in her lap and at her feet. A longing came upon her, so deep and pulling that she sighed out loud. How could she settle for anything less and be happy?

She turned and plodded the length of the drawbridge. In light of the good abbot's absence, her yearnings were selfish. Her mother and sisters suffered on, while she pined for something that was more than most women ever attained.

The Slayer offered her his sword arm and shattering physical ecstasy. Unless Alec could top that offer, it would have to be enough for Clarise DuBoise.

Was it a boar or a deer? Christian couldn't readily tell by the color of its fur. The animal froze as though sensing that it had become a target. He pulled his bowstring taut until it creaked ominously in the silent clearing. The birds were dumb with terror. The leaves on the trees ceased to tremble. In the meadow nearby, the pure, high scream of the gyrfalcon signaled Sir Roger's success in his portion of the wager.

Christian gave a determined smile. By felling this animal, he might still come out the victor and produce the biggest game.

The animal suddenly bolted. Through the underbrush it crashed, snapping twigs, crushing ferns. "Don't shoot!" it cried.

Christian brought his arrow down. *A talking boar?* Nay, it was a monk. He could see that clearly now. The man wore the dun-colored cloth of a novice. The bottoms of his sandal's flashed as he ran.

"Hold!" he called out. "I mean you no harm."

The monk disappeared behind a tree, then peeked around it.

"What are you doing on my lands?" Christian snapped. It irritated him to be reminded of the Abbot of Rievaulx right now. He'd been enjoying this challenge between himself and his vassal. It had been a long time since he'd taken part in the hunt. More than that, every pheasant, every rabbit felled would find its way to the banquet table in celebration of his marriage to Clarise. Provided she agreed to wed him.

"I've been following you," the monk admitted feebly.

"What the bloody hell for?"

The man blanched at his foul language and crossed himself. "I . . . I have a package for you," he replied. An arm jutted outward. Dangling from the monk's hand was a large leather satchel.

"What is it?" Christian demanded, suspicious of anything the Gilbert might have to give him. Two possibilities occurred to him: a ransom note for Ethelred—he dismissed the notion, as the bag was too big for a note. Or a body part of the good abbot—a hand, perhaps.

"Letters!" cried the cleric. "Letters from Clarise DuBoise to her lover, Alec Monteign."

Those were not the words Christian expected. He heard a buzzing in his ears that might have been caused by a fly. *Clarise and Alec? Lovers?* He recalled that they had been betrothed at the time he seized Glenmyre. But he'd assumed their marriage was a legal arrangement, an alliance between Monteign and Ferguson. It was the catalyst to every event that followed.

He sat astounded in his saddle. Shock gave way to denial. Gilbert was meddling again. "Come forward," he growled.

"Will ye kill me?" the man inquired. His eyes darted to the warlord's sword.

Christian could see his reputation was alive and well at the abbey. "I don't kill clergy," he growled.

When he seized the bundle from the man's shaking hands, he was instantly impressed by the quantity of letters inside. "Stay a moment." He loosed the cord and withdrew one of the parchment tubes. He would determine at once if the letters were real or forged. *My beloved Alec*, he read, struck by the flowing script of the writer. *You have been gone but a month and already I feel that years have passed.* He released one end of the parchment and it sprang closed.

He could not begin to name what he was feeling. A vise had closed about his chest, squeezing so hard that he could scarcely draw breath. Without a word to the watchful monk, he jerked his horse around and galloped from the glen. He rode blindly in the direction of the field where he'd left his hunting partner. Through the green canopy overhead, he caught a glimpse of the gyrfalcon circling the sky. Sir Roger would know what to do.

Hours later they sat in Christian's solar with the table between them and Clarise's letters lying in two piles: those they had read and those yet unread. He'd refused to let his vassal read the majority. The messages were too intimate, too sensual. They made him burn with jealousy and shame.

Dearest One, read the letter in his hand. *When you lie on your narrow cot at night, do you not dream of me? The marriage bed is a warmer place and softer, I trow. To sleep with your hand on my breast were as pure an act as prayer.* He dropped the letter out of Sir Roger's reach and snatched up another.

Alec My Love, if you knew the humilities I endure under Ferguson's rule, you would not have abandoned me so cruelly. Have you forgotten the kiss we shared at the Feast of St. Michaelmas? We strolled by the lake, and you held my hand. Have you forgotten that you pledged your heart to me that day while a starling serenaded us? I have not forgotten. I dream of kissing you again. All that I have are my dreams, now. Ferguson and his men roam the halls of Heathersgill looking for wenches, willing or nay. I try to stay clear of them. Do you lack the courage to rise up for me? You took your horse and armor with you when you left. In the name of chivalry, how can you leave us to suffer so?

Even with a bitter taste in his mouth, he was not immune to Clarise's desperation. Had she directed such words to him, he would have snatched up his sword and leaped on his horse at a full run. Yet, these pleas were not for him, which was precisely the rub. They were for Alec, her beloved, her Dear One.

In a violent gesture he scythed his arm across the table and swept the letters to the floor. "Enough!" he shouted, scraping back his chair. He stalked to the window and stuck his head outside to find a breath of air. The wind had turned and was coming from the north. Clouds bruised the afternoon sky, bringing the threat of a storm.

"'Twill rain," Sir Roger observed from where he sat. "This front will bring relief from the heat," he added.

Christian wondered how his man could even think about the weather. "What shall I do?" he asked, feeling perfectly violent. He rubbed his forehead where his scalp seemed to be pulled too tight. The alliance he had terminated by killing Monteign had been a love match! He reeled with the truth of it.

"What had you intended to do?" Saintonge inquired easily.

"Kill Ferguson," he retorted. It had all been so simple. He would kill the Scot, thereby earning the right to wed Clarise. But everything had changed with the appearance of her letters.

"And then?" prompted Saintonge.

"Wed Clarise," Christian admitted, feeling the bite of jealousy in his gut. He darted his vassal a warning scowl. "Don't laugh," he warned.

Sir Roger glanced at the letters scattered all over the floor. "Your plans have changed?"

A streak of lightning jagged from the clouds, drawing the warlord's gaze outside again. "She loves Alec," he said, forcing the words through his clenched teeth. "She would never have me."

Trees foamed on the horizon. A breeze stirred his hair.

"Why would the abbot give you these letters?"

Sir Roger's question forced Christian to *think* and not to feel. He watched the storm surge closer. "Clearly, Gilbert wishes to expose her," he said. "He lives to strike misery into the hearts of everyone."

"True enough," said the knight. "But there is more to this picture than pettiness. Gilbert suspects that you covet the lady for yourself. He means to drive a wedge between you and Alec in the hopes that you will withdraw your offer to return Glenmyre to him."

"How could he know such things?" Christian demanded, referring to his intentions toward Clarise.

Sir Roger shrugged. "He must have put a spy among us."

That gave him pause. "You think he wants me to withdraw the offer to Alec."

"Alec's lands are forfeit to the Church," the knight pointed out, "but only as long as he remains a monk."

The warlord raked a hand through his hair. Following Sir Roger's logic was like wending along an ancient riverbed; he never knew where it would lead him. "I presume we are speaking of Glenmyre, which is presently in my control."

The knight tapped his fingers on the table. "Gilbert will question your right in due time. He means to absorb Glenmyre into the abbey's holdings, mark my word on it. Alec knows nothing of your offer. Nor will he ever know. He is completely cut off from the world, just as the abbot designed."

It was true. Alec had never replied to his offer.

He thought of the distress in Clarise's letters. *Alec, in the name of God, you must answer me.*

A disturbing notion settled in the pit of Christian's stomach. If Alec did accept the offer of Glenmyre, he stood to gain more than his own lands. He would need a bride to run his household, and he would logically ask for Clarise.

His teeth clicked together. *Nay.* If her love for Alec had been earlier revealed, then maybe. If he hadn't raised his own hopes falsely, perhaps he could be generous. But it was too late now. Either he would have her for himself, or no one would get her!

The darkness in his heart mirrored the storm outside. He could not stand to think of another man touching her!

Suddenly a horrible notion struck him. Perhaps Clarise had come to Helmesly, not only to poison him, but to be closer to her betrothed. He turned around, his fingers curling into fists. He'd caught her trying to leave once. She'd said she was going to Abbingdon to hear the Abbot of Revesby preach in English. Hah! Likely she intended to steal off toward Rievaulx and tryst with her lover!

A sharp rap at the door jerked him to the present. "Who is it?" he shouted.

"'Tis Clarise," called his nemesis. "I would speak with you about Ethelred."

Christian darted a look at his vassal. The knight shrugged. "Come in," he growled. He would have the satisfaction of witnessing her mortification. Aye, he would squeeze the truth from her this time and make her weep for the heaviness that was in his heart.

She tugged on the latchstring and pushed. He could see at once that she had his baby in her arms. His anger died to a seething bitterness.

Clarise wondered what lord and vassal were up to. They rarely cloistered themselves in the solar during the day. She hoped they weren't discussing Ethelred's plight without her. "Gentlemen," she began, "I have something to tell you." She had just closed the door behind her when she noticed the mess on the floor. It looked as though someone had lifted one end of the Slayer's table and dumped its contents.

"What has happened here?" she asked, staring down at the letter that was touching her toe.

With a sense of unreality, she recognized the handwriting on the edge of the vellum. Holding Simon to her body, she leaned over and plucked it up. Her heart began to pound in earnest. *My Dearest Alec,* she read.

She felt as though her feet were driven into the ground with spikes. Quickly she estimated the number of letters on the floor. She had written Alec over fifty pleas. There were at least that many here. A hot wave of self-consciousness rose toward her cheeks. "How did you get these?" she croaked.

"Gilbert sent them by messenger," said the Slayer, watching her through half-closed eyes.

Clarise wasn't the least bit fooled by his sleepy look. He was furious. "The Abbot of Rievaulx?" Anger rushed out to replace humiliation. "He gave you these!" she cried, her volume rising. "How dare he? How dare he meddle in something that has naught to do with him?" Even holding the baby, she managed to rip the parchment in her hands, tearing it first this way and then that. "I should like to put an arrow through his shallow heart!"

"Compose yourself," the warlord warned. He looked nonplussed that she was shouting. What did he expect? Repentant tears?

"How simple for you to say!" she yelled, forgetting that the baby grew distressed at the sound of raised voices. "Do you know the hours I spent laboring over these letters? I called upon every creative power I had to persuade Alec to quit his studies and defend us. I'll wager he never even got these letters. The abbot kept and read them for his own perverse pleasure!"

The warlord was looking at her very intently now. With her fury exorcised, she grew calmer, more aware of the currents weaving through the chamber. He, too, had read her letters, she realized. She felt exposed to him now, completely vulnerable. So many yearnings she had poured upon the page. But more than that, in attempting to entice Alec from the church, she had displayed the depths to which she would sink.

What did he think of her now? she wondered, laying the shredded letter on the chest piled with books.

"You think Alec never read them?" Behind the glimmer of his green eyes, she saw that his mind was busy calculating.

"I think he would have helped if he had," she said with more certainty than she felt.

The warlord crossed the room to approach her. She locked her knees to hold her ground. As her gaze fell to his lips, she experienced the wistful urge to be kissed by him. When they kissed, she felt treasured and revered.

"I should have you punished, lady," he said in a voice devoid of emotion.

"Why?" she asked, taking a startled step back.

"You swore to me, no more lies." Thunder rumbled outside, adding a menacing undertone to his words. "You told me you came here because Ferguson sent you to poison me."

"I did!"

"Another lie," he snarled. "You came to Helmesly to be closer to your beloved."

"Nay, if I wished to be near to him, I'd have stayed in Abbingdon."

"The day you wanted to go with the servants to pray, you had planned to meet with him, hadn't you?" He tilted her face up, putting his fingertips beneath her chin. His touch was searing.

"I meant to speak with Ethelred," she corrected, "so he could contact Alec for me."

"Ethelred," said the warlord, stunned. His mind was quick to grasp at clues. "Is he even now at your behest?" he guessed. "Is that why he's gone to the abbey?"

"Of course not. He has gone to see the papal seal on the interdict."

"Is that all?" he pressed, his gaze incinerating.

She jerked her chin free and stepped to one side. "Nay, that isn't all," she admitted, darting him a wary look. She had come to his solar to tell him the truth. So be it. According to Ethelred, truth was a stronger fortress than deceit.

The sound of rain showering the cobbles told her that the clouds had buckled. The room gave an eerie flash as lightning forked the sky. The warlord made a sound of disgust and stalked back to the window.

Clarise looked to Sir Roger for help. The knight sat straighter. "My lord, make no rash decisions," he warned uncertainly.

Decisions? "What will you do?" she asked. Volatile currents filled the chamber, making her uneasy.

Simon seemed to sense her agitation. His round face crumpled with distress. He sobbed against her shoulder. Clarise felt like weeping with him.

The Slayer stood with his back to her. "I have had enough of your lies, lady," he announced grimly. "I will not be used to reunite you with your lover. Nor can you convince me again to raise arms on your behalf. I will return you to Ferguson," he announced, against the backdrop of pouring rain. "You and the Scot have more in common than you think. You are both dissemblers."

She soothed the baby with automatic gestures. Shock settled over her, leaving her emotions in frozen limbo. "Return me?" she cried. "What makes you think Ferguson would want me back? He will see that I have failed and he will hang me, along with my mother and sisters. Aye, he'll hang us all!"

The mercenary shrugged, still presenting her his back. "What does it matter to me, Clarise DuBoise? I have tried to turn myself toward righteousness, and you and others have taken advantage of me. Leave me to my sins. You had no intention of staying with me, anyway."

Clarise frowned as she struggled to interpret his words.

She gave up trying. All she knew for certain was that he'd sentenced her, her mother, and her sisters to be hanged. It was too horrific even to envision. Even the Slayer of Helmesly was incapable of such malice!

"Er, my lord, why not take some time to think about it?" Sir Roger asked. Alarm had turned his face into a map of battle scars.

The Slayer flicked him an obstinate look. "I have made up my mind," he snarled, his profile unfamiliar against the screen of rain.

Sir Roger closed his eyes and dropped his face in his hands. He said nothing.

"You've forgotten about Ethelred," Clarise offered in a quaking voice.

The warlord swiveled abruptly. "What did you ask him to do for you?" he demanded.

"Simply to see if Alec had received your offer."

"So, you take on yourself to settle my affairs for me," he observed, his eyes as silvery as the rain, "and in the bargain you get yourself a landed husband."

If she had a knife, she would carve a matching scar on his right cheek. "He was *my betrothed* before you stripped him of his inheritance," she shot back, fisting her hands.

Simon matched her volume with a deafening wail.

"I do not recall meeting him on the field of battle," the warrior rebutted. "He ran like a coward for Rievaulx. Or mayhap he was simply grateful for a reason not to wed you!"

With his face still in his hands, Sir Roger groaned.

Clarise went perfectly still. The pain that diced her heart gave her something to cling to. "Do what you will with me, you monster." Her voice turned fearless and resolved. "I pray one day that you will eat your words, for I will have naught to do with you even if you crawl on your knees, begging my mercy. You do not deserve this babe that I have loved. . . ." Her voice broke and the dam burst behind her

eyes, flooding them. Before they betrayed her, she spun
around and raced to the door.

She slammed it behind her, startling Simon into silence.
Then she hesitated, pricking her ears to the quiet on the
other side. Just when she despaired of hearing anything
through the thick wood, Sir Roger drawled with irony. "Well
done, my liege. Your father would be most proud."

Chapter Fifteen

Clarise worked the laces of the boy's braies tighter and marveled at how quickly her circumstances had changed. One day the Slayer was determined to have her for his mistress, the next he wished never to lay eyes on her again. The pain of his rejection made her fingers stiffen as she tightened the last two stays.

Nell had secured the boy's clothing from one of her brothers. "The lord told me to bring all manner o' knowledge to him, and he would ease yer circumstances," the young girl whispered as she arranged the pillows on the bed to take the form of a person sleeping. Clarise could tell that Nell was torn.

"That was before he threatened to return me to my stepfather," she retorted. "He suffered a moment of human compassion, 'tis all. Do you put faith in his promises, you will be sore disappointed."

"But why must ye travel at night?" Nell complained as she straightened from the bed.

In the darkness Clarise could just make out the golden halo of Nell's hair. She nosed through the oversize tunic until her head popped through the proper hole. "Do I look like Callum?" she asked, holding her arms out to her sides.

As she was standing in the only puddle of moonlight, she was certain the maid could see her.

Nell shook her head. "Nay, m'lady. Me brother ne hath such a bosom as thine."

"That is precisely the reason I must travel at night," Clarise pointed out. "Now remember what I said. You last saw me when I went to sleep earlier this evening. When asked, you don't know where I am, or how I ventured through the gates. You must lie to protect yourself. Is that clear enough?"

Nell mumbled an unhappy answer.

"Where are those awful boots I have to wear?" Clarise asked, peering around the perimeter of the moon's glow.

She had lived through the past few days as in a dream. The warlord was too busy tracking down Ethelred to make good on his threat. The Slayer had ventured to the abbey twice now to demand an audience with Gilbert. According to the monk at the gate, both abbots had fallen ill. There was nothing the warlord could do to gain entrance or prove otherwise. The abbey was sacrosanct. To attack it would be a violation of the Church proper.

He sent a message to the archbishop of York, stating his concerns. All they could do now was wait.

In those two days Clarise had joined the servants in lighting candles for the good abbot's health. In silence she added prayers for her own deliverance. As the hours crept by, her dread mounted to unbearable proportions. She could only hope that the warlord had changed his mind about returning her to Ferguson.

The sound of the baby fretting next door jerked Clarise to the present. It was Dame Maeve who had moved Doris to the nursery in order to care for Simon. Yet Doris snored so loudly at times that she failed to hear the baby's cries. His pathetic wails tugged at Clarise's heartstrings. She refused to consider that she might never see him again.

Focus on the present, she told herself, blowing out a slow breath. She would need to find the secret entrance Ethelred had mentioned. The fate of her family still rested on her shoulders. Once Ferguson realized her plan had failed, they would all be killed. Alec was now her only hope.

Gathering her hair into a hat, Clarise pulled the brim over her ears and carefully opened the door. Nell followed her down the tower stairs and through a deserted corridor. It was well past midnight, and the torches had burned themselves out. Only a few sputtered intermittently, casting grotesque shadows on the walls. Clarise found herself wishing this were all a dream. She pretended she was slipping down to the goat pen to fetch Simon milk. The fantasy brought a lump to her throat.

As they scurried along the gallery, past the Slayer's solar, she was beset by memories. She recalled the evening she and Christian had watched over Simon in his illness. She recalled how he had prayed by his son's cradle. Her heart softened briefly toward the warlord. Surely he had reconsidered his threat to cast her off to Ferguson; after all, he'd yet to execute it.

Where was the chivalry Sir Roger had remarked in him? It seemed anger had the power to douse the flame of goodness that burned in him. Even if he did recant his threat, all that he'd ever offered was his bed. She burned in shame to think that she'd nearly agreed to become his mistress. Where was her pride? The man had accused her of liaisons with a monk!

Nell still tiptoed behind her. Clarise hurried down the grand staircase, drawing the notice of the wolfhound that stirred the rushes with his tail but couldn't bring himself to slit an eye. Alfred was used to her midnight ramblings.

Clarise's heart raced with unnatural urgency as she lifted the crossbar on the double doors and slipped through them. She gave Nell the signal that all was going as planned. The maid would wait until her mistress had passed through both gates. Then she would replace the crossbar.

The plan was a simple one of assuming another's identity. The gatekeepers were accustomed to Callum's midnight outings. Rumor had it that Nell's brother had several sweet-hearts in Abbington and devoted his nights to keeping them all content. As he worked in the castle's brewery, it was his custom to reward the guards with ale. In exchange they left the pedestrian gates unlocked between the hours of twelve and one.

Callum always returned at dawn to commence his work in the brewery. Clarise, disguised as Callum, would not re-turn.

That realization struck her forcibly as she stepped off the drawbridge and onto the well-worn path to Abbingdon. Her passage through the pedestrian gates had gone unchal-lenged. One guard even called in drunken encouragement, his crude words making her ears burn. The sweat that had gathered between her shoulder blades quickly dried. She'd escaped the castle without raising a hue and cry.

The sweet night air filled her lungs but failed to lift her spirits. The rain that had deluged the land for the last two days had passed, sweeping away the last lingering cloud. The moon was a half crescent, hanging like a pointed pen-dant in a star-spangled sky. It shed just enough light to guild the hilltops in gold and gleam on the puddles of the muddy road. *A good omen,* she thought to cheer herself.

Listening to the squish of her boots, her short-term wor-ries faded and the larger issues loomed. A wolf howled in the distance. She couldn't help but consider that she was right where she'd been a month ago. Yet so much had hap-pened since her first attempt to reach Alec! She had dwelled in the stronghold of a much-feared mercenary. She had eaten at his table, cherished his son, bantered with his master-at-arms. She had even kissed the beast and quivered with plea-sure at his touch!

But because of Abbot Gilbert's interference, the Slayer had discovered her original intent. Dimly she realized his pride had been wounded by his discovery. He hadn't liked to find himself second to Alec in her choice of champions. Yet it was his violent overreaction that left her with no choice but to seek Alec's help again.

In the process she would try to locate Ethelred. It seemed impossible that he would be stricken by the illness within a day of visiting the abbey. *The plague is the least of my concerns,* he'd told her. He wasn't sick at all, she'd decided, but held prisoner by the Abbot of Rievaulx.

Her plan was perilous and impractical. She would find the secret entrance described to her. She would seek out Alec and enlist his help in determining Ethelred's whereabouts. If she could do that much, then she wouldn't feel so bad about steering the good abbot toward his ruin.

Now, as she sidestepped puddles and listened to the eerie call of wolves, she had to wonder if she shouldn't have tried to convince the warlord that her letters were dated. They were not at all a true reflection of her feelings. It wasn't Alec who occupied her thoughts, waking and sleeping, but Christian and all his myriad complexities. Getting to know him had been the most disturbing and, ironically, the most rewarding experience of her life.

If only he knew how desperate she'd been when she wrote her pleas.

The road curved, bringing her around a shadowy mound of earth. Clarise looked up and spied the outline of Rievaulx against the starry sky. She drew to a halt. A tremor of dread shook her as she thought of the sickness fouling the air there. She wished suddenly that she could turn back and trust Christian to come to his senses. It was too late now. She'd said she would have nothing to do with the beast, even if he crawled on his knees, begging her mercy.

She lifted her chin and struck out boldly for Rievaulx. Her stride was jaunty, even confident. Her heart sank like a stone down a wall.

Christian knew what it felt like to be a hound after an elusive hare. He felt desperate enough to foam at the mouth, perhaps even bay at the sun rising over the treetops.

The laundry maid cum lady-in-waiting was as crafty as any rabbit. She had led him in a pretty chase this morning, disappearing from the very places where she'd been seen just seconds before.

She had not been in Lady Clarise's chamber when he knocked at her door that morning. What he'd found instead was enough to make him forget the speech that kept him awake the night before. What he'd found had made his blood run cold.

The lump under the blankets was not Clarise. The gowns that he had gifted her were neatly folded in the open chest. Her slippers had been cast beside the bed and forgotten. Her chemise had been flung over the top of the dressing partition. She was clearly gone, and from what he could tell, she was naked to boot.

He'd dashed to the great hall to advise his master-at-arms.

"Find the lady's maid," Sir Roger retorted, smirking over his mug of morning beer. His eyes said, *You get what you deserve.*

Christian made inquiries. A page had seen Nell in the kitchen breaking her fast. But when he raced to the separate building, the girl was already gone. "Laundering," said Dame Maeve in her terse manner. "You will find her by the well."

He skirted the main keep to avoid Sir Roger's mocking salute. The courtyard was alive at this hour with servants rushing through their chores. Stalking across the courtyard, the warlord drew more than a few startled gazes. He scattered the chickens pecking at their feed, upset a bucket of water placed by the well, and ran smack into a wheel of cheese that a youth was rolling to the kitchens. Nell was nowhere.

He spied Sarah making her way toward the gates with a basket in her arms and jogged to intercept her. "Have you seen your sister?" he demanded, blocking her path.

The girl squared her shoulders and stared at him stoically.

He recalled that he'd threatened to make her scrub the garderobes for life. Given the look on her face, he'd get nothing from her.

"I saw her by the well but a nonce ago," the maid said mildly.

"Obviously, she's not there," he countered, gesturing toward the well.

"I ne do not know where she be," Sarah insisted. She glanced nervously toward the brew house.

The direction of her gaze betrayed her.

Without a word he strode to the squat brick structure that was a stone's throw from the kitchens. The scent of hops wafted from the brewery's open windows. He dived straight into the dark rectangle of the open door and collided with a figure in an apron.

Nell squealed in fright.

"There you are," Christian said, laying hold of her. He could feel her trembling beneath his firm grasp. His eyes adjusted to the gloom, allowing him to see the many barrels stacked against the wall. A fire flared at the end of the room, making it unmercifully hot. Servants paused to observe the interchange.

"Where is she?" he asked, drilling Nell with a look that had always earned him quick results.

"Wh-who, m'lord?" the servant stuttered.

He tightened his hold for good measure. "Don't play games with me, Nell. This is not the time to forget where your loyalty should lie. Or have you no dreams for your brothers?" he threatened.

In contrast to the glaring fire, her face was as pasty as a lump of dough. Yet he saw the same flash of defiance that he'd seen once before. "She said ye would withdraw yer promise," she accused, her voice wobbling.

"What?"

"Ye made me a promise!" the girl insisted. "Ye said me brothers would have land o' their own. And ye made milady a promise to defend her against the Scot. Ye haffe lied on both accounts now!"

Christian sucked in a breath and released her. He glanced at the servants who huddled together for safety's sake. There was more contempt than fear in their faces. "You grow impertinent, Nell," he said under his breath. "Yet I give you credit for your bravery. My offer to your brothers stands," he said, raising his voice. "As does my intent to defend Lady Clarise from Ferguson."

"But ye tolde her ye would return her to the Scot!" the maid insisted.

And he had. But that was two days ago, when he'd spoken in haste. Since then, he'd had two interminable nights to help him reconsider. And he'd concluded that he couldn't live with himself if he executed his threat. "For reasons of security, I can tell you nothing more. Suffice it to say that I have no intention of returning the lady to Ferguson. She has made herself your mistress. I will make her my lady."

Smiles of delight lit up the servants' faces and took the edge off his own humiliation. "The fact is that if she is not within these walls, then she is very much in danger. Tell me where she went," he pressed, turning on the lady's maid once more.

"Tell him, sister," urged a youth, coming forward.

Christian looked into the sweaty countenance of a young man and saw at once his resemblance to the laundry maid. The youth looked him bravely in the eye, but he did so with respect. "Aiden or Callum?" he wanted to know.

"Callum, m'lord," said the young man, tugging his forelock. "Spare me sister and I'll tell ye where the lady be."

"Nell will be spared," Christian reassured him. He thought, with some disgust, that he was all bark and no bite these days.

"The lady haffe gone to the abbey," said the boy succinctly. "She wears me best tunic and braies." He cast an accusing look at Nell.

Christian's gut tightened in response to the news. So, she

had fled to be with the man she loved, he thought gloomily. Yet how would they meet, when the abbot had sealed the doors as tightly as a tomb?

Nell touched his sleeve. Her eyes were bright with hope. "She made mention of a secret entrance, m'lord. The good abbot Ethelred tolde her how to find it. But she ne woulde tell me where it was."

A secret entrance! He felt like putting his fist through the wall. "God's teeth and bones!" he hissed, pivoting toward the exit. Had she been meeting Alec after all?

Nay, everything inside him refused to believe it was true.

Alec had never read Clarise's passionate letters, he was certain of it. If he had, then he would have rescinded his vows long ago. Her words could have convinced the pope himself to defend her.

If not for love of Alec, then, she had left Helmesly for one reason alone: he had driven her out. His own violent humors had betrayed him.

By God, it was up to him to get her back. If he did not, then he'd lost his only chance for redemption.

The bells at the abbey tolled the ninth hour of morning when Clarise stumbled on the cave. By then she was convinced she would never find it. Someone was bound to see her scurrying along the rows of barren trellises and send a person up—or down if they happened to spot her from the abbey— to question her.

There were hundreds of rocky overhangs. This alcove of rock was no different from the ninety-nine she'd already peered inside of. In fact, it was so shallow that she could hardly bring herself to bend over and peer inside. But when she spied a hole the size of an animal's burrow at the rear of the cave, the sight gave her pause. Ethelred had said the hole was small.

She squatted down and shuffled under the overhang. From here she had a view of the bare vineyards, the steep slope, and the river stitching through the town below. The

cave was cooler than the air outside. She was tempted to remain where she was and forget all about her foolhardy mission. But then she thought of the Slayer's threat and the
good abbot's plight. She could not afford to be passive.

Using her hands, she widened the hole that had apparently grown over. Sunlight disappeared into the dark maw.
She would have to crawl through a space no wider than her
shoulders, no taller than a small child. She imagined briefly
coming across an animal, dead or alive. She wished she'd
thought to bring her flint and taper.

Well, she could sit here all morning dreading the task at
hand, or she could put it behind her.

Like a swimmer plunging into unknown waters, Clarise
took a deep breath of air and crawled into the tunnel hewn
from earth. The scent of mineral stone and moisture assailed
her nostrils. With every hair on her body cocked in anticipation of creeping insects, she nosed blindly forward.

Pebbles gouged her knees, yet she could feel that the land
was sloping upward. Her cheek brushed a root that dangled
from above. The air grew thicker, and she breathed through
her mouth, gasping for air to feed her thudding heart. She
knew a real and sudden fear that the ceiling would collapse
and drown her in rock and dirt. Yet she was too deeply en-
trenched to reverse direction. The passage was too narrow
for her to turn around.

Just when a cry began to gurgle at the back of her throat,
her hands met with a low wall. Had she come to a dead end?
Nay, it couldn't be, for a rush of cool air kissed her cheeks.
Patting down the floor and walls, she found them smooth,
cut by man and not by nature. She realized the roof was no
longer right above her head, and she cautiously stood.

It was then that she spied a line of light overhead, so faint
that she feared she imagined it.

She put her foot over the low wall and discovered it was
a step. She was standing at the bottom of a set of stairs! With
relief and mounting excitement, she climbed it. The stairs
were steep and slick. They seemed to rise forever.

At last, with her temples throbbing, she gained the last step. Light filtered around the edges of the door before her, yet the door was made of stone. She pushed. It didn't budge.

Running her hands over the slimy surface, she discerned two iron pulls. Tugging them toward her, she was astonished when the door popped inward and rumbled to one side. It traveled in a stone trough, giving off a sound like thunder.

Her lungs swelled as she waited to be discovered. She realized she would give anything at that moment to have Christian with her, wielding his monstrous broadsword.

No voices called out. All was still in the sunlit chamber before her. It was a little workroom, cluttered with desks that were designed for the illumination of manuscripts. Hundreds of loose sheaves littered the tabletops. Jars of gold-leaf paint and horns of black ink lined the edges of the parchment. But the scent of ink had long run dry. Dust motes swirled in the rays of sunlight streaming through the window. The brilliance of the detailed paintings was dulled by time. Projects seemed to have been abandoned in midsentence.

The scourge, thought Clarise. She wished she had brought a sachet of herbs to cover her nose.

Stepping into the room, she dusted the dirt from her hands and knees and kept her ears pricked for sounds in the hallway. The abbey seemed as deserted as it had on the day she'd inquired at the gate. Finding grooves in the stone door, she hauled the door shut again. It closed with the finality of a crypt. She knew an urge to push it open and leave while she could.

She took a moment to consider how to execute her rescue. To skulk around the abbey unnoticed, she would need a monk's robe. Such apparel might be kept in the cells where the monks slept. No one would likely be *there,* she comforted herself, providing they were well enough to be about their prayers.

The stark hallway was devoid of human life. She raced down the lengthy passage to the window slit at the end and caught a glimpse of the abbey's gardens. Beautiful! Who would have suspected such variety of color behind the austere walls?

She took the stairwell to the right. It spiraled upward to a higher level where she supposed the men slept. The sounds of many voices had her hesitating. Was the refectory above her? she wondered. She had imagined it on the first level, as it was in most holy buildings.

Hugging the wall, she crept upward, if only to orient herself. As her gaze rose over the topmost stair, she was astonished to see a large chamber filled with rows upon rows of cots. Each bed was occupied by a groaning invalid. Only a few men tended them, moving among the rows to ease their companions' suffering.

An infirmary, Clarise decided, freezing in terror at the grotesque scene. The ill lay struggling for breath. The pustules that reddened their skin seemed most virulent about the mouth. As she listened to the coughing and wheezing, she wondered if the blisters coated the victims' throats.

Swallowing hard, she backed down the stairs, desperate to escape the horror. She could not go through with this plan. God forgive her, but she was mad to leave the Slayer's castle and to strike out on her own. She would rather face Ferguson than this!

She did not even see the shadowy figure slipping up the stairs behind her. He clapped a hand on her shoulder, and she screamed so loud that her voice reverberated in the stairwell. The hideous countenance of Horatio swam into her view. As he grinned at her, his grip became an unbreakable hold.

"What have we here?" he leered in a rusty voice. His gaze was greedy as it absorbed the boyish garb. He wrenched off her hat, and her hair came tumbling down. "Hah!" proclaimed the monk in wonder. "So, yer back. The abbot will be pleased to see you." He dragged her, kicking and cursing, down the stairs with him.

Above them, in the infirmary, a monk rose slowly from

the side of a cot and listened. He'd thought he heard a woman screaming. The sound of it still rang in his ears, defying the logic that said he'd imagined it.

Two nights ago the Abbot of Revesby had halted him, while following Gilbert to his office chambers. He'd grasped his arm and quickly divulged two pieces of news that had him reeling with concern. Clarise DuBoise was looking for him, the abbot had said, and the Slayer wanted to give him back his lands.

Alec frowned as he stirred mush in the wooden bowl. It must have been the abbot's words exciting his imagination. The woman who screamed had sounded just like Clarise, but that was impossible. She would not have been admitted to the abbey with the quarantine in place.

He shook his head in puzzlement. It was just one more mystery in the conundrum of riddles at Rievaulx. Why did the ailment afflict only some men at the abbey and not others? What were the animal cries that rent the nighttime quiet?

Something more than the scourge disturbed the peace of the tranquil monastery, and Alec dared discover the true nature of evil lurking in its halls.

Chapter Sixteen

Clarise measured the width of the windowless chamber, using the torchlight in the corridor to guide her steps. Seven . . . eight . . . at nine paces, her toe hit the stone wall. It was ten paces deep, and barely tall enough to keep the dripping spiderwebs from sticking to her hair.

She backed up to the middle of the room and wrapped her arms around her shivering frame. Her gaze was drawn to the chains dangling from the wall. This room was clearly used to detain prisoners.

What would an abbot need with manacles? she asked herself. Criminals were sometimes granted asylum in the holy houses, but never imprisoned in their cellars. Perhaps the chains were not for prisoners, but to discipline the monks. Aye, that made more sense, given Gilbert's grim hold at Rievaulx.

The sound of footsteps in the corridor had her scurrying in vain for somewhere to hide. Yet there was no escape in a cell with only a crude table, a mat of hay in one corner, and a waste hole in the other. Clarise heard the jangling of keys. She saw the tonsured pate of a monk through the bars at the top of the door. When the abbot edged into the room, her worst nightmares seemed to be materializing.

She would rather have the grotesque Horatio keeping her

company. The abbot had read her letters. She felt violated by him already.

He bore a tray in his hands, with a cup, a loaf of bread, and a candle on it. The flame sparked a mad light in his countenance, making him look oddly happy to see her. And yet the cruel twist to his mouth told her that his joy was a perverse one, whatever the reason for it.

"Clarise DuBoise," he crooned, shutting the door behind him. Her gaze darted to the loop of keys he carried on a cord around his hips. "How good of you to come." He laid the tray on the rickety table. The gems at his fingers caught the glow of the candlelight.

She backed cautiously away from him, saying nothing. The door was unlocked, she thought. Perhaps she could make a run for it.

"Like a proper host, I have brought you food. Sit," he invited, nodding at the lice-ridden pallet. "Take nourishment. God knows how long you will feel well enough to eat. The illness is likely in your veins already." Baring his sharp teeth in a smile, he came forward and extended the cup to her.

Clarise knocked it from his grasp, casting a sheet of wine onto the wall beside her.

The abbot gaped with astonishment and then hissed in outrage. "Why, you perfidious bitch! Have you any idea how precious that wine was?" He flew at her, arms raised like bat wings. His palm made stinging contact with her cheek.

Clarise reeled back. One of his rings had bruised her cheekbone. With righteous anger giving her courage, she barreled past the abbot and raced toward the closed door, pulling on it. The door swung open with astonishing ease. She threw herself into the corridor and ran headlong into a human wall.

Horatio. He'd been standing guard.

He held her fast, and she screamed until her throat felt raw. Certainly someone at the abbey could hear her. The corridors seemed to magnify her shrill cries.

"Chain her," said the abbot, coming up behind them. He straightened his silk stole and handed Horatio the keys. "Give her nothing to drink until she begs for it," he added in disgust. "Then post yourself outside the door. If the Slayer comes to call again, I will send another in your stead," he added to his henchman.

Horatio manhandled her back into the cell. She was made to face the wall and breathe its damp, musty odor. The manacles banded her wrists with cold implacability. Using the keys, he locked them tight.

"I am sore tempted," grunted Horatio, "to treat you like a lady." He allowed himself the liberty of squeezing her buttocks. Clarise yelled in outrage and struggled to kick him.

Horatio grunted as her booted heel slammed against his shin. He stepped back quickly and spat at her.

She closed her eyes, willing him to leave. At the sound of his retreating footsteps and the click of the outer lock, she wilted in despair. The chains, with their short leash, kept her from reaching either the loaf of bread or the candle that beamed upward in the stillness.

You've done it this time, Clarise, she railed at herself. She had always been too impulsive, too quick to act before thinking. Rather than plead with the warlord, she'd come to Rievaulx alone and defenseless. In doing so, she had spurned the only person mighty enough to dispatch Ferguson. No, that wasn't right. He had spurned her.

Dear God, don't let me die here, she prayed, dropping her forehead against the wall. It was hardly comforting to learn that her instincts were right. The Abbot of Rievaulx had some wicked plot afoot, though she could not imagine what it was.

She huddled for warmth against the hard wall, feeling homesick. Only it wasn't Heathersgill she missed, but Helmesly. She was assailed by the memory of Christian's scent, his disturbing kisses. He would have made her his mistress. So what? She could have accepted that much for the time being. Then eventually, she would have done some-thing to secure her footing.

She could have taught the warlord to love her.

She could have convinced him to marry her, for Simon's sake.

But now it was too late. He wouldn't know where to look for her, so long as Nell kept quiet. And she would waste away in this bleak, damp hole under the abbey.

Hot tears filled her eyes, spilling over her lashes to track down her dusty cheeks. What would become of her mother and sisters if she died in this musty cell? They had less than a month to live before Ferguson would hang them.

"Oh, Father," she choked, invoking the memory of Ed-ward DuBoise, "I have tried to protect Mother, Merry, and Kyndra—I have. But everywhere I've turned for help, men have betrayed me. I've done all that I can do. Please forgive me."

Over the sound of her weeping came a low humming that recalled her from her pain. Clarise caught back her sobs and listened. The sound seemed to be coming through the wall. She pressed an ear to the stone. Someone was chanting a canticle in the chamber next to her. "Who's there?" she called, unwilling to alert Horatio, who was standing guard in the hallway.

The chanting stopped. She heard the eerie scrape of chain across stone. "'Tis I, Ethelred. Lady Clarise, is that you?" She barely recognized the good abbot's voice. It sounded raspy, weak.

"It is I, Your Grace," she answered with happiness and sorrow intermixed. She was so relieved not to be alone, yet so remorseful for not bringing help.

"Why did you follow me? Is anyone else coming?"

She swallowed the bitter taste in her mouth. The abbot sounded terrible. He must have caught the scourge, after all. Those lesions she'd seen on the monks' mouths must be popping up on his throat and tongue.

"Lord Christian has come to the abbey twice now," she

sought to encourage him, "but they won't admit him. He's sent an urgent message to the archbishop. Oh, Your Grace, please forgive me," she added, bursting into tears anew. "I ought to have told the others how to get inside the abbey, but I didn't. I followed you on my own."

"Why?" he asked. She thought she could hear him sinking onto the floor.

Why, indeed? What in heaven's name had she hoped to accomplish, but to prove to Christian that she didn't need his help—not that he had offered it. "Lord Christian and I had a falling out," she admitted.

Ethelred said nothing for so long, she thought he'd fallen asleep. "Don't drink the wine, my child."

"What's that?" She pricked her ears to his sudden warning.

"Don't drink the wine," he rasped. "You will . . . seem to show the symptoms of the plague."

"Show the symptoms? I don't understand. If the wine makes you sick, then it cannot be the plague."

" 'Tis a simulation."

"Quiet in there!" Horatio shouted through the bars. "You two are not meant to talk."

She obeyed the monk, too stunned by Ethelred's news to think of anything to say. So, the disease was a fraud, no doubt made possible by the many plants growing in the abbey's garden! What on earth was Gilbert hoping to accomplish by poisoning his monks?

When she whispered this question to Ethelred moments later, she got no reply. He had either fallen asleep or fainted. The chill of isolation struck her to the bone, and she sank to her knees. The chains weren't long enough to let her sit. She was left in a posture of penitence that was supremely painful. How long could she stand it? she wondered, beset by panic.

Ironically, this was the treatment she had feared from the Slayer. Instead he'd given her a feather mattress and colorful gowns. Even when he learned the truth of her identity, he'd forgiven her and offered her his sword arm. His stipulation had been simple enough. A warm embrace. A body willing to receive him.

Hadn't he proven that his touch was more than tolerable? She spent a moment warming herself with the memory of his intimate caresses. Oh, what she would give to feel his arms around her now, to curl herself into the security of his sure embrace.

Then she remembered her anger and his cruel words. Was his threat prompted by jealousy? Did he really think her in love with Alec?

She found a ray of hope in the thought. If he were jealous, then it meant he truly cared for her. Her heart expanded, then folded in on itself. His feelings would have little impact on her situation now. No one knew where she was, at least not until Nell admitted to their scheme.

How long would that take? Knowing her lady's maid, no more than three days. Could she live that long without a drop to drink?

"Psssst. Clarise, is that you?"

Clarise shook her head. In her misery, she must have imagined the ghostly whisper.

"Lady, look to the door!" This was said more urgently.

She looked. Her eyes widened, and her heart leaped up at the sight of Alec's boyish face. He peered through the bars at her, looking amazed and nonplussed. "What are you doing here?" he asked.

She struggled to her feet, her chains jangling noisily. Alec, of course! She'd forgotten all about him and the possibility of his help. "Where is Horatio?" she asked, hopeful that Alec had clubbed him over the head.

"Supping in the refectory."

Some of her elation dimmed. Alec didn't have the keys to set her free. "Oh, Alec," she stammered, not knowing where to start. "I've been trying to reach you." Now that she could finally speak to him, she found that the words she had poured to him on printed page would not come forth. "I have long needed your help," she managed lamely.

"For what?" he asked, glancing fearfully over his shoulder.

He was afraid. She understood that he would fear his abbot, and yet his temerity only dampened her spirits.

If he couldn't even face Gilbert, there was simply no hope that he would battle the burly Ferguson. "Can you get me out of here? The Abbot of Revesby is in the chamber next door. They have tortured him, I fear. He sounds unwell."

Alec gazed at her, stricken by her predicament and clearly stunned by her words. "I have no key," he said after a moment. "But I will try to get it. I don't understand what brought you here."

She sighed. "You left me to live with Ferguson," she accused him flatly. "You abandoned my family to his treachery and fled to Rievaulx."

"The Slayer seized Glenmyre," he defended himself, curling a hand around one of the bars. "I had no choice. He killed my father; he would have killed me, too!"

She shook her head at him. "He had no intention of killing your father. He's been trying for weeks now to give you back Glenmyre."

"That's what Ethelred told me," the young man admitted. "But why would he do that?"

"Remorse," she answered simply. "He only meant to put an end to our marriage alliance. Your father, who was no doubt given false information, mistook his intentions." She changed subject midstream. "You never wanted to marry me, did you?" She felt only calm acceptance in the asking; her bitterness had faded.

Alec took his time in answering. "Clarise, my calling was always clear to me," he said uncomfortably. "That doesn't mean I didn't love you."

"As one Christian loves another," she finished for him.

He gazed sadly into the light of the candle.

Clarise looked, also. The candle's wax was melting at an alarming rate. Soon the cell would be plunged into darkness. "You have to help us," she told him firmly. "Your abbot is a madman. Listen to me. The wine here is poisoned, you mustn't drink it."

"I never have," he said. "I'm allergic to elderberry."

So that was why he hadn't caught the illness. "Gilbert is making the monks here very ill. I don't know what his purpose is, but Ethelred knows. That's why he is imprisoned here. Gilbert fears that he will reveal his depravity to the archbishop."

Alec's brow furrowed with disbelief. "But he preaches the Word of God. How can this be?"

She had once found his innocence appealing. Now she wanted to shake him until his teeth rattled. "Alec," she said succinctly, "your abbot is making me thirst until I beg for the wine. You must find a way to set us free. There is another way out of the abbey besides the gate. Just get these doors open, and no one will know it was you who helped us. We will disappear without a trace."

He gazed at her with thoughtful gravity. "I will find the key," he promised at last.

Her knees quivered with relief. "Horatio has it," she said. "Hurry." She put her forehead to the wall. When she next glanced at the door, he was gone.

The disappointment he had seen in Clarise's eyes reminded Alec of the looks his father had often sent him.

Alec tried to force his mind back to his morning meditations. Normally he didn't notice how hard the flagstone flooring was or that his legs had fallen asleep beneath him. But this morning he could not abandon himself to spiritual ecstasy. Reality intruded. The knowledge that Clarise had been chained in a cold cell all night kept him from peace with his God. The knowledge that the abbot was causing innocents to suffer disturbed him greatly. But who was he to rebel against authority?

If not you, who else? asked his conscience. His bedridden brethren were useless, though he'd dumped all the wine he'd come across down waste holes, giving water to the sick, instead. If he had doubts about the poisoning, he had only to consider the evidence. He was one of a handful who hadn't yet fallen ill.

There were other things about Gilbert that had troubled him over the months. The unseemly fits of laughter, the stains on his hands and vestments. He had overheard the abbot boast that he would heal the ill at Rievaulx with his knowledge of herbs. Perhaps he meant to make a name for himself by reversing the process he'd initiated.

With a sigh Alec abandoned his prayers and stood. Fortunately, most of his other brothers had left the chapel before him. He bowed to the host and wandered to the nearest window slit to look outside. The walls at Rievaulx were impossibly high, obscuring the view of the countryside from nearly all the windows but this one.

What man could concoct evil in the midst of such beauty? The morning sun spun a coppery web across the sky. The land below undulated like a counterpane quilt, with patches of earth tones, patches of green. Helmesly loomed in the distance, a mighty stronghold, holding up the horizon with its four towers.

Alec's gaze fell to the winding cart road that passed below. A cloud of dust told him that even at this early hour, horsemen were approaching the abbey. He hoped mightily that it was the archbishop, come to make inquiries. He, Alec, had never been one to take initiative. To defy his abbot and the vows of obedience required more of him than he had to give.

Perhaps he would be spared having to wrestle Horatio for the keys. The envoy drew closer. He counted five horsemen all together. It wasn't the archbishop. These men were heavily armed.

The warrior at the lead was the largest. His very darkness compelled Alec to focus on him. When he spied the white cross at the corner of the black shield, he gasped with recognition. The Slayer was coming a third time to Rievaulx.

Rumor had it he'd come twice before while Alec had been busy tending to the ill. The last time he'd seen the warlord with his own eyes, he'd been watching his father's ambush from the wallwalk at Glenmyre. He'd seen his father's chest crack open like a nutshell under the Slayer's sword. And then he'd run.

If Clarise had spoken the truth, then the warlord was neither vicious nor greedy. He wondered how she would know that. Perhaps she had gone to the Slayer with her plight. Perhaps the man was looking for her even now.

Hope dawned like a blinding sunrise. Here was the answer to his prayers! With speed he'd forgotten he possessed, he bolted to the steps that would carry him to the courtyard. Normally Horatio answered the bell at the abbey's gate. This time Alec would answer it and let the Slayer in.

Christian ground his back molars together and tugged with impatience on the bell rope. He had no hope that the monstrous creature who usually answered the summons would let him in. Nor would he let him speak to the abbot. He was wasting his time.

He would have to find the secret entrance that Clarise herself had used. God knew how long that could take. He had no idea where to begin looking for it.

The sound of someone running caught his attention. The peephole snapped open. There stood a young monk, panting from his haste and staring at him through wide, gray eyes. "Are you looking for Clarise?" he said.

Amazement kept Christian mute a moment. "Are you Alec?" he guessed.

"I am," said the monk, paling slightly. He glanced anxiously over his shoulder. "She is on the lowest level, the Abbot of Revesby, also. Both of them are chained. Will you help me?"

"Open the gate," said Christian steadily.

Alec drew back the bolt and pulled the gate open. Christian motioned for his men to dismount and follow him. They led their horses into the empty courtyard. Iron shoes rang smartly against the cobbles. The monk seemed to shrink into the shadows at the noise. "Leave the horses," Christian instructed, dropping his reins. He looked at Alec. "Show us the way."

Alec took a visible breath, then darted across the courtyard. The men followed him. As they passed under the archway with its Latin message, *Hic laborant fratres crucis,* Christian felt a blade of fear bisect his spine. The monk had said Clarise was chained. He couldn't stand to think of her enduring any mistreatment, especially when he was responsible. He should have governed his jealousy!

They strode along the abandoned passageway. The stink of illness seemed to permeate the cool shadows. Christian ignored the stench and stared at the baldpate on Alec's tonsured head. The youth was as handsome as an angel. In his eyes he read not only fear, but determination and honesty. No wonder the lady loved him. Walking in the monk's wake, he felt like an animal, rawboned and scarred.

Could she bring herself to love the Slayer?

He focused his attention on the route they were taking. At one point Alec froze in his tracks. As the murmur of voices drew closer, he motioned the men to retrace their footsteps. They took an alternate route and managed to avoid detection.

At last they stopped wandering through the maze of corridors. "They're down here," said the young man, pointing down a flight of stairs. "Horatio is guarding them. You will have to fight him."

Christian knew a moment's surprise. "Aren't you coming?" he asked.

Alec glanced down the stairwell. "I set aside my sword

when I joined the brotherhood." A self-conscious blush made his ears turn pink.

The warlord felt suddenly better about himself. "Does that mean you will remain here?" he asked. "Have you no desire to rule your people?" *Marry your betrothed?*

Alec lifted an earnest gaze at him. "Clarise told me of your offer. I never expected such magnanimity of spirit. If you show equal kindness to my father's serfs, then Glenmyre is better in your care than in mine. In truth, I would be too often in my prayers to rule wisely."

So much was said in so few words. There wasn't time now to beg the handsome monk for his forgiveness. Christian looked into his trusting countenance and his heart gave a pang. He thrust his hand out and prayed the man would take it.

Alec put his own hand forward. The squeeze of his fingers was a balm to Christian's soul.

"Hurry," Alec encouraged as he glanced down the stairwell. "You may find Horatio sleeping. He sometimes naps through prayers at prime."

Christian pulled his broadsword, *Vengeance*, from its leather scabbard. "Stay here," he told his men. "Don't come unless I call for you." He wanted to rescue Clarise singlehandedly. Holding the sword before him, he ducked his head and charged down the shadowy stairway.

The light of a torch steered his passage. He rounded a turn and came face to face with a robed figure. It was the monk who normally answered the gate.

Horatio's flat face registered surprise. His mouth popped open and he backed up, giving Christian a view of the space behind him. A row of doors lined one side of the wall. The silence behind the barred windows was alarming.

"I've come for the abbot and the lady," he growled, sizing up his enemy. Horatio was a hulking man and not to be taken lightly.

"Humph," the monk snorted. "Ye cannot have 'em. They're ill," he added, showing his rotten teeth in a snarl.

"Stand aside, monk, or I'll shave your head with my sword."

"Not exactly a fair fight with that sword o' yours is it?" Horatio taunted. "But then I don't expect fair play from the likes o' you."

"You know nothing about me." Christian slammed *Vengeance* back in its resting place. "I don't kill clergy."

The monk gave a grin that betrayed his relief. He put his fists up, ready to fight.

The man's hands were the size of hams. Christian gave an inward groan. It was a tiresome thing to have scruples, he thought, putting his fists up slowly. Then, without warning, he sent a jab at Horatio's nose that brought a fountain of blood gushing out of it.

The monk howled and gingerly touched his wound. When he looked at Christian again, there was fury in his eyes.

"My lord, is that you?" called a woman's voice from one of the closed cells.

The sound of her voice was so welcoming that he forgot about Horatio. *Wham!* A full set of knuckles slammed into his right eye and had him staggering against the wall. Christian regained his balance just in time to see another fist flying toward his face. He twisted out of the way. His gaze snagged on a heavy iron cross hanging on the wall beside him. Without a second's hesitation, he wrenched it off the peg and, taking advantage of Horatio's forward momentum, landed a stunning blow to the monk's head.

Horatio stared at him in amazement. Even with a crimson stain spreading on the side of his skull, he remained on his feet for what seemed an eternity. Then he keeled over, face first, onto the stone floor. A cloud of dust rose up around him. Christian glanced gratefully at the cross and hung it back on the wall.

"Clarise," he called into the sudden stillness. "Where are you?"

A soft cry guided him toward one of the closed doors.

The torches wagged eerily, making him fearful of what he would see. He peered through the bars into the darkened cell and made out a figure in the corner. "Lady? Is that you?"

The figure moved. "Oh, you are a blessed sight!" she cried. "Horatio has the keys on his belt."

He hurried to the unconscious Horatio, then returned to the door and unlocked it. Wrenching it open, he peered in as the torchlight illuminated the cell. Clarise flinched from the glare, and he faltered at the vision of her, shackled like a thief to the wall. Her hair hung in a disheveled curtain about her pale face. A great surge of emotion rose up in him. He didn't know whether to unlock her first or clasp her to his pounding chest.

He fell to his knees on the hard floor. "You'll be free in a moment," he rasped. His fingers shook as he guided another key into the manacles' locks. Her wrists were chafed and swollen. He released them as gently as possible.

"Ethelred is next door," she whispered. "I fear he is fairing poorly. Either he has drunk the poisoned wine that is making the monks ill, or he is dying of thirst."

The words were pouring out of her, almost faster than he could absorb them. As the last chain fell away, he scooped her into his arms and carried her from the cell. Stepping over the stricken monk, he rushed her up the stairs. He meant to pass her to one of his men-at-arms, but he found he couldn't let her go. She had looped an arm about his neck and was holding him fast.

Instead, he gave the keys to his men and ordered all four of them to fetch the abbot from the other cell.

Waiting, Christian leaned against the wall and savored the feel of Clarise in his arms. The urge to shelter her shuddered through him. He had wondered if he would ever hold her again. There were so many dangers on the open road! A lone woman could disappear without a trace. What would have happened to him if he could never look into her glowing countenance again? He would have been lost to the darkness, forever.

At last she lifted her head from his shoulder and pushed the bright strands of hair from her face. He saw at once the shadows of exhaustion under her eyes and a vivid bruise on her cheek. He swallowed a curse.

"I prayed that you would come," she admitted. Her soft mouth curved in a fleeting smile. "I suppose Nell admitted everything almost at once?"

"I had to find her first," he drawled. He was startled to feel the heat of anger pulsing through him and growing stronger with each beat of his heart. It was a by-product of fear, he knew. He gripped her tighter, hoping to rein himself in.

"I am sorry for the trouble I have caused you," she whispered, as though sensing his volatility. Her gaze fell to the swelling under Christian's eye. "Oh, look what you've done!" she cried, lifting a hand to caress the angry flesh.

His anger subsided to a steady boil. After all his blustering and accusing, she found it in her heart to feel concern? He couldn't speak for the humility that clogged his throat. Shamed by his unworthiness, he kept his eyes downcast.

"My lord, I want you to know something," she told him, wresting his gaze upward. "I have not loved Alec for a very long time. Perhaps I never loved him but only thought I did. I was more in love with the hope that he would rescue us from Ferguson."

Christian had to wonder if Horatio hadn't killed him, after all. She didn't love Alec? Not even a little? It sounded too good to be true.

"I only sought to appeal to him one more time, because . . . well, because you threatened to return me to Ferguson."

He shifted her in his arms and looked away again, scowling. He had forced Clarise to do the very thing that had caused him to burn with jealous rage.

"Alec won't leave the abbey anyway," she added, without a hint of sorrow. "I've been wasting my time. He doesn't even want his inheritance back."

Their conversation was abruptly terminated by the reappearance of his men. The Abbot of Revesby was propped between them. The little man flinched against the sunlight in the open corridor. Christian assessed his health. His skin looked dried and shriveled. His shrunken frame betrayed starvation. But there was no sign of sores on his face.

The abbot moved his lips only to emit a croak.

"Find him water," Christian commanded one of his men.

The man had taken no more than a step when Alec materialized again, bearing a full bucket and a loaf of bread. He placed it before the good abbot. Christian saw a flicker of gratitude in Ethelred's eyes before he sank to his knees and began scooping water into his mouth.

Alec turned to Christian. He appeared a little shocked to see Clarise in the mercenary's arms but not at all dismayed. His mouth hardened in a manner that reminded Christian of Monteign's face beneath the visor of his helm. "Abbot Gilbert is in the herb garden," he announced. "I told him that I turned you away from the gate."

Again, Ethelred tried to speak. At first he choked, for he was still desperately drinking the water. "We need proof that he is sickening the monks," he rasped. "The College of Cardinals must have proof to condemn him."

"Sickening?" Christian asked. Clarise had said something similar when he freed her.

Alec summarized the abbot's foul experiment, offering himself as evidence that the wine, which he never drank, had been tampered with. "He means to make a name for himself by curing the monks of the very sickness he conceived."

"Do you know where he mixes his herbs?"

The young man nodded. "I will take you there," he said. His gaze shifted to Clarise, who was watching from the circle of Christian's arms. "I won't let you down this time," he told her.

She gave him a faint smile. "Thank you."

Christian insisted that his men-at-arms take Clarise outside the gates. He was gratified to hear her protests.

"Nay, I will not let you go alone," she said, with the same haughtiness that had drawn him to her in the first place. The worry in her eyes was a novelty. No one but Sir Roger had ever spared a thought for his safety.

"My lady, you are in no condition to accompany us." He pried her gently from his shoulders and made her stand. Her knees folded under her weight, lending proof to his statement.

She cast him a pleading look.

"Go," he commanded, forcing himself to sound firm.

Ethelred rose shakily to his feet. "I must accompany you," he said. His voice had gathered strength.

The abbot was in worse condition than Clarise. "If he goes, then I am coming, too," she argued, shaking off the arm of the man who tried to help her.

Christian rubbed his jaw with agitation. Clarise had no business in the abbot's affairs, while Ethelred had initiated the inquiry. She would have to wait at the gate. "Give her some water," he commanded to his men, turning quickly away so he wouldn't have to face her pleas or her anger. "Then take her to the gate."

"This way," Alec gestured.

Christian put a helping hand under the good abbot's elbow and trailed Alec down the corridor. He threw one last look over his shoulder and encountered Clarise's worried stare.

Alec led them clear to the other end of the abbey. Their footfalls on the flagging invaded the hush of the long corridors. "Down here," whispered the monk, pushing open a door.

The hinges gave a low moan. Stairs hewn from the rocky hillside beckoned them downward. The barest light guided their footsteps. Strange animal noises greeted them, fluttering, scuffling, and grunting. Alec paled and stepped aside. "I can go no further," he admitted.

Christian noted the bead of perspiration sliding from the young man's temple. "You have been most brave. Tell me how to repay you for the losses I have caused."

Alec looked him in the eye, his expression somber. "Take proper care of Clarise," he urged. "She is worthy of great loyalty and love, as those are the very traits she shows to others. I let her down. See that you do not."

He nodded, seeing wisdom in the young man's words. "Come, Your Grace." He motioned for Ethelred to take his arm as they descended the stairs to the abbot's laboratory.

The faint light, he ascertained, came through a ventilation slit at ceiling level. Christian was first impressed by the number of boxes and cages piled about the room. The chamber reeked of waste and feed and the overlying scent of drying herbs, suspended in clumps from pegs along the ceiling and walls.

Ethelred released his arm and headed toward a table. It was littered with mortars and pestles, a crucible for heating herbs, and bowls that overflowed with seeds, roots, petals, and leaves. A collection of blue bottles lined the shelves above. Ethelred unstopped a bottle and sniffed it.

His attention fell on a scrap of paper, and he turned it toward the window to read the scribbled words. "Infusion of Henbane," he murmured and reached for another bit of paper. "Bark of Mezereon Spurge, just a pinch. Devil's bit, with Honey of Roses."

Christian caught sight of a scrap by his toe. Thinking it another ingredient, he picked it up and unrolled it. *Archbishop Thurstan denies interdict at Helmesly. Ethelred comes today to make inquiry.* As he read the warning a second time, the full implication of its existence came to him.

Someone at Helmesly had been spying on Gilbert's behalf! It was just as Sir Roger suggested the day he was given Clarise's letters. The evidence was overwhelming. The culprit could be just about anybody. He felt a stirring at the nape of his neck.

"Excellent," said Ethelred, holding several bits of parchment together. "This should be enough to implicate Gilbert." He looked at Christian. "I think we should go now."

Christian heartily agreed. The damp air of the cellar was worming beneath his armor. He felt distinctly chilled. "Just one more thing," he said, turning toward the cages behind him. Reaching high and low, he twisted the latches that held the animals captive. The first to break free was a filthy pig, who nosed his way free with a delirious squeal.

Ethelred gave Christian an approving look. Together they approached the stairs. With the good abbot still weak from his captivity, the climb up the narrow passage was laborious. Christian was tempted to pick the man up and carry him. There were so many matters to attend to.

They had ascended little more than halfway when the door above them yawned open. The Abbot of Rievaulx appeared with a candle in his hand. As they were disguised by the darkness, he failed to see them. But the noise of the liberated animals alerted him to trouble. He thrust the flame of his candle to a rush holder, and the tallowed rushes flared into life. The stairwell blazed with brightness.

"You!" cried Gilbert, his gaze sliding from one to the other. The sight of the Slayer so unsettled him that he dropped his candle. It sputtered on the steps and died. "What . . . what are you doing here?" he cried. "Brother Alec said he sent you away!"

"He misled you," Christian answered coolly.

"What have you got there?" Gilbert demanded, his gaze lighting on the paper in Ethelred's hands.

"Your notes," said the good abbot, with more strength than he'd shown previously. "There is evidence here that you have sickened your monks. Soon you will be thrust from office."

Gilbert began to breathe like a man running for his life. "You don't know what you're doing!" he cried. His hand went to the wall for support. "I have discovered a cure for the plague. If you destroy my work, the disease will continue to run its course. It will kill everyone, including you." He pointed. "You should never have come here!" He backed up a step, distancing himself.

Christian doubted his conscience would trouble him if he overlooked his scruples just this once and sent Gilbert on his way to his just reward. Despite the trappings of a monk, he was surely no servant of the Church.

The abbot withdrew another step. Christian suddenly realized that he intended to bar the door, locking them in the cellar. His first thought was for Clarise. He'd promised her he would hurry. With the window too small to slip through, his only alternative was to reach the door before the abbot had a chance to lock it.

Just then, he felt something brush by his feet. He glanced down and recognized the tail of a weasel as it streaked past. Gilbert failed to mark the animal's approach. A second later it rippled against his ankles. The abbot gave a cry of alarm and jerked his leg back. The weasel turned and sank his teeth into his leg.

Gilbert screamed. He tried to kick the weasel free. In the process, he lost his footing.

Christian watched in fascination as the abbot flailed. He seemed to hang for a moment in thin air before he lurched forward, pitching down the stairs. Christian snatched Ethelred out of harm's way. The two of them hugged the wall as Gilbert tumbled past. Together they winced at the sound of snapping bones.

Gilbert came to a rest at the bottom of the steps. He didn't move. A hedgehog trampled over him as it crossed the room.

It was clear even at a distance that the Abbot of Rievaulx had snapped his neck. His head lay at an odd alignment to his body. Christian and Ethelred shared a look. Without a word, they turned and followed the weasel up the stairs.

A reward for righteousness? Christian asked himself. So much had happened when he'd expected so little. It all seemed fantastical when considered in the light of logic. Yet of all the events of the morning, none seemed so miraculous as Clarise laying her palm against his cheek and announcing that she didn't love Alec. That she likely never had.

Suddenly it seemed a simple thing to shuck the mantle of darkness that had consumed him for years and trade it for a cloak of another color.

Clarise DuBoise wanted a champion? He would be the noblest hero she could possibly imagine.

Chapter Seventeen

Clarise felt as light as a feather as Christian swept her onto the back of his huge destrier and swung himself into the saddle behind her. She felt no fear as the midnight warhorse plunged down Rievaulx's steep hill, for his arm was locked beneath her breasts.

From the abbey's open gate, Alec waved farewell. It was up to him to advise his brethren of their circumstances. They were all still shaken by the news that their abbot was dead, killed by his own fall down the treacherous stairs. Clarise was thankful Ethelred could corroborate the tale. The warlord's reputation was such that he might fall under suspicion without a witness to the accident.

She glimpsed at Ethelred to see how he was faring. The good abbot rode double with one of the men-at-arms. It was agreed he would go with them to Helmesly to recover. Later he would travel to York and carry evidence of the abbot's treachery to the archbishop. He looked pale, but stronger for the warmth of the morning sun.

The fresh scent of heather helped to nudge their shock toward relief. Everything would return to normal at the abbey. The men would shake off the effects of the malignant herbs and rise again to their prayers. The vineyards would enjoy pruning and reseeding and would soon yield a harvest of green grapes.

From the circle of Christian's arms, Clarise gave a sigh of contentment. The wind rushed through her hair and whistled through the threads of her boy's attire, carrying away the musty odor of her prison cell. The sun shone warmly on her face. She was pinned securely to the man who'd snatched her from the clutches of evil.

After all the lies, the difficulties she had brought to his entangled life, he was willing to shelter her. Did this mean that he would help her with Ferguson?

"Relax," he said in her ear. "You are safe now." The words seemed a message to her anxious heart.

They thundered into the valley, past the waddle and daub structures of Abbingdon. Merchants peered from their window shops to identify the passersby.

Clarise experienced the peculiar contentment of going home. She reminded herself that there were many unanswered questions, not the least of which was what the Slayer intended for her. He'd said nothing about his threat to return her to Ferguson. Rather, the tender way that he held her close gave her hope that he would not. The spark of anger she'd witnessed earlier was gone.

She could only assume he would ask her to be his mistress again. While that prospect hadn't looked so grim from the vantage of a prison cell, it rankled her pride in the light of day. She would give anything to set her family free, but she couldn't give the Slayer her body without also giving him her heart. And to get the latter, he would have to profess an emotion other than lust.

The rise and fall of the horse's back lulled her into a trance. She stared at Christian's grip on the reins. The sun had tanned his long fingers to a shade of golden brown. She remembered how gently, how persuasively those hands had coaxed her toward surrender. A sigh escaped her lips. Her eyelids grew heavy.

She must have drifted off to sleep. When the rhythmic

movement of the horse ceased, she came awake. The warrior
had pulled them to a halt in the meadow outside his castle's
walls. His men-at-arms filed over the moat and out of sight.
"What are we doing here?" she asked, twisting around.

She felt him dismounting. Several strands of her hair
were caught in his mail. "Ouch!" she cried, reaching up to
save them.

He snatched her off the saddle with him and in the process lost his balance. They tumbled from the stirrups into the
stalks of wildflowers, with Christian taking the brunt of their
fall.

"Sorry," he managed to groan. He lay flat on his back beneath her, peering up at her with worry. "Are you all right?"

"Fine." She took her weight off him, rising to her hands
and knees. "My hair is caught in your armor." She tried to
free the troublesome snags. "Why did you stop here?" she
asked again. The strands had worked their way between the
links. She doubted she could pull them out without tearing
them.

He didn't answer right away. She stabbed him a look.
"Well?"

"You said you would have naught to do with me even if
I crawled on my knees begging your mercy," he reminded
her, his green eyes watchful.

Guilt elbowed its way to the forefront of her feelings. Her
heart beat faster. "I said all that?" she asked, wincing inwardly.

He nodded very seriously. "I intended to apologize before we entered the castle."

"You were going to apologize?" The very sweetness of
the gesture made her light-headed. "Why out here?"

He gave her his endearing half-smile. "So no one would
see me?" he admitted.

She punched him in the ribs and came away with bruised
knuckles. "Oh! Help me get my hair out," she snapped,
shaking her wounded hand.

His clever fingers went to work, and in seconds she was

free. "Thank you," she said, rolling away from him. She came to her feet and brushed the grass from her boy's braies. "You can get up now," she told him.

He pushed himself to his knees and reached for her. "Give me your hand," he said.

"My lord, you don't have to do this!" She had to wonder if she wasn't dreaming. The scenery was stunning. The petals of the flowers rippled under the breeze. The moat danced about the castle in sparkling, little waves. And the most notorious warrior in the borderlands was on his knees before her.

"Your hand, lady."

With a sigh she stuck her hand out for him to take. Pleasure feathered up her spine as he stroked her palm and brought her reddened knuckles to his lips. "I am groveling," he informed her as his mouth brushed her skin. "Perhaps you could still bring yourself to forgive me?" He darted her a pleading look from under his lashes.

The heat of his mouth reminded her of the scorching kisses they had shared the night he made his demands. "There isn't a need to apologize," she said breathlessly. "I brought it on myself. I was most deceitful, and I am sorry for the mistrust my lies had spawned."

"Forgiven," he said, cutting her off. "However, do you attempt anything so rash as worming your way inside an abbey again, you will answer for it."

She regarded him closely. Was he angry or merely concerned? "Will you get up now? You're going to snap the buckles on your knee-guards."

"I'm not done yet. There is something else I need to ask you while I'm down here."

"What?" The question came out on a breath of disbelief. Nay, surely he wasn't going to . . .

"Will you wed me?"

She told herself the wind was rustling the stalks of wildflowers. "What did you say?"

"Lady, will you marry me?" The naked fire in his eyes matched the intensity of the question.

The sun gathered warmth on her shoulders, but still she couldn't speak. Could this be the realization of her fantasies? Had a handsome warrior fallen helplessly in love with her? Did he want to cherish her always, give her children, gather her close on winter nights? "Why?" she asked in a thin, little voice.

He paused a moment. "Simon needs a mother" came his reasonable reply at last.

Some of her delirium dimmed. "Ah."

"And you need a knight to challenge your stepfather."

It was all so reasonable. She tugged her hand free and stalked a short distance away. Amidst a patch of tangle roses, she forced herself to forget her pique and think of the benefits.

He was right. She still required a champion. And Simon needed a mother—oh, how lovely it would be to claim him as her own! This was not some romantic fairy tale with a prince and a princess. He was the Slayer, for mercy's sake! Tying her name to his meant accepting the darkness that hovered around him and rose to consume him at unexpected moments. Could she live with that?

"Why not just demand that I be your mistress?" she asked with her back still turned. She needed more time to think.

He remained on his knees. "Two reasons," he said. "The first is that you deserve more."

She felt herself wavering toward acceptance.

"Secondly, I would like . . . a more permanent arrangement. I have a son to think of and no time for courting."

A thorn of disappointment pricked her heart. She hoped he would admit to harboring a *tendresse* for her. After all, he'd once admitted that he liked her. Wasn't love just a step above like?

She sternly put a stop to her runaway thoughts. Love was a fickle emotion. She'd fancied herself in love with Alec once, and those feelings had done naught but die a slow, frustrating death.

Nay, Christian was right. It was better to marry for the sound reasons he'd supplied.

As for his bleak reputation, she would let it work for her own ends. The Slayer would destroy her stepfather as only a ruthless warlord could. Following that, she could only pray that his sense of right and wrong would reemerge, bringing a balance of humors to his inner darkness.

With her decision made, she pivoted and came to stand before him. "Very well," she said, ready to set a seal on the bargain. "I agree to marry you."

His eyes blazed with triumph. He grabbed her wrists and tugged her down until she dropped to her knees before him. "You will never regret it," he vowed, cupping her face.

She wanted badly to believe him. She was keenly aware of the leashed strength in his fingertips against her delicate skull. She shuddered with mixed ecstasy and dread as he pulled her close to claim her with a kiss.

Five days later Clarise descended the tower stairs with the feeling that moths were eating holes in her belly.

It was natural for any bride to feel nervous. Yet it wasn't solely the prospect of marriage to a warlord that worried her; it was the knowledge that Ferguson had come to the wedding as planned. He had pitched his tents outside the walls in the very meadow where Christian had proposed to her. He had come believing that an alliance was about to be forged. He had no idea that the Slayer intended to kill him during a joust tomorrow.

It was Christian's notion, drawn from the game Ferguson had invented when he sent her mother pounding at the gates of Glenmyre. Clarise had doubts that Ferguson would accept the offer: he'd wanted the Slayer dead, after all. But apparently the lure of having the Slayer for an ally was even more tantalizing than having him dead. The promise of a wedding and a tourney had lured the Scot to Helmesly. Clearly he was all too eager to expand his power.

Perhaps if Clarise knew more details about the Scot's ultimate demise, she could focus on her marriage. But Christian had been stubbornly silent on the subject. "Am I not the warrior?" he'd pointed out one night. "Are you not the maid? You've carried the burden of your family's plight long enough, Clarise. Leave the rest to me." It wasn't that she didn't trust Christian; rather, it was Ferguson whom she did not trust.

"Do you see any wrinkles in my gown, Nell?" she asked, trying to recall the wedding vows she'd committed to memory.

"Nay, milady," assured the servant, descending the tower steps behind her.

"What about my hair? Is it staying up?"

"Ye look perfect, milady. Like a queen."

Her gown had been cut from a cream-colored bolt of Normandy silk, procured from a silk merchant who'd come to Abbingdon. It clung to every curve of her body before streaming behind her in a shimmering cascade. Her hair was caught up in a tiara of pearls with a matching girdle slung low on her hips. She believed that she had never looked lovelier in her life. Would it make the mercenary speak the words of love she still foolishly wanted to hear?

Given the scents wafting up the tower stairs, the wedding feast would be one befitting a queen. Christian and his master-at-arms had gone hunting every day to procure the necessary fare. Clarise doubted she would manage to eat any of it. What if Ferguson had a plan of his own? What if his toxic powders found a way into the food?

Surely Christian would have taken measures to prevent that. She considered the man she was about to wed. It still came as a shock to think of herself as the Slayer's bride. At the mere mention of his name, peasants still crossed themselves and fled. The tragedy at Wendesby would live with him forever.

She asked herself for the hundredth time if she was making the right decision. His behavior since the day of their proposal had given her no reason to change her mind. He'd treated her with abundant generosity and unfailing chivalry, assigning her a seamstress to provide her with a new trousseau. A perfume merchant arrived yesterday morning bearing an assortment of oils and perfumes. A tapestry weaver, hired to create five new tapestries for the castle, had requested her input on the size and color of each. Her groom gave her leisure to do all this while he planned the details of the wedding and tourney.

She knew that the Abbot of Revesby would marry them. Ethelred had procured a special license while conferring with the archbishop. Elections were already in process to determine who would take Gilbert's place at Rievaulx. It was no secret that Ethelred, desiring to see his former abbey flourish, would be happy to accept the position if offered.

One villain down, thought Clarise as she edged toward the balustrade to peer down into the bustling hall, *and one to go.*

She braced herself for the sight of her stepfather. She saw at once that Ferguson had brought more than half his men with him. Their pea-green plaid was unmistakable, as were their bare knees in kilts. They milled impatiently in the great hall, gathering closely about the fire pit as though anticipating the fires of hell that awaited them.

She backed up until her spine was pressed to the wall. Her mouth had gone dry at the sight of their too familiar faces. Kendal, Rowan's father, stood with his shoulders hunched and his eyes glittering with the desire for vengeance. It came as little comfort that his only weapon was a costume sword, its scabbard encrusted with rubies, emeralds, and sapphires. Clarise didn't doubt it was sharpened in anticipation of conflict.

She summoned the courage to look again. Her eyes sought and found her stepfather. He lounged behind his men, using them as a shield in the eventuality of a scuffle.

The smirk that rode the edges of his orange mustache contrasted sharply with Kendal's fury. He looked well pleased, she thought, thinking himself allied with the Slayer. Hatred and grief wound themselves about her throat and squeezed. He did not deserve to be happy, she thought, when he had brought her family so much pain.

Her gaze slid to the women huddling beneath the window, and she gave a gasp of mixed delight and dread. Her mother and sisters had come! Jeanette was even wearing a presentable gown, though her hair was still gnarled and her expression haunted. Merry looked nearly as distressed as her mother. Her fire-red hair had been covered with a headdress, but she stood with her arms crossed and her green eyes darting nervously. Only little Kyndra, her hand tucked in Merry's arm, looked pleased to attend a wedding. Blond and guileless, she was too young to scent the current of danger in the air.

If God were merciful, Clarise thought, they would all be free of Ferguson by the morrow.

Suddenly a Scot caught sight of her. He nudged his partner, and a dozen curious gazes rose above the tapestry of the hunt. A rash of pinpricks broke out on Clarise's skin.

"Daughter!"

The cry startled her. Her mother had seen her as well. Clarise watched with alarm as Jeanette struggled to claw through the wall of Scottish soldiers to get to her.

"Get back, wench," one of them growled, shoving her into the wall again.

"Leave her go," said Ferguson. His eyes glittered with contempt. "Let her make a fool o' herself."

Jeanette shot through their ranks, not waiting for her daughters, who trailed behind. Up the stairs she scrambled, leaving Clarise torn between panic and the desire to greet her halfway. She took several steps toward the stairs. Her mother gained the last step and raced forward, her eyes wild with alarm.

"Daughter!" she cried again. She flung her bony arms around her and held her tightly.

Clarise felt her mother tremble. Her own arms folded protectively over her. "Hush, Mother. Everything's all right."

"My dear, how have you been?" Jeanette cried. She pulled away and clasped her daughter's face in her hands. "Oh, but you look so beautiful!"

She wished she could say the same of her once-lovely mother. Jeanette was as thin as a wraith. Her cheeks were now hollow, and her hazel eyes had lost their luster. "I am well, Mother," she answered earnestly. Her gaze moved beyond her mother's shoulder to Merry and Kyndra, now gaining the second level. "Sisters!" she cried, holding her arms out to them, also.

They huddled together, embracing fiercely, their eyes wet with tears, their hearts aching.

"I have found help," Clarise whispered, taking care not to be overheard. "The Slayer will reclaim our home."

The blare of a trumpet signaled that the wedding was about to commence. All and sundry began to file through the forebuilding and out to the chapel. "Stay with me," Clarise implored, gripping them tightly. "You need not go with them."

The Scots looked to Ferguson for permission to proceed. In a tightly knotted group, they marched toward the chapel, ignoring the women who remained on the gallery.

At last the only people left below were the servants laying out the fare.

"You don't have to marry him!" Jeanette blurted. She seemed suddenly stronger than she had seconds before.

"I have a poison for you," her younger sister added, pressing a satchel into her hand. "You can kill him ere he takes you to his bed."

Clarise regarded them both with amazement. "Nay," she said, "you misunderstand, both of you. I am not being forced in any way. 'Tis my choice. The Slayer is going to help us."

"Hah, he's another like Ferguson," her mother insisted. "He has killed women and children. I heard he even killed his first wife."

She gripped her mother's arms. "Mother, I am not being coerced. You have to trust me in this matter. Christian is an honorable man, not a murderer. I will wed him of my own free will," she insisted.

Merry hissed a breath through her teeth. "He's put you under a spell!" she guessed, her green eyes enormous.

"Stop it!"

"How could you want to marry such a man?" her mother asked. "Do you want to end up like me?"

A movement drew Clarise's gaze to the window. It was a pigeon, launching itself into flight. Could her mother be right? She shook her head. Nay, she believed in the better side of Christian de la Croix. Besides, if she didn't marry him, who then would save her family from their misery?

No one.

In truth, she had no choice. But it didn't help to have them planting doubts in her mind.

There was more to this marriage than the promise of Christian's help, wasn't there? After the tourney tomorrow, their marriage would hinge on something other than Ferguson. The question was, what?

Nell called her name. "Milady, Sir Roger doth give his summons," she pointed out. Indeed, the knight had poked his head through the double doors and was signaling them to descend.

"Hear me out," Clarise said firmly to her mother and sisters. "This marriage is our best chance at destroying Ferguson. Do not meddle in the matter. The Slayer is not like him," she added. "He's a far better man, an honorable man. I do not need this poison," she added, thrusting it back at Merry.

"Come," she added when they simply gawked at her. "The sooner this is done, the sooner you'll be safe." Taking her mother's hand, she led them down the sweeping stairs and across the hall, where Roger held the doors. As they approached the knight, she could see the interest and the pity in his eyes as he beheld her mother. "My lady," he said, bravely addressing her. "May I have the honor of knowing your name?"

Startled, Jeanette looked to Clarise for instruction.

"This is my mother, Lady Jeanette," Clarise said, making the introductions. "My sisters, Merry and Kyndra."

He repeated each of their names, giving them all a gallant bow. Then he turned his focus to Jeanette. "Will you grant me a token for the tourney tomorrow?" he begged her.

Flustered, Jeanette looked down at herself in vain, for she wore no jewelry of any kind.

"Give him one of your ribbons," Clarise suggested.

It was a simple task to tear a pink ribbon from Jeanette's dress. Sir Roger smoothed it reverently between his thumb and fingers. Then he led the way through the forebuilding to the chapel, gesturing for all the DuBoise women but Clarise to enter. He then offered her his arm, and she took it gratefully.

The harp fell silent at their entrance. Clarise was struck by the utter stillness of the vaulted chamber, especially given the number of witnesses standing wall to wall. Incense hung in fragrant spumes above their heads. The flames of a dozen torches kept a steady glow.

The aisle was a clear-cut path between the Scots on one side and the people of Helmesly on the other. Doris stood with Simon in her arms. As Clarise passed the baby, her heart swelled with love for him. *Soon, my sweet, I'll be your mother.*

Her gaze slid over a row of familiar faces and came to land on her groom. The Slayer stood before a candelabrum of five bright candles. They cast a brilliant haze about his torso. He wore a tunic of emerald silk—not black, she marveled with a curious sense of relief. The tunic deepened the green of his eyes as his gaze probed hers. Awareness plunged through her, deep and keen.

She felt much the way she'd felt at their first encounter. She was still struck by the size and breadth of him. The aura of power radiated from his being. Yet now she knew that the look in his eyes was neither ruthlessness nor a quest for blood. Instead, he looked worried she might change her mind and bolt from the chapel.

She looked at Christian's scar for the courage. More than anything, the scar was a reminder of the faithful child in him. The band of apprehension eased around her chest. She took a cleansing breath. Despite the doubts her mother and sister had spawned, she believed he would overcome the demons of his past. She had no choice but to believe it.

As she slipped her fingers into his warm grasp, she felt his squeeze of reassurance. "You steal my breath, lady," he murmured in a voice threaded with awe.

Bemused by his compliment, she looked down at their hands. His strong, tanned grasp looked enormous in contrast to her pale, slim fingers. The sight was both reassuring and disturbing.

Ethelred launched into the Latin service. In a matter of minutes she was bound to the Slayer for a lifetime. For the sake of fulfilling her father's request, she said, "I do."

For the sake of her own private yearnings—a warrior to retake her home, a lover to cherish her, and a friend to keep her company through good and through evil—she sealed her promise with a kiss.

"Will my lady eat?" Christian asked in her ear.

Clarise eyed the lozenges of curd cheese, bacon and walnut stew, hazelnut crumble, and crustade of chicken with mistrust. The centerpiece was a whole, stuffed swan, dressed in its own feathers and swimming on a sea of lettuce. The fare surpassed anything she had ever seen before, but she couldn't bring herself to take a bite.

"I cannot," she admitted. She cut a distasteful glance at her stepfather and found him enjoying himself immensely. His beard was sticky with grease. A horn of ale was clutched

in his left hand. He looked happy indeed thinking himself allied with the Slayer.

Just you wait, she thought.

Her groom leaned in closer. The warmth of his shoulder
spread quickly through the silk of her gown. "The food has
not been tampered with. I posted guards at every door. Look
you, even Ferguson is eating."

Nearly everyone was enjoying the feast. Trestle tables
groaned beneath the weight of so much food. Wine and ale
warmed the blood of those imbibing freely, especially the
Scots who celebrated the forging of an important alliance.
Tongues began to wag, and boasts could be heard over the
jangling of the juggler's bells. A minstrel of far better skill
than Rowan sang both Scottish ballads and Norman tunes,
while fighting men tapped toes beneath the boards. Given
the bright ribbons that festooned the lord's table, one might
be deceived that the atmosphere was gay.

"You should not have let them bring their swords inside
the walls," she whispered tensely. "Look at Rowan's father.
See how much he hates you."

The warlord cast Ferguson's henchman a considering
look. "Hush, sweetling," he soothed. "Our broadswords can
cut those paltry blades in half. There will be no uprisings.
Mark you how they drink and eat. They think their futures
secure. Besides, if there were danger, Sir Roger would sense
it. He has a gift for that sort of thing, you know."

She looked to Sir Roger for confirmation. The knight
took his ease in a chair opposite her mother and sisters. He
had eaten a good portion of his trencher and was sipping the
mulled wine with narrow-eyed satisfaction.

"I'm worried about tomorrow's tourney," Clarise admitted, turning back to her husband. "How will you kill Ferguson without starting a war?"

He silenced her with a sudden kiss. Her eyes flew wide
as she found herself gazing into his pupils. "Not now," he
whispered against her lips. "Tonight."

The recollection of the night to come sent a cataract of

chills down her spine. In response to her shudder, the warlord kissed her more deeply, his tongue stealing between her lips. The warmth of his kiss weakened her instantly. Over the thudding of her own heart, she heard the hoots of encouragement coming from the men at the boards. She imagined what she and Christian looked like to the assembly—newlyweds eager to spend time alone.

In her preoccupation with the tourney tomorrow, she had almost forgotten about their wedding night. Now, with his thorough kiss, she was startled by her own anticipation. If the preview he'd already given her was any indication, this would be a night she wouldn't soon forget.

He lifted his head at last, and her eyes floated open. She found him gazing at her with toe-curling intensity, a hint of color in his cheeks. "Perhaps you would care to retire, since you have no appetite," he suggested in a voice that made her stomach flutter.

She darted a look out the windows. It was shockingly early for them to retire. The sun was still a hot ball of fire sinking toward the west. "'Tis not yet sunset," she protested, though the notion greatly appealed to her. She didn't want to sit another minute watching Ferguson feast on his final supper.

The knowledge of tomorrow's violence left her queasy. She felt strangely guilty for plotting Ferguson's demise in such a cold-hearted manner. Moreover, it troubled her that Christian had not considered that war might break out.

"Will you come, too?" she asked. She yearned to speak with Christian in private, to calm her fears.

"In a while," he promised. "You should take some rest." His eyes glinted with sensual warning. "I vow you'll need it."

Her heart skipped a beat. To distract herself, she glanced toward her mother. Jeanette was seated next to Ferguson. She appeared to be in deep contemplation of her trencher. She had eaten no more than her daughter, though a fork was poised over the food in readiness. She hadn't been given a knife, apparently.

Clarise couldn't help but sense an air of determination about Jeanette. At Heathersgill, her mother had always behaved passively. Perhaps it was Sir Roger's flattering gaze that caused her mother to sit straighter, to hold her chin higher.

But Merry was another matter altogether. Clarise realized how little she had seen of her sister, even before leaving Heathersgill on her dangerous mission. Merry had taken to living in the hills with the cunningwoman who taught her of herbs and their powers. Even with her flame-red hair out of sight, there was something wild and reckless about the look in Merry's eyes. It pained Clarise to discover that her sister dabbled in poisons as well as herbs. *Look what Ferguson has done to her,* she thought. He deserved to die tomorrow. She wouldn't waste another drop of guilt for plotting his death.

She turned back to her husband. The strain of smiling under so much tension had drained her. "I think I will retire," she informed him wanly.

He pushed back his chair and helped her to rise. All conversation dimmed at once. Clarise concentrated on picking her way past the many guests at the table and ignoring the jests called out by brave or foolish soldiers. They wove their way among the trestles and came to the stairs. There Christian passed her on to Nell, who was waiting with the bloom of pleasure on her round cheeks.

"Anon," the warlord promised, bringing his hand up to caress her jaw.

He seemed distracted, Clarise thought, turning away with Nell. She looked back at him once, overcome by curiosity. Was he up to something? she wondered. She found him studying her ascension to the second level. He raised his goblet in salute, and she blushed at the attention, looking away.

Above the solar door was a garland made from lily of the

valley blossoms. She paused to admire it. With a proud smile, Nell opened the door to the bridal bower. The servants had thrown themselves into the wedding preparations. Even Dame Maeve had contributed her share of help, undertaking a frenzy of activities that included looping garlands around the bedposts and laying Clarise's new wardrobe in the chest toted from her bedchamber.

The room smelled of summer lilies and heliotrope. The tallow lamps splashed white light onto the tapestries. Her new collection of perfumes was posited on the table next to Christian's books. A nightdress fashioned from the sheerest silk lay across the bed like icing on a cake.

Clarise absorbed every detail with a sense of unreality. Was this just a dream? Everything had come so easily. Even the passion and romance one normally associated with a love match seemed to find its way into the atmosphere, despite tomorrow's conflict. It left her wondering if she wasn't trying to delude herself. This *was* just a marriage of convenience, after all. No one had mentioned a word of everlasting love.

The train of her gown crackled over the rush mat as she crossed to the open window. With the onset of evening, the horizon was turning pale pink. A cool breeze stirred the loose tendrils of her hair. She sent her gaze over the outer wall and spied the collection of Ferguson's tents. Other competitors had come to test their skill at the tourney, adding a sea of bright canopies to the open field.

She turned away. This was her wedding night. Tomorrow would bring a deadly tangle of arms and the unexpected death of the Scottish leader. Would the Scots suspect foul play and rally behind their murdered lord? Would a war break out at Helmesly?

She wanted to address these fears to Christian, only he had avoided all discussion of it earlier. And now he was lingering in the hall, playing the gracious host.

Clarise pressed a hand to her roiling belly. She wished she hadn't insisted that Ferguson be destroyed at once. Tomorrow's violence diminished tonight's possibilities. She felt as though something breathless and beautiful were on the verge of bursting from its chrysalis, only to be discouraged by the threat of winter. She wished she'd been more patient, allowing time for her marriage to mature.

Tonight, she wanted Christian to herself, with no worries intervening.

She comforted herself with the thought that she would have him every night hereafter, for the rest of their lives.

Chapter Eighteen

She was dozing against the heap of pillows when the door groaned inward. Clarise's eyes snapped open. Her indrawn breath congealed. She couldn't see the door for the bed curtains that barred her view. The room was steeped in stygian darkness.

If the intruder were her husband, she would have heard the revelers accompanying him to the bridal bower. Tradition dictated that they create a great clamor, thereby advising the bride of the groom's imminent appearance.

The door closed quietly behind the interloper. It couldn't be Nell, for she'd sent the maid away after brushing out her hair, applying more perfume, and donning her nightdress. Besides, Nell's footfalls were lighter.

A nameless fear raked Clarise's spine. It had to be a Scottish intruder, intent on murdering the bride. Poor Christian, she thought, unable to move for the terror that gripped her. He would be accused of killing her himself, just as he'd been accused of murdering Genrose. She could not allow that to happen. For his sake, she must summon the courage to move.

Now! She threw herself to the far side of the bed and dived under the closed drapes. Thudding to the floor, she scrambled up again. Her heart strained against her ribs. She lurched blindly toward the door, intent on ripping it open and running onto the gallery to scream for help.

She never made it to the door. Two powerful arms snatched her from behind, lifting her into the air. She screamed, and a hand clasped over her mouth. "Quiet!" commanded a familiar voice. " 'Tis I, Clarise. Why are you fighting me?"

Fear drained away in such a rush that it left her limp. She sagged in her husband's arms, her legs useless to hold her weight. He lifted his hand from her mouth. "Are you all right?" he asked.

She nodded, dumbly.

The arms that held her became a tender circle.

Clarise was grateful for his support and the radiating warmth that soothed her trembling. Would she always associate his scent with comfort and security?

"Come back to bed," he urged, taking her hand. He stubbed his toe in the darkness and cursed. "Who doused the flames?" he asked irritably.

"They were never lit," she said. "I went to bed when it was still light out."

He pulled apart the bed drapes while keeping one hand on her silk-clad waist. "Did you rest?" His palm smoothed upward to linger under the weight of one breast.

"Aye." His heat seemed to burn her through the flimsy fabric. "I was asleep when the door opened. I heard no revelers, my lord, so I assumed you were an intruder, intent on murdering me in my bed."

"Hush, that's an evil thought." He cupped her breast, his thumb rubbing over the nipple, pearling it instantly.

"And not beyond the scope of Ferguson's mind," she added breathlessly. "Why didn't I hear the revelers announcing you?"

They had been standing toe to toe in the darkness. Suddenly he stepped away from her, dropping his hand. "You must have slept through their noise," he said, crossing to the table. She heard him strike a flint before the room flared into view.

Her husband looked forbidding with the light shining on his face. Indeed, he was scowling. His scar stood out in pale relief.

"I hope I haven't upset you, my lord," she said, dreading the appearance of his darker side. He seemed preoccupied.

"Hmmm?" He glanced up from the flame. "Nay, 'tisn't you." He gazed at her thoughtfully a moment. "Your sister Merry, has she always been so fierce?" he asked.

"Merry?" *Oh, mercy, what has Merry done?* "She didn't try to poison you did she?" she asked, covering her mouth with her fingertips.

"Worse," he said. "She cursed my manhood."

Speechless, Clarise could only stare at him.

"'Twas during the toasting. She stood, and before the Scots and everyone, she said—let me see if I recall the words correctly—she said, 'To the groom. May your ballocks shrivel and fall off if you dare ever to strike my beautiful sister.'"

"She didn't!" Clarise gasped, appalled that Merry could have made such an unladylike threat. "I'm so sorry," she added, trying to guess the extent of his upset.

He shrugged. "I don't fear her threat," he said. "Only cowards use their strength against the weaker sex. Besides, she was right." He flicked her a look. "You are beautiful."

"My lord, she doesn't know you," Clarise explained. "All she knows of warring men is what Ferguson has demonstrated. Do you see what he has done to our family?" She gestured. "He has made my mother but a shadow of herself. He has made my sister crazed!"

"Let's not talk of Ferguson," he curtly interrupted, turning to the window. As he opened the shutters, the light of the full moon flooded the chambers, lending an ethereal glow to their boudoir. "Perfect," he said, with forced satisfaction. "Can you see the moon from the bed?"

She could see nearly the whole face of the moon through

the open window. For modesty's sake, she thought it better to keep the room in darkness. Clearly, her groom thought otherwise. "'Tis lovely," she relented.

He turned and looked at her, and his expression transformed from brooding to awestruck. "Nay, 'tis you who are lovely," he corrected her. His gaze fell to her bosom, outlined in a gown so sheer it might have been woven by spiders. She had a feeling he could see straight through it.

Her recent fright was forgotten. Tomorrow's tourney seemed eons away. There was only the two of them now and a night that promised so much. His admiring gaze made her feel alluring, a siren beckoning him into the seas of bliss. Suddenly she was happy to let the moon reveal her best-kept secrets.

His hands went to the buckle on his belt. The thick strap dropped to the mat with a soft *chink.* He put one boot on the chest, unbuckled it and cast it off. The other boot followed. With his gaze still intently on her person, he unwound the leather strips that crisscrossed the length of his legs. The tunic he yanked over his head followed by his undershirt. In a single movement, he pushed his chausses over his hips, drawing them off, drawers and all.

Clarise could scarcely breathe by the end of his undressing. She reeled to find him suddenly naked, muscles oiled in moonlight. The size of the weapon jutting from the thatch of dark hair at his groin had her sinking weakly onto the bed.

Her gaze traveled wondrously over his naked form. Every muscle stood in stark relief, enticing the light to gleam on the upraised surfaces and the shadows to linger in the valleys. The closer he sauntered, the more details sprang into view. She felt herself growing dizzy.

"Are you afraid?" he asked, sitting smoothly beside her.

She marveled at the breadth of his chest, dark hair gleaming on it like a shield. "Nay," she admitted, surprised by her own realization. She remembered the tenderness of his kisses. He would be gentle with her, she was certain.

He let out a long breath. "I am," he admitted gruffly.

She looked abruptly at his face. "You are?" She would never have thought he would admit to such masculine insecurity.

"Afraid I'll hurt you," he told her, raking a hand through his savage hair. "You're an untried maiden, and I am not a small man. I want to give you pleasure tonight, not pain."

"Afraid of my sister's threat?" she teased, glancing down at his upright member. "'Twould be a shame for it to wither and fall off."

Despite the seriousness of the moment, she managed to make him laugh, a rusty sound that made her want to reach for him and kiss him soundly. "You won't hurt me, my lord," she added, smoothing a hand over the muscles of his upper arm. So much latent power! "I promise, 'twill be all right."

He leaned slowly toward her. With aching tenderness, he kissed her mouth, gaining entrance so painstakingly that she looped her arms around him and pulled him harder to her. The feel of his bare skin was intoxicating. Both times he'd had her in his bed, he'd been fully dressed. Now, she could not get enough of his warm, densely muscled body. His skin felt like silk over steel. It smelled of manliness and juniper-scented soap.

He pressed her down onto the pillows, then rolled abruptly onto his back, taking her with him. "You set the pace," he said, his hands searing through the fabric of her gown. She lay sprawled across his hard body, one leg between his. He waited.

"I . . . I have no idea what to do," she said, flushing self-consciously.

"Aye, you do," he replied. "Just kiss me."

She shyly complied, putting her mouth to his, her hair falling in a silken curtain around them. He responded with retrained savagery, and she found it exhilarating to control how long, how deep. She drove him to hungry desperation, then pulled away, placing petal-soft kisses at the corner of

his mouth, along his jaw. She nibbled daintily on his ear-
lobe, drawing a groan from him.

His reaction mounted her excitement. She squirmed
against him, seeking his hardness instinctively, not knowing
where or how to focus the growing hunger inside of her, the
ache in her breasts.

"Put your knees here," he instructed, patting the mattress
on either side of him.

He helped her, lifting the silk of her gown so it wouldn't
tear. Its hem rode the tops of her thighs, giving him a
glimpse of her bright woman's hair. Christian closed his
eyes in pleasure as she settled down on him, not penetrating
but touching thigh to thigh.

Stunned by their closeness, Clarise tensed, half fearful of
the thick column pressed against her tender flesh. "Get used
to me," he said. "Touch me as you please."

She obeyed, her hands trembling with awe as she spread
them on his raised chest muscles. Her fingers tangled in the
crisp mat of his chest hairs. She caressed the tiny male nipples that grew erect at her touch. She drew her fingers lower,
across the armor of his rib cage to the flat plane of his belly,
where a line of hair tapered to his loins. His indrawn breath
made her ask in deight, "Are you ticklish, my lord?"

He grabbed her wrists before she could tickle him.
"Don't," he warned.

She longed to make him laugh again, but then he released
her to caress her thighs, and she forgot her intent. He caressed her, using the silk of her gown to enhance his touch.
The cool glide of the material ignited a shimmering heat in
her belly. She rocked her hips instinctively, encountering his
hardness.

Very gently Christian rolled her over. It fulfilled an in-
stinctive need in her to feel his weight pressing against her.
She'd touched and explored him; she was ready to join with
him if the time was right. He pressed a kiss to her temple, to
her cheek, her jaw. He nuzzled her neck, making her giggle
as the bristles on his chin tickled her.

"Are *you* ticklish, my lady?" he countered. Laughter became a gasp as he nipped the crowns of her breasts through the fabric of the nightdress. He slid the capped sleeves over her shoulders, baring her breasts one at a time to his view. The firm orbs glowed in the moonlight. He took them deep in the heat of his mouth, sucking as he'd done before. Clarise's gasp became a moan. Pleasure arrowed downward, summoning warmth and wetness between her thighs.

Feeling his knee between her legs, she parted them, tensed for the thick invasion that was to come. But then he moved clear down the length of her body, pinning her thighs wide open with his hands. He kissed the insides of her legs where her skin was the most sensitive. She leaped and squirmed to keep the rasp of his jaw from scraping her.

All at once his mouth landed on the curls between her legs, and she froze in astonishment. She could scarcely breathe. Then Christian delved deeper, tasting her.

She lurched to her elbows. "What are you doing?" she gasped.

The firm, moist ridge of his tongue slid into the folds of her flesh. She tried to twist free, but he held her fast and repeated the scandalous caress. "My lord!" she cried, amazed by the searing pleasure washing over her. "Oh, heavens!"

"Relax," he said. "Feel me."

She fell back with a cry of surrender. How could she do anything but feel him? He caressed her intimately, acquainting his tongue with every one of her secrets. Driving her relentlessly to a place she'd never been before. Sensations built one on top of the other, threatening to wash over her.

He slipped a finger inside of her. She bit her lip to keep from screaming. He stretched her gently, never ceasing his scandalous caresses. Her muscles tightened. A scalding flush brought perspiration to her skin. She felt fevered, a little frightened by the intensity of her pleasure. Surely, if she let herself go, these feelings would consume her.

Without warning, he covered her again. His mouth sought hers, and he kissed her deeply, hungrily. Tasting her woman's musk on his lips, she became a creature of instinct. Her hips rose to greet his tumescence, needing, longing for him to ease the sudden emptiness.

She expected some measure of pain, but it would be far worse a plight to be deprived of the sensations she'd just felt. He continued to kiss her as the tip of his manhood nudged her opening. Then with a sudden surge, he tore through her resistance, and sank himself to the hilt. The sting of pain was so intense, she failed to swallow her cry. She tried desperately to back away from it, but she could not. She was impaled by him.

Just as suddenly the pain receded. She let out a sigh of relief. And then she became aware of a gratifying, overwhelming fullness.

"Clarise?" he whispered, his voice strained by some private torment. "Are you all right?" He lifted his head and looked at her, his eyes glazed with passion.

"Fine," she reassured him, though her own voice was thin and high. "The pain is gone."

He pulled out of her slowly, leaving a trail of fire along her woman's passage. Clarise hissed at the scalding heat, yet at the same time she felt a sudden deprivation.

He sank back into her softness, making her sigh. There was no pain this time, only a warm rush of fullness. "Again," she cried, as the pleasure she'd felt before gathered unexpectedly.

"By God, I don't deserve this," he murmured, breathing heavily. "You are so lovely, so sweet." He raised her legs higher, so that on his next thrust, he sank even deeper. Clarise moaned at the sweet satisfying sensation of his claim.

Their shadowed gazes merged. Buttered in the moonlight, he looked somehow familiar to her, his body ridged with passion. Had she dreamed him? Their lips gently touched. Their bodies came together, sweaty now, taut and straining. She arched her hips, craving more. He set a tempo that nudged her higher with every thrust. She fisted the bed-sheets in one hand and clutched him with the other.

He began to whisper as he'd done before, scalding words that made her shiver and pant. She clung to his broad shoulders. *I am one with the Slayer,* she marveled. *He is part of me forever.* She opened herself to be ravished. Gently, but inexorably, he slid inside of her, again and again, deeper and deeper. He told her how she made him feel—how sleek, how wet, how tightly she held him.

His words pushed her over the top. With a soft cry, she came undone. Her pulsing muscles beckoned him to follow. He groaned against her mouth, thrusting three more times. Then he stilled, his heart thudding hard against her breasts.

After a moment he took his weight on one elbow and tucked a lock of hair behind her ear. Then he traced the graceful arch of her eyebrow, the full sweep of her lower lip. "You make me forget," he whispered on a note of wonder.

"Forget what, my lord?" She could barely think, let alone remember anything.

"Christian," he said, reminding her to say his name.

She smiled, cherishing the intimacy. "Forget what, Christian?"

He looked down at her breasts, pressed to his chest. "Who I am," he said at last. His lashes swept up again. He gave her his semi-smile and kissed her, lingering with such tenderness it made her eyes sting.

She didn't know what to say to his confession. She savored the closeness of their bodies, of their mind and spirits. "What will we be when tomorrow is over?" In the unguarded moment the question slipped out of her.

He held her more firmly. "What do you mean?" he asked, sounding as worried as she felt.

She smiled ruefully and looked away. "Never mind."

"Nay, tell me what you meant," he insisted.

How to put it in words? "Will I ever be more to you than a mother for Simon?"

Her question visibly startled him. He took a deep breath

and pressed himself deeper. She fancied she could feel him swelling inside of her again. "You are already more," he growled.

The answer pleased her, as did the echoing tingle at her core. He caught her mouth in a kiss that was frankly ravenous. His sudden hunger sparked her own. She met his thrusts with a deep, answering need.

A long time later they lay among the twisted sheets, a sheen of sweat on their skin. She asked him another question that was nagging her. "How will you kill Ferguson tomorrow and make it look like an accident?"

She felt him tense against her. "I don't want to talk about the morrow," he replied, his tone suddenly dangerous.

The sound of his voice made her shrivel inside, but she was not so easily turned away. "Why won't you tell me what you've planned?" she persisted. "All you've said is that you'll kill him in a joust. How, without rousing the suspicions of his men, without causing a war?"

A full minute passed, and still he did not answer. Disappointed, she laid her head back on his shoulder, fearing she had angered him.

"There will be no war," he whispered with certainty.

She wondered how he could be so sure. She listened to the even thud of his heart. Her fingers coiled gently around the soft whorls of his chest hair. She closed her eyes and breathed a sigh of repletion.

They would still have *this* when tomorrow was over. Perhaps their passion would deepen to abiding affection. It was a simple thing to imagine, a natural thing. She snuggled closer. She felt treasured and replete. She had a strong arm to protect her. A lover to warm her on winter nights. It was more than most women had in a husband.

A soft snore followed on the heels of her observation. Christian had fallen asleep. At least he had the peace of mind to do it. Her mouth quirked. For herself, she doubted she would sleep at all on the eve of Ferguson's demise.

•   •   •

At the crack of dawn Christian garbed himself in chain mail and led his mount across the drawbridge. With the visor of his helm open, he absorbed the scene that awaited him. Ferguson's warriors were up and stirring, their green plaid buried under thick, steel hauberks. They had traded their costume swords for sturdier weapons.

They milled about a campfire, their expressions grim. What had begun as an alliance would end in war if Ferguson failed to meet the challenge the Slayer had put to him last night.

Christian recalled the Scot's expression when he'd charged him of his crimes before the wedding guests. He had sent Clarise to their bridal bower to shield her from any potential ugliness. He wished he could have done the same for her mother and sisters, who'd looked on, as pale as ghosts.

At his challenge, the Scot had spewed ale across the table. He'd blustered and protested. He'd turned an alarming shade of red. Kendal had lunged across the table with his costume sword in hand, only to be restrained by his own men. The Slayer's men-at-arms displayed the points of their swords to discourage the Scots from reacting rashly.

Ferguson's protests could not sway the warlord from standing in judgment of him. *To prove your innocence, Ferguson, you must meet me tomorrow in a contest of arms, a battle to the death.*

In declining, the Scot would have found himself and his men slaughtered in the Slayer's hall. The gauntlet had been tossed, and Ferguson accepted it, with no other choice.

How quickly the night had sped by! The sun was already edging over the treetops. Peasants tromped across the meadow from their far-flung huts in order to satisfy their curiosity. Did they know the tourney had given way to a deadlier sport? Christian wondered.

He glanced over his shoulder at the sharply rising wall of the castle. He couldn't see the solar from his present vantage, but he imagined that his bride still slept. She was rarely

up before mid-morning. Had he done the right thing to keep
the truth from her? It had been hard to think of little else
when he joined her in the bridal bower. But later, as he drew
her tender body close to him, he'd felt a peaceful certainty
in his soul. And then he'd slept—by God, he'd slept the entire night without waking! It had been the best sleep of his
adult life.

He wondered, now, if he should have told her everything.
She'd assumed the Scot would come to some accidental end,
that Christian would kill him by devious means. She did not
fully realize the metamorphosis for which she was responsible. The only way to prove his worthiness was to slay Ferguson by honorable means: by Ordeal by Combat. That way
Ferguson, at least, could defend himself, and neither Christian nor Clarise would be troubled by their conscience later.
He knew too well the torment of a troubled conscience. His
wife would never suffer such agonies, he vowed.

Still, he wished Clarise could watch him do it. *How he
longed to be worthy of her!* But her peace of mind and her
physical safety came first. He could not trust her to remain
an impartial observer. Clarise was too loyal, too protective.
She forgot at times that he had spent his adult years learning
to fight. She thought she could do it better.

Nor did he trust the Scots not to target her in some way,
thereby forcing his surrender. Nay, it was best she remained
where she was, sleeping peacefully in bed, her body soft and
warm beneath the coverlet.

Sir Roger scurried around the front of his horse, breaking
into Christian's thoughts. "My lord, I have a bad feeling
about this," he volunteered, catching his liege's arm.

Christian shook him off. This was not the time for
Roger's sixth sense to kick into action. "'Tis too late to
change my mind," he snapped at his vassal. All he could do
at this late point was to calm his roiling nerves.

"Look for trickery, then," Sir Roger cautioned, his scars
bulging with concern. "He knows he cannot defeat you. He
will try something underhanded, mark my word!"

They led their horses off the drawbridge and onto the road. Christian's armor made a chinking sound with every step. "We fight hand to hand," he told his vassal. "Do you remark any trickery, then by all means strike the Scottish forces. But do so hard. I would not have any finding their way into the castle. Signal for the drawbridge to close."

"Aye, my lord."

"Should something happen to me—"

The knight cursed, looking away.

Christian stopped and put a gauntleted hand on his vassal's shoulder. It took effort to push the words past the constriction in his throat. "Do whatever it takes to keep my lady content in life and to assure Simon's inheritance. Remember we suspect a traitor in our midst."

Sir Roger's mouth thinned. "It *will* not come to that," he growled, as if to convince himself.

The fighting had been moved from the outer ward to the meadow outside the walls. The field afforded them more room for maneuvering. It would keep the Scots from spawning mischief in the castle to distract them. "They're waiting," Christian urged, nodding toward the area that was already roped off.

As they neared the meadow, the sun spilled over the hill in a bloodred stain. Christian's gaze fell upon a blackbird as it swooped from the sky to steal a hot bun dropped by one of the spectators. When he next looked toward the tents, he was looking at Ferguson.

The Scot had emerged from his tent wearing English armor, his helm in his hands. Despite his indulgence the night before, he looked fit and fierce. His eyes were focused and clear above his burnished beard. At the sight of his double-edged ax, several onlookers backed away, giving him clear berth to approach the field.

Christian looked for Ethelred, standing alone with his cowl pulled over his head. A more reluctant participant could not have been found to shrive the two combatants.

The good abbot gave him an imploring look as they came closer.

Unable to meet the abbot's gaze, Christian focused on Ferguson instead. To bolster his enthusiasm, he recalled the nineteen peasants cut down at Glenmyre, the ravaging fire, Clarise's mother begging to be let through the gate. He gave a thought to Clarise's father, brought to an early demise by the Scot's artifice. And lastly, he thought of the pink scars on Clarise's beautiful back, put there by this barbarian.

By the time Christian's soul was properly commended to God, he was fully ready to spill the Usurper's blood.

"Choose your weapon, Ferguson," Sir Roger charged, acting as intermediary.

The Scot gripped the handle of his ax and grinned like a cunning fox. Christian reached over his shoulder to pull the hilt of *Vengeance* from its sheath.

"You will begin at the sound of the horn. May the first to be unseated defend himself as best he can. Any violation of the code of honor shall end the tournament." Sir Roger's tone became threatening. He made it clear to everyone gathered that a breach of the rules would result in war. Behind them, men-at-arms watched each other warily.

"Mount your horses." Sir Roger's final words saw Ferguson spinning away toward his sorrel. Christian tightened the girth on his saddle. With nothing left to delay him, he heaved himself onto his mount and gave the destrier a jab. He trotted to his position on the far side of the field.

Turning by a copse of beech trees, he waited for the horn that would hurl him into combat.

Time stood still. Only the rapid beating of his heart assured him that the seconds ticked by. He found himself wishing suddenly that Clarise were in attendance after all. With the light of her eyes on him, he would feel himself cloaked in her protection. He imagined her standing at the edge of the field, a faint smile of encouragement on her lips. She'd believed in him last night. *'Twill be all right,* she'd assured him. He repeated the words to himself. *I promise, 'twill be all right.*

He had to win. There was no room for defeat.

If he did not emerge the victor, he would never know if his plot to win her heart bore fruit. Or withered like an unplucked grape.

Chapter Nineteen

The blast of a war horn caused Clarise to bolt upright. The shutters were ringed with morning light. Memories of her wedding night flooded pleasurably into her mind, and she fell back onto the blankets with a sigh. Her muscles were sore, as was the tender place between her legs. But she felt like a new woman, a butterfly freshly sprung from its chrysalis.

How foolish she was to have feared that marriage to the Slayer would bind her to a beast! He'd been gentle, considerate, unbelievably giving. She dragged a hand over her sensitive breasts. No longer did she worry what would become of their marriage after Ferguson's demise. A world of possibilities lay before them. With Christian's sword arm to defend them, their security at Helmesly was unbreachable. They would raise a family behind Helmesly's impenetrable walls and never know the terror of being overcome, displaced, violated.

Her palm smoothed the sheets where her husband had just lain. She found them cool to the touch. He'd been gone longer than she thought.

She sat up again, experiencing an odd sense of abandonment. Had the tourney begun already? Of course it had. A horn had just bayed outside her window. Being the host,

Christian had no choice but to rouse himself early and attend it. He had kindly thought to let her sleep.

Flinging off the coverlet, she crossed the room and threw the shutters wide, heedless of her naked state. She sensed a great stirring of activity on the eastern side of the field, but the window gave only a view of the tents with their pennants snapping.

She heard the telltale thunder of two combatants coming together. The repercussion of the blow carried clearly to the window. A roar went up in the crowd, conveying a sense of urgency.

She had planned to bathe and dress in one of her finest new gowns. But something came over her, gripping her with nameless agitation. She couldn't spare the time to bathe. She was galvanized to join the spectators right away.

Spotting the dress Nell had laid out for her, Clarise slipped it over her head, leaving the laces to dangle at her sides. Unable to locate her slippers, she gave up looking for them and dashed out of the room. The great hall below her was empty. Was she the only one missing the day's events?

Barefooted, she skipped down the wide stairs, shot through the double doors and down the steps of the fore-building. The courtyard was also deserted. She crossed it quickly, braving the cobbles that gouged her bare feet. She was hardly dressed like a proper hostess, yet she couldn't shake the feeling that something momentous was underway.

Lengthening her stride, she ran through the first gate to the outer ward. There she faltered at the sight of the empty lists. The tourney must have been moved to the field outside the castle. The urgency in her belly hardened into apprehension. Why would they have moved the tourney outside?

She bolted through the outer gates, pushing aside the guards that stood beneath the barbican. One of them tried to restrain her. "Let me go!" she demanded, sending him a look so fierce that he snatched his hands away.

She crossed the rough planks of the drawbridge, amazed to see that a throng had already gathered to witness the spectacle. More amazing still was the daunting display of weaponry on the men who jostled for a better view. She rose on tiptoe to catch a glimpse of the combatants. They must be well-known knights to have gathered so much attention.

Their mounts sailed off toward opposite ends of the field in preparation for another clash. She sought the insignia of the knight nearest her. When she saw the double-edged ax resting with deceptive ease on his thigh, she knew at once that the first opponent was Ferguson. Could this have something to do with the accident that would befall him today?

Her gaze swiveled to the second combatant. On the back of a huge black destrier sat a warrior of immense proportions. Her brain refused to believe what her eyes were telling her. But as his shield tilted in her direction, there was no mistaking the white cross on a black field.

She felt the blood drain from her face.

He'd never warned her that he meant to oppose Ferguson himself. Surely he didn't intend to kill him now, in this very event! As they raised their shields in a signal for readiness, the truth slowly penetrated.

He did. He intended to kill Ferguson in hand-to-hand combat, nobly and without deceit. That was the reason the tourney had been moved outside the castle, to more neutral ground. She gave a cry of denial. Didn't he realize it couldn't be done? Ferguson knew dozens of deceitful ways to fell his opponent, and Christian would suspect none of them!

That awful realization kept her rooted to the dew-laden grass, her toes curling to keep her upright. With the sound of thunder, the combatants converged in the center of the field. She told herself to rise from what surely was a nightmare. They collided in a screaming tangle of steel. This was not a dream.

The crowd roared with dismay as the horses parted with no advantage to either man.

Clarise plunged into the throng of spectators and pushed her way to the rope that kept them off the field. The sound of ringing metal had her peering over a woman's shoulder. She glanced up in time to see her husband thrust in slow motion from his horse. "Nay!" she screamed in denial. He managed to roll to his feet, but his helmet flew into the ankle-deep flowers, leaving his head vulnerable to attack.

Mercifully, the blow had also unhorsed Ferguson. The Scot was slower to rise, but his double-edged ax rose with him, singing a song of death as he arced it in a figure eight through the moist air.

With a distracted glance Clarise realized the woman in front of her was her mother. Jeanette stood very still by the rope partition. This morning she seemed in full control of her faculties. She watched the fight with steady eyes.

Clarise redirected her attention to the struggle now ensuing on foot. Why was this happening? Ferguson was to die in an accident, not in a blatant challenge. *Not in a scenario where he could easily cheat to meet his ends!*

What would happen if he won? My God, what would become of her if Christian were killed? What would become of her family?

The enemies circled each other cautiously. Ferguson was the first to strike. The blade of his ax slammed into steel as Christian lifted his shield at the last second. Clarise could imagine the impact shuddering down his arm. She winced for the pain he must be feeling.

Her husband stepped to one side, turning at the last moment to bring down his sword. The edge of *Vengeance* made sharp contact with Ferguson's arm, and the Scotsman howled in pain, clutching his wound. Clarise smiled grimly, her confidence returning.

Of course Christian would win. Was he not perceived as the mightiest warrior in the borderlands? Hadn't he earned the position of seneschal for his skill with a sword?

Ferguson recovered swiftly from the blow. Grinning beneath his helm, he calmly moved his ax into his left hand. The weapon whistled through the air as he closed in on his foe.

The Slayer bided his time, evading attack after attack with quick footwork and masterful use of his shield. His tactic was clearly to tire the Scot.

Soon enough, Ferguson's ax grew heavy. He lowered the weapon, and it was Christian's turn to be the aggressor. *Vengeance* caught and held the sun's fire as it sang through the air, seeking weakness in the older man's defense.

Though not as quick on his feet as his opponent, Ferguson held his ground. A blow from the broadside of Christian's sword sent him staggering backward. He stepped into a low area where he lost his balance. Then he toppled sideways into a thatch of carrot weed.

A joyous cry escaped Clarise's throat. It looked as though her husband would win the contest. Suddenly she realized that her mother had ducked beneath the rope and was racing into the field. Clarise called for her to stop, as interference at this point could escalate the conflict into war. But her mother was deaf to her cries, leaving Clarise with no option but to chase after her.

To her dismay, she saw her husband hesitate, his sword raised for the deathblow. The movement on the field distracted him. Her gaze flew to Ferguson, who was grappling in his boot for a second weapon. She screamed a warning to Christian.

But the shouts of the crowd drowned her cry. Ferguson surged from his crouched position. His hand sprang open, releasing a fine powder into the air. Christian staggered back, blinded by the invisible weapon. His broadsword fell heavily to the grass as he clapped his hands to his eyes and doubled over.

Ferguson adjusted his grip on the handle of his ax. Just as he hefted it to pursue his helpless opponent, Jeanette hurled herself onto his back. Clarise watched in wide-eyed shock as her mother sank a dinner knife deep into Ferguson's neck.

The Scot roared in surprise and shook off his assailant. Pawing at the haft that stuck from his throat, he gurgled words impossible to understand. All the while, Jeanette watched his contortions with indifferent calm. Ferguson spat blood. His face drained of all color, and then he fell face-first into the fragrant grass.

A hush of amazement had fallen over the crowd. Clarise transferred her attention to her crouched husband. He had sunk to his knees, his hands still pressed to his eyes. In contrast to his dark hands, his jaw looked ghostly pale. She hastened toward him, skirting her mother, who stood with arms akimbo over her dead husband.

"Christian!" she cried, dropping on her knees on the clods of dirt left behind from their battle. She grabbed his wrists and tried to pull his hands away. "Look at me!"

He groaned in agony. "I cannot. My eyes are on *fire*."

She gasped in alarm and twisted around to seek help. What she saw made her skin crawl. The Scots and the Slayer's men bristled with weaponry. They paired off, posturing their willingness to fight. "Oh, God!" she cried.

A shrill war cry broke the feeble thread of peace. With roars in their throats, men clashed with the intent to spill blood. Women screamed and ran. Peasants broke for cover.

"We have to get out of here," she told her mother and her husband in the same breath.

He made a sound like an animal in rage. "I cannot see!" he shouted.

"Hush, no one knows that but us. You must stand up. Stand up!" she ordered, tugging at his elbow. He came obediently to his feet, his palms still pressed to his eyes. "Take your sword," she said, heaving the heavy blade from the grass and holding it out to him.

He put a hand out, and she thrust the hilt into his palm. It frightened her to note the trembling in his fingers. She glanced with dismay at the wet bubbles seeping from beneath his eyelids. "Now take my hand," she instructed, darting a look at the men hacking one another just a few yards away. "Mother, stay close!" She grabbed her mother's arm and tugged her companions toward the castle.

"The drawbridge will rise," Christian advised them. "We must hurry."

"We will run, then. Hold your sword before you, my lord. Do not let go of my hand."

The three of them charged for the moat at a full run. Clarise steered them through the battleground. Screams of agony surrounded them. Blades bit into bone. The grass was slick with blood. Mercifully, no one challenged their passing.

At last they arrived at the drawbridge where the chains were already rattling the cogs. It was just beginning to go up. "Hold!" Clarise called, pulling her husband behind her.

Fury and the reluctance to flee from any battle made it difficult to persuade him. "You will come with us!" she insisted. "You are useless to your men right now."

She glanced at the skirmish behind them. The conflict had broken into pockets of fighting. Sir Roger led the largest contingent of men in pushing Kendal and his followers away from the field and off into the woods. Several were breaking away, fleeing into the vegetation for cover.

"'Tis almost over," she added to persuade him. "Sir Roger has it well in hand."

As they hurried along the planks, Clarise's temper rose in proportion to her relief. How dare her husband risk his own life just to kill her stepfather? For the first time in over a year, she had felt secure in the knowledge that she was wed to a man who could protect her. Yet he had nearly made her a widow within a day of her wedding. How dared he jeopardize that union as if it meant nothing to him!

"My lord," she pronounced as they passed through the inner ward, "I am furious with you!"

Christian stared through the film that blurred his vision and pieced together Clarise's features, relying as much on his memory as on what he could see. She sat at his writing table, reading the missive that had just arrived from Heathersgill. Her hair, recently washed and dried, gave off a luster that could be seen clear across the room. It fell in a glossy curtain over her shoulders, smelling of flowers. The scent reminded him of their wedding night, six long days ago.

He saw her mouth curve into a smile, and curiosity got the better of him. "What does he say?" he prompted.

She shifted, drawing up one knee. If he wasn't mistaken, she was dressed in a linen chemise and little more. It was nearly the end of summer, and the sun injected its last blast of heat into the air before the winds of autumn would drive it away. His wife dressed appropriately—which was to say that in the environment of their bedchamber, she wore only her undergarments.

For a man who hovered on the brink of complete recovery, it was sheer torment.

Not that he was ready to admit that his vision was practically restored. Though he was fit enough to resume his duties as seneschal, it had been only six days. Why admit to recovery when his wife pampered and fussed and cosseted him like a child? Given such gentle treatment, he found himself tempted to trade in his broadsword for the life of an invalid.

Every afternoon she read to him. How he coveted the sound of her voice, modulated to fit the text in her hand. As she read of Ulysses's trials at sea, her voice grew tremulous and brave. Boethius's *Consolation of Philosophy* made her soft and contemplative. Her emotional state seemed to alter with the direction of the wind at the window, while his could be summarized under the single heading of *Randy as a Bull*.

And there was no sign of relief in sight.

His wife's gentleness belied the physical distance she strove to keep between them. Her stinging declaration still echoed in his brain, murdering the hopes that died with gasping stubbornness in his breast. *I am furious with you!*

How could she have said such crushing words when he had sacrificed his very life to win her? If such a profound act failed to draw a proclamation of love, then nothing would. He consoled himself with the knowledge that he would always have her near him. Whether he might yet win her affection over time remained uncertain.

He was sure that she cared for him. Why else would she read and pass all idle hours in his company? Was it simply to exacerbate his constant state of arousal that she bathed and dressed and flitted around the room half-naked? Or did she mean to comfort him with her chatter?

He'd heard her in-drawn breath yesterday when the patches over his eyes were removed. Had she gasped because his eyes were swollen and ravaged, or because she cared for his pain as he flinched against the brightness?

Can you see, my lord? she'd asked so tremulously. He could have sworn there was a sheen of tears in her own eyes, but then his vision was hardly perfect. And he was annoyed that she'd gone back to "my lord" over his given name, further distancing them from their intimate encounter. Was he fooling himself in his need to hear a confession of love, or did the woman comfort him because it was her nature to do so? One cold truth remained, mocking his hope that he could still win her. *Ferguson was dead. She didn't need him anymore.*

"What does it say?" he repeated, refusing to give credence to his own depressing thoughts.

"All right, I'll read it." She cleared her throat and adjusted the letter. "'My Liege and Good Lady, I greet you with news that the random attacks on Heathersgill have abated. Kendal's followers have fallen off one by one, leaving him with too few soldiers to cause anything but spurious and ineffectual attacks. Our watches continue their vigilance at all times, and we will soon capture our foes, putting an end to this uncertain time.

"'Lady Jeanette is much improved in health. She and her daughters have given the Scots' goods to the peasants who continue to serve them. Revenue will be needed to restore the stronghold to its full potential. I would like your permission to purchase sheep. The terrain is craggy and the soil too shallow for planting, but the manufacturing of wool is quite promising.

"'We pray daily for your quick recovery. All is peaceful both here and at Glenmyre. Let naught trouble your mind. Yrs, Sir Roger.'" She laid the letter down. "What do you think?" she demanded.

"About what?" The patterns of her thoughts still mystified him.

"About my mother. Do you think she will recover from the violence she's endured and been a party to?"

He heard the thread of pain in her voice and it tugged at him. "Clarise," he soothed her, "you fret about everyone but yourself." He saw her look at him sharply, and he deliberately fastened his gaze on the wall beside her. "Your mother is stronger than you realize. She must have known about the powder in his boots. If she hadn't acted, I would likely be dead. And fortunately, there is no one with any legal right to accuse her of wrongdoing. In time, she will recover."

"She loved my father to distraction," Clarise added wistfully.

"In time she will love again," he promised. "She is but a rose in winter, awaiting the warmth of the sun."

He could see his wife was looking at him strangely. A painful longing carved at his chest. He, too, awaited warmth—the warmth of her love.

Clarise uncoiled from the chair. He pretended to squint at her as she approached the bed and stood before him. Through the flimsy linen undergarment, he could make out the fiery red curls at the juncture of her thighs. He felt his manhood stir, but that was nothing new.

"Do you have a headache today?" she inquired.

"A small one."

"Drink your infusion, then." She reached for the goblet perched on the headboard and gave it to him.

Christian took a tentative whiff. "I think not," he said, handing it back.

"Shall I dump it in the jake as you do?" she asked more sharply.

He'd been caught. He felt a blush stealing toward his cheeks, and he willed it away. "I'm a grown man, not an infant," he grumbled. "I mistrust any herbal remedy, no matter who blended it."

She thinned her lips and put the goblet back on the head-board. "How many fingers am I holding up?" She held her hands before his face.

He hesitated. Nay, he couldn't lie that baldly and witness her disappointment. "Three," he admitted.

"Excellent." She started to turn away.

Christian grabbed her wrist and yanked her back. She fell sideways into his embrace, and he pulled her close, burying his nose in the fragrant mass of her hair. "I love this scent," he admitted with a groan.

Predictably, she stiffened in his arms. He quelled his dis-appointment and held her tighter.

"Let me go," she said, with a catch in her voice.

He thought about it. "Nay," he said. "You cannot con-tinue to avoid me, lady. I'm your husband. Think you that you can parade about the chamber in your chemise without rousing me?"

"I think your vision is more improved than you admit," she answered coldly.

"Why must you be like this?" he asked, lifting his head. "Why are you angry at me when I only meant to do right?"

She struggled so earnestly that he let his arms fall away. She thrust herself from his lap but remained on the bed, scooting mistrustfully to the end. He watched her frown and scratch her shoulder idly. She was thinking about his words, at least.

"Would it have been the right thing to widow me and to orphan your son?" she demanded. She was angry now. Twin spots of color bloomed on her cheeks. "I married you for your protection, not to be left for the next opportunist to come along and alter my life! How dare you fight to the death and not warn me first. How dare you!"

Ah, now he understood the reason for her hurt. He leaned forward under the pretext of needing to see her better. "Sir Roger would have protected you," he assured her softly. "Besides, I had no intention of dying."

"You almost did! If my mother hadn't interfered, Ferguson would have killed you, you said so yourself." She snatched up a pillow like she meant to thump it on his head.

"By trickery alone," he pointed out. "Had he fought honestly, he never would have defeated me. His weapon was too heavy; his feet too slow."

"You challenged him on our wedding night, didn't you?" she pressed with the dawn of realization in her eyes. "That was why I never heard the revelers approach the door. You challenged him and everybody left." She jumped from the bed and began to pace the room.

Christian rubbed his eyes. It drove him mad to have her coming in and out of focus. "You have it all figured out," he told her wearily. *All but the most important part.*

"You were in a dark mood yourself," she added, putting more pieces together.

"Not for very long," he said wistfully. Visions of their wedding night flickered behind his eyes.

She threw her hands up. "Why didn't you do as I suggested? An accident was supposed to befall him. It happens all the time at tourneys!"

"Come here," he commanded, desperate to make her hold still, and to understand.

She edged reluctantly toward him, but only in response to the threatening tone of his voice. He disliked having to speak to her that way. "Listen, Clarise," he pleaded, locking her hands in his. "If we had designed some seeming accident, we would still have been guilty of Ferguson's death. Aye, he was a blackguard and doomed to hell no matter the circumstances. But to execute him in cold blood would have made us no better than butchers ourselves. I have killed too many men, my love." He squeezed her fingers to convey the horror. "I didn't want the guilt of his death on my conscience. But mostly, I didn't want it on yours."

He could see that his words had hit their mark. She stood before him, revelation on her face. He wondered, hopefully, if she could see the love he harbored for her, if she would answer it.

"You risked your life to protect my conscience?" she inquired with wonder in her voice.

He loved how soft and breathless she could sound. "To prove myself worthy," he said, releasing her hands.

"Worthy?" She held perfectly still. "Of what?"

He looked straight into her amber eyes. For a heart-stopping second, there were no walls between them. "Of your love," he admitted.

It was not the answer Clarise expected. She forgot how to breathe. *Of your love.* The words replayed themselves over and over. *Of your love. Of your love.* She heard a humming in her ears. Her heart expanded and rose into her throat.

She had tried to convince herself that love was not an essential part of a good marriage. Until Christian said the word, she might have been content with the passion between them and the security of Helmesly's high walls. But once it was spoken and hovered in the air between them, she knew that to be loved was the one thing she craved above all else. The one thing that assured her that her husband had overcome the demons of his past and let the light of goodness flood his heart.

"Oh, Christian," she whispered. "How could you think that you had anything to prove?"

He gave her an incredulous look. "In case you hadn't noticed, lady, I am feared by the people. I was born on the wrong side of the blanket. I have a scar running down one side of my face, and a wicked temper to match it."

"I know how you came by that scar," she told him, notching her hands at her hips. "And as for your temper, you are careful to guard me from it."

"The people, my lady?" he prodded, entranced by her ability to reduce his fearsome qualities into nothing.

"The people have been fed lies by the Abbot of Rievaulx and by others. Gilbert wanted them to fear you. Elsewise he would not have poisoned their ears by predicting you would kill Genrose."

Christian felt himself pale. "You know about that?" he asked.

She kneeled on the mattress beside him. "Husband," she said, cupping his jaw in her delicate hand and forcing him to look at her. "There is something you should know about yourself; something someone should have told you long ago."

"What is it?" he asked, feeling poised on the brink of self-discovery.

Her amber gaze warmed him like the sun. "You, my lord, are a good man. You are honorable and noble, chivalrous and incredibly brave." This time he could not mistake the sheet of tears that slipped across her eyes and made them glitter. "And I am honored to be your wife. I am honored that you nearly laid your life down in the belief that it would make you worthy. But if you ever do anything so rash again, you will answer for it," she added, using his own words against him.

He'd never been called those things before. Christian felt a silly smile overtake him. The urge to laugh out loud tickled his lungs, but he feared he would croak if he tried.

"I love you," she added, throwing her arms around his shoulders. She buried her face in his tunic as if she would cry.

"I'm up here," he reminded her, desperate for a kiss.

She beamed up at him. "I love you," she repeated, pressing her mouth to his. "I have loved you since the night you prayed by Simon's cradle. I knew then that you were not what people said, but a man with a pure heart and pure needs."

Aye, and his manly needs were about to explode if they

did not find immediate relief. Her words rushed over him like springwater over mountain stone. Their mouths fused in a heady blend of hunger and joy. As his hands sought the weight of her breasts, they fell back together in a frenzy of need, too long restrained.

An hour later Christian lay on his back, thoroughly replete and damp with sweat. "Will you always forgive me so thoroughly, wench?" he panted. He felt utterly relaxed.

Clarise rolled on her side to face him. "Think you that I'm done?" she asked, in mock seriousness.

He groaned in surrender. "Hundreds of warriors have raised their swords against me, yet you bring me to my knees with your wanton appetite."

Clarise laughed out loud, delighted by his wit. How was it that she'd overlooked this lighthearted vein in him? Now that she considered it, she remembered several instances when he'd injected humor into their exchanges. She'd been too blinded by fear to see it.

"My lord," she purred, rubbing her sweat-slicked body against his side. "Did you ever think that everything would end so well?"

He gave her a look, then fastened his gaze on the cobalt bed canopy. "Too cynical for that, I fear."

"What is there to fear?" she asked. "The abbot is gone; Ferguson is dead."

A moment passed when all that came from Christian was the sound of his breathing. "Someone at Helmesly was loyal to the abbot. They sent him missives informing him of certain matters. He was advised of Ethelred's visit, for example. I saw the warning myself written on a small scrap of paper in Gilbert's herbal."

A chill settled on Clarise's moist skin. "Will it matter now that Gilbert is dead?" she asked.

He hesitated again. "I cannot say. But as long as there is reason for caution, Simon is in danger. We should advise Doris never to let him out of her sight."

She suddenly recalled the mysterious offerings of goat's milk. "Do you recall the day that Simon fell ill?" she asked.

"How could I forget it?"

Gooseflesh prickled her tender skin. "The milk I had given him that day was not milk that I fetched myself," she admitted. "I found a full bucket awaiting me that morning. I thought it might have been left behind by one of the milk-maids. Simon was due to waken at any moment, so I took it, loath to make him wait any longer. I think, perhaps, that it was poisoned."

He stared at her in silence, lines of his face growing suddenly harsh.

"Please don't be angry with me." She put a hand to his cheek to calm his wrath. "Believe me, there is nothing you could say to me that would chastise me any more than I have chastised myself. But here is the strange part, my lord. The bucket was there again the next day and the next. I poured it out," she hastened to assure him. "I may be impulsive, but I'm not stupid."

"Of course not," He rolled onto his side to face her. "Thank you for telling me. And thank you for using your wits, even though you ought to have told me the truth by then."

"I need to go get Simon," she said, overcome by sudden panic.

"Stay but a while," her husband begged. He dipped his head and flicked his tongue across the sensitive peak of her breast. "I trust Doris to guard him."

"Nay, I have to check on him. I will bring him here, and we can play with him until supper."

"No rest for the weary," he groaned, burying his face between the swells.

She nipped him on the shoulder, then wriggled quickly off the bed.

"Vixen!" he shouted, reaching out to pinch her buttocks as she fled.

The banter continued as she quickly washed and dressed.

Brushing the tangles from her hair, Clarise glanced out the window. The ground was scorched and thirsty for rain. The wildflowers had wilted in the heat. Yet, deep in her heart, a river of contentment flowed.

But then she remembered Christian's suspicions, and alarm shivered through her. Putting down her hairbrush, she hastened from the room, blowing a kiss to her husband as she went.

Chapter Twenty

Rushing up the tower stairs to relieve Doris, Clarise barreled into Harold, who was hastening down the stairs. "Oh, Harold, I'm sorry. I didn't see you."

He mumbled an apology under his breath and kept right on going, his chin tucked against his chest.

Clarise watched him beat a hasty retreat. What was Harold doing on the third level? He didn't usually venture beyond the great hall or the kitchens, especially in late afternoon with preparations for supper under way.

Determined to assuage her curiosity, she ascended the remaining steps as quietly as possible. Christian's suspicions came sharply to mind as she tiptoed along the corridor. She peeked into the room she had formerly occupied and spied Doris, straightening the rumples from the bed.

Clarise drew back with a gasp. The evidence was overwhelming. Suddenly she knew who'd fathered Doris's unborn child. It was Harold. Because of his mental infirmities and odd manner of speaking, she had placed him above suspicion. Now she recalled his agitation when Doris had gone into labor. He had feared that Doris would die as his niece had done.

Did Dame Maeve know about her husband's liaisons? Could that be the reason for her bitterness and spite?

Clarise waited a minute longer, then stepped forward to knock on the door.

"Come, milady," Doris sang out, clearly expecting her. As Clarise entered the room, the woman turned with the baby clasped to her ample bosom. "He is just waking from a nap," she announced. Seeing the look on her mistress's face, she faltered. Her doughty cheeks fell as her smile died.

"Doris," Clarise said, sternly enough to make the nurse pale. "You have not been honest with me or, for that matter, with yourself."

"Milady?" Doris croaked.

Clarise shut the door so they wouldn't be overheard. "I just saw Harold leave," she announced. "He was the father of your baby, wasn't he?"

Doris cast a miserable look to the floor. "Aye, milady."

"How long has this been going on?"

"Twenty years an' more."

The answer staggered her. Twenty years! Her outrage frittered away like so much hot air.

"It were me he was going to wed," Doris admitted, as great tears welled up in her hazel eyes. "But his father, bein' a powerful man, arranged a marriage for him with a wealthy merchant's daughter. He were forced ta wed Maeve, as he ne did have a choice. But 'tis me he loves, and I him."

All this was uttered with such wrenching emotion that Clarise felt a rising empathy for the woman. She approached the former cook and gave her a searching look. "Does Maeve know?" she asked.

"Aye, milady. She watches us close, though not for love of her husband, but to own him. When she learned I would have his babe, she called the midwife. Together, they forced me to drink a potion boiled with brakefern bark. It expelled the little babe from my womb, as ye know."

Clarise's gaze fell to Simon, who blinked sleepily against the woman's shoulder. "*Jesu,* Doris! Why didn't you say something? 'Tis a horrible crime. Maeve should have to answer for it."

The old woman blushed like a maiden in her prime. "Don't ye see, milady? Harold and I would be publicly exposed. We were the ones what sinned in the first place." She lifted the baby from her shoulder and passed him to her mistress with a wistful look. Clarise could tell that she was thinking of her stillborn son.

"'Tis not a sin to love for more than twenty years!" Clarise insisted, settling Simon in her arms. "You are wed to Harold in your heart, are you not?"

"Aye, milady. He is a good man, a gentle man," Doris proclaimed on his behalf.

"Then I will tell Lord Christian of Maeve and the midwife's attempt at murder. Mayhap she'll be made to leave the castle and her marriage to Harold annulled."

Doris staggered to the bed and sank heavily upon the mattress. "Do ye think so?" she breathed. Her eyes were filled with such longing that Clarise experienced a pang of doubt. She wondered if she'd raised the woman's hopes too high.

"I will do my best for you," she promised, turning away. "Oh, Doris, there is one more thing," she added by the door. "We must watch Simon as close as ever. Lord Christian believes there is still good cause to fear for his safety."

Doris nodded dumbly. As Clarise turned away, the nurse heaved a great sigh. "Oh, Harold," she overheard her whisper.

Clarise lay in bed that night, too hot to sleep. Though the window was open, the air lay thick and close, making it difficult to breathe. The stars pulsed feebly in the midnight sky, shedding little light on the bed she shared with her husband. She should be sleeping in the happy knowledge that her husband loved her. Instead, she was plagued by dark suspicions.

Thoughts spanned her mind like intricate spiderwebs. Christian had agreed that Maeve should be tried for contributing to the death of Doris's baby, but, he pointed out, she would have equal right to demand that Harold and Doris face judgment for their illicit affair.

Was there no way to ostracize Maeve from the castle and leave the lovers in peace?

Clarise replayed her various conversations with Harold, seeking the signs she'd missed that would have pointed her to the truth. *Doris is well,* she remembered comforting him. *'Twas her baby that died.*

He'd seemed to confuse the death of his baby with the plight of his niece. *She was a babe once, my Rose. I rocked her on my knee. Here's your horsey.*

Doris was right. He was a good man, despite his differences, and clearly well bred without an Anglo accent of any kind to blunt his Norman tongue. Likely he had been a dutiful son to his father, who Doris had said was a powerful man. Powerful implied noble. Yet as no noblewoman would want to wed a halfwit, perhaps Harold had been made to marry a merchant's daughter, causing him to sink into anonymity.

Hadn't he told her something of his family? She tried to reconstruct their conversation.

You must have been a wonderful uncle, she remembered telling him.

Harold, he'd said. *Brother of John.*

John. John who?

John of Eppingham, Baron of Helmesly?

Clarise sat up slowly, careful not to awaken her husband. Her heart thudded loudly in her chest. Perspiration coated her skin. Could it be? She racked her brain for any evidence that her wild guess was right.

If Harold was the brother of the Baron of Helmesly, then he was also uncle to Genrose, the baron's only daughter.

Rose, that's a pretty name.

Yet why didn't anyone acknowledge Harold as a nobleman, as Lord Harold, the baron's brother? She could only assume his family had been ashamed of his infirmities. Had they given him the title of a steward, found him a wife, and left it at that?

Yet no amount of concealment changed the fact that he was second in line to inherit the baronetcy.

Our pretty Rose has wilted.

He'd said those words in the lyrical voice he used when repeating people. The words, sounding so poetic at first, took on a sinister edge. *Our pretty Rose has wilted.* Who would have said those words for Harold to repeat them? Neither of Genrose's parents, for Lord John and his wife were dead before their daughter.

A vision of the gnarled midwife sprang to the forefront of Clarise's mind. With the midwife's help, Maeve had managed to kill Doris's baby. Could the pair of them have forced Genrose to drink an infusion of the same toxic bark?

Clarise smothered a gasp. Without a baby to inherit or a niece to deliver another son, the baronetcy would fall to Harold. And who was the driving force behind her husband but Maeve?

Galvanized by her guesswork, Clarise slid off the bed and stalked to the open window. She hoped for a breeze to bring relief to her fevered skin. But it was useless—there was absolutely no wind in the air tonight. To cool her neck, she gathered up the heavy fall of her hair and looked at her sleeping husband.

Should she wake him now and tell him her suspicions? She wanted to, but the darkness strained his eyes, and sleep was precious to him. Hadn't he marveled just this morning that he had slept through two nights straight? She was loath to affect his recovery, even temporarily. Her news could wait until morning.

She turned and looked out the window again. Tension gripped her shoulders in a vice. Christian's belief that Simon's life was still in danger had overworked her imagination. Either that, or there was every reason to take action right away.

A tendril of fear tickled her nape. Clarise let her hair fall.

She crossed to the desk and snatched up a tallow lamp and flint. In deference to her husband's eyes, she closed the door before lighting the candle on the gallery.

The great hall below was deserted. Holding the candle aloft, Clarise lifted the hem of her chemise and approached the tower stairs to Doris's chamber. She would check on Simon and at the same time ask Doris if her suspicions were right. The plump nurse clearly knew of Harold's past.

The light barely illumined the steps beneath Clarise's feet. They seemed to rise more steeply in the darkness.

At the top of the stairs she paused. She could hear Doris snoring from where she stood. The servant's door was open. Gooseflesh ridged Clarise's back. With her eyes wide open, she sought to see beyond the candle's flame as she inched down the corridor.

Nothing is wrong, she told herself. Christian's concerns were playing with her mind—that was all. She reached the door and peered inside.

The shutters were pulled shut. She could see no farther than the periphery of candlelight. Doris's snoring sawed over her senses, increasing her agitation.

Clarise forced herself to march straight for Simon's cradle. She did so, fully expecting to find the baby sleeping within. She would carry him downstairs, thus ensuring herself some rest. She stepped right up to the box with the flame held high. Gold light plumbed the depths of the empty cradle. Simon was gone.

With a gasp and a leaping heart, she spun around. The candle sputtered. She hastened to the side of Doris's bed and yanked open the drapes. "Doris!" she cried. Her tone was so sharp that the woman lurched into wakefulness. "Is Simon in the bed with you?"

A disoriented pause came from the large woman. She patted down the bed around her. "Nay," she answered in bewildered tones. "Is he ne in the box? I left him there but a nonce ago."

Clarise had a feeling they were wasting precious time.

"Hurry downstairs, Doris," she commanded, already halfway to the door. "Awaken Christian and tell him Simon has been taken!"

Doris leaped from the bed. As the woman thundered down the turret steps, Clarise edged into the hall, not knowing where to start her search. The flame of her lamp dimmed as if deprived of air.

She thought hard, calling on every one of her senses to aid her. When she'd stepped onto the gallery, not a soul had stirred on the steps or in the hall. Every instinct shouted that the kidnapper either lingered on the third level or had taken an alternate route down. For Simon to be so quiet, he would either have to be sleeping or . . . nay, she couldn't bring herself to think of an alternative.

She crept down the length of the hallway in the direction of the eastern turret. Hadn't she encountered Dame Maeve on the stairs of that turret once before? A sound reached her ears and she drew up short, listening. There it was again, a metallic jingle that came from the garderobe, immediately to her right.

Clarise approached the shut door. She tugged at the latch and shoved it open with her foot. The room was poorly ventilated. Though not in heavy use, it reeked nevertheless on such a still evening. She caught her breath and bravely stepped inside.

It was then that she saw her. Maeve cowered in the far corner of the chamber, next to one of the holes that passed waste into the moat. Like a wild animal, her eyes seemed to glow in the lamp's light, and like an animal she looked terrified at being cornered. Her breath came in ragged pants. In her arms was a swaddled bundle. Simon! Clarise's heart threw itself against her ribs. *My Simon.*

"Give him to me," she commanded in a voice that sent chills down her own spine. She stalked the woman.

"Get back!" Maeve cried, her eyes darting in desperation. "Get back," she repeated, "else I'll drop him through the hole!" With that, she ripped away his swaddling cloth and threw it down into the void. Simon cried out, protesting his rude awakening.

Clarise stifled a scream. A vision of Simon's little body plummeting toward the moat stopped her short. "I'll kill you," she answered back, meaning it. "You've been caught now, Maeve. Even if you killed Simon and your husband were the only heir remaining, you would never live to see it! The Slayer will cut you into little pieces with his sword!"

Even in the murky shadows the woman's visage seemed to pale. She took a furtive step toward the door, and Clarise moved to block her path.

With the knowledge that help was shortly coming, Clarise desperately sought to buy time. "Did you think you could manipulate so much and get away with it?" she scoffed. "I know that you poisoned your niece, Genrose. Mayhap you even killed her parents," she added with sudden inspiration. "'Tis said they died of dysentery. Did you poison them as well?"

"Aye!" screeched the woman, losing her composure. Wisps of her hair had escaped her usually tidy bun. "I killed them all, and I'll kill you, too. As soon as I've rid the world of this parasite." Simon emitted another cry.

"You've tried already to poison him," Clarise quickly interjected. "Was it you who left the buckets of milk in the nanny pen?"

"Aye, and you would have been blamed," retorted the woman, even as she quaked with fear. "All the servants knew ye were a fraud."

Not far away, Clarise heard her husband call, his tone filled with urgency. Dame Maeve heard it, also. With a muffled cry she stooped to toss Simon through the hole. Clarise dropped the lamp and leaped forward. As darkness swallowed them, her fingers groped for the baby. She encountered Maeve's bony elbow and wrenched it upward. Simon tumbled from the woman's arms, and Clarise barely caught him, her fingers closing around his thigh. She hung on tight.

Shoving Dame Maeve against the wall, she rushed from the room, gathering Simon closer.

She came within an inch of skewering them both on her husband's sword. "Clarise! My God, is he hurt?" he panted, reaching out to touch them.

Simon howled, forcing her to raise her voice. "I don't know," she admitted. "Maeve was going to drop him through the waste hole. Oh, my saints!" she exclaimed in the aftermath of horror. "She's still in there!" She pointed, despite the fact that the hall was nearly black and he couldn't see.

"Maeve? But why?"

"I'll tell you later," she promised. "Just get her. Kill her if you must, I don't care."

And she didn't. A mother's instinct had risen up in her, making her fiercely protective and completely unforgiving. "But how can you see?" She caught him back when he made to move past her.

"I've been blind for a week," he reminded her.

The assurance was comforting. So was the sound of others pounding up the stairs, bearing torches and raised voices. Her husband disappeared into the garderobe. Clarise strained her ears for sounds of a struggle.

"Come out, old woman," she heard him threaten, "else I'll run you through with this sword. You know its name, do you not? I call it *Vengeance*. Wherever there is evil, *Vengeance* draws blood."

Maeve whimpered loudly enough to be heard over Simon's cries.

Clarise ran her fingers over the baby's naked body, seeking signs of injury. There was nothing to cause her further alarm, save for his trembling distress. Men-at-arms came up behind her, hushing each other as they realized that their liege lord was already handling the villain in the stinking chamber.

"Should we go in?" one of them asked Clarise.

"Stand fast," she said. "He will have her shortly."

Indeed, he appeared at that very moment, escorting the woman out of the darkness, the edge of his broadsword pressed to her throat. She didn't dare to struggle. Her eyes darted wildly as she took note of the many witnesses.

Clarise reached out and grabbed the ring of keys, snapping the cord that held them to the woman's waist. She was stripped of her authority.

"Hagar," Christian called, waving the dungeon guard forward. He lowered the sword only to thrust the woman into Hagar's beefy hands. The mute man toted her off, deaf to the invectives that came spewing from her mouth the moment the Slayer set her free.

Simon's screams quieted as the woman was dragged from sight and sound. The remaining men-at-arms awaited orders from their liege lord.

Christian tucked his sword under his arm. "May I hold him?" he asked hoarsely.

Clarise put the baby gently in his father's hands. He laid Simon against his shoulder and turned from the glare of the torchlight to soothe his son. Or was it the babe who soothed his father?

A streak of moisture shone upon the warlord's cheek. She didn't know if her husband was weeping, or if the strain on his eyes had caused them to tear. Deciding it was the former, she put her arms around father and son. *My men,* she thought, feeling the fullness of her love.

"Return to your beds," Christian rumbled, directing this suggestion to the men. "I thank you for your timeliness."

"First, my love, I think we should send a party to arrest the midwife," Clarise spoke up suddenly. "She and Maeve are responsible for the death of Doris's baby, as well as"—she hesitated, loath to shock him—"as well as Lady Genrose."

"Genrose," he whispered, blinking away his disbelief. He lifted his gaze to the men's stunned faces. "Do as she says."

"Aye, my lord. What about Harold?" asked the oldest man.

"Harold is innocent," Clarise supplied, before her husband could speak. "Question him if you must, but this plot was engineered by Maeve. You have my word on it."

A thoughtful soldier left his torch for them and turned away, encouraging the others to follow.

The warlord stood gazing at her with amazement. "How did you come by all this knowledge?" he asked her. Simon's sobs had become mere hiccups.

"I couldn't sleep," she admitted. "I lay in bed, and my mind started churning. I knew that there was something I had overlooked. Something I could almost put my finger on if I thought about it hard enough. And then it came to me. I rushed upstairs to check on Simon, and he was gone."

He shook his head in wonder. "God knows what would have happened if you hadn't come sooner. Why didn't you wake me?" he demanded, suddenly angry. "When will you learn to garner your impulsiveness and stay out of danger?"

She felt the flexing of his muscles under her fingertips. "If I hadn't acted when I did," she soothed him, "then Simon would likely be dead."

He took a sharp breath and reined himself in. "She was going to drop him down the waste hole?" he asked incredulously. "Why?"

"I will tell you everything in a moment," she promised, "but first we need to get a soiling cloth on Simon before he wets you." She stepped over to fetch the torch and bring it with them.

"Are you hurt at all?" he asked, betraying his concern with worry this time.

"Not even a scratch," she answered, urging him to follow. "Now hurry, or you'll need another undershirt."

He trailed her down the hall to Doris's chamber. "You wrestled the babe from her, didn't you?"

"Of course I did. Think you that I would let that woman kill him? I'd have torn her into shreds first."

Her proclamation impressed him into silence. She motioned for him to lay the baby on Doris's bed while she foraged for linens. The heavy nurse had yet to return to her room. She would hear the news of Maeve's arrest from the men-at-arms. And then she would go to Harold to explain matters to him. At last the lovers would be free to proclaim their affection for each other.

"This reminds me of the time I found Simon naked in his box," he mused, looking down at his son. "Do you remember that night? My first thought was that you'd performed that mischief to avenge me."

She remembered perfectly. The terror she'd felt for him then seemed unreasonable in light of their newfound love. "Maeve was likely the one to do it. She hoped he would take chill and die as many infants do."

Christian's fingers scraped the bristles on his chin. "I remember now that I sent her up to waken you. She had the perfect opportunity to kill him then. Why not take it?"

"She would have been suspect right away," reasoned Clarise. "Better to drop him in the moat where his body . . . my God, I can't even speak of it, 'tis so horrifying. I have so much to tell you, Christian," she added, "but I think you should be sitting when I say it." She looked around. "Have a seat on the chest," she said, waving him toward the chest he'd sat on once before.

"Christ's toes, what do you think me made of?" he exclaimed.

She turned toward his stunned expression. "I think your heart is far more tender than you realize," she told him earnestly.

He glowered at her. "Think you so?" His bloodshot eyes gave him the appearance of a demon.

"I know so." She picked up the securely girded baby. "When you hear the extent of Maeve's wickedness, you will think yourself an angel by comparison."

He gave a tortured sound that had her looking at him sharply. "What was that? Did you just laugh?"

His expression was composed. "I never laugh," he said grimly.

"Hmmm." She trusted her ears more than his words. "We have work to do," she announced. "As you imagine yourself undaunted, I will tell you what I have pieced together on the way. Would you kindly bring the torch? And the keys, we'll need Maeve's keys, most likely."

"Where are we going?" he asked, bewildered.

She scooped up the baby. "To look for proof."

"Proof of what?"

"Proof that Maeve sent messages to the abbot. Proof that the two of them collaborated to see you thrust from Helmesly."

"Maeve and the abbot? I doubt they even knew each other."

"Don't be so quick to judge, Christian. Think about it. What was the purpose of the interdict but to breed discontent among the people? The abbot instilled resentment into the hearts of the peasants. He wanted them to fear you. Elsewise he would not have predicted you would kill your lady wife. The idea was to cause the people to rise against you in the hopes that they would thrust you from Helmesly.

"You were too much a danger to Maeve's plans," she continued, leading the way toward the east tower. "She feared you would get a boy child on Genrose, which you did, of course. She then plotted to get rid of the baby. With the midwife's help, she poisoned Genrose with the same infusion of brakefern that they gave to Doris."

"Why the devil would Maeve do such a thing?"

Clarise touched her husband's arm before delivering the coup de grace. "Harold is the brother of the late baron of Eppingham. After Simon, he is next in line to the seat of Helmesly."

"What!" he cried, coming to a startled halt.

She quickly related the scraps of information she had pieced together. "Harold mentioned that his niece, Rose, would ofttimes read to him. I didn't make the connection at first. All I knew was that they were close." She urged Christian to precede her down the tower stairs, holding the torch aloft so they could see.

"Genrose never told me Harold was her uncle," he puzzled aloud. "Neither did Baron John."

"He was apparently an embarrassment to the family. As no noblewoman would wed him, his family settled on a merchant's daughter, Maeve."

"Who soon had ambitious thoughts," he concluded, his voice echoing in the stairwell.

"Aye, only you ruined her plans by getting her niece with child. She couldn't run the risk that the baby might be a boy, so she sought to kill him. If you hadn't saved Simon, Harold would be baron, despite his shortcomings."

"Especially if the abbot Gilbert sealed his right to rule."

"Exactly."

"How much farther?" he asked. The stairs were steep and slick with moisture in the lower regions.

"Maeve's retreat is down with the storerooms. One more level, I think. I've been here before," she volunteered when they reached the lowest level. "The goods that were stripped from the castle were piled in one of the storerooms like a hidden cache. Sir Roger said Genrose had wanted to give her parents' riches to the poor. I suspect Maeve was holding on to them for the time when she would rule as baroness."

They moved from door to door, finding the keys in precise order on the key ring. More goods littered the dusty floor.

"There's another room around the corner," Clarise informed him.

As they turned the corner, Christian pulled her back. "Wait," he whispered. "There's a line of light under the door."

His vision was much improved, she thought, to discern the coppery glow. "Try the key," she whispered. Nervously she patted Simon's back, though the baby had already dropped off to sleep.

But the key wasn't necessary. The door swung silently inward, and a pungent odor greeted their nostrils. The room was illumined with tallow candles, betraying Maeve's recent presence. It was clearly an herbal of sorts, as a number of dried plants were suspended from hooks and littered the tabletops. What drew both their gazes was the cote of carrier pigeons. The birds fluttered in alarm as the couple edged into the room.

They stared at the cage in contemplation. "Was the message you discovered at Rievaulx small enough to be carried by air?" Clarise inquired.

"Aye," said her husband, who had come to the same conclusion. He turned and gave her a respectful look. "It seems you have figured it all out, my love. I shall have to make you my chief tactician."

She sketched him a curtsy. "We have yet to know the reason why Maeve and Gilbert would help each other."

"Greed motivated both of them," her husband guessed. "Gilbert desired power and fame."

"And Maeve wanted to be mistress of Helmesly," Clarise finished for him.

"They might have been lovers."

She shook her head. "He could never have loved a woman. They were siblings, most likely, with those dark eyes so much alike. We have only to ask Doris. She is one of the few servants old enough to recall when Harold wed Maeve."

He gave the rest of the room a quick inspection. "Maeve and Gilbert shared an interest in herbs as well. This herbal reminds me much of his."

"It is done, then," she said, feeling the tension rush out of her. At last the security and peace she had craved for so long was theirs to enjoy. "Simon is safe. Nothing else will ever threaten him," she swore with a mother's determination.

Christian's bloodshot gaze lingered on her profile as she kissed the baby's cheek. "Can we go to bed now?" he asked with his lids half shut.

"Oh, my love," she said, remembering his condition with

sudden contrition. "I hope you haven't strained your eyes with all this nighttime activity."

"Lady, you will turn me into a pudding-heart," he swore, moving to snuff out the candles.

"Not at all. You are welcome to as much nocturnal activity as you please, so long as it's restricted to the bedchamber."

His answer was a laugh that was cut short.

Clarise allowed herself a smile. She had fulfilled the vow she had made to her father. She had surprised Simon's would-be murderer and unveiled the plot to usurp the baronetcy from the rightful heir.

Making the Slayer of Helmesly laugh out loud was a challenge she looked forward to.

Epilogue

A man once called the Slayer gazed into the lilac eyes of his newborn baby girl and saw his reflection in her pupils. In a former life, he'd been a dreaded warlord. Now he was an ordinary man. A profoundly humbled father.

The infant who was no more than a minute old was still wet from her passage into the world. Her lungs swelled with air as she cried, heralding her birth. Sunlight streamed through the open shutters to guild her bright red hair. An April breeze carried the scent of hyacinths from the meadow. Her weary mother groaned.

"I am never doing that again," she vowed, lifting her lashes to observe them.

Christian lowered their daughter to the bed so Clarise could share in the miracle. "Look," he urged, his eyes stinging with boundless joy. "Look how beautiful she is!"

He watched his wife's expression as she absorbed the baby's heart-shaped face, the cherry-red hair and bowed lips. Their daughter ceased to cry. She stared back at her mother, as though in recognition.

"Her eyes are violet," Clarise whispered.

It was a self-admitted weakness that the warlord loved to watch his wife's expressive face. Her intelligence and pathos never ceased to stir him. And while he'd nearly sacrificed his life to be worthy of her, he couldn't help but confess himself a blessed man.

Ignoring the young midwife who pressed a compress between his wife's legs, Clarise bared her splendid bosom and guided one ripe, pink nipple into the baby's mouth.

The infant thrashed just once before she fastened on. "That was easy enough," she commented, with relief.

"You've had practice, remember?"

She flicked him a patronizing look. "I don't want to hear a thing out of you right now. You could never have survived what I just went through."

He loved it when she scolded him. "Likely not," he agreed, thrusting aside the nightmare of her twenty-four-hour labor.

"I am *not* doing it again," she repeated. Her head lolled upon the snowy pillow.

He indulged her in all things, but he could not agree to this whim. Already he was looking forward to the day she healed, so they could resume their lovemaking. There was nothing in the world remotely like the passion that they shared.

He leaned over the suckling baby and dropped a gentle kiss on his wife's lips, bruised from biting down on them while pushing. "Did I tell you that you're beautiful today?"

She gave a snort of disbelief. "A bald-faced lie," she retorted. Her lashes floated upward. "Will you bring Simon in?" she said. "I want him to meet his little sister."

"In a moment." He smoothed a flyaway curl from her cheek and watched her eyelids sink closed. His daughter sucked contently. "What will we name her?" he asked as the question suddenly occurred to him.

Clarise gave a sigh. "Rose," she murmured.

The name was perfectly suited to the baby's coloring. "Harold will be happy," he added, thinking out loud.

Harold executed his duties as steward these days with newfound confidence. His marriage to Maeve had been quickly annulled, thanks to the efficiency of Ethelred, newly elected Abbot of Rievaulx. Harold still wandered in his speech and lacked an awareness of his surroundings, but he was loyal. And loyalty meant a lot in the household of a future baron.

As for Maeve, she had succumbed to a fate similar to that of her brother, the Abbot of Rievaulx. But instead of falling down a set of stairs, she had hung herself with her own hair, in the dungeon of Helmsly.

"Rose," Christian whispered, shaking off the memories of the past. He caressed the back of his daughter's head, then gave in to the urge to put his arms around both wife and baby. The midwife had traveled all the way from York to attend the birth. He wondered what she would think to see a mighty mercenary cry like a baby.

I've grown soft, he admitted, swallowing down a sob. He would never say it publicly, though his wife accused him often enough.

He had outgrown the unreasonable need to stir fear in strangers' hearts. Now he used his sword for practice only and for protection. With Heathersgill and Glenmyre under his supervision, peace and prosperity cast their blankets over the land. And both seemed settled in for good.

He couldn't help but reflect how much his life had changed since the fateful night he'd cut Simon from the belly of his dead first wife. The pivotal point had been when Clarise marched into his world and snatched his son from certain death.

As he sat basking in the bounty of their love, a shaft of sunlight warmed the disfigured half of his face. He believed beyond a doubt that Clarise had come to him as a reward for righteousness. The words from Ethelred's book had come true!

"My sweet?" he whispered, leaning forward. He was filled with a need to share his gratitude.

"Mmmmm?" she grunted.

"Thank you," he told her, pressing his lips to hers.

She cast him a feeble smile and kept her eyes shut. "You

won't be needing a nurse," she remarked over the musical sound of their daughter sucking.

"Nay, but I may have to send Roger looking for a leman," he replied with mock despair. "My own lady has decided to forsake the marriage bed."

She was silent so long he thought she'd fallen asleep. "Try it, my love, and you will have a second scar to match the first one," she muttered acerbically.

He threw back his head and laughed out loud. "You know I couldn't bring myself to look at another," he added, nuzzling her neck.

"I made you laugh," she pointed out.

"Aye, you did." It was their favorite game. One of so many private games they shared. To hell with the midwife, he thought, letting a tear of joy roll unchecked down his cheek.

He was not ashamed to admit that the Slayer of Helmesly had shucked the mantle of darkness.